"Only ...

—*Romance Junkies*

"One amazingly phenomenal sexy novel that will keep the pages turning, your imagination running, your dreams carnally vivid, and your partner very happy."　　　—*Bitten by Books*

"Joey W. Hill impresses me with every word she writes."
　　　　　　　　　　　　　　　　　—*Joyfully Reviewed*

"Ms. Hill is a talented writer with a style that can only be deemed exclusively hers . . . All of the books in this series are ardently poignant romances at their finest . . ."　　　—*Risque Reviews*

VAMPIRE MISTRESS

"Keep a fan and a glass of ice water handy; this one will raise your temperature."　　　　　　　　　　—*RT Book Reviews*

"The Vampire Queen novels are more than a reader ever needs to indulge in a world where connection with the characters is amazingly intense and all-consuming, leaving you very, very satisfied."　　　　　　　　　　　　　　—*Fresh Fiction*

continued . . .

BELOVED VAMPIRE

"Lock the door, turn off the television and hide the phone before starting this book, because it's impossible to put down! . . . The story is full of action, intrigue, danger, history and sexual tension . . . This is definitely a keeper!"

—*RT Book Reviews*

"This has to be the best vampire novel I've read in a very long time! Joey W. Hill has outdone herself . . . [I] couldn't put it down and didn't want it to end."   —*ParaNormal Romance*

A VAMPIRE'S CLAIM

"Had me in its thrall. Joey W. Hill pulled me in and didn't let me go."   —*Joyfully Reviewed*

"*A Vampire's Claim* is so ardent with action and sex you won't remember to breathe . . . Another stunning installment in her vampire series."   —*TwoLips Reviews*

"[Will] enthrall and delight not only existing Hill fans, but also those new to her writing."   —*RT Book Reviews*

"A great vampire romance . . . [An] enticing, invigorating thriller."   —*The Best Reviews*

MARK OF THE VAMPIRE QUEEN

"Superb . . . This is erotica at its best with lots of sizzle and a love that is truly sacrificial. Joey W. Hill continues to grow as a stunning storyteller."   —*A Romance Review continued . . .*

SOMETHING
ABOUT
WITCHES

Joey W. Hill

BERKLEY SENSATION, NEW YORK

THE BERKLEY PUBLISHING GROUP
Published by the Penguin Group
Penguin Group (USA) Inc.
375 Hudson Street, New York, New York 10014, USA
Penguin Group (Canada), 90 Eglinton Avenue East, Suite 700, Toronto, Ontario M4P 2Y3, Canada
(a division of Pearson Penguin Canada Inc.)
Penguin Books Ltd., 80 Strand, London WC2R 0RL, England
Penguin Group Ireland, 25 St. Stephen's Green, Dublin 2, Ireland (a division of Penguin Books Ltd.)
Penguin Group (Australia), 250 Camberwell Road, Camberwell, Victoria 3124, Australia
(a division of Pearson Australia Group Pty. Ltd.)
Penguin Books India Pvt. Ltd., 11 Community Centre, Panchsheel Park, New Delhi—110 017, India
Penguin Group (NZ), 67 Apollo Drive, Rosedale, Auckland 0632, New Zealand
(a division of Pearson New Zealand Ltd.)
Penguin Books (South Africa) (Pty.) Ltd., 24 Sturdee Avenue, Rosebank, Johannesburg 2196,
South Africa

Penguin Books Ltd., Registered Offices: 80 Strand, London WC2R 0RL, England

This is a work of fiction. Names, characters, places, and incidents either are the product of the author's imagination or are used fictitiously, and any resemblance to actual persons, living or dead, business establishments, events, or locales is entirely coincidental. The publisher does not have any control over and does not assume any responsibility for author or third-party websites or their content.

SOMETHING ABOUT WITCHES

A Berkley Sensation Book / published by arrangement with the author

PRINTING HISTORY
Berkley Sensation mass-market paperback edition / February 2012

Copyright © 2012 by Joey W. Hill.
Excerpt from *In the Company of Witches* copyright © 2012 by Joey W. Hill.
Cover design by George Long.
Cover art by Don Sipley.
Interior text design by Tiffany Estreicher.

ISBN: 978-0-425-24613-9

BERKLEY SENSATION®
Berkley Sensation Books are published by The Berkley Publishing Group,
a division of Penguin Group (USA) Inc.,
375 Hudson Street, New York, New York 10014.
BERKLEY SENSATION® is a registered trademark of Penguin Group (USA) Inc.
The "B" design is a trademark of Penguin Group (USA) Inc.

PRINTED IN THE UNITED STATES OF AMERICA

10 9 8 7 6 5 4 3 2 1

ACKNOWLEDGMENTS

Many thanks to Rick of Shooter's Choice for helping me understand a gun store operation better, as well as correcting some of my more outlandish notions related to the use of specific firearms. Any errors that remain are all mine. Long live the Second Amendment, and bless the founding fathers for understanding its key importance to our remaining a free nation.

DOUBLE, DOUBLE TOIL AND TROUBLE; FIRE BURN, AND cauldron bubble. The *Macbeth* quote fit to a fucking *T* as Ruby stared through the ten-power Nightforce scope of the McMillan 50-caliber military-grade sniper rifle and saw 100 percent trouble coming her way. Complete with battered cowboy hat, his own Chris Cagle "Chicks Dig It" theme song and honest-to-Goddess dragonskin boots. How the hell had Derek Stormwind found her?

Okay, scratch that. She'd always known he'd find her. She'd just nurtured an unrealistic hope that he would be like most men and, once he realized she didn't want to be found and that she'd made following her trail a real pain in the ass, he'd sniff out easier prey. But Derek Stormwind was definitely not like most men. Which was why she'd rather be stuck up the backside of one of Artemis's hunting hounds without a flashlight than face the next few moments.

Putting the rifle down on the counter, she uncapped a mini-sized vodka bottle and dashed the contents into her open Dr Pepper can, then brought the soda to her lips for a healthy swig. Too healthy. She choked, hacking over the part of it that had gone down the wrong tube. Meanwhile, he was crossing the street, seconds away from putting his hand on the brass doorknob and invading her store. Unless she was mistaken and he was in town for a French manicure from the salon next door.

Hell, she needed an extra moment. Flicking a glance down at her feet, she wheezed out the command. "Theo. *Kill.*"

The elderly mastiff erupted from behind the counter, a bulldozer of rippling muscle and sheer bulk that would have knocked her off her feet, if she wasn't practiced at flattening herself against the ammo case behind her to give him take-off room.

As Derek came through the door, the dog was clattering across the floor like an approaching herd of marbles, making menacing and somewhat asthmatic noises similar to low-level wheezing thunder. A froth of drool hit the front display case, spattering the glass and obscuring the array of handguns there. Ruby stuck the soda back under the counter and pummeled her chest with a decisive fist at the same moment the dog launched his considerable weight onto his hind legs and hit Derek's chest with both front paws.

"You great big baby." Derek tried to fend off a tongue that Ruby knew was like a lukewarm and slimy hand towel. "Still a crappy security guard, buddy."

He should look ridiculous, struggling with the dog, but of course he didn't. He'd braced all that well-sculpted muscle against canine attack, which just emphasized the fit of his T-shirt over his broad shoulders. The way his thighs and ass flexed in his worn jeans basically screamed sex-in-faded-denim. The hat was low on his brow, nearly hiding the brown hair teasing at his collar, but which he usually kept trimmed short. He'd not yet looked her way, but she knew what kind of impact those eyes had when they turned toward a female. His handsome, shit-eating grin could disarm a woman at twenty paces. But every time Ruby looked into those dark blue eyes, the country-boy theme segued quite decisively into the Khazad-dum score from *Fellowship of the Ring*. She could see Gandalf standing before the Balrog, his voice thundering like the word of God.

You shall not *pass.*

Her gaze dropped. Anyone else would think the scuffed-up dragonskin boots were some kind of alligator skin. He had a healthy reverence and respect for dragonkind, particularly the non-shifters. However, when she'd pressed him for an explanation of those boots, he'd simply said, "I had a disagreement with that one." She'd caught a dangerous glint in his eye, the honor-bound sorcerer crossed with the gunslinger who'd be pushed only so far, something between Merlin and Wyatt Earp. That observation had earned her a flash of that devastating grin.

He was one of the most powerful sorcerers she'd ever known, directly or by reputation. He flew so far under the radar that to most he was a myth, or a scary bedtime story. But she'd had him in her bed, and while the feelings he conjured from her there could be overwhelming, they were far from nightmarish. In fact, the only good dreams she had anymore were about him. Which just pissed her off. If she could have banished him from her mind without banishing other important things, things she couldn't afford to lose, she would have. That was what she told herself.

Pull it together, Ruby.

When he finally managed to shove the dog back down to all four feet, which put his gigantic head at the height of Derek's waist, she had her hip propped against the shelf behind the cash register and was eyeing them both, hopefully with a faint trace of disgust in her eyes. "I'm trading him in for a Chihuahua. The littler they are, the nastier they are."

"Make sure it's a female. I hear they're even meaner." He glanced up at the marquee. "Arcane Shot. Firearms, shooting range, safety courses and permits? Pretty radical shift from Witches R Us outside Carmel."

She shrugged. "I got tired of the Wiccan wannabes, who think granola, hugs and ten-sticks-for-a-dollar incense will change the world."

"And this works better?" He eyed the sniper rifle under her hand.

"Sometimes magic comes through; sometimes it doesn't. But superior firepower never lets you down."

"No argument there. I prefer the pump-action riot gun myself. A classic. Took me a while to find you. Your magic's gotten stronger."

And darker. She could tell he thought it, but, points for him, he didn't say it. "Told you I didn't want to be found." She tried to modulate the energy around her so it was more candy and flowers, less the ominous stillness and yellow jaundice of a pre-tornado sky. On second thought, since he knew her prickly nature, candy and flowers might trip all his alarms. His current uncomfortable scrutiny might upgrade to full-body-cavity search.

Okay, that was entirely the wrong thought to have.

"So you ran away and decided to open a gun shop because . . . people suck?"

Her lips twitched. Three years since she'd seen him, and he still knew how to pull a smile out of her. She suppressed the reaction, told herself not to give him that advantage. "I didn't run away, but that last part works. Why are you here, Derek?"

He seemed in no hurry on that score. He sauntered up to the counter, giving her a nice eyeful of how the man could walk. Damn him. "I understand you followed Raina out here. She still operating her overpriced cathouse with succubi and incubi disguised as hookers?"

"Escorts," she corrected him. "And yes. It's doing well here, with the military base nearby. Her cover's safer than it was on the West Coast. She'll last longer here."

"She should change professions."

"She would, but this one pisses you off." She flashed a humorless smile. "That's a perk to her."

"I'll bet." That good-ol'-boy languor only enhanced the sexual confidence that made any wise woman wary. "I'm here about a job for you."

When disappointment twisted inside her like a poisoned athame, she cursed at herself. *Cerridwen, Circe and Cassiopeia.* There was only one thing she'd wanted more than for him *not* to find her, and that was for him to find her. To feel absurdly insulted that he'd come this far merely to find her for a job made it official. Female perversity was the bane of her existence.

She guessed she could find a spell that would turn her into a guy, but she liked her long, streaked brown hair, her gray-green eyes and curvy figure. *A better-than-decent rack and wrap-them-around-me-tight-and-fuck-me-all-night legs.* Raina's description, of course, delivered in her typically colorful fashion.

Delicate as a Fae sprite and yet somehow lush as a siren. Derek's description, eliciting different emotions.

Her self-deprecation didn't make her feel one whit less different about seeing him. As if he was picking up on it, he took off his hat, dropped it on the counter. All her senses went on alert. A lazy lion had pushed up to his feet, and she was one of the caribou on the open plain. Waiting to see if he was changing position to lick his balls, going to get some water, or had decided it was time to check out the drive-through menu.

"So what's the real reason you left me, Ruby?" His tone was conversational, mild, but she wasn't fooled. Not when those intent eyes were focused on hers, probing.

"You were too old for me. You literally know what kind of fruit pie George Washington liked."

It was true. He'd never said for sure one way or another exactly how old, but from things he'd told her, she knew he'd actually been alive during the Crusades. He'd aged *extremely* well.

He slid behind the counter. Her hand, resting on the rifle, instinctively tightened. He registered it. "Gonna shoot me just for giving you a friendly hug hello? We are still friends, aren't we?"

One wouldn't think so, when she'd basically told him to stay out of her life. But for some reason, she didn't reply. She couldn't, because he kept coming on, and then he was there, right in front of her. Goddess, he was a big man, and she remembered way too well how much those broad shoulders could bear. She remembered his scent, a subtle magical heat like the residue of a unique gunpowder, infused with an extra explosive kick. Mixed with something even more potent: the sheer warmth and strength of the man. He was *here*. Within touching distance.

She'd known him almost all her life, had loved him about as long. Then she'd shoved him out the door like garbage she couldn't get rid of fast enough. She'd done such a good job of it that it had taken him three years to recover from it and come looking for her.

She would not start shaking. She was not going to break. Yeah, she could have told him to keep his ass on the other side of the counter, or backed away, but she had to prove she was indifferent, right? Friendly hug, a peck on the cheek, then she'd tell him to shove his job up his muscular, far-too-fine butt and get the hell out of her store.

As his arm slid around her, he kept his eyes on her face. She kept hers on his chin, stubborn. He knew her so well, it was like fitting a key to a lock, the way his fingers cruised under the hem of her snug Arcane Shot tee, a forefinger sliding along the valley of her spine, his thumb hooking the waistband of her jeans, stroking the elastic of her panties, so casually seductive.

He tightened his grip, let her feel all that strength reeling her in. She was too stiff, had gone as inflexible as a corpse, and his brow creased. She was proving there was something way wrong, because if she was over him, the hug would have been done by now. Thoughtfully, he leaned down, and she closed her eyes as his lips landed on the corner of her mouth. Just rested there, like a morsel of chocolate icing that had escaped when eating a really, really good fudge cake. The desire to lick at it, rather than reach for a napkin, was almost overwhelming.

The rest of her body wanted to roll the same way. She wanted him to press her back against the ammo case, his oak-like strength against her willowy flexibility, and hook her leg over his hip, bringing him even deeper into the cradle between her thighs.

"I smell Deception potion on your breath, Ruby. You're double-dosing these days. The Dr Pepper isn't covering it."

"I've never had a good poker face. You need one in this job. It helps." She managed a casual shrug, one that she turned into a step back, knowing she was almost against the cash register. But she refused to give off trapped vibes. Sliding a hand in her pocket, she leaned against the ammo case. All by herself. "Okay, you've had your hug. Now give me some room and tell me what the job is so I can tell you I'm not interested."

"Wasn't much of a hug. You didn't hug back."

"You just wanted me to grope your ass, and I'm not in the mood." *Yeah, that was the biggest lie in the history of the world.* "I mean it, Derek. I'm busy. Talk."

The tension was building in her breast, because of the things unsaid, the things she suspected were happening under that casual demeanor. *Goddess, hold it together, Ruby.*

Giving her a long look, he inclined his head at last, but he didn't retreat. He propped a hip against the front counter and crossed his arms, keeping her boxed in. His hat was at her elbow. She didn't want to remember, but she did. That wonderful weekend they'd spent at the beach together. The sun had been so bright, he'd put the hat on her head to protect her fair skin from the rays. They'd walked hand in hand along the shore, like innocent lovers. He'd made love to her later, her wearing nothing but that hat, her sandy toes curled against his calves.

Thank Goddess he started to talk.

"There's a coven in Florida that needs your help."

"Tell them I offer group discounts. They can buy thirteen Sigs for a ten-percent markdown, and I'll throw in a free box of hollow points."

He ignored that. "They're on one of the magical fault lines, and there's been some bad activity brewing there. It's not a quick fix, so they need training, a way to keep it managed themselves. You're one of the best instructional priestesses I know."

"And one of the lousiest practitioners."

"That's your mother talking, not you." He frowned.

"There are better people to do what you're wanting."

"That's your opinion."

"Mine's the only one I'm counting."

He straightened, moved from behind the counter. Though it gave her room to breathe, it didn't give her any relief, because he stopped, hooking his hands in his back pockets to stare up at the row of assault rifles mounted and locked on a metal backboard. "What happened to you, Ruby?"

When she didn't answer, he sighed. "They let it go too long. It's going to take some work to get it all in balance again, and the fight may get ugly. You won't be in the line of fire; that's my area, but I need to know they can hold it after I'm gone. That's where you come in."

"How ugly?" she asked, then cursed herself for appearing the slightest bit concerned.

"I think it's torn up enough to attract attention. I've heard murmurings in the Underworld Asmodeus is headed that way. I want to fend that bastard demon off before he gets there."

As she went still, he turned. His eyes narrowed. "Ruby?"

She was pushing the roaring back, wasn't sure he hadn't said her name several times, because when she focused on him again, he was right up at the counter, his hand landing over her ice-cold one. "Ruby, what the hell—"

"I'll think about it. Can't give you an answer right now." Though of course she already knew that was a lie, and now he probably did, too. Asmodeus made all the difference in the world.

"Maybe you're right. This isn't the right job for you." He studied her face, stepped back. "My mistake."

"Give me the number of the coven priestess. I'll call and talk to her." At his expression, she rolled her eyes. "Stop being such a ninny and give me the number. I was just day-dreaming about how high you'd jump if I peppered your feet with my AK-47, that's all."

"Yeah. I'm sure that was what made you turn white as a sheet." But he wrote down the number on the order pad on the counter, pushed it toward her. When he did, his fingers closed over hers, drew her eyes up to his. "Tell her when you're coming so she can make arrangements for you. I'd wait and take you down there myself, but I've got a couple details to wrap up before I can head that way."

"I'm crushed." She arched a brow. "Here I thought we could do some shopping and get our hair done together."

He gave her a narrow look. "I'll be down there within the week."

"No rush."

"Yeah, there is. They need you to train them. But you need me for the rest. I'm not taking a chance of leaving you to face Asmodeus. That's my job, if it happens."

"My knight in shining Wranglers."

Another one of those intent looks, and then he picked up his hat, put it back on his head. To her relief as well as dismay, he moved toward the door, tousling Theo's ears as he passed the dog. "Keep your mistress safe, Theo."

Glancing back, his hand on the doorknob, he raked his

gaze over her. "You still wear those Victoria's Secret cotton bikinis. Still prefer pink?"

"You're losing your touch," she returned sweetly. "I'm wearing a pair of my boyfriend's briefs. More comfortable than girl's underwear, you know."

He pursed his lips. "Hmm. You may be right about that. I'm not wearing any at all, and I couldn't say where they got off to this morning."

She tightened her jaw. "You're not my boyfriend, Derek Stormwind. I'm long finished with you."

He didn't smile. "You may be finished with me, Ruby Night Divine, but I'm far from finished with you. See you in a week."

AFTER HE LEFT, SHE SLUMPED AGAINST THE COUNTER, her knees buckling. Fortunately, she kept a stool back here to do computer work, and now she slid onto it, taking another sip of the soda with the potion he'd correctly detected on her breath. Hell, if she were a better liar, she wouldn't need it, but that part was the truth. She'd always had a sucker's face, showing every emotion. The Deception potion helped to keep those muscles locked down, which stopped the flickers of the gaze, flushing or nervous body movements that could give things away.

Every part of her was still tingling, her mouth wishing she'd taken that lick. Wishing she'd turned her head and met the kiss full-on, given him everything and taken just as much back. But that was the bitch of it. Some things you just couldn't take back.

That one touch had brought so many memories to mind. The way he would lie curved behind her in her bed, his arm over her body, his hand clasped around her wrist as they slept. Sometimes she'd wake to feel his thumb tracing slow, sensual runes in her palm, along her pulse points. Protective runes, to keep her safe. She could close her hand and still feel them there. Realizing she was doing it now, she opened her fingers, shaking off the feeling.

It didn't work, Derek. Damn you.

That day they'd been at the beach, they'd seen two children playing in the waves, a brother and sister, probably no more than six and seven years old. The boy had his plastic sand shovel and was sweeping it through the water in dramatic, sword-swirling motion, sending out geysers of water toward his sister. She was ineffectually trying to use her spread-fingered hands to splash back at him. It was as if males came out of the womb with that warrior instinct, and women . . . women learned too late.

Asmodeus. Bringing the unloaded sniper rifle determinedly back to her shoulder, she lined up the sights with Derek's retreating form, headed down Main Street. Never again. She'd never be too late again. No matter the cost.

* 2 *

DEREK STARED MOODILY UP AT THE ANTEBELLUM PLANtation house. The driveway to reach it was a mile long, winding through oaks draped with Spanish moss, and punctuated by views of marshland and waterways, since the place used to be a rice plantation. Once near the house, the natural beauty gave way to sculpted gardens and statuary that ranged from sensual to whimsical. In the side yard was a large bronze that looked like children running along a fallen log, a dog chasing after them, while in the front, a large fountain poured water over a pair of naked alabaster lovers.

They were flush against each other, the man's fingers buried in her hair, her head tilted, lips parted, while his mouth was on the tender spot beneath her ear, as if he were whispering his passion and promises to her. The water slid over the shallow valley of their backs, the smooth buttocks, inviting fantasy and touch. Derek remembered how it felt to trail his fingers along Ruby's nape, down the delicate valley of her spine.

The carved oak sign welcomed the visitor to Sweet Dreams.

Like a freaking bed-and-breakfast, which was actually how the place was listed for tax purposes, but he'd bet money no one had ever come to this bordello to sleep, despite the heavy, languorous feel that lay over it like a fantastical mist.

The three-story Queen Anne structure had an elaborate roofline of cross gables and a block tower, a chaotic design he knew was helpful to box in and contain energy flow where needed. On top of the tower was a wind vane, a wrought iron depiction of a witch riding a broom. The fronds of the broom curled like the witch's long streaming hair.

The wraparound porch on the first level matched the balcony on the second and third, with elaborate turned posts and lots of bead- and spindle work. The upper corners of the outdoor living space were embellished with brackets and delicate arches. A wide front door displayed original colored-block stained glass windows with a matching transom. On that small tower balcony, there was a similarly impressive entrance.

He suspected the tower was where Raina's personal rooms were. The laws of gravity made it far easier to disseminate protection spells and other magics over the square footage of the large house from a higher point. And considering the only reason the succubi and incubi in residence didn't fatally drain the clients was the moderating effect of Raina's spells, her location in the house was vitally important to its feng shui.

His lip curled. The whole place suggested an escape into lush, unhurried fantasy, with a subtle undercurrent of erotic danger impossible to resist. A perfect reflection of the female who owned it.

"It's about time you got here, you worthless piece of shit."

It should have bugged him that he hadn't sensed her approach from the side porch, but the list of things he was fucked-up about right now was at capacity. "Could have been here sooner if someone had told me where the hell she was."

"Doesn't work that way. Unfortunately friend loyalty trumps friend stupidity. Plus, I didn't expect it to take a big bad sorcerer three years to find one broody little witch. Oh, let me guess." Her sultry laugh had a sharp edge that could cut off a man's balls. "The world was in peril half a dozen times and you just couldn't pull yourself away."

"Pretty much." It was that, but something more as well, something that had him lifting his gaze and locking with Raina's, showing her this dog wasn't in the mood to have his chain yanked, unless she wanted to see teeth up close and personal.

He'd gone over it a hundred times since Ruby had sent him away. She'd always kept her soul open to him, so they could increase their intimacy, feed that energy, but the day she'd tossed him out of her life, she'd been cold, locked down. The woman he'd seen today was still battened like a ship in a gale. The only good thing about that was it had helped him rein in the million things he'd felt when he turned the knob and saw her standing behind the counter. Controlling his own reaction had helped him notice the big thing that *had* changed.

Ruby had always lacked the confidence to explore her magical potential on a deeper level. In contrast, the woman he'd seen today had enough energy hovering around her it was like watching Pandora's box throw off sparks. Of course, given what had finally brought him back to her side, finding she'd embraced her potential was a bitter confirmation, not a surprise.

He'd *never* have left her under the circumstances in which he had in fact . . . left her. For three years, it had bugged the hell out of him. He'd known something was terribly wrong. Any other time, he would have hung around, dragged the truth out of her. Instead, he'd convinced himself it was best to give her some space. He'd come back later when she'd settled down, figure it out then.

Unfortunately, it had taken months to get back, one thing

or another cropping up, and she hadn't answered calls. Always the same damn answering service, and he didn't carry a phone. Since their romantic relationship had begun, with one vital exception; they'd never been out of contact for more than a few weeks at a time. When he finally got back to the West Coast, he discovered she'd not only pulled up stakes; she'd locked down her essence, making herself virtually invisible. An effort that could only be targeted at him. A big *Leave Me the Hell Alone*.

He'd respected that. What the fuck? His need to find her would ebb and flow, and whenever it hit a big-time flow, he'd be interrupted by other inescapable responsibilities. Then, a couple months ago, he'd heard she was involved with someone.

Bullshit. He knew her, down to blood, heart, soul and the dust of her bones. Yeah, he was possessive, but mere male territorialism hadn't put the hot iron to his blood. The moment he heard the rumor about another guy, it was as if he were in a movie where the fake fog got sucked up by one of those high-powered fans, clearing everything out of his path. The aching need and pain, the loss of her in his life, clamped down on his heart like a bear trap. It was as if he'd been doped up all these months, and now he felt in full force the way he should have been feeling all along.

He'd taken a good hard look at what had happened and considered the unthinkable. A sorcerer guarded himself against spells cast by enemies. Long before McAfee and Norton existed, sorcerers had their own personal virus protection. But they had a similar limitation—they couldn't anticipate everything. And an inside attack was the hardest to predict.

When he'd considered the possibility, done a soul sweep with the new configuration, something had burst inside his unconscious like a stretched chain link finally breaking. It had been the mother of all sucker punches, chilling him to the bone and pissing him off at once.

Ruby had used Dark soul magic to drive him away. That was why none of it had ever made sense. Not his reaction, not hers. For fuck's sake, except for the requirements of the occasional Great Rite he'd had to do, where he channeled the Lord and a priestess channeled the Lady in a physical coupling to raise energy, he hadn't been able to touch another woman for three years, even after Ruby made it clear she had no hold on him.

If anyone could confirm what Ruby had done, it would be the black soul in front of him now. Which was why he was here. He wanted answers.

"She should have fallen for a plumber," Raina remarked. She fastened those exotic green-and-gold feline eyes on him. "Living with someone who gets called out to unstop someone's toilet at two in the morning is a lot less lonely than being with a man who has to unstop the cosmic crapper all the time."

"Lovely language. Quite the Southern belle."

"Oh, I can talk dirty when it suits, Derek. You have no idea." She propped a hip on the front porch rail, which undulated her body into a sinuous *S* of curves designed to make a man's blood drain straight to his cock. Most men.

A long time ago, he'd made Ruby laugh when he suggested Raina sat around in flannels when nobody was around, eating ice cream and watching white-trash reality TV. The truth was she probably lounged on a divan in some dim room scented with money candles, her eyes glowing in the half darkness. Incense would curl around her as she meditated and spun webs to entrap men in her wiles, like a spider plotting against flies.

When she wasn't doing that, she'd be busily tapping keys with her wicked long nails, figuring up her profits. If Hell ever needed a business manager, she was probably on Satan's A-list. If he could handle her, which Derek doubted any male could.

Her hair was blue-black and fell to her hips in curls and

waves, with a few select streaks of red ochre at the temples. Since right now she wore a silk gold robe that clung to her curves, it was easy for a man to imagine that hair tangled in his fingers as she wrapped her arms and legs around him, allowing him to bury himself in that wet dream body. Her fingernails trailed along the rail like a man's arm, drawing his gaze despite himself.

He'd tell her to tone it down, but he knew this was just Raina. Daughter of a witch and an incubus, she could no more turn it off than he could turn off how he felt about Ruby.

"You're still a bitch, you know that?" he grumbled.

"Good thing we both love the same person. Else we might be tempted to maim one another beyond repair."

Goddamn it. He was frustrated, hurting, pissed off, and he had nowhere to go with it. He couldn't change the past three years. In Ruby's shop, he'd picked up on the well of pain trapped behind that smart mouth and hazel eyes. Something unbearably fragile was behind the brick wall she'd constructed against him. So fragile, it might destroy her if he blasted that wall the way he wanted. He had to convince her to open the door, and that wasn't usually the way it worked between them.

She had teased him about his cowboy side, but she liked the way he could rope her down, body, heart and soul, and get her to surrender it all to him. She didn't realize, when he held such gifts in his hands, how their power overwhelmed and humbled him.

He'd seen her potential for a long time, what she could become. Thank God that harpy of a mother of hers was dead, may the Powers that Be forgive him. With Mary Night Divine gone, Derek had been sure Ruby would embrace that side of herself at last. He'd even arrogantly assumed the love he could give her would help fill in that foundation, make it solid.

Well, she'd built herself a foundation, all right. It worried him to the bone what kinds of things were in that concrete.

While he didn't know what the hell had happened, he should have been here to help. Even if he had to let the world fall to darkness.

For every day he'd ever spent with her, he'd had to spend a hundred times that away from her. He had no right to feel this way. Fuck that—he had every right. He knew a lot of things about time, and one of them was that in things like this, it didn't mean shit.

"Where are you staying tonight? You *are* staying."

He looked up to see Raina studying him with narrowed, kohl-rimmed eyes. Though her tone warned him against the wrong answer, the set of her mouth wasn't completely fuck-you-and-the-horse-you-rode-in-on. "I'll find a dive to catch a few hours; then I'll hit the road." Before she could retort to that, he added in a curt tone, "I have some things to set up. I've asked Ruby's help on a job in Florida teaching a coven to contain a fault break. Think she's going to do it."

Raina tapped one of those inch-long nails on the railing. Interestingly, it was painted a delicate frosted pink. "Isn't that like throwing molasses against glue? Taking a woman playing with Dark forces to fight Dark forces?"

Derek set his jaw. So she'd decided to take the bull by the horns. Good. Suited him fine. "What *is* she playing with, Raina?" At the woman's closed expression, he restrained the urge to come up the stairs and throttle her. Instead he simply braced his stance, hooked his thumbs in his jeans pockets and took a gamble on one sure thing. "I know you love her. Else you wouldn't still be here. You could make ten times more in Manhattan with this little gig of yours."

"Yes, but the cost of living is higher. And I couldn't be within a stone's throw of a military base. You know how I feel about men in uniform."

Derek imagined the bruises his fingers could leave on that fragile throat, then swallowed pride. "She used soul magic on me. That's how she drove me off. And it took me too fucking long to figure it out."

The sardonic look on the witch's face vanished as if it had never been. It was one of the few times he'd ever seen her without it. She straightened from the rail, the Lilith seductress routine becoming more Shiva the Destroyer, her eyes like his six-inch switchblade. "Damn her lying bitch ass. Goddamn it. I should have known. You have the stubbornness of the bloodhounds that abound in this backwoods. But she did such a good job . . ." Her eyes became ominous slits. "She used it on all of us. I didn't know she had the ability . . . Well, yes I did. But I never would have thought Ruby . . ."

"Yeah, welcome to my world."

Raina paced along the porch. She was barefoot, which increased the energy connection between her and the house. Heat magic shimmered through the boards like a flash of interior lightning as the witch channeled her anger. When he sensed the stirring of her sleeping succubi and incubi as they registered the formidable heat, he reached out with his own abilities to stabilize and soothe. It was probably unnecessary, though, since Raina had good command of her impressive powers. And, used to the volatile nature of their Mistress, the creatures probably rolled back over almost before her tantrum passed.

The witch stopped at the porch steps, her hands on her hips. "It's stupid for you to pay for a hotel, even with your limitless resources. I'll put you in a room for the night. My cook might fix you a decent steak. Two inches thick and at least two pounds of meat. Plus a bowl of mashed potatoes and gravy that'll fill even your bottomless pit."

He eyed her. The steak offer was appealing, since he always needed calories for his freakishly high metabolism. However, the meat would have to bunk down in his lean stomach with his bile over Ruby, so it might not be the most settling meal he'd ever eaten. Particularly considering his added wariness of the offering and what lay in that house. The Shoney's all-you-could-eat buffet might be the better bet. "What's the catch?"

She sighed. "You're not the only one who operates on a code, Derek Stormwind. My house has a life of its own." She stroked the pillar at the top of the porch, hand molding over the rounded shape. The gesture immediately conjured the vision of her cupping a woman's breast, or trailing her hand along a generous female hip. "Even if I'd like to take a pitchfork to your tediously noble heart, my house tells me when someone comes to my door needing what I can offer. And, like every successful businessperson, I don't ignore or neglect the advice of my assets. This is sort of like that."

"I think I'll find the motel."

"Don't be such a pussy. You came here because you think I'll tell you what you want to know about Ruby. I won't, but that doesn't mean you won't learn things from me that will help you. You already have. So don't pretend you're not coming in. I read men for a living. You may be a great sorcerer, but you have a dick, and that pretty much dictates everything else about you."

"I don't want anything your house has to offer."

"So faithful. You're wrong. Everything you want you'll find in here. I promise you that. What you do with it . . . that's up to you."

* 3 *

RUBY HAD CALLED THE COVEN PRIESTESS IN FLORIDA. Linda Egret was not only Wiccan; she was an engineer and middle manager at a nuclear plant. Her technical, left-brain background was evident by her cautious and practical demeanor, relieving Ruby considerably. While she knew Derek wouldn't train a coven to protect a fault line if they weren't serious practitioners, it was good to confirm Linda knew her stuff, which meant her coven did as well. It told Ruby she wasn't being sent in as a kindergarten teacher to teach ABCs and wipe noses. Derek was dispatching her as an expert consultant, augmenting a local spiritual force's arsenal of skills. She'd be teaching higher levels of energy manipulation, geared to keep a fault line reinforced and stable. Once she showed them the basics on that, they'd take it from there.

However, even the estimated two weeks away from her business required a certain amount of preparation. The firing range was handled, because the facility was off premises, and she contracted with a trio of local cops to handle its open shifts for supplementary income. John, the most dependable of them, would come open up the store for a few hours each day to handle shipments and pending orders, and she could manage their Internet store from wherever she was. The constant work to try to restock inventory from overtaxed suppliers would just have to wait, but she at least needed to make sure the most recent log entries and 4473 forms for purchases were in order, in case the trip took longer than expected and a random ATF visit happened in her absence. She didn't carry a lot of cheap guns, so ATF flagged her place a lot less frequently than they did the local pawnshop, but if they called in for a trace, she didn't want John to have any trouble locating the right information.

The government insisted on knowing every last detail of every firearm sale, making sure she hadn't peddled her wares to a six-year-old wanting to play Rambo, or the felon with a yard-long rap sheet. There was even more red tape on the front end, verifying her suppliers weren't black-market operators. So in short, if she got behind on the paperwork, catching up was like a root canal without painkillers.

Which was why she had no idea why she'd set all that aside to go to Raina's.

As she drove her beat-up van down the winding road leading to Raina's place, her lip curled at the thought of the latest stack of invoices on her desk. The current cost of keeping an adequate inventory made black-market prices way too tempting. Demand was high these days, not only for guns, but munitions and accessories for them, and the prices she was paying reflected that. Many gun brands were back-ordered for months at the manufacturers, so the bulk of her time was spent figuring out how to get what her customers wanted quicker.

Mikhael—an acquaintance, in lieu of a better word for their complicated relationship—had offered to get her military surplus fast if needed, but his secretiveness about his sources made her wary. That wariness had been replaced by outright rejection when he added he could get her certain gun brands for 30 percent under her supplier's price, which meant they were stolen. When she asked him point-blank about it, his response was that they'd been liberated from those who shouldn't have them. He also courteously noted that he could make the paperwork pass inspection so she wouldn't have to worry about that. *Yeah, right.*

Actually, from what she knew about Mikhael, she didn't doubt it. She still wasn't touching any deal he offered with a ten-foot pole. ATF could shut down a store at the drop of a hat if they scented even a whiff of something out of order. Mikhael kept offering, however, and she kept telling him he was Satan, tempting her with water in the desert. Mikhael had replied with his usual indifferent shrug.

The Devil isn't to blame for offering the temptation. The weakness of men is, for taking it. Fast-food employees sell hamburgers to overweight people with heart problems. I sell guns to people who may or may not do bad things with them. It is not up to me to make others' choices. I am not worried about going to Hell, Ruby. Haven't you been paying attention? Hell lurks in every corner of this *world.*

Despite her unwillingness to accept his offers, or sign off on straw purchases he requested, gun purchases he was coordinating for someone sight unseen, Mikhael had proven useful for other things, as most sources of seductive Dark power were.

Maybe it was the paths she'd traveled in the past three years, or maybe it was being without Derek. She didn't like to think about which reason gave the knife such a cruel edge, but at times her body burned for release so badly it was painful. Her hand and modern electronics could do only so much. She couldn't relax enough, couldn't get there, and it could make her cry with frustration in the small hours of the night. The Darkness would roll through her, taunting her with erotic whispers of forbidden things, needs that grew desperate and volatile. That was when she'd met Mikhael.

In reflection, he *had* been the Devil, only it wasn't his offer of low-cost guns that made damnation look irresistible.

Mikhael, with his apathetic attitude toward good and evil, his pure physical intensity. He fucked women. Never made love to them, wooed them, romanced them. The first time she saw him, he was sitting at a bar, spinning a half-empty glass of whiskey while he pointedly studied the over-flowing cleavage of an animated blonde chattering to him. It was a trade show, a big one that catered to gun suppliers and store owners, so Ruby had been at a table with an owner from Texas and two guys who ran a machine shop. The first was trying to flirt with her; the other two wanted to help with the repair side of her business. They interested her far more than the flirting gun store owner.

But when her gaze flickered over to the bar, she'd been caught by the way strands of dark hair fell over the tall man's brow, how his sensual lips were set in a stern, cruel line. He'd turned his head, as if feeling her regard. Brown eyes the color of deep-below-the-surface earth had swept over her with the same deliberate appraisal he'd had for the blonde's tits, only he seemed to like what he saw in Ruby's direction more.

He finished the drink in a swallow, stubbed out his ciga-rette and left the woman in mid-sentence, not saying another word to her. As Ruby watched him come, all that heated need boiled up in her, but a deep panic as well. She wanted to cry out for Derek, run away from this approaching threat, but Derek wasn't there. He was never going to be there for her again, because she'd sent him away. Because he hadn't been there when it mattered, and that changed everything.

Leaning down to her, the dangerous male cupped the side of her neck, strong fingers stroking beneath her ear as he murmured into it, his voice flavored by a Russian accent.

"There is a stockroom by the elevators on the mezzanine level. You will meet me there in fifteen minutes. I will fuck you like a whore, and give you the pleasure and pain you

crave. I will not ask you the questions you do not want to answer. That is not what I care about."

Then he was gone, the shockingly intimate touch and words vibrating through her. She'd gone to the stockroom, and he'd done things to her in the dark that left her gasping and in tears. Her whimpers had only fueled his rough handling of her, as if he knew that was what she needed. She'd wanted punishment and release, and he'd given her both. She hated him, and yet he was in that desolate part of her soul, such that when she met him several times a year, it always resulted in the same. Shameful acts in the shadows that left her crying for Derek in her heart, even as her body spasmed under Mikhael's ruthless touch.

Dark and Light. She wasn't yin and yang anymore. Dark and Light had become so mixed she was a permanent, storm-cloud gray, a color she was pretty certain was becoming blacker and more ominous-looking every day.

SHOWN IN BY RAINA'S DAY HOUSEKEEPER, WALKING THE long hallway to the parlor, Ruby remembered why she didn't come here that often. It whetted that cruel need. The hallway was lined with erotic oil paintings, blatantly depicting every imaginable sex act. Vanilla missionary, ménage couplings, a chained male on his knees being whipped by a pair of females in only corsets and stockings. Spankings, doggie style, oral . . .

But the most disturbing piece was mounted over the fireplace in the parlor. In the lush oil painting, a rugged, virile male stood over a woman, kneeling naked before him. He was wearing black-tie formal, only he'd shed the coat, rolled up the sleeves. He'd lifted her chin, his fingers stroking her throat. Her hands were tied behind her back and bound to her ankles, so she was helpless to him. But her eyes, riveted with absolute attention on his face, were adoring. As he gazed upon her, his expression made it clear he was completely in control, yet somehow he conveyed how much he cherished her. They belonged to each other, complex nuances of surrender and possession. It was a decadent, graphic and reverent vision, all at once.

She hated that one, mainly because she couldn't ever stop looking at it.

The pictures weren't here merely to torture her. Being close to the military base and a major seaport, Raina had a plethora of international clients. Even those who had a good command of English could stumble when they tried to voice their fantasies. A picture was worth a thousand words, and having the visual à la carte menu was a bordello tradition that dated all the way back to the times of Pompeii. Typical Raina, none of the pictures were cheap porn renditions, but all fine, expensive pieces done by masters. Walking that hallway fueled the libido, the eyes gulping down the offerings like an all-you-can-eat buffet that never filled the stomach, resulting in a ravenous body that wanted more and more. The soul could get lost here forever, like Ulysses on Circe's island. Why the hell had she come?

The housekeeper had said Raina was with someone, but she'd join Ruby shortly. She was brought a glass of her favored white zinfandel and some chocolate truffles and tea cakes, without requesting either one. Raina's customer service rating put even Disney to shame.

What the hell. She finished off about half before she heard the brush of Raina's bare soles on the polished winding staircase in the main foyer. She was moving at her usual casual saunter, that pendulum sex walk that was impossible not to watch, whatever the viewer's gender, orientation, species or religious affiliation.

"You know that act's wasted on me," she commented out loud, knowing Raina was within hearing. "You could clop down here like a Clydesdale, for all I care."

"Your first mistake is assuming it's an act. Your second

is lying. I know you'd do me in a heartbeat, if you could afford me."

"Yeah, right. Bitch."

Ruby meant it with the usual acid affection, but when Raina stopped in the doorway of the parlor, her true greeting, her intention to pour out what had happened, where she was going, her desire to confide in one of her closest friends, faltered. She detected genuine anger in Raina's gaze, even some hurt. But then it was gone as if it had never been. Raina's usual expression was back in place, cool, indifferent amusement.

Unlike Mikhael's true indifference, however, there was a softness to Raina, a kindness and generosity of spirit that had made them fast friends all these years. Regret came with that thought, but Ruby pushed it away, knowing that was a road she couldn't go down.

"Everything all right?" Ruby asked, rising. Recognizing that Raina's mood might have nothing to do with her, protective concern filled her instantly. "Something wrong with a client? Do you need help kicking someone's ass?"

Raina's expression eased a bit. "Always riding to the rescue, so unwilling to let anyone help you. You missed your calling, my dove. You should have been a martyr."

She was used to Raina's bitter tongue, but that cut a little too deep. She shrugged it off. Maybe she wasn't going to get the friendly reinforcement, the girl talk she'd hoped to find here, but so be it. "I came to say good-bye for a few days." She took a breath. "Derek's found me, and he's asked for my help."

Raina barely blinked, but it was rare she gave any emotion away. In her business, having ironclad control of facial expressions was a key job requirement. Which was why that brief flash of hurt and anger still had Ruby a little rattled. "Of course he has," Raina said dryly. "Figures he wouldn't show up unless he needed something."

She'd made Raina and Ramona, her other closest friend, believe that Derek had been the one to leave her. It hadn't been fair to him, just as leaving Raina's accusation hanging out there now wasn't. But she couldn't change that. "Good cause, though." Ruby pushed forward. "Coven needing help, demon army on the march, blah, blah, blah."

"And aren't you the good little Buffy, riding to the rescue?" Raina shifted to her opposite hip, moving to another topic in the same flowing motion. "Then I'm glad you're here. I need you to test something for me before you leave. Given how tense you look, I think it would do you some good."

"Raina, I told you, I don't really feel comfortable with one of your—"

"Oh, pure illusion, dove. Smoke and mirrors. It's a charm room, designed to manufacture a favorite fantasy straight from your mind. I've been spending my few off-hours perfecting it, and I think it's ready to go. And before you balk, it has a benevolent purpose, a public service for a private cost." Her small, even white teeth flashed. "Military spouses can imagine being with their loved ones. Those who have private fantasies they can't bring themselves to share with their significant others can act them out, gain the confidence to do so. Or enjoy them like a dream, no guilt of having committed actual physical adultery." Her dark eyes flashed. "Let off that steam pressure, so to speak."

"Raina, I really don't have time—"

"Another magic user needs to feel it out before I make it operational. Just in case it gives someone rabbit ears or a third eye, some nasty business like that. With Valentine's Day coming up, I'm launching it with a formal tea to attract the women in the area. The first twenty-five military wives will get a free hour, my gift to the community." Putting a hand on her generous breast, Raina made a beneficent expression that elicited a snort from Ruby.

"You know I can't ask poor Ramona to test it," she added. "With her random chaos issues, the thing would detonate, blow pure emotional fantasy into a nightmare of one's worst imaginings. Hannibal Lecter meets *Debbie Does Dallas*."

Ruby's lips quirked. Ramona ran an herb; novelty and magic shop. The white-rabbit-and-disappearing-handkerchief kind, which was a good cover for the fact that her magic was wildly unpredictable yet somehow always appropriate to the situation, no matter how roundabout its path to the final goal. Amusingly, the waiflike woman's demeanor was similar, her focus always seeming to be else-where, yet always attuned to what someone's emotions really were. Which was why Ruby had avoided seeing her more and more.

"I'm going to tell her you said that. All right. I have an hour, but then I really have to get back to the shop."

"More than enough time." Those jewellike eyes gleamed, making Ruby somewhat uncomfortable. What the hell was going on with Raina today?

Striving to take it to more normal footing, Ruby switched back to the issue at hand, at least for her. "Would you keep Theo while I'm gone? He doesn't do so well traveling any-more because the arthritis in his hips is getting bad. He jumped up on Derek today, so excited to see him, but that's the first time I've seen him do that in ages."

"Apparently, Theo doesn't share our mutual disdain for the asshole. I'll have to talk to him about that."

"It's water under the bridge, Raina," Ruby said quietly. "Just let it go. We're working together on this, and it will be better if we do it as friends, not enemies."

"Yes. Trust is important between friends."

Ruby swallowed, fumbling out an envelope from her purse. "I need a favor. Probably the biggest favor I've ever asked you."

She met Raina's green-and-gold eyes. "This envelope is spelled so that it can't be opened unless I'm dead. I know you're probably powerful enough to undo it, but I'm asking you to respect that, not try to unravel it. Okay?"

Raina's brow creased, some of that reserved look disappearing. "Ruby, you're teaching a coven how to do protection work. Not usually fatal or all that dangerous. Unless you can die from an overdose of hen party."

"I know. It's just a precaution." Ruby's lips tightened. Derek thought he would handle Asmodeus, but things didn't always happen as planned. Not if Ruby had anything to say about it. "If something does go wrong, I need you to open that and follow it to the letter. It's the most important thing I could ever ask of anyone, and I ask it of you, because I trust you more than anyone. I . . ."

Those pressure cracks that Derek's presence had created ran a little further into her heart, making her pause. "I know I haven't been a good friend, not for the past several years. You've known it, yet you've been a far better friend than I deserve."

Raina's dispassion disappeared. Snatching the envelope out of Ruby's hand, she tossed it to a side table and put both hands on Ruby's shoulders. "Okay, you're acting like this is the last time we're going to talk, which is making it really hard for me to be pissed off at you. And that just annoys me more."

"Why are you pissed off at me?" Ruby blurted out.

"You have your secret. That will just have to be mine." When Raina pulled her down on the velvet sofa designed for longer male legs, she curled her legs up beneath her. Ruby did the same, so they faced each other. In the mirrors scattered around the room, Ruby thought they looked like bookends, connected by their joined hands, elbows propped on the back cushion between them. She stared at her friend, wishing she could say so many things. Raina shook her head, sighed. "Don't know why you bring this out in me. Come here."

As Raina drew her closer, Ruby laid her head in the other woman's lap, curling her arms around her hips as Raina stroked her hair. "You're a pain in my ass," the witch said, tugging Ruby's ponytail. "And you better come back, or I will give that slobbering dog to a cult and let them torture him to death."

"You won't. He's the only male you ever let sleep in your bed."

"Well, he is warm and he doesn't hog the sheets. He might drool and have terrible gas, but as long as I don't light a candle, he's a lot safer than most bedmates."

"Men aren't really all that bad."

"Occupational hazard, dove." Raina twisted Ruby's ponytail around her fingers. "This is a place for men to come and be vulnerable. That's fine, but what I want is a man without his vulnerabilities hanging out like sloppy shirttails. A real man can lower his shields and still be a man. Too many these days are children masquerading as men, suckled at their mother's tit for far too long. I'll give Derek that much credit. He's a man in every sense of the word. They're few and far between."

Ruby was quiet a moment. "You know he didn't dump me."

"I figured that out some time ago. So did Ramona. A dumped woman has a grieving process, usually involving alcohol, anger and bitter jokes about the tiny size of his penis and brain, which are interchangeable at that point. You're carrying a deep, frightening anger, Ruby, but it's the kind that pushes a man away from her, not the other way around."

The lump in Ruby's throat was painful and immediate, and she turned her face into Raina's thigh, fighting back the tears. *Damn it, not now.* Raina respected her attempt to bring it back under control, rubbing her nape and shoulders without saying anything for a while.

When they'd slept in the same bed, Derek had done that. Closing her eyes, Ruby gave herself the contraband memory, probably the real reason Raina didn't sleep with men. The intimacy of it was overwhelming. Addictive, when it was the right male. She missed it as much as the sex. Often more, and given how much she missed the sex, that was saying something.

"Well, he's free, by my choice." Ruby forced out the words. "Go for it. I don't have any claim on him."

Raina tugged her head up. "I like all my limbs in the proper places. Don't try to convince me you wouldn't turn me into a warty toad, because I know better. Ruby . . . was it losing the baby? Is that why you sent him away?"

"Raina—"

"I know. You don't want to talk about that, not now, not ever. You told me as much, when you made me swear he would never know." Raina cupped her face when Ruby would have looked away. "That man is a pain in the ass in so many ways. But I will bet every dollar I've ever earned that he's missed you as much as you miss him. And you know how I feel about my money. I only bet on sure things."

She was already aching. She didn't want this conversation. The look in Derek's intense dark blue eyes was already haunting her, vibrating through her body. "He's probably been with hundreds of women since three years ago." Ruby tried to shrug, shoulders weighted down with an avalanche of hard emotions. "Derek Stormwind is far too virile, too close to nature . . ."

That was the thing about him. Though Derek said he was human, she'd felt things from him that were far more than human. When they'd walked on a beach and he embraced her, she'd felt the movement of the tides and currents through his kiss, inhaled salt and sea through his skin. In the mountains, it was as if the grand panorama of peaks, the smallest woodland creatures, the silver winding ribbons of creeks, streams and rivers, all of it, were coursing through him. When she'd visited such places alone, that quiet tranquility she felt, a sense of the powerful energy of nature itself, that connected animal, rock, tree, sky, stars and moon . . . They all made her realize it wasn't in his magic. It was *him*. He was a conduit to the Earth, to all four of the elements and the sacred energy that connected them. He was pure power, gentle rain and terrible thunder both, and no woman with a pulse could resist that. Even zombie women would probably respond to him.

"Raina, with the Great Rite alone, he could get himself all sorts of available pussy. I'm sure he hasn't been hurting for it."

"You are far more than sex to him. And misusing the Great Rite is the last thing he'd ever do. He is tediously noble, a true white knight. With a deliciously demanding, alpha dominant edge to him when it comes to that out-front sexuality of his."

"Thanks for twisting that knife."

"Oh, I'll bet he twists his knife quite capably . . ."

"Raina." Pushing up to her knees, Ruby snatched a pillow, swatted it at her. Raina grabbed the other cushion and returned blow for blow, until Ruby was laughing despite herself. She stopped in the middle of the room, breathing hard. The swirling laughter stirred up other things, sediment that shouldn't be disturbed.

"Sweetheart." Raina's arms were around her, Ruby's suddenly wet face pressed into her shoulder. Ruby fought it back, but it was too hard. She had to let some of it out, one tiny sentence.

"I've missed him so much." She gripped Raina harder to contain the sob behind that simple, devastating truth. This was so not good. "I can't have him, Raina. I just can't. Don't ask why."

"Bullshit, dove." But Raina's voice was gentle as she rocked her, held her together. "Maybe this trip to help the coven will be good, help you both figure some things out. Though fair warning—if you invite him back into your life, I'll continue to treat him like the sanctimonious prick he is."

Ruby shook her head, stepped back. "This may bring closure, but it's not a new beginning for us, Raina. That part of my life is done." *It has to be. There's too much blood, too much pain . . . Too much water has gone under the bridge. And that water is the River Styx, all about death and endings. Not life and new beginnings.*

"All right, then." Raina gave her a piercing look, but

didn't push it further, to Ruby's great relief. Moving to the bar, she fished around, found what looked like a deep purple wine and splashed a small amount in a shot glass, pushing it over to Ruby. "That's all the more reason you should try this little room of mine. You're an emotional mess, and it will help you get the physical urges under control. You're emanating sexual need a ten-cylinder Dodge Ram vibrator couldn't handle, darling."

Still holding the pillow, Ruby pantomimed another swat at her. Raina countered with a wave of her hand that pulled the cushion from Ruby's grasp and returned it to the couch with her own pillow. It was a demonstration of the witch's effortless control over her magic, a control she'd always had.

Ruby grimaced, affecting a look of resignation, but she knew too much about the pleasures of Raina's house, at least by description. She wasn't going to resist Raina's demand. Her body was revved up way too high to do any well-grounded energy work, but because of what was in that letter, she *had* to do energy work tonight. Her paperwork was important, but not as important as the protection spells she had to lay down before she left. She took the shot glass, sniffed at it. "Raina, there's nightshade in this."

"Yes, it helps the room do what it needs to do. Not enough to poison you, dove, I promise."

"How comforting." *What the hell.* Ruby downed it in a quick movement, was surprised to find it potent and sweet. "Okay. Let's go do the 'Escape from My Agonizing Reality Room.'"

"What a catchy title. Thank God guns don't require clever marketing campaigns. Just, 'If you want to kill something, I'm here to help.'"

"Good customer service doesn't have to be complex."

"Too true."

* 4 *

DESIGNED TO MANUFACTURE A FAVORITE FANTASY straight from your mind . . .

"Focus on the candle, think of your fantasy, and the magic unfolds. The client also has the option of not thinking of a fantasy at all, letting the magic choose from the unconscious. The stronger that unconscious fantasy, the more likely it is to take precedence during the session, no matter what you actively choose." At Ruby's alarmed look, Raina's tone gentled. "It will be what you want, dove. Don't worry about that."

Then, becoming brisk once again, she added, "Don't use any active magic to force it, because my clients won't be able to do so. Just the focus of your own desires, where your mind takes you. When you're ready for it to end, there's a candle present throughout the session, in one guise or another. Blow it out. But don't blow it out too soon, or I'll call you a fat-assed chicken and make you do it all again."

"Your ass is bigger."

"Unlike you, I believe eating is required to sustain life."

A complex, powerful spell designed to be harmless fantasy.

This was the type of thing that drove Derek crazy when it came to Raina. But Raina was Raina. Sometimes Ruby thought Raina's mother had chosen her name based on the adage: "Might as well try to stop the rain from coming down."

She tried to relax, but apprehension still knotted the muscle group between her shoulders when Raina closed the door, leaving her in a chamber the size of a bedroom. Nothing was in it except a polished oak pedestal and the burning candle sitting on it. Though mundane eyes couldn't see them, Ruby discerned the circle drawn on the floor, the symbols marking thirteen evenly spaced points. Symbols also marked the key compass points on the walls and ceiling. Noting their placement and meaning, she appreciated the elegant craft that had allowed an enclosed space for magic to ricochet and become four-dimensional.

Her apprehension had nothing to do with a lack of confidence in Raina's abilities. Probably just the opposite. Fantasies weren't harmless, not for her. That driving hunger came from a black well inside her, and it took very little for it to boil forth. Just being here, in Raina's house of nonstop fornication, was enough to have it doing a clog dance on her uneasy stomach. Most days she could put a tight lid on it, but then yearning desire, a prettier but no less demanding face of that hunger, would sneak up on her in dreams. Sometimes it chased her through the day. If it became unbearable, she was like an AA-attending alcoholic, overwhelmed by the never-ending craving. A quick trip out of town and a violent binge with Mikhael was followed by the hangover of shame and renewed resolve, couched in the battered lie that it would never happen again.

In short, she spent more time quelling such imaginings than dwelling upon them. So why the hell had she agreed to do this?

She was being a drama queen. This was just a favor for Raina. A test. Like she was in a laboratory, wearing a white coat, very clinical. Of course, it was far more likely she was the lab rat and Raina was wearing the white coat. A sexy, tailored lab coat, made by a French or Italian designer. Cheap synthetic blends had never touched those silken shoulders.

Ruby put her hand on her abdomen, soothing that clog dance. Okay, she could do this. She'd fantasize about a long bubble bath with a good book. The New Kids on the Block and the Backstreet Boys would be serenading her from a corner. A few of them could multitask and give her a foot and back massage. Wash her hair while crooning one of their love songs. That would be perfect. A perfect, safe fantasy.

She positioned herself in one corner of the room. She didn't have to act as obliviously defenseless as most humans did. It didn't affect the activation of the spell, after all.

Interestingly, the very moment she decided she was ready, the room darkened around the candle like a movie theater, only this was a deep gray mist, swirling around the flame and outward. It closed in on her, took up all the available space. She could still see the candle's flame, but she lost her tame fantasy, her mind swiveling toward fearful memory. Things could come out of the mists, things that were far from harmless. Panic drilled holes in her diaphragm.

A breath away from tossing up protection spells that would take out that candle with the force of a Cat 5 hurricane and blast away all of Raina's painstaking work, she saw the mist start to clear.

The rush of ocean waves reached her ears, the comforting salt aroma filling her nose. Powdery white sand was under her feet. She stood on a moonlit beach, the water stretched to the horizon, the white curve of sand inviting long, romantic strolls. A hammock was strung between two palm trees. On a table next to it was a platter of fruit and cheese, glasses of wine picking up the glimmer of the moonlight.

All it needed was a zoom-in on the wine label and an invisible announcer intoning, "Please drink responsibly."

But it was okay. This was beautiful, serene. Only the two wineglasses bugged her. One would be better, more aligned with the fantasy she had in mind. Or a stack of the plastic kind, to accommodate both bands if they needed to wet their throats between sets for her private concert.

When her gaze strayed back to the shoreline, her heart accelerated like one of those maniacal cymbal-clashing monkeys. Derek was coming out of the water.

Like that night on the beach over three years ago, he was wearing only a pair of jeans, plastered to his long thighs. He hadn't had any trunks, and the beach had been a little less private than this one, so he'd stripped off his shirt, shucked the boots and socks, diving in after her in denim. That lack of privacy hadn't mattered so much in the water. He'd untied her bikini bottoms with deft fingers and then, with a smile made for sin, tied them around her wrists. Linking her bound hands around his neck for an anchor, he'd proceeded to do things that had her clinging helplessly to him, gasping. She remembered the heated strength of his hands pressed against her wet flesh, his husky voice against her ear as he held her so close, all her limbs locked around him because she never, ever wanted to let him go, to let that moment go.

Goddess, he looked so good. The water sluiced down his wide chest. Unlike the hairless boys of the current popular pinups, he had a silken mat of dark chest hair narrowing to that appealing arrow that cut straight down his ridged abdomen. The water weighed the jeans down enough that his hip bones showed, the musculature over them. His lean form had never experienced an ounce of fat, let alone the blasphemy of a love handle. Being a Guardian of the Light meant battles where his life depended on quick reflexes, stamina and a body in top peak form. He took his workouts seriously. He ran, kickboxed, did a dozen different types of martial arts, lifted weights with the dedication of a Mr. Universe.

However, because the magic gobbled calories as fast as she could down a pound bag of M&M'S, he didn't have a body-builder's thick physique. Instead, he had the build of a quarter-back, ready to throw a seventy-five-yard pass to win the game.

She wanted the fantasy to freeze-frame here. She at a

safe distance, looking at him like any woman on the beach would, imagining all the things she could do with him. That he could do to her. The moment she touched him, even as illusion, need was going to overwhelm her. But she didn't have the strength to deny herself, just as she'd feared. As Raina had known. Her gaze followed those drops of water over firm skin she wanted to touch, lick, bite. She wanted to rub herself all over him like an animal, re-marking him with her scent. He'd been hers. He *was* hers. The power of it rolled up in her, a savage, feral female animal.

His broad chest expanded further, getting his breath back from his swim. His gaze covered the beach like he was seeing it for the first time, evaluating it for threats, things hidden in the shadows. That was so Derek, it almost made her smile, except the pain of memory was squeezing her heart too hard. He found her pretty quickly, standing out there in the open, staring at him with such hunger in her face.

"Hey, girl," he murmured.

That was what he called her in their intimate moments. It wasn't the affected "giiirll" of the urban scene, like "Girl, where *did* you get those earrings?" It was the cowboy, meeting her for the first time at the church social, doffing his hat and giving her a slow smile. When he said, "Hey, girl," those concentrated blue eyes said he thought she was the prettiest girl in three counties, and she'd always be that way to him, even when she was eighty years old.

She'd been raised in a host of cities and towns, part of her mother's divination tour. Those travels had always been overpopulated with eccentric wealth and pretentious academics, so she was as country as a New York cab. But her heart had responded to the wide-open-range and quiet-nights-by-a-fire in those eyes the first time she'd seen him, as if that was really where she was meant to be.

She swallowed. "Hi."

His firm mouth curved, his eyes glowing, taking everything away but this moment.

This was too emotional. She needed to get out of here. The candle was on the table between the wineglasses, somehow undisturbed by the ocean breeze. She didn't move toward it, though. She wanted the physical, wanted it badly enough that she didn't have the strength to end this, but it couldn't happen here. This was where he'd first told her he was in love with her, the words murmured against her ear as he entered her, slow and deep. His fingers had tangled in her wet hair so she met his eyes as he said it, saw how much he meant it.

This wasn't fantasy; it was a trip to heartbreak. But damn it, she wanted to immerse, purge, pleasure. Raina said she couldn't use active magic, but she'd implied simple thought could change the setting. Shutting her eyes, Ruby wished for a different venue, fierce as a child following the track of a shooting star. She didn't have a specific scenario in mind. Anywhere but here would do.

The smell of the ocean disappeared, as well as the sense of being outdoors. When she opened her eyes, she was hell and gone from the beach. She'd let the magic choose, and just as Raina had warned, it had delved deeper into her unconscious. Ruby hadn't really believed it was capable of plucking a fantasy from the darkest part of the psyche, but she was looking at proof it could.

Like so many others, she sometimes forgot that behind Raina's sultry Belle Watling–meets-Jezebel routine was an extremely powerful witch. Ruby was impressed as hell—and thrillingly terrified.

This scenario was something she'd never done with Derek, but she'd certainly fantasized about it. She was in a stable. A stable with the smell of fresh-cut hay, warm horses, saddle leather, wood. The candle was a lantern, sitting on a rough-hewn table next to a hoof pick and a few bits of harness. Rain was drumming on the tin roof, so the sound of water was still here. She was entirely naked, except for a red corset that cinched her in like an hourglass and restricted her breathing. Her breasts were pillowed up high, her waist tiny, and her bare ass was braced on her heels. That was because she was kneeling on the ground, her wrists tied behind her, and those wrists were tied to her ankles, so she couldn't pull against them without the danger of toppling herself over.

She'd co-opted the picture in Raina's parlor. She looked like a man's fantasy, and it made her tremble, because she knew she looked like one particular man's fantasy. A man who had a propensity for saloon girls and the John Wayne cowboy code of the Wild West, a code he claimed was directly connected to the code of knights and chivalry. Since he'd been alive back then, he should know.

When she lifted her gaze, he was standing a few paces away. He was still wet, only now he wore a duster, chaps, boots and spurs. He carried a bridle and a coil of rope on his shoulder, as if he'd just come in from tending stock. As he studied her, he let them slide off that broad perch, tossed them onto the back of a chair with a clank of metal and a muted thud. She clung to the way the rough twine passed through his fingers, and she shivered as she imagined that against her skin. He saw it, the blue eyes becoming more intent.

"You're a fantasy, for sure," he rumbled. The sound of that sexy voice, low and filled with lust, made her rib cage strain for more air in her boned confinement. "All tied up so you can't run from me." Picking up the rope, he twisted it in his hand, and she noticed it had a couple knots in the end. "Maybe I should put you over my knee and beat you, for all the bad nights you've given me. Or keep a bit in your mouth until I've had my say and that sharp tongue doesn't interfere. But I think I've got a better use for your mouth."

He moved to her then, bringing the smell of leather and denim close. "Lift your face up to me. Close your eyes."

She did, and gasped as cold rainwater splashed across her cheeks, over her breasts. Opening her eyes, she saw he'd taken off his hat, angling it so the water still captured in the brim trickled slowly over her. He watched the water run down her breasts, some of it funneling into the cleavage. "I like you all trussed up, in just that corset."

The bikini bottoms tied around her wrists hadn't been the first time their lovemaking had taken this kind of turn. She'd been innocent when he'd first lain with her, but their couplings had integrated this element almost from the beginning. She'd spent her life so guarded, so many things locked up inside. Through restraint and command, Derek was able to free her. Though not all alpha men had it, she'd recognized that dominance went naturally with his personality, and something in her craved and responded to it. Every time he won her surrender, that boulder of responsibility, guilt and insecurity was removed, letting her breathe.

It was part of what had pulled her to Mikhael, she couldn't deny it, though she knew there was a pretty big chasm between this and that. Mikhael's dominance helped her appease her body's hunger. Derek's helped her stretch her wings, let her fly. With Mikhael, she found a way to numb her aching heart. With Derek, she surrendered it utterly. It was chicken and egg. Maybe Mikhael had given her the bravery to flesh this particular fantasy out in her head. Or maybe her needs with Mikhael had become even more explicit, the more she fantasized about and missed Derek. As closely linked as Derek and she had once been, she wondered if maybe this fantasy had crossed his mind a couple times.

Oh, Goddess, this was a huge mistake.

She saw something warring in his expression as well, likely a projection of what was going on inside of her. She told herself she wanted to be used hard, fucked senseless. She wanted an act devoid of tenderness. And yet she hungered for him to bend down, put his mouth on hers, give her one of those soul-stealing kisses where she'd open herself up and hand him her heart anew, everything she was or wished to be.

"Please," she whispered. She didn't know how to choose, but it was okay; it was her fantasy. It would know. Raina had said so.

"So afraid of letting go, but all sweet honey when I take control. Fuck, you're killing me."

Shrugging off the duster, he tossed the rope aside so it hit the table with another heart-stopping thud. The lantern trembled, and so did she, afraid it might go out. But this was her fantasy. Only she could blow it out, though of course if he put it out, it would be an extension of her mind, ending the fantasy. It was so dangerous to get lost in this.

Shut up and just enjoy it.

His hands moved to his belt, loosening it from the buckle. "Your shirt," she breathed. "Please." She repeated it, wanting to see him. She wanted to rub her cheek against his hard stomach, take him in her mouth. Looking up at him like that, her mouth stretched over him, had always stirred him to an even thicker girth. She'd loved it.

His biceps rippled with casual power as he pulled the cotton shirt over his head, tossed it to the side. When he opened the jeans, her thigh muscles tensed, lifting her up so she was dead eye level as he reached in and drew out what she wanted to see. He'd already been noticeably thick against his jeans, but seeing it up close and personal made things between her thighs contract, hard.

"You work hard, girl, and I'll bend you over that saddle over there. Put every inch of me in that wet heat of yours."

Yes, that was what she wanted. Rough male demand. Even so, her heart betrayed her as she leaned forward. A lump formed in her throat, making her want to weep. For all that this seemed down and dirty, it was still Derek. And that moved it right from crude, simple satisfaction into the more complicated maze of intimacy. She parted her lips, tasted him, welcoming him the way she wanted to welcome him inside other parts of her body. Inside all of her.

He dug his fingers into her hair, controlling her movements as he pushed in deep. But once there, he stopped, a hard shudder going through him. She found herself doing the same at that contact. Closing her eyes, a moan caught in the back of her throat. Two stingy tears had squeezed out from beneath her lashes.

His taste, his heat and life. So close to him, touching him. Contact. He would take her after this, and no matter how rough he threatened or promised to make it, he knew everything about her, how her body responded, what her soul needed. Not just the dark, ugly part of her soul that Mikhael knew. Derek knew all of it, the dark and light.

But she wasn't that same girl. As Raina said, Derek was one of the good guys. If he knew just how dark she'd gone, he'd no more have sex with her than he would with a harpy straight from the fetid depths of Hell.

Stop it. This is your fantasy. All yours. Don't ruin it. She hollowed her cheeks, flicked her tongue over the base of his cock, and the spell was broken. His hand convulsed on her. The jeans were gone from under the chaps, but he was still wearing those sexy, flank-baring leathers. It made her thank Raina's skill anew for allowing her mind to dispense with the improbable clothes-coordination issues. She wished her hands were free so she could trace that buckled line just above the pubic bone, though. When he thrust harder, she made a noise of urgency and distress at once. She wanted him to demand more of her, make her strain to pleasure him. She needed oblivion to leave the rest behind, and Derek had always had his own unique way of making that happen, ways she didn't anticipate, like now.

He pulled her off him. In that blink, the jeans were back and fastened, but he left the belt hanging loose. Before she could figure out why her mind would want him more clothed in *any* fantasy scenario, he was reaching behind her. The angle pressed his body against her and she burrowed her nose in his abdomen, putting her mouth on him there. He made a noise, freed her wrists from her ankles, though he left both still tied. Picking her up under her arms, he put her over his shoulder, his hand spreading out on her buttocks. She moaned again as he fingered the petals of her sex between her bound legs, and she writhed, nearly choking on the desire that swept through her.

"You're going to sit here now." He placed her on the table, her feet on the bench, bottom firmly on the surface. "Don't squirm. You might get splinters in places you don't like. Though I might like plucking those out for you." A flash of that devastating grin.

Putting his knee on the bench to the right of her feet, he cupped her breasts in that tight corset, his gaze assessing, pleased by what he saw. She swallowed, quivering, as he freed the first several hooks so he could slide a finger inside, tease over her left nipple. At the first contact, she cried out, arched into the touch. "Still have those responsive tits. Remember how I could just look at them, and you'd get two hard little points? I could see them even under your bra, begging for attention."

Bending down, he put his mouth on top of her left breast, giving her a heated, openmouthed kiss on that curve, pushed up like a ripe offered fruit. His head, his hair, brushed her jaw, her cheek, and she closed her eyes, taking in his scent, her fingers clenching in the bindings. Had she been that smart or that masochistic in her fantasy, denying herself touch, because she knew that might take things too far into the emotional realm? The ropes around her ankles and wrists were a reminder of what she couldn't have.

"Derek . . ." She breathed his name, because she had to say it. Earlier today, she'd had to say it in scorn, but here she could say it the way she wanted. With need, desire, yearning.

"I'm here, baby. I've got you. Give it all to me."

I didn't mean it, when I sent you away and said I didn't love you anymore . . .

She couldn't bring herself to say it aloud, but since she hadn't let herself even think it for three years, she'd give herself that at least. She cried out again as his tongue found her nipple, teasing it on the inside of the corset's loosened hold so the friction of the stiff fabric was enough to make her squirm, just as he'd warned her against. But he slid his hands down under her backside, cupping each cheek in one broad palm. It brought his fingers in contact with the wet folds between her legs and she writhed harder. She would have picked up every splinter on the table without his protection. He had the nipple in his mouth now, his sandpaper jaw against the tender skin of her breast.

"Oh God . . ." She was going to come just from this. Go right over. She could climax three, four, sometimes five times with Mikhael, astounding him with her responsiveness and sometimes frightening her, because she knew part of it had an unnatural source. With Derek she might come twice that amount, because it was him. She'd come so intensely she'd be in danger of blacking out, particularly in the oxygen-depriving corset. But it made her feel so erotic, so restrained . . .

"You're so close, you're rippling against my fingers," he muttered. "So wet and needy. You've been wanting it bad. Beg me for it, girl."

"Please. Please, I need you inside me."

"Keep begging. I like your voice. Long as you keep talking, I'll keep doing the things I'm doing."

He was a sensual sadist of the first order, and she managed to do as he ordered, begging for his cock, to be taken, to be fucked hard, even as her voice faltered beneath his clever fingers and tongue, her breath laboring, body trembling so hard she felt close to seizing. *"Derek."*

He picked her up, but instead of bringing her to the saddle as he'd threatened, he took her to the ladder that led up to the hayloft. He'd retrieved the rope as well, so now he used it to pull her hands over her head, binding her to an upper rung. It put a strain on her shoulders, until he lifted her knees and placed them a few rungs below. She felt a jerk as the ankle rope was released, but then there was the click of a blade as he deftly split the rough twine and retied her just above the knees, binding her legs to the insides of the ladder step, spreading her in that narrow space. So quick and easy, all smooth motions, his skill with the knife and rope enough to make her stomach jump with butterflies of apprehension and lust at once.

Her breasts were on the platform of a step and now her eyes widened as he came around with another length of rope. He positioned the rope horizontally over them, looped it around her back, then brought the ends under the step, tying the knot beneath. He'd made it snug so the rope constricted over her breasts, holding them there. Then he did another wrap so there was a taut line positioned just in front of her nipples, the twine pricking and teasing the tips.

"Derek." All she could do was repeat his name now. Her sex was contracting, impossibly aroused. She was helpless, panting. Stepping back, he hooked a thumb in his pocket and studied her with approval, her body naked but for the corset, pulled below her breasts. But his chest was rising and falling like a man who'd been running, his cock a bar of steel against straining denim. Every muscle was delineated in his beautiful body like priceless erotic art of the male form. All of it told her he was far from affected.

"You're not begging, Ruby." He glanced left, and when she followed his gaze, her heart thumped into her throat. He was studying a barrel of assorted cattle brands, and next to them was a lit brazier.

She'd conjured it, so she couldn't deny the primal, crazy desire. Whether or not she'd ever have the bravery to acknowledge or do it in real life, the idea of him marking her as his in some permanent way in this fantasy was overwhelming, tripping up her tongue and silencing any protest she might have.

"I want to put my brand on you. Doesn't much matter how wrong that is; it is what it is." He brought his face to hers, his hands closing over her tied wrists. His chest pressed against her distended breasts, and the sensitized tips screamed in a mixture of pleasure and pain at the stimulation of his body pushing the rope into them. It made her quiver harder against the ladder, made the wood rattle. "You tell me, Ruby. Tell me who you belong to, no matter how much you try to deny it."

"You," she said. Her voice choked with the emotion of it. "You know it's always been you. It always will be you. Please, Derek. Be inside me. I've needed you for so long. I've died a hundred times of loneliness and pain. I need you."

"I've always been here, damn you." She saw emotion in his face now, the same pain of loss, of betrayal. "Ah, hell. It's a fantasy, right?"

He moved away, two steps, and lifted the brand from the fire, brought it back. Shifting behind her, he closed his hand on her shoulder, at the juncture of her throat. His thumb swept the tender section of skin on the inside of her shoulder blade, telling her where he intended to put it. "Say it, Ruby," he said harshly. "Say it again, and keep saying it until I tell you to stop."

"Yours. I'm yours. *Yours.*" She screamed it as the brand pressed to her flesh. It was less than a blink of time, but the pain seared through her instantly, white-hot, incredible. She embraced the agony, the purging. When he threw the hot iron aside, so violently it hit the wall with a clang, she began to beg again. He opened his jeans, and her eyes closed as he fit his sizeable organ at the wet entrance that welcomed him. Putting his hand on her opposite shoulder, that same juncture, he tightened his fingers on her throat. His mouth was close to her ear.

"You're mine, Ruby. I don't care how far you run, or how you try to push me away. I've lived for centuries. I'm never giving up on you."

He pushed inexorably into the narrow opening provided by the spread of her legs. It had been over a month since her last time with Mikhael, so she was tight. The tissues, though soaking wet, weren't used to loosening for a man's penetration. Derek gave them no choice, demanding entry.

She took him in with a deep groan, and when he was in to the hilt, his hands came around, captured her breasts. That rope constriction made her shriek from the stimulus.

"Has there been anyone else? Anyone else been inside you like this?"

"Not like you. Not the places you can take me."

He set his teeth to her throat then. "But there has been someone."

She swallowed, not sure how to respond. It was something so different from Derek, and it was about the pain, about not letting the hunger become a monster that could consume her. She didn't want the fantasy to take this turn, so she didn't answer.

He deepened his penetration, making her whimper as he bumped her cervix, an intentional discomfort. "That won't happen again. Ever. Say it."

"Only you." She could say it, because though she knew it would have to happen again, here in her fantasy she could pretend that Derek would be with her, that he was as much hers as she was his, and nothing else mattered.

"Little liar." Withdrawing and pushing back in, he made her whimper again. Then he started to torment her in earnest, thrusting slow and fast, teasing her by pulling out to rub against her clit, then going back in again, sometimes pulling out only to fondle her breasts while he stroked his cock up the channel between her buttocks. Her sex wept in need for him.

He was a big man all over, such that the wood of the ladder protested. Her body might be fragile in comparison, but her need gave her the strength to meet him on every stroke. She took the punishment, the rough contact of his chest hair against that brand, the stretch of his cock inside of her, the pinching of her nipples.

She'd taken punishment from Mikhael to get a climax, but Derek brought true fulfillment with his demands. He wouldn't let her get away with anything less than complete surrender. So it was that the tears were streaming down her face, her heart giving in with her body when he pulled out again, holding the climax just out of reach.

"Say it again, girl, and you damn well better mean it this time. You won't ever lie to me again."

"Only you. I'll never . . . let another man touch me again . . . but you. Please, I can't bear it. I'm yours. I belong to you."

"Damn right you do." He slid back in, and now he pushed her hair out of the way, nuzzling her throat, his fingers closing back over her breasts as he brought himself flush against her, thigh to thigh, his pelvis in tight against her backside, chest against her shoulder blades, the abrasion of that brand between them. He pinched her nipples and made a subtle, incremental adjustment, slid back in. Tiny, tiny movements of his cock inside her, rubbing in all the right places. He had her pushed full against the ladder steps, and, true to a fantasy, one of those steps was right against her clit, so that minute friction, within and without, the ruthless manipulation of her nipples, took her over. Everything else began to disappear.

"Derek . . ." It was a desperate wail.

"Come for me. And don't hold anything back."

The climax crashed over her. She screamed herself hoarse, unable to stop when wave after wave swept through her. Then he took her up impossibly higher by beginning to pump hard and fast, releasing within her. Her fingers dug into the rope above her, head dropping back against his shoulder. She turned to snap at his throat, held on as he kept pummeling her against that ladder.

It went on a long, long time. Bliss, ecstasy, the best parts of Heaven and Hell. Long after she was rippling in aftershocks along his length, he kept going, apparently wanting to underscore the lesson, the binding between them. She took it, her chest near exploding with feeling.

Hearing his erratic breath as he at last came down, she wondered if he was choked by some of the same emotions she was. Then, like a cold-water shock, she remembered it was her fantasy. That lantern was still burning strong. Whatever he was experiencing, it was what she wanted him to be feeling. Her sense of loss was so great, she'd needed to share it.

Raina had herself a winner here, though it was a double-edged sword. A military spouse could share emotional and physical release with an absent husband or wife. But it might be too adept at what it did. Too painful for it to seem this real, when it really wasn't. She needed to warn Raina about that, since Raina wasn't as in tune with the emotional ramifications of sex as the physical ones.

However, as far as the physical part of it went, if it got much better than this, Raina would need to post warnings like they did for roller-coaster rides—no back problems, heart conditions, risk of seizure or stroke, etcetera.

Derek was placing long, lingering kisses on her throat, her shoulders, stroking his fingers through her hair as he did it. Then he dropped his touch to slide along her sides, relearning her shape, obviously enjoying the corset's hold and indulging himself as she remained tied. "I want to do this to you all night long," he said, making it sound like the enticing threat it was. "In a hundred different ways. I want you to be so sore that the last time I do it, I'll need to ease into you. I'll go so slow, so I don't hurt you. You'll take me despite all that, because that's the way it is between us."

She nodded, sniffling. She could deny him nothing, because as he'd said, she was his. "I love you."

It was out there before she could stop it. The first time she'd ever said it, she'd barely been out of girlhood. The declaration had terrified her, because she'd realized it was more than infatuation, a young woman's crush. The all-powerful sorcerer was a charismatic part of him, but it was the man, Derek Stormwind, the one who liked to swim with her at the beach, who didn't like raisins but loved oatmeal-raisin cookies, who preferred riding horses to driving a car, the one who got cranky if she tried to elicit dialogue more complex than grunting before he had his morning coffee . . . That was who she truly loved.

Even more remarkable, he'd said it first. And he saw all parts of her the same way. Though he'd told her she had tremendous potential as a witch, when it came to this, it was more basic than that.

At the end of the day, doesn't matter who or what you become. It won't change how I feel. We're just two people doing our best to figure out each other's hearts, and that takes more lifetimes than even I have. But I'd spend every one of them with you trying to learn. Trying to make you happy.

But what she'd become *could* change how he felt. She knew it. "I love you," she whispered again, her voice broken with the weight of all the knowledge she now held about love and loss.

"I know that, girl." He put his jaw alongside her temple. His hands cradled her breasts gently now, his body a reassuring bulwark. "Though it's nice to hear."

She closed her eyes. She shouldn't have said that, even here in this fantasy world. It was time to end it. "Will you turn off the lantern? I want to sleep with you in the hayloft." *Touch you in the dark.*

"I'm sure I could conjure a saddle blanket or two to make that happen, protect this pretty, soft skin of yours. Hold on." His hands slid away, though one lingered on her buttock, gave it a firm squeeze before he moved to the table, leaned over the lantern. She turned her head to savor that one last look at him before the fantasy was gone. It was good she was going to be leaving tomorrow. She needed to put some distance between her and this room. She'd never, ever use it again. She'd make Raina promise not to let her.

He was studying her in almost the same way, as if memorizing the way she looked. She imagined what he was seeing; her in the red corset, tied up for him, his seed still damp on her thighs.

Leaning down, he cupped the top of the lantern, blew it out.

* 5 *

SHE WAS AGAINST THE WALL, EXACTLY WHERE SHE'D started, except at some point she'd slid down to sit, her legs folded up in front of her. She was still fully clothed, though her panties were soaked, telling her she'd actually had the intense orgasm she'd experienced in the fantasy. The skin between her shoulder blades was sore and throbbing, as if the brand had marked her in truth. That bit of information startled her, but not as much as what was directly across the room from her.

Braced against that opposing wall, though still standing, Derek stared at her. Between them, next to the candle and pedestal, the branding iron lay on the floor. The residual magic was still sparking off it.

She was sure she lost all color in her face, because when she shot to her feet, she swayed, uncertain of her balance. Fumbling for the latch, she flung the door open and fled into the hallway.

The room was on the second level. Though she knew navigating the steep winding staircase of an antebellum house when one was reeling from universe-altering climaxes and complete panic was inadvisable, she hit it at a run. As a result, she stumbled on the third step. Grappling for the banister, she lost purchase, flailed.

In that harrowing moment, when she teetered on the brink of physical catastrophe, she wasn't too worried. She'd given Raina the most important instructions, after all. Dying might deal with all of it, and wherever she ended up, Heaven or Hell, she wouldn't have to face this. She wouldn't keep making the wrong choices, over and over.

"Ruby." She fell against a dense wall of air, one that caught her at a forty-five-degree angle before she could pitch down the stairs. True to a sorcerer's nature, he pulled that power right from the closest elemental, the sturdy old oak of the stairs. For a second, as that energy surrounded her, she could feel the last day of the oak's life, the recipe of a summer day; warm wind, animals foraging and hiding among the full greenery of the trees, the intent heat of the sun.

She struggled against it, the unique, seductive touch of his magic, but it held her as easily as a butterfly in a net, easing her upright without damage. Unfortunately, it also gave him the needed moment to catch up to her. Heedless of their precarious perch, she tried to shove him away. In answer, he seized her arms, swung her to face him, one foot braced on the stair above hers, the other just below, caging her against the railing. It also put them almost eye level despite the significant difference in their heights. "Slow down, damn it."

"You son of a bitch. You had no right. *No right.*" She punched at him. "Let go of me. Let go of me now."

Catching her wrists, he set her down hard on her backside. He put himself on the step just above, clamping her between his thighs as she struggled. She snapped at his arm like a rabid coyote before he pulled her wrists out from her body, taking his flesh out of reach.

"Calm down. It wasn't him."

Ruby's gaze jerked to the base of the stairs where Raina leaned against the rail. Though it was her usual provocative pose, the woman's gaze was hard, her mouth tight. "He had no more idea than you did. I gave him the choice of using it, just like I gave it to you."

No one blames the Devil . . . They make the choice.

It took a full minute for her to process it, to believe it, and when she did, what swept through her was devastating. If Derek hadn't made her sit, her legs would have buckled. "Raina . . . why would you do this? You're supposed to be my friend."

Try as she might, Ruby couldn't keep her voice from breaking. Derek's grip eased, registering her distress. She wouldn't look at him, though she couldn't push away from the strength flanking her when she didn't seem to have any of her own.

"I *am* your friend," Raina said sharply, though she'd gotten a little whiter. "And you never asked if anyone would be sharing the room with you."

"Oh, Raina. That is total bullshit." Ruby fought to rein in her emotions. It was like trying to call back a flood after the dam had shattered, but she had contained a lot worse than this, right? She had to pull her shit together to get Derek to let her go. Though it was painful, she made herself look up at him.

At least Raina was telling the truth there. He looked as floored and pissed as she felt, but there was speculation in his gaze, too. That quick mind was reviewing what had happened, what the magic had revealed about her true state of mind. Panic gripped her anew. "Let go of me, Derek. Please. I'm not going to fall now. I'm going to go to the bottom of the stairs and kill Raina."

"As much as I've dreamed of hearing you say that, now's not the time." His jaw flexed. "Maybe this opens some things up. Things we need to talk about."

"No, it doesn't, and no, we don't." She extricated herself,

relieved when he released her, though he rose with her, his alert expression showing his readiness to catch her again if she started to fall. It made things hurt, made her want to scream and rage further. Instead, she bottled it up like a potion, put all those incendiary feelings under pressure and stalked down the stairs.

She ignored the fact her body was still trembling from what she'd experienced with him. Not only that, but it now wanted the real thing, merely from sitting that close to him. Her shoulder hurt. What the hell had happened there? Reaching back awkwardly, she clawed down the neck of her shirt. Nothing. The skin was smooth, but the nerve endings were acting as if the skin had been seared by that brand.

It was probably one of the perks Raina offered. The client got a souvenir, a magical hickey with an intensity and placement appropriate to one's deepest needs. It would probably linger in nerve memory for several days, drawing the mind back to that room like a lemming to a cliff edge.

Raina held her position. If she'd suspected the state of Ruby's mind, she would have run. Or maybe not. From the flash in her gaze, Raina looked like she was spoiling for the fight. It made the ache in Ruby's gut worse. She reached the bottom step.

"Why would you do this to me?" she repeated. "Why, Raina?"

"Why would you lie to me for three years? Use fucking *soul magic* on me?"

That panic frog jumped in her throat, but it also triggered shut-down mode. Her emotions closed up like slamming doors. Ruby couldn't say she was sorry, couldn't take it back, so she simply went wooden. "This was about payback?"

"No, damn it. You've been tapping Dark magic."

Ruby tightened her hand on the banister, suppressing the knee-jerk reaction to look toward Derek. It didn't matter. Raina scoffed. "Yeah, he knows, too. He picked it up the first second he saw you at your shop. Messing with Dark forces is like being strung out on drugs, dove. It gets harder and harder to hide the addiction, and it's starting to show on you, big-time."

Derek had come farther down the stairs. Ruby was sure those dark blue eyes were as keen as the blades he usually carried. "You can turn off the lights," Raina continued. "Hide all you wish, but that room proved what you want is still in there, still haunting you in the dark. If you don't think forcing you to see that is what a friend does, then you don't know what friends are. Something is eating you alive, and if you don't figure out a way to let it out, to let us help, it's going to swallow you right up."

Ruby stared at her. Every muscle was rigid from hurt and betrayal, but she couldn't really blame them. They didn't understand. They would never understand. It already *had* swallowed her right up. "Did we actually . . ."

"No." Raina shook her head. "It's all mind interaction. Until you were on these stairs, you didn't even physically touch."

There was something so sad about that, having such an intimate fantasy, with no actual touching. It all made her sad.

"I'll be taking Theo with me," Ruby said. Her voice was even. Calm as death. A stupid metaphor, since there was nothing calm about death. Death was just . . . silent. Eternal. A cold wind blowing across stone on a desolate hillside. "I'll give him a sleeping draught to make him comfortable. For the sake of our friendship these many years, and with no other choice, I'll have to trust you with that other matter I gave you. But when I get back, we're done. This is unforgivable, Raina."

"Nothing is unforgivable, Ruby. Not when it's done out of love."

The Darkness surged forward at that. It barked out of her throat in a harsh, shrill laugh. From the startled look on Raina's face, and the sudden tension she felt from Derek, Ruby knew they detected it, that force that gave her laugh a sibilant echo. "Yeah," she said. "You keep thinking that."

I hope you never have to face the truth the way I did.

Pushing past Raina, she left the house, her back straight,

though her body felt brittle as glass. Neither one tried to stop her.

THE MOMENT THE DOOR CLICKED SHUT, DEREK WAS down the stairs. He looked torn between wanting to go after Ruby and having to deal with Raina. Raina would have preferred the former, because she wasn't in the mood to deal with a male tantrum, but he pivoted on one booted foot, squared off with her. "What the *hell* is the matter with you?"

Raina arched a perfect brow. "You should be thanking me. I'll bet you didn't know your little witch had such naughty thoughts—"

Derek caught her by the throat. Raina found herself slammed against the wall, pinioned there not just by a powerful, angry man's strength, but by the energy that swirled out from him like a furnace blast. She faced the sorcerer who was a Guardian of the Light, who'd gone toe-to-toe with some of the Underworld's most frightening demons.

"You forget yourself, witch," he said with chilling menace, underscoring it. "Cut the shit." That branding iron was suddenly in his hand, called from the room above as simple as a blink, a mere rearrangement of matter and air currents. He pressed the unyielding steel against her windpipe. "This part was real. You made me hurt her, cause her pain. You betrayed her trust."

"It's a tracking mark," Raina said with a calmness she didn't feel. He could shove the iron up into her brain with one effortless movement, charge it with energy and turn her into a shower of confetti over her pricey Persian rugs. But that didn't bug her as much as him holding her helpless like this. Being manhandled just pissed her off in ten different ways. "Unable to be removed. You'll never lose her again. That brand is your mark, a physical connection between the two of you that can't be broken. You can thank me after you get your goddamn hands off me."

With an oath, he threw the branding iron away from himself. It shimmered and vanished before it touched the floor. He let Raina go, though, his lip curling in a silent snarl as he moved back to the stairs, rubbing a hand over his face and the back of his neck. "I'm going to ask you a question, and I want an answer. I won't ask twice. What happened to her, Raina?"

She had half a mind to give him a nasty jolt, try to turn him into one of Circe's pigs, but she couldn't outmatch him. Beyond that, something more important was at stake than his bad manners, or the possibility that she *had* pushed things a little far. Well, tough shit. She had as much right to act on her hurt and anger as they did.

"I can tell you what I know, but it's what I don't know that's key to it all. She lost a baby, Derek. Yours, in case you had any doubt."

The anger evaporated, sucked out of the room. When he turned, a stunned look on his face, Raina's own temper settled. He actually went a shade paler, making her feel an annoying pinch of regret. "Derek . . ."

He held up a quelling hand, his jaw tightening. "Keep talking." But his voice had a hoarse note, and there was a swirl of thoughts moving behind the keen eyes. She pressed her lips together.

"It was during the Unseelie conflict."

He'd told Ruby he had to deal with a problem in the Fae world, and, of course, while he was there, he wouldn't be able to contact her. While he'd teasingly assured Ruby it wouldn't be like the stories, where he emerged three hundred years after everyone he knew was dead and gone, he had warned time moved a little differently there and he might be out of touch for a few months. Raina had seen the worry in Ruby's eyes, the worry she always had when Derek left her to face Goddess-knew-what.

It turned into the second longest stretch of time Ruby had been out of contact with Derek since their relationship had begun. As a few months stretched into more, the impending baby had been a blessing for a lot of reasons. Aside from the obvious distraction it provided, Raina could tell carrying his child changed Ruby for the better, settled some things in her. Gave her more confidence in herself. She'd told Raina straight out that when Derek came back this time, she was going to want to make some commitments with him she'd never been willing to consider before.

"That's a good thing," Raina had told her bluntly. "Because Derek Stormwind is as old-fashioned as they get. I don't care how old he is; that baby's not going to be born without a ring on your finger."

If he gets back in time. Raina had held that thought back, but she knew Ruby appreciated hearing the other, even if the thought of marriage turned her an amusing three shades whiter. Raina guessed that Ruby's idea of commitment with Derek had been a more gradual plan. But no matter how much she goaded him, Raina knew men pretty damn well, and she had no doubt that Ruby Night Divine was it for Derek. He'd just been waiting all these years for her to become her own person, and reach that point herself.

The tragedy was, for the first time in her life, Ruby had hit that sweet spot. With the baby growing inside her, there'd been a peace and quiet strength to her that Raina and Ramona both had been glad to see, even as they teased her unmercifully about it.

"The Unseelie conflict." Derek's expression clouded. "I was there for two months, and when I came back out, thirteen had passed here. Damn mage tricked me, got the upper hand and distorted time."

Raina nodded. "She discovered she was pregnant about a month after you left. She made it to eight months. Knew it was going to be a girl."

Her voice had softened, her words getting more clipped, because, hard-edged as she could be, they'd shopped for that baby, planned for it. She and Ramona were going to be her god-aunts, Goddess help the poor babe.

Derek sank down on the bottom steps, a big man whose strength was suddenly not so certain. Damn it, she really was a complete and total bitch. She'd told the man he'd lost his daughter the same way she'd tell him the basement of his house had flooded, or his car had been wrecked by a careless relative.

She couldn't fix that, but she did keep her tone quiet, gentle, now. And she kept going, because she knew he needed to hear all of it to understand. "She was crossing the street with some groceries, was thinking of other things, in her head like she can be sometimes, and a car came around the corner . . ."

"You were already out here. In North Carolina. She was all alone." He spoke stiffly.

Raina recalled that anguish, a familiar constriction in her chest. "Yes. She didn't let me know what had happened until she was out of the hospital, a week after. She called, told me not to come, if you can believe it." Her tight, hard smile had nothing but brittle pain in it. "I should have known something was wrong, because as closely linked as we three are . . . we should have felt something when it happened.

"I was on the next plane out, and of course Ramona went with me. Shows how upset I was, not thinking how likely it was she could have caused the plane engine failure." The grim humor was a quick flash, not enough to dispel the seriousness of the moment. "When we got there, Ruby had changed. She would get cold so abruptly, so distant. In hindsight, I was catching the whiff of Dark magic infecting her, but it was overlaid with so much grief, I missed it. Then you came back. I thought that would break her out of it, but instead you left."

"The soul spell." He spat it out like the vile curse it was.

"Yes. I really wish I'd figured that one out sooner. But here's the deal, what I don't know."

His head lifted as she moved to stand before him, gripping the banister rail. "I got hold of the police report, Derek. The driver was drunk, so they dismissed his story as alcohol and covering his ass. He said she didn't step in front of the car. She landed on his windshield, as if she'd been thrown there. And he said when she landed, there was a shower of sparks, like a fireworks show."

The coldness in those dark blue eyes was back, only even more dangerous than a moment before, which had been scary enough. "A magical attack?"

"I believe so. I never brought it up with her, because you've seen her. Right after the baby died, she was so much worse. All we cared about was breaking her out of it. So after you were gone, even though we knew she was still messed up, we took it as a good sign that she wanted to come out here and set up a new business. And she's functioning, talking, sometimes laughing and smiling on a good day, but there's this big part of her that's just locked away and gone. Neither Ramona nor I have been able to find out what really happened, and what changed her. But what you discovered and confirmed for both of us tonight, no matter how much you disapprove of my methods, is that she's still in there. Ruby is still there."

"She shouldn't be taking this job. I'll call Linda—"

"You should let her go," Raina interrupted him. "I know that might not suit the task, but I think it will help *her*. To be honest, I don't give a damn about the higher good or how many lives are at stake. It's her turn, Derek. You fight battles to keep Darkness in balance, at bay, whatever, all the time. That's what this is."

She took a deep breath, looked toward the ceiling. "In her entire life, she's never trusted anyone the way she's trusted you. So, to my way of thinking, you're the only one who has a chance of finding out what happened and then figuring out how we can help her make it right."

He raised a brow as she leveled her gaze back on him. "It must have been hard for you to spit that out."

"Worse than enduring the seven rings of Hell. Or my client who has a fetish for bear grease. *Don't* ask what that is." Raina gave him an acerbic look. "If I'm wrong, and you can't help, the one comfort I'll have is ragging your ass for failing her. And I swear upon every demon and saint, I'll do it until the end of my days."

He rose. "The brand was still way over the top."

"It's also a very impressive and complex magic that even you didn't see coming." At his expression, she was smart enough to lift a quick hand of truce. "Ruby won't be able to shake it, even if she figures out what it is. The Underworld knows and fears you, Derek. Whatever she's doing, it's dangerous, and detecting your protection mark might give them pause."

"This other guy," he ground out. "How does he figure into this?"

"He doesn't. Give the testosterone a rest." Raina shot him an annoyed look. "I've never even met him. He's some hookup she meets away from here a few times a year to scratch the itch." She paused. "You'll think this is an overshare, but it's relevant. It's a pretty violent itch. She comes home bruised, but purged, if you get my drift. She's using him to lance a boil."

At the flash of rage in his expression, Raina added, "I only have a first name, but I'm going to hold it, because I don't want every guy with that name in the continental U.S. dropping from the plague."

"The plague is contagious. I'd have their hearts explode in their chests."

"Much more elegant. Still not giving you the name."

He gave her a narrow look, but he didn't argue it. "The fantasy in that room. Whose was it?"

"Both of yours. I think you know that. Places you'd like to go again and wish you'd never left. Places you two touched upon before, only in that room you went to a deeper level, more vulnerable, more raw." She nodded. "It's a truth room as well as a fantasy. It can be dialed for either one, a balance between the two that I can direct with the will of the magics I use for it. So Ruby's fantasy was a true fantasy, but directed by the deepest truth of her heart. The truth is what makes the room work; without that element, it would be only a drug, because pure, uncut fantasy is destructive."

Derek studied the witch. Though he still wanted to strangle her, he saw her earnest frustration beneath the caustic exterior. He'd heard the darkness in Ruby's harsh laugh, and with Raina's information, so many things were clicking into place.

To say he was rocked on his foundation didn't come close to covering it, but he'd lived long enough to know the hard things had to be put away to deal with the immediate threat. Grief and loss were painful luxuries he couldn't afford to indulge right now, and maybe that was good, because he wasn't sure how to process the deeper wounds.

The Darkness that Ruby carried would spread like an infection. At a certain point, it would become unstoppable. However, Fate had aligned to bring him back to her door. He was enough of a magic user not to discount the timing, though he felt a boiling fury that Fate hadn't seen fit to put him here when it mattered most, before Ruby lost their child. Their daughter. It wrenched painfully in his gut. He didn't even know where she was buried. He'd ask Ruby, demand to know.

"I know you deserve answers from her." Raina proved how good she was at reading a man's face, his rigid body language. "But save her soul first. Then you can ream her out about the rest. The love she has for you is the only thing that might save her, and if you take out your anger first, you'll lose her for sure. We all will."

That raised another concern, a fear he left unspoken. His anger and the universe's plan aside, his love *had* failed her. As the witch before him had noted, until he'd come into her life, Ruby had never had a love she halfway trusted. Because he'd fallen short, she might not give him the *chance* to save her.

Raina was right about something else, though. Despite the many times he'd been pulled from Ruby's side, that wasn't happening this time. If the Darkness wanted her highly shielded heart, her fragile soul, it was going to have to come through him.

* 6 *

IT TOOK AN EXHAUSTING, PUNISHING NIGHT TO PREPARE for the job ahead—her own plans for it, as well as what Derck was sending her there to do. It also took those long hours to ensure everything was protected at the shop the way it should be. None of that involved the paperwork sitting on her desk, so in the end, Ruby banded up her accordion file and threw her manual logs and her laptop case into her van. She'd work on it in the few hours she wasn't teaching the coven.

Despite all the effort, she was glad for the distraction, because she sure as hell wouldn't have slept. She jumped at every noise, but neither Derek nor Raina showed as she'd dreaded. Of course, considering how often her time in Raina's diabolical sex room replayed in her head—Derek's mouth on her skin, his arms around her, his voice commanding her senses, surrounding her like a magical cocoon she never wanted to leave—his physical presence practically would have been redundant.

She'd let Raina call Ramona, tell her where she'd gone. She just wasn't up to it, and Raina owed her. At least, she told herself that, even though she knew it was a lie. If she'd been in Raina's position, suspecting what she did about Ruby, Ruby would have done the same thing to help her friend. Knowing that didn't make the betrayal hurt less, but it was a different kind of pain. Sometimes what was fair and sensible didn't mean shit.

She'd known the path she traveled required a cutting of all ties, and yet she'd hung on to Raina and Ramona, too weak to go it completely alone. That was what really hurt about that moment in Raina's foyer. She'd faced the stark truth that she *was* completely alone, and she couldn't allow anyone to penetrate her isolation.

Well, nothing human. As he always did, Theo managed to wrest a painful smile out of her. He'd put his front paws on the back fender of the open van and was giving her his patient look, waiting for her to heft his back legs up into it.

"Sure, you leap on Derek like a track star, but now you're all two hundred plus pounds of helpless again."

She'd brought the van with her from California, and it was the flamboyant stereotype. The dented side panels were painted with flowers and unicorns, a swirl of glittering sparks across them to follow the track of dancing fairies. But every stroke of that paint was infused with magical properties. When properly reinforced, the van was as much an impenetrable fortress as a medieval castle, and it could be a backup reservoir and an extra weapon when she needed that as well.

"There you go, big guy. Settle in and I'll make it better." The dog circled on the mattress she'd laid in there, then came down on his aging frame with a grunt. When they'd driven from California, she'd slept on it at rest areas, curled up next to his warm body. She didn't like hotels, had spent too much of her childhood in them, never having a room of her own. Cork was glued on the van's curved insides so she could keep pictures and mementos tacked all along them. Dried flowers, a piece of ribbon, a napkin from a restaurant. Ordinary things that meant nothing to anyone but her, and of course that was the point. She had some photos of Raina and Ramona. Shopping, having coffee, hanging out at one another's homes for wine-drenched sleepovers. She'd boxed up all her pictures of Derek, along with other memorabilia she couldn't bear to see anymore. But she'd kept one out, to have in this van.

He was resting easy on his haunches in a pair of cutoff shorts and nothing else, his bare feet sunk into the wet sand of a tidal pool. Looking toward the camera, his eyes had a softness to them, his firm mouth seconds from kissing her. Hair tousled over his forehead, he sported a day's growth of beard, because they'd woken at dawn to go play on the beach, take their bath in waves drenched by pink sunrise colors.

She tore her gaze away from those blue eyes that even now saw too damn much. Murmuring the sleep spell, she made a stroking motion over Theo's reclining body. His liquid brown eyes followed her; then the lids drooped, more than usual, as the energy she pulled from the earth beneath her bare feet took effect. He puddled into the mattress, a soft sigh leaving him.

She'd also given him a sleeping draught a half hour before, so the two together should keep him down for the twelve-hour drive to Lilesville. Once he woke, she'd massage his limbs back to life again. Part and parcel of being a witch, she had a variety of certifications—massage therapy, Reiki, herbalist. On past visits, she'd used the massage therapy on Derek, because he had a couple old wounds that could tighten up his back like a clenched fist.

She'd spread her hands over that broad expanse, her thighs straddling his fine ass. A tender smile had crossed her face at his incoherent grunts while she worked out those knots, the grumbling retorts when she teased him about being ancient and creaky.

A different emotion took over when her fingers passed over the scars, reminders of battles where he hadn't been quite quick enough, and luck and sheer nerve had saved him.

She was all too aware his immortality applied to his age only, not an inability to be harmed or even killed.

Shutting down that memory as firmly as she did the van doors, she secured Theo. She did a quick check of the building, ran back down her list of things to take to make sure she hadn't forgotten anything, double-checked she had the necessary permits to transport the guns she was carrying, then got into the van herself.

As she pulled out of town, the vehicle belching small puffs of black smoke that had stained the "Go Green" bumper sticker on the back, nothing was stirring. That was the way it was in small towns. She wondered if Derek had already left. He'd said he needed to do other things first, would meet her there in a few days. Fine by her.

Ah hell, she did love him. Loved him so much, but it was wrapped up in all of it, so that she couldn't separate the pain of loss from those feelings, couldn't heal enough to take him back. It was too late. She knew this shit; he was just stirring it all up again.

That jagged ache was back in her throat, so she started to hum a lullaby. Theo made a contented noise in his dreams. Her chest tightened as she imagined such a contented noise coming from a baby, her baby. The lullaby had its own magical properties, taking her mind to the secret that meant more than anything. The only thing that *could* have meaning for her now.

Raina and Derek were wrong if they thought she didn't understand what she was doing. She knew the path she was taking was fraught with wrongness, but it was also right. Besides which, once a certain point was reached on a wrong road, there was no turning back. Darkness sure as hell didn't offer exit ramps.

She picked up her Dr Pepper. She'd infused it with a mega-pack caffeine boost, enough to send a herd of strung-out elephants stampeding a village, and now she took half of it down in one go. She had no interest in sleep, or dreaming. True nightmares weren't about fears. They were about the things lost that could never be gotten back, no matter how much the heart cried out for them.

To some degree, most serious practitioners of the Craft studied the areas in which Ruby was proficient, but she'd pursued academic study to a level most never did. Initially, she'd applied herself so diligently to please her mother.

You have no natural ability, dear. No use whining about it. It always seems to skip a generation. But study hard, and you'll prove yourself useful to others who have it. Great magic users need invaluable assistants, after all. Perhaps you can also teach beginning novices, those starting their Craft studies. After all, those that can't do, teach.

Mary Night Divine had been an exceptional Seer, one consulted by magic users the world over. She'd maintained a mundane facade as a fortune-teller to neurotic high-profile stars. That paid the bills for their expenses, including a home in Monterey. A home she and her shy, awkward daughter rarely visited, until Mary had contracted severe dementia in her early forties, an unexpected development likely connected to her gift. She'd drowned herself in the tub when she was forty-three. Ruby had found her.

Soon after, it was discovered that Mary had wanted all her assets liquidated, and the money ejected from a plane over the Nevada desert during the Burning Man gathering. The will had been written in her thirties, when there were plenty to testify she had been of sound mind. A relative statement, Ruby had realized. In the document, she simply stated, "My daughter needs nothing further from me."

All the assets included the contents of the house, so Ruby was left with nothing but her few books, her clothes and some personal items. She'd been the indispensable shadow behind Mary, handling all the domestic chores and tedious magical preparations so her mother could apply herself to the higher arts of her particular gift. The salary Mary had given her was little more than a stipend to cover a restaurant meal or the occasional clothing need. As a result, she didn't have any money set by.

Fortunately, she had Raina and Ramona, friends she'd met in the years on the road with her mother. Through letters, calls and the occasional visits when Mary's entourage was passing through, those friendships had stuck. Ramona's contacts secured Ruby the job at Witches R Us, and she soon proved her worth there, in spades.

Though she'd begun studying to please and serve her mother, a natural desire to learn, to embrace that knowledge, had unfolded over those years. Mary's prediction that she could help "beginning novices" was an understatement. There was no aspect of the Craft Ruby didn't know. The things that drove witches with natural talent crazy, she could do effortlessly. The proper way to charge a potion, how to combine difficult ingredients correctly, how to read between the lines of a grimoire and make a spell even more effective. She could teach experienced witches how to get more out of an energy raising, enough that the spiral could light up the night sky with its charge. She just couldn't channel the energy herself. But the energy fascinated her, and she studied the underlying science of it via any text available on the subject, and met with metaphysical theorists to learn even more.

So in no time, she acquired the reputation of being an excellent teacher. So excellent, it had moved her out of her mother's shadow and she'd begun to grasp at a nebulous idea. Did Ruby Night Divine have the courage to be more than what her mother thought she could be? Derek had said Ruby's lack of confidence was the only thing blocking her from her true gifts. Then Ruby got pregnant. Overnight, Derek's viewpoint had been hammered home like nails in a cross.

The first time the power made its presence known was when she was infusing a simple cold remedy at Witches R Us. It was a low-level magic use, little more than positive thinking. Power had sparked from her fingertips, shattered the vial. The liquid contents lit up like reactor fluid, and a flower sprang out of the middle of it, the charge resurrecting one of the herbal ingredients.

At first, she thought it was the fetus. After all, she was carrying Derek Stormwind's child. But as the power grew, whether or not the growing child was a magic user, Ruby could tell the pregnancy had activated abilities that were all her.

It thrilled her for about thirty seconds. Then she was terrified. As if summoned from the grave, Mary's sharp voice started reciting a mantra in her head.

When I say you lack natural ability, dear, I'm not saying you don't have any powers within you. I'm saying that you lack the ability to use them properly. If ever you show an ounce of true power, don't let anyone talk you into using it. It's best for you to hide it, because people in our world always want you to use power. If you do, it will only come to tragedy. I sense it, see it. And no matter what you think of me, you know my Sight is always true. Don't try to be more than you are, Ruby.

She wasn't an idiot. Her mother had emotional issues, a competitive streak so destructive she applied its poison to her relationship with her only child. But Mary was also a great Seer, and the words *It will only come to tragedy* rang with that otherworldly resonance that came through when she was foreseeing. It pulled the rug from beneath Ruby's feet, made her feel like the small kernel of pride she'd nurtured was being punished by this reminder.

Don't try to be more than you are, Ruby.

With each passing month the fetus had grown, that energy had as well. At times, she struggled with serious spikes, as much chaotic kinetic energy swirling around her as around Ramona. It frightened her. So she hid the power from her friends. In fact, during her pregnancy, it was the only thing she learned to do with it, cranking up her Deception potions to greater and greater levels to hide knowledge from the people who knew her best. When she had to make the harrowing foray into soul magic, for the first time in her life she regretted having friends who were so powerful a simple lie wouldn't work.

If Derek had been there at the beginning, she knew she would have told him about the power. He made her feel beautiful, capable of so much. Plus, he would have detected it anyway. He could see through the strongest Deception spell. The main reason the soul magic had worked was the element of surprise. He never expected a friend, a lover, to use such a spell on him. Because for so long she'd had to rely on skills that had nothing to do with magic, she never underestimated the power of distraction, sleight of hand, to augment a spell.

Unfortunately, she'd forgotten that if a powerful magic user of Derek's caliber could detect her latent powers, so, too, could another equally powerful magic user. One not blinded by love.

Asmodeus.

COMING BACK TO THE PRESENT, RUBY DASHED AWAY unbidden tears with the back of her hand, then took another liberal swig from the Dr Pepper can. She grimaced at the caffeine additive the Dr Pepper taste couldn't completely conceal. Tears happened; she couldn't stop them. She had no poker face, as she'd said. But it didn't mean anything.

She started that lullaby again, imagining the soothing tendrils of it winding around her baby, keeping her dreaming good dreams. A dream where she crawled into a father and mother's waiting arms, where a plastic shovel and bucket waited on a beach and her parents helped her make a sand castle with them. She could knock it down if she wanted, because it could be rebuilt again and again. In this dream, all she would know was how loved, how special and amazing she was.

Ruby didn't mind giving her soul away for that to happen. She didn't want anything else. Her baby would never know sorrow or pain, because for her, Ruby had done what no other magic user had done before.

She'd made time stop.

During that fateful, tragic night, she'd embraced her power, discovering she could keep a foot in both the Light and Dark pools, twisting their disparate forces together to create a highly effective and dangerous energy she could channel for various purposes.

She had no aspirations to serve the Darkness, with its meaningless promises of power and glory. But walking the line with Dark forces got things done. Other magic users like Derek and Raina viewed it as a death wish, since one could interact with Dark forces for only so long before being pulled into full servitude to them. To avoid that fate—or delay it—she disintegrated pieces of her soul to balance what she took from the Dark side.

In the process, she'd made herself into a formidable witch, one who wasn't afraid to embrace her damn powers, no matter what they looked like. Or what her mother had foretold. Tragedy *had* happened, and nothing worse was possible.

Put that in your pipe and smoke it, Mom. You cruel, fucking bitch. I still love you.

LILESVILLE WAS ON THE GULF SIDE OF THE FLORIDA PANhandle, a hole-in-the-wall town ninety minutes away from a town of any size. It looked much like the North Carolina coastal town she'd left behind twelve hours ago. Shacks crowded up around the waterfront next to homes that pulled in six figures. The town was surrounded by acres of protected wetlands and vibrant green marshes. It was a community of displaced Yankees seeking warmth, eccentric intelligentsia, native old salts and redneck fishermen. It was also bifurcated by a major magical fault line.

While the rest of the world saw longitude and latitude, magic users knew about another kind of map. Lines of power crisscrossed the earth, some fixed in predictable patterns, some constantly shifting due to unknown forces. Whether conscious or unconscious in intent, sacred sites were often built on the fixed lines, like ancient Stonehenge or a plain mountain chapel emanating tranquility. The fault lines weren't merely feel-good spots, however, though it was certainly helpful that most humans thought of them that way, visiting them with starry eyes, New Age ideas and chakra stones.

Fault lines provided the divine arteries that kept the earth flourishing, a spiritual flow as essential as the rivers and waterways that nourished physical life. Sorcerers like Derek knew how to draw on them at the deepest levels, all magic users connected to them in certain ways. At specific points, the fault lines also contained portals to other realms. Even after centuries of awareness, ongoing studies by magic users kept finding out new things about those lines.

Quite helpfully, Linda's place was on the fixed fault line that needed reinforcing. Her home was a spread of twenty acres, the surrounding woodland and marsh ensuring privacy. As Ruby bumped down the gravel drive through a thick cover of pines and scrub, she frowned. The old energies were strong here, and there was a decent overlay of recent ritual to bolster them. A lot of solid Earth power clustered along the line to use for its reinforcement. What weakness had the Underworld detected to make this a target? She needed to quiz Derek further, but even if she hadn't made such an abrupt departure from him, she preferred to get her own first impressions.

Just as she was beginning to wonder when she'd reach the house, the forest thinned and she pulled into the small clearing that had been allowed for Linda's home. It was a charming two-story log cabin, with several guesthouses and a large gazebo on the property. The gazebo had swings Ruby suspected could be removed for rituals that were done under its cover. The house was North point, the three guesthouses at the other compass points and the gazebo in the exact center. To avoid the aesthetic faux pas of it looking too symmetrical, the guesthouses were angled differently, but there was a ritual purpose to that as well. Magic was often an important balance between harmony and a sprinkling of chaos for reinforcement. The theory was similar to allowing metal a certain amount of flexibility and movement to keep a bridge standing.

Winding stone paths ran between the buildings, expanses of grass liberally broken with natural areas dotted with flowers and frond-type plants that flourished at the southern coast. There was an herb garden near the kitchen entrance of the house. When she stopped the car, got out and stood in front of the van's heated bumper to study everything in silent evaluation, she located statuary, wind chimes, rock formations. While they were well integrated into the landscape, everything was chosen and placed so it provided the maximum reinforcement to protect the home and guide and raise the spiritual awareness of the inhabitants. Someone had put a lot of care and planning into the design.

As she heard the screen door from the house thud, she turned to see a woman come down the steps. Linda Egret had thick blond hair cut in a shoulder-length style around her attractive forty-something features. The slacks and blouse suggested she'd recently come home from work. Her body was in the comfortable thickening stage that softened the face and padded the hips in middle age. Her earrings were simple, silver-wrapped clear quartz for focus. The pentagram nestled between her breasts, visible from the blouse neckline, had two silver crescents flanking a center round gemstone of calcite. It was well charged, such that Ruby could feel its protective and calming power like the heat coming from the van's grill behind her.

"I would have come out earlier, but Derek said to give you about five minutes when you arrived." Linda had a warm voice, smooth and assured. "He knows you well. You didn't even look for me until about that fifth minute."

"Well, I realized I need to go to the bathroom, and I didn't want to water your azaleas."

Linda smiled at that, extended her hand. Ruby took it, pleased with the firm grip. "He also said you were a smart-ass. I told him every woman worth something is. Come on in. You can use the bathroom; then we'll get you settled in the guesthouse."

"I brought a dog," Ruby said as they moved in that direction. "It was last minute. He's a good guy, won't cause any problem."

"My two Australian shepherds will be delighted. They love to herd guests, four-footed or two-footed."

"Herding Theo will be like directing a lumbering elephant with a cat's brain, but they can knock themselves out."

THE GUESTHOUSE WAS ALSO A COMFORTABLE, REIN-forced space, a one-bedroom with kitchenette, bath, screened porch. With the angling of the house, the screened porch was private, not in direct view from the main house.

"This place could be a bed-and-breakfast," Ruby commented.

"It's fairly new. The owner built it as a B and B, a spiritual retreat destination, or his home to raise children and retire, depending on where the years take him. He asked if I'd like to live here rent-free in return for watching over it and keeping it up, because right now he travels a lot. And he has a house in town."

Ruby stepped back out on the front stoop of the guesthouse, her eyes narrowing. "So the owner . . . he set all this up?"

"Yes. And yes, he is a witch. Actually, a fairly powerful priest. I'll tell you about him at dinner if you'd like. He's an interesting story."

Linda elevated herself further in Ruby's eyes by helping her wake Theo, massaging his front limbs while Ruby took the more affected hips and rear haunches. The dog nosed Linda thoroughly, checking her out. When he got drool on her blouse, it didn't faze her. The two women hefted him out of the van, steadying him until he woke up enough to become interested in his surroundings. Then Linda let the shepherds out so they could become friends. As Linda helped Ruby carry in Theo's mattress, Ruby saw Theo lumbering off with them to investigate his new place.

She had forgotten what it was like to interact with a practitioner who understood what being a witch was about. Except for Raina and Ramona, Ruby didn't often trust women or relax around them. While she certainly didn't need a shrink to help her understand that, it didn't change the fact she was always looking for that backstabbing competitive trait that most women carried in their X chromosome. In this case, it would have been pretty detrimental, so she was glad not to see it in Linda.

Probably sensing Ruby's impending caffeine crash, Linda had encouraged her to turn in whenever she wished, and they could get started in earnest tomorrow. Because Ruby did have some questions she wanted answered tonight, however, she took Linda up on her offer of an early dinner. The woman proved she had awesome culinary skills, putting together a lightly spiced tomato-cheese spread on focaccia bread with a side of pita chips.

During the dinner, Ruby got her second wind and asked Linda some pointed questions about the other twelve women in the coven. If Linda was surprised about the intimate details Ruby requested, she didn't show it. For the serious nature of the work they were doing, Ruby would need to know weaknesses and strengths of the group. For her part, Ruby found Linda's answers thoughtful and not defensive, even when they were asked about herself.

In short, Linda was a well-grounded, quietly confident

woman who seemed more interested in serving the Light than in proving herself more accomplished than the unknown magic user Derek had sent to help her and the coven.

To finish out the evening, Ruby joined Linda on the screened porch of the main house, curling up on a comfortable papasan chair to listen to the forest night sounds. Theo lay at her feet, his nose almost touching the flank of one of the sprawled Australian shepherds. Linda had changed out of her work clothes into a long patchwork skirt and a snug wraparound top that made the most of her voluptuous Renaissance figure. It gave her a sensual Earth-mother look.

Ruby cupped her hot tea, blew on it, keeping her eyes on the caramel color. "So, now that we have the preliminaries out of the way, how do *you* feel about me being here?"

"I'm relieved," Linda said frankly. "I have the most experience in our coven, because I've been a practitioner for most of my life, learned the Craft from my grandmother, but I'm very much a hearth witch. Potions, spells, crystals, general energy raisings for the highest good. We have the foundation to do what Derek says needs to happen, but I'm in the dark about the best way to go about it. Do I need to be scared, for me or my ladies?"

Ruby gave her an honest answer. "To fight what comes out of the Underworld requires a Guardian of the Light, or a serious kick-ass magic user. A witch's magic is often very intuitive, connected to Earth energies, related to maintaining balance or making slight adjustments to it as needed. For this, you're the peacekeeping border patrol. Derek's job is being the invading force, taking back territory from the enemy."

Linda pressed her lips together. "Sometimes the border patrol gets shot."

"Yeah, they do. But I'll teach you how to heighten your senses, give you more lead time if hot spots happen. I'll also give you ways to protect and defend yourselves if you miscalculate." Ruby held her gaze. "It's like having a firearm in the house. You train with it, make sure you're comfortable using it, but in the end it's for self-defense. If you have a way to get away from the threat, that's always your first option."

"Well, as long as whatever boils up from the Underworld isn't here for my limited-edition Fairies of the World plate collection, that'll work. Otherwise, I'll fight to the death."

Ruby didn't smile. "You know you don't have to do this. It remains a choice, for you and the rest of the coven."

"I know." Linda set her jaw. "Derek made that very clear. But this is our home, Ruby. The Craft has been my way of life since I was a little girl. What does it say about my faith if, the first time I'm called to use it in a way that I'm uniquely qualified to do, that can help others, I turn my back because I'm afraid?"

"It says you've joined the billion other species that instinctively know what most humans are too dumb to figure out. Running from a fight is the best way to survive."

Linda raised a brow. "You don't look like the type who runs from a fight."

Ruby yawned. "I didn't say I was any smarter than the average human."

Linda smiled at that. Leaning forward, she covered Ruby's hand, gave it a quick squeeze. "I'll yammer at you half the night, so you just tell me when you need to go to bed. I know you're done in. Per your instructions, I've set it up so the coven won't come until tomorrow at dusk. You can sleep in, recover from your drive, and then I'll help you with any setup you need for your teaching strategy. Today was my last day at work for the next couple weeks. I've taken my vacation time to dedicate myself fully to this, and the other women who could do so have done the same. The full coven will be here every night and on the weekends."

Ruby nodded. "Good. It sinks in better that way, like a language immersion course."

"That's what we figured. Now, would you like me to freshen your tea, so you can take it to bed with you?"

"In a minute. Just a couple more questions. I want some things to mull over tonight, get a head start on tomorrow."

Despite her exhaustion, Ruby knew other things would kick in and stir when she went to bed. It was best for her to have something to occupy her mind, distract it, so she could slip past that darkness, escape to oblivion. Only of course it was never oblivion. Her dreams were getting more and more surreal, disturbing, leaving her with the acrid taste of nausea when she woke.

"Your coven is all women. But you said the guy who owns this place is a priest. Is he not a joiner?"

"Justin actually was a part of our coven. Or, rather, is a part, whenever he can be here. He's a very powerful witch, a very good man. He got married, and as you know, that can change some things. His wife, who is our sheriff, had a commitment to help out with a task force in Chicago for six months, so he closed his shop for the next two seasons to be with her there." Linda gave her a mischievous look. "Justin runs an erotic boutique for women."

"In *Lilesville*?" Ruby thought of the sparse, eclectic, but mostly conservative populace she'd seen when she'd driven into town late afternoon.

"Women come all the way from Tampa to shop there." Linda winked. "He could have left it open while he was gone, but he's tried employees before and they just . . . Well, women come as much for his understanding of their needs as they do for what the shop has to offer. He says you can't really teach that kind of intuition. They come for the full experience. Though he won't be there, I'll take you through it if we have time. I have a key so I can check on the place. If you see anything you like, I'll just deposit the money in his account."

The planted suggestion, as well as the fading effects of the caffeine high, stirred that heated need the exertion of the drive had blissfully quelled. Ruby managed to stifle a curse as it swept low through her vitals. It was Derek's fault. She'd had it leashed down, and he'd gotten it all worked up again, like a bronc goaded with an electric prod in the chute.

How is it a guy a jillion years old still likes sex so much? Shouldn't you be beyond such earthly cares by now?

She remembered teasing him about that once. While she'd been cooking them dinner, she'd extended a wooden spoon for him to sample her sauce, and some of it had dripped on his hand. Quickly putting her mouth on his flesh, she'd given him a playful lick to soothe the burn. That was all it took to have him carting her off to the bedroom.

He'd brought that sauce with them, dropped it on her like hot wax. He'd done just as she had, sealing his mouth over each place, licking her slow, making her imagine where else he'd put it before he was done. But when she'd asked the question again, much more breathlessly, he'd lifted his head, stared into her face that way he did, as if she were the eighth wonder of the world.

Do you know, in a jillion years—his lips quirked—*I've never seen the sun rise in exactly the same way? The colors, the clouds, it's always different, sometimes a lot, sometimes a little, but always different. And I never get tired of the pleasure of it. Earthly pleasures were meant to be enjoyed for all eternity, Ruby. Else it's an insult to the Powers that made them.*

Yeah, immersing herself in a store full of sex toys and lingerie would *really* help with this burning need. While she was sure Derek would approve wholeheartedly, there was no chance in hell she was going to that shop. "We'll be pretty busy, but thanks." She managed to inject dry humor into her voice rather than whining, resentful regret. From Linda's odd look, she wasn't entirely successful. "So does Justin know what's going on this week?"

"He said he could come back for this, that Sarah could spare him, but I could tell he was torn. He loves her so much, and the task force she's on is a dangerous one. Derek talked to him, though. He told Justin he could handle the Great

Rite or any other areas where male energy was needed, so Justin reluctantly agreed to stay in Chicago and let me call him if I need anything. Men. They can be so overprotective."

Derek could handle the Great Rite. Yeah, sure he could. Remembering the catty comment she'd made to Raina, Ruby knew being married did, in fact, change things for some couples. While the Lord and Lady were channeled into the priest and priestess during the Great Rite, it didn't change the fact two earthly bodies were coupling. A man and woman needed to achieve some level of intimacy and pleasure, some familiarity and trust with each other, to give the energy a free flow. And the practical facts of life—that birth control and disease protection had to be used—underscored that "sacred" or not, it was real sex between two real people.

If she were this Sarah, married to the remarkable Justin, she wouldn't be thrilled about him doing a Great Rite with another woman. After all, Ruby wasn't married to Derek, and she was having a hard time quelling an ugly, unpleasant tide toward Linda, her warm face and soft body. Ruby knew she was too skinny right now, had seen it in Derek's assessing look. According to medical professionals, Dr Pepper and M&M'S weren't the world's best diet, but what the hell did they know?

"So no other guys practicing in the area?"

"Not to my knowledge." Linda grimaced. "I wish it was different, but you know how it is. Modern-day Wicca, where most of us have landed, attracts far more women than men. As the Craft has always done. Of course, we have a good mix. Three of our ladies are actively Wiccan, and four are churchgoing Christians, who recognize this path reinforces the mystical side of theirs. The others have chosen not to categorize their faith, but they believe in what we do here."

A good mix of belief systems, and from what Linda had told her about the women, they were well-meshed friends. That would be helpful. It was important in this type of teaching situation to be working with open minds, willing to learn and confident enough to tolerate new paradigms.

"Derek said you used to work in a Wiccan store out in California? And now you run a gun shop? That was quite a switch."

"It was time for me to move on." Ruby shrugged. "I'm not one of those witches who looks down her nose at the mundane practitioners. I know we all have the personal power within us to connect to the Lord and Lady, use energy. But the shop in which I worked . . . I had some life changes, ended up in a different place. I didn't fit there anymore."

Linda digested that. "Would you like some wine?"

"Did I just give the impression I needed some?" Ruby asked wryly.

Linda smiled. "I thought it might also help you sleep. Sometimes when you're as exhausted as you are now, you lie down to sleep and end up staring at the ceiling."

"All right. But if I end up sacked out here, you'll just have to live with my snoring."

"I'm sure it's no worse than Theo's." Linda poured her a glass, settled back down across from her. "So what was it about the people at the arcane shop that no longer fit with your perspective? I don't want to pry into anything too personal, but I'm the curious type."

After an hour of being quizzed in detail on her own life, and that of her friends, as well as being told there was a real element of danger involved, Ruby suspected Linda felt it was quid pro quo to seek more information about the woman to whom Derek had entrusted her coven. Ruby didn't blame her a bit.

"At Witches R Us, they saw the world as a matter of Light battling and overcoming Dark. Really, it's about Light *balancing* Dark. Human beings will always have killers, megalomaniacs, sexual predators, because all of us have the capability for that darkness. Our circumstances or genetics will manifest it. Saints and Good Samaritans happen the same way. To pretend that we'll one day have this peaceful world where there's no war and no money, that we'll all live in this happy bubble hugging one another, is not only faintly nauseating, but it completely overlooks what human nature is. Hell, it overlooks Nature itself."

Linda blinked. "So it's wrong to hope for world peace?"

"No more wrong than it is to strive to lose those ten vanity pounds. It helps you keep it from becoming fifty, right?"

The woman chuckled. "I've never heard it put in quite such . . . applicable terms. That must be why you're such a good teacher."

An opportunity to teach always unfurled a certain private pleasure inside of Ruby, a sense of ease and satisfaction that helped keep other things at bay. A small form of balance, even though Ruby knew it was like tossing a marble on the scale across from an anvil.

"And thank you for being kind," Linda added. "These hips carry about twenty extra pounds."

Ruby shrugged. "They're nice hips. What I'm saying is this. If world peace suddenly happened, and we did have the big happy bubble, something would be wrong. The fault line is a scale, equally weighted. What if the Darkness disappeared tomorrow, and it was the counterweight to the Light? The Light would flip over, spin, fall, break; you name it.

"It's better to change small pockets than to try to change the world. Because the pockets of Light balance the Darkness, and in some way, the Light is stronger that way. You can hold a pebble in your hand, use it to create ripples in a pond. You can't hurl a boulder, and even if you could, it would displace the water and the pond would dry up."

Linda pursed her lips. "I get it. It's like that *Forrest Gump* quote, about dying being a part of life, but wishing it wasn't. I wish the other was possible. I hope somewhere, somehow, the answer is hiding in the shadows, that it's doable."

It is. It just comes at a terrible price. One that keeps that balance in place. "Don't look too hard at the shadows, unless you really want to know what dwells there."

Speculation etched Linda's face in the growing darkness.

Ruby cleared her throat. Looking out toward the marsh, she let the wine she rarely drank take her to a more whimsical place. "Do you know every body of water has a spirit? Even a puddle. A swimming pool does, too, despite the chlorine. A sleek, polished kind of spirit. Saltwater bodies have male spirits; freshwater have female. No one knows why, but it's said that salt water has a male spirit because he's surrounded by female tears. All the bodies of water squabble about who's more important. Lakes argue with the rivers connected to them; rivers argue with the ocean; so on and so forth."

"What's your opinion?" Linda raised an amused brow.

"I think it's like the joke about the argument between body parts. The brain, heart and lungs all thought they were the most important, until the rectum got offended and closed down. In about three days, they figured out the one who handles the shit they cause was the one they couldn't do without."

"You are a disturbing woman."

Ruby gave her a half smile. "Derek did warn you tact isn't my strong suit."

"He told me he was sending the most gifted practitioner he knew. Are the two of you together?"

Ruby studied the other woman. "No, we're not. Do you want to be with him?"

Linda flushed. "Touché. I guess I was a little rude, asking it straight out like that."

"Doesn't bother me." *Liar.* "Has he shown any interest?"

"He worked with me here for a month before he went to find you. He was so . . . All that energy that comes off of him . . ."

In short, he did the oblivious-Derek thing, which made a woman fall for him like a toddler hitting a trip wire, the detonation just as fast. In the space of time it took him to put a fistful of candy bars on the counter and reach for his wallet, Ruby had seen grocery clerks decide they'd give up indoor plumbing *and* chocolate for him. And he never noticed his appeal, always infallibly courteous and warmly attentive.

It was enough to make a woman want to shoot him. Or keep him chained and naked on a cot in her basement so she could ride him like a carnival ride with the "on" lever stuck in a permanent *up* position.

Okay, *wow*. She really shouldn't have gone there. The sleeping rabid dog of her libido came fully alert. She tried to fake it out, concentrated on what Linda was saying as if she were offering the formula to cure cancer.

"I admit I've been a little intimidated by him, awed by his skill." The woman firmed her chin. "I need to take the bull by the horns. I've made him dinner before, but next time he's here I'll make him a meal in the date kind of way, and see what reaction I get. It's been a while since my last disastrous relationship, so I guess I'm a little gun-shy. The police chief in the adjoining county, Eric Wassler, got divorced a couple years back, and to be honest I've always had a little bit of a thing for him. But I haven't been able to make step one."

"Well, Justin hooked up with a cop and they sound pretty devoted. Maybe you should give Sheriff Eric a shot. You'd probably have a better relationship with him than a sorcerer who's always on the move. Long-distance relationships suck."

Of course, Derek was technically a cop as well. A sheriff of the Light. With the hat and dragonskin boots, all he needed was a silver badge. She should pick him up one from the dollar store. With handcuffs.

Down. Sshh . . . go back to sleep.

Linda gave a little laugh. "This sounds terrible, but I wasn't seeking anything permanent with Derek. I'm old enough to know better than that. But I was thinking he might give me . . . confidence. You know how it is. Every woman wants to have a crazy, romantic, passionate night with a guy who's all the best parts of the fantasy. I expect men are the same way. You know, running into the starlet whose car is broken down . . ."

"And thus countless Penthouse Forum letters are born."

Linda snorted. "I'd like to write at least one of those letters in my life, and Derek Stormwind looks like publishable material."

You've no idea. Ruby pantomimed another yawn, rose. "Well, good luck with that." *Not.* "Time for me to turn in. I'll probably go walk the fault line, get a feel for things, then head to bed. Okay?"

"Oh . . . sure." Linda rose. "There's a phone in the guesthouse. If you need anything, just hit one. That dials the main house."

As Ruby nodded and took her leave, she could feel Linda studying her. As an accomplished priestess, the woman had intuition skills of her own, and Ruby was sure she sensed something off about her houseguest, a lot of mysteries she didn't care to share. But that was okay. She was here to teach them, not work magic with them, so there was no need for open flow. Derek would handle the magic part. Great Rites and all.

The irresistible bastard prick.

She was so exhausted her head was a block of concrete on her shoulders, but she needed to walk that fault line now, before the other coven members were here. Nothing disrupting her focus, the night aiding her concentration.

She was in no hurry to get back to her guesthouse, anyway. The anger about what had happened at Raina's was gone, and all that was left was the yearning created by that experience, exacerbated by the sheer pleasure of it. She could recall every moment, every touch. If she closed her eyes, she could still smell him, feel his heat against her skin. Linda's innocent imaginings of plundering Derek's virtue had fed it like kerosene on a fire.

Hoping this exercise would mute that raw edge, help her get things under control, she went to the gazebo, where

Linda and the coven did their circle castings. It was on one of the wider parts of the fault line, so Ruby stood in the center, her eyes closed, feeling its shape. She'd slipped off her shoes, so it was with bare soles and eyes still shut she moved away from the gazebo, following that line, seeing it in her mind, experiencing its shape. She drew its power through her feet and the channeling centers of her own body, cycling it back to the earth as she released it through the crown chakra. It was dense, pure. Settling.

She moved through the woods like a shadow, the soles of her feet coming down light, barely breaking the thinnest twigs as she breathed in the elemental energy sources that raised their heads at her presence. Birds and squirrels in their nests, foxes and possums that gazed at her through the darkness. One lone deer, a male.

When she set all her personal shit aside, focused on being the witch Derek expected her to be, she finally detected what he had. There *was* a problem here.

It emanated from those animal watchers as well, the trees and nearby water bodies—small creeks and tributaries to the marshes and the Gulf. Something had been scooping energy away from the underside of the fault line, like an army of prisoners tunneling out of their cells, one scoop of sand at a time. Not an entirely inaccurate description.

Creatures in the Underworld could wreak all sorts of havoc and mischief through projection of their spirit into the Overworld. However, some of them seemed to have a real hard-on for getting their corporeal selves here. Their personal motive for doing so was complicated, but Derek had once likened it to the way the 9/11 terrorists had gone off to party and hang out with strippers the night before they crashed into the WTC to register their abhorrence of Western capitalism. It wasn't a direct answer, maybe not an answer at all, but it had some oddly right-feeling logic to it.

As far as the higher-level motive, the eternal battle between Dark and Light, an Underworld being could do a lot more damage on the surface than a spirit one. Since a spirit one could fuck things up pretty well, that was really saying something.

But why here? Linda had mentioned a murder in the area a couple years before, the first in the county in nearly a hundred years. Despite the official report of local law enforcement, the motive had been paranormal in nature. It had apparently brought Justin and Sarah together. Linda thought the weakening had started happening then, but she just wasn't sure, given that hindsight could be misleading. But if she was right, the simplest explanation was that the paranormal activity in the area drew attention and certain beings in the Underworld saw an opportunity to exploit a possible weakness.

Or, like terrorist cells, it might be a plan that had been years in the making. They had all the time in the world, after all, and gradual incursions were far less likely to be detected until they reached this level of intrusion. Dropping to a squat and putting both hands on the earth, Ruby concentrated, reaching. It felt somewhat older than the murder time period. Perhaps the murder simply heightened the coven's awareness, such that what they had noticed was something already in process.

She walked the fault line back to the gazebo, stood there, breathing deep. Could she reach deep enough in that fault line, follow it to Asmodeus himself? No Guardian of the Light had ever brought the fight into the Underworld. The tug-of-war for balance had always been fought on the borders. You couldn't kill a demon, after all. You could only send him limping back to the Underworld, and no one wanted to fight one on his own turf. But she'd gone places other magic users hadn't.

She had a weapon she'd worked on for so long, knowing an opportunity like this would eventually come. If she could get the barbs of that magic into him, she would cause him such pain, he'd beg to destroy himself. He'd cower in the

Underworld like a rat for the rest of eternity. But she didn't want him there. She wanted to make the impossible possible. She wanted to obliterate him.

As she gazed out toward the water, she pulled the vitality from the circle to her like a long, dark cape, the kind the witch wore in *Sleeping Beauty*. The stepmothers had always gotten a bad rap in those films, women of strength and ambition who weren't afraid to grasp power. The lingering energy shimmered, disturbed, and she knew it wasn't from the fault. She draped herself in that cloak, pulled it closer to breathe it in, imagining mayhem and death. Asmodeus in bloody pieces, her raining fire over him, over all of it. A warrior Goddess of vengeance and death.

A growl disrupted her concentration. She'd put Theo to bed, knowing he was worn-out, but now, lowering her gaze, she saw Linda's Australian shepherds sitting on the other side of the circle, regarding her steadily. The way dogs watched intruders. Their earlier friendliness was replaced by wariness, hackles raised, the growl continuing to rumble in the female's throat.

With one sweep of her hand, she could turn them into nothing but ash for daring to challenge her. Doing so would be no more difficult than breathing.

Ruby shut her eyes, hard, breathed deep. *Steady, steady.* There was a line here, and everything depended on her being able to stay on that line. She had a circle cast in her mind, and if she stepped outside that circle, she'd lose it all to Darkness. It was inevitable; one day it would happen. She had no illusions about that. But not yet. Not until she'd done what she swore she would. She'd bided her time like an Underworld demon. It was pure tragic irony that it was Derek Stormwind who'd brought her this chance.

As she opened her eyes, throat aching with emotion, she was relieved to see those red edges had faded out of her vision. "What's the matter, darlings? It's okay."

Their ears pricked up, the moment gone. Despite her

resolve, it still wrenched something in her gut. They reacted as they should to something unnatural. Something evil. Starting to hum that lullaby again, she moved away from the circle, back toward the guesthouse.

JUST AS SHE'D FEARED, SLEEP WOULDN'T COME. SHE stared at the ceiling, listening to Theo snore. She wanted to call Derek, wanted to hear his voice. Thank God he didn't carry a cell phone. He never got reception within his dense aura. Closing her eyes, she felt his hands on her again.

She'd picked up a new burn phone, but she hadn't given him that number, either. He could call the infatuated Linda from whatever pay phone he found and learn that she'd arrived safely. It would give them a chance to talk, flirt, have phone sex, whatever.

Fuck. If she couldn't escape it, she'd embrace it, damn it all. Her mind wanted to take her back to the beach, kiss those drops of moisture from his mouth, feel his smile against her, his arms lifting her as he carried her to that hammock. Instead, she forced herself to return to the stable, focusing on the ropes, the more violent emotions that had driven their fantasy. Which, of course, came with a whole different set of problems. Her body heated up like a volcano about to erupt.

"Fine." She punched in the number, forced herself not to hang up, even as her mind screamed at her to do so. When the throaty Russian voice answered through her hands-free earpiece, she couldn't speak for a moment.

"Ruby? What is it you need tonight?"

She didn't know how he knew it was her. Though, in truth, Mikhael probably had GPS coordinates on every major world leader, and the ability to off them with no more than the press of a button.

Or maybe, less dramatically, he just knew the sound of her erratic breath, because she couldn't form words.

"Hmm. You have not called at a convenient time, and that irritates me. Your clothes are not off, so you have not prepared yourself for me. You expect me to wait on you?" His voice had that tone that pressed jagged glass against her broken heart. She wanted him to press harder, sever the muscle.

She stripped off the big sleep shirt, shoved off the panties. "I'm naked. Make me come." She couldn't keep the desperate demand from her voice, and his cold response was exactly what she told herself she craved.

"You give me orders? Who do you think you are, you little cunt?" The crudity prickled over her nerves like poison ivy . . . both unbearable and irresistible to scratch. "I am hanging up now. You will spread your legs as wide as you can, keep them open for me, and you will pinch your nipples, Ruby. Pinch them so hard, that if I cared to stay on the phone with you, I would hear the pain in your breath. You will keep pinching them that way until I decide to call you back. Then you can beg to stop. Being the dirty little fucked-up whore you are, you will be dripping wet for me by then."

She was now. But she didn't say it. He clicked off. She scissored her legs out wide, the air generated by the ceiling fan blades raising goose bumps on her naked flesh. Grasping her breasts, she began to pinch as he'd ordered. She thought of Derek, the intensity of his blue eyes . . . the way he'd touched her so ruthlessly, yet with such . . . care. Love. She pinched herself so hard a whimper came from her throat and Theo's head rose groggily from his mattress. *Forget, forget, forget.* She thought of Mikhael, how he would take off his belt after he fucked her, then whip her until the welts he made broke and bled; then he would fuck her again. Even if she begged him to stop, like he demanded now.

He punished her because that was what she wanted, what the Darkness demanded, and perhaps even the Light demanded it. *You have no natural ability . . . Make me some tea, dear. You're so helpful . . . Don't do magic. It will only lead to tragedy.*

She wished her mother was alive. She'd go back to that clean, loveless house, destroy all the beautiful clothes that Mary had bought on Rodeo Drive. She'd smash every tray of expensive makeup, tear apart every prop she used to disguise true power as parlor tricks to make more money. Oh hell, why bother with those things? She'd tear apart her mother's perfect face, make *her* beg through the blood and pain, and she'd laugh and laugh . . .

Ruby stopped, hands still on her breasts, fingers clamped on her nipples so shards of pain radiated out from them. Horrified, she let go. The blood surge was an even worse pain, but she barely felt it. She curled in a ball on her side, hiding her head beneath her arms. *No, no, no . . .*

"Derek." She whispered it. Pulling off the earpiece, she put it in the nightstand drawer, turned off the cell phone. Then she rocked, and made herself remember every single moment of the time on the beach. The way Derek had spoken against her ear. *I love you, Ruby Night Divine.*

He'd loved Ruby as she was then. This, no one could love. But she'd made her choice. In the darkness, like this, she could cry over it, wish things could be different, but in dawn's light, she had to be what she'd chosen to be. With Derek coming back, and her being here . . . It made her feel an end was coming, for certain.

But if that end meant a chance to face down Asmodeus, it was okay. She'd even welcome it.

In the words of the Collin Raye song, that was her story, and she was sticking to it.

* 7 *

"LIKE EVERYTHING ELSE IN THE UNIVERSE, FAULT LINES have a topside Light energy that feeds the surface, and a Dark energy beneath that feeds the Underworld. As long as everybody stays on their side, all's well, but of course it doesn't work that way. Magic users dabble where they shouldn't, and Underworld beings seek ways to tangle Light energy up with Dark for purposes that could unbalance things. And if those fault lines get messed up, Mother Earth gets messed up. The saying, 'If Momma ain't happy, ain't nobody happy,' becomes true in a big way."

A ripple of chuckles ran through the women sitting in the circle. They'd completed a casting, called Quarters, welcomed the energy of the elements and the Lord and Lady, and warded out harm. An hour before they'd arrived, Ruby had done the same, since she didn't yet have direct experience with the group. She needed to ensure they weren't overheard by forces that could penetrate a weaker warding. But she was pleased with how they performed, the cohesive energy they had as a group.

Still, once they'd cast, she'd had them hold position and focus while she walked the interior perimeter, touching each woman to gauge her unique signature and strength. They'd sent a few quizzical glances toward Linda, who nodded reassuringly. Once she did that, they waited Ruby out in respectful silence. Also good. No power egos in the group who couldn't take direction.

"Next time the circle is cast, you'll have a different arrangement," she continued. "The four strongest will be on the Quarters, and those most aligned with a specific element will be placed in those quadrants. The choice of Quarter callers is not a judgment. All parts of a fence are important, both the mesh and the post. But the post has certain properties, just as the mesh does. All right?"

As they nodded, Linda spoke up. "Ruby, would our normal five-minute meditation disrupt what you're intending to do? It's how we connect, prepare ourselves for whatever task we have before us."

"Not at all." Ruby swept her gaze over the group. "However, keep something in mind. What we're going to do these next couple weeks will be like basic training. You'll do certain key things, like casting and reinforcing your circle, over and over. We may even do an emergency drill or two in the middle of the night, where I'll call you out of a sound sleep and tell you to get here immediately. You'll get into position, cast and protect this area as fast as you can. That spontaneous casting will need to be as strong and unshakable as what you can do when you spend time meditating and preparing for it." At their expressions, she added, "It's like loading a gun when someone is breaking into your house and the children are upstairs, no time to get them out. You don't have time to read a manual or fumble it. It has to be instinctual, fast and steady."

Miriam raised her hand. As the youngest coven member in her early twenties, she had a quiet intelligence Ruby liked. But of course she was a little more uncertain of herself, a privilege of youth. She currently held the Air Quarter, but was one Ruby would move, knowing she was better as "mesh" than "post" until she gained more experience.

"Ruby, Linda said we'd be learning how to strengthen and reinforce the fault line so nothing . . . bad can get through. You sound like you think something *is* going to get through."

"Derek didn't send me to prepare you for the best-case scenario. If something does break out, you ladies are what stands between it and harm to your community." Remembering her earlier thought, Ruby added, "Think of Derek as a sheriff, and he's pretty much decided you're capable of being deputies. That's what I'm here to train you to be."

Miriam pressed her lips together, but nodded. When they'd arrived, there'd been the usual atmosphere of chatter that punctuated an amicable female get-together. On a normal night, after the Grounding, when the general energy work was done, Ruby knew they usually sat down to the wine and tempting hors d'oeuvres Linda had waiting in her fridge. Hundreds of years ago, when the very first all-female coven had been formed, Ruby suspected it had been that way. They'd performed their vital magical function to help crops, protect or heal family, but in the aftermath, they'd bond over discussions of family, marriage and service, the building blocks of the female world. A different, but no less important, kind of circle.

She'd just introduced a new element to this coven, one most modern-day groups didn't face. As a result, Miriam's somber expression, her trace of uncertainty, was now reflected in the other faces in the circle.

"Let's do that meditation," Linda interjected. "The Lord and Lady are with us. They'll guide us, steady us. Help us learn what needs to be learned, and know what questions need answers."

The ladies settled into their preferred resting states, eyes closing. The five-minute meditation started with a Goddess chant to focus the mind. Once it was done, Marie lifted the flute she had resting next to her and began to play a haunting Native American piece that spoke of blue sky and grass-covered plains.

It was easy to imagine oneself lying between those two wide expanses, connecting to the energies above, below and within, as well as the surrounding elements, all infused with divine power. The focus of the coven intensified, that energy condensing around them. After several moments, Marie, her eyes closed throughout the playing of the piece, set the woodwind aside and joined them fully in the meditation, letting the night sounds take over as a natural extension of her music.

Ruby kept her eyes open throughout. She monitored the rate at which the auras changed around each of them, confirming her opinion of which coven members were strongest, most focused. But beyond that, she didn't need the meditation. She could ground herself in a blink, pull magic into herself as needed, as easily as picking up a pencil to write.

A pink moon was rising over the trees while the dusk light settled. It looked vulnerable yet enduring, something she used to feel and no longer did. At least not until Derek Stormwind had walked back into her shop.

Holy Goddess, could she string three sentences together in her mind that didn't involve that man? Closing her eyes, she took a few deep breaths, synchronizing with the others. While she didn't need it for her magical purposes, the preparatory meditation connected the circle, connected her to the other women, and that was important, though she'd held off from it as long as she could, curiously reluctant.

As she tapped into that flow, the alluring peace and tranquility that came with such spiritual sisterhood, no matter how transient to the moment, filled her. It brought a bittersweet feeling. Grief. An emotion that would find familiar ground among thirteen women who'd experienced the joys and sorrows of marriage, childhood—of life itself, from the uniquely female perspective.

The Dark part of her recoiled from the dangerous provocation. Then Linda reached out, took her ice-cold hand. Robin, the woman on the other side of Ruby, did the same, connecting them as a natural part of the circle binding. Ruby had an overwhelming urge to squeeze those hands tight, to imagine Raina's long-nailed, elegant fingers, or Ramona's chapped palm. Her chaotic friend's nails were usually jagged, chewed off. Raina had sometimes playfully rubbed one of her own wicked nails across Ruby's palm to tickle it and disrupt her circle casting, make her laugh.

"Blessed be," murmured Robin. It was picked up and continued around the circle until it came back to Linda. When she lifted her head, Ruby sensed it, opened her eyes. Linda looked at her expectantly.

"Blessed be," Ruby said, though the words stuck in her throat. "All right, then." Giving Linda's and Robin's hands a brisk, functional squeeze, she drew her hands back to herself. "First lesson is feeling the fault line itself, its contours and shape, and taking our wards and protections with us when we stretch out in a line to do that. This circle is a powerful place, but that fault line is even more so. You can draw on that power even as you're strengthening it, which is a different kind of 'circle,' just as three-dimensional, because remember the circle itself is a sphere . . ."

She hadn't been lying. True magical energy work was an extremely intense workout, particularly while learning to do it properly, correcting bad habits or carelessness that developed from doing monthly routine prayer circles. When she called for a break three hours later, that moon was high in the sky and the women were drained. Some were sweating, the cotton ritual robes they'd donned clinging to their skin. As soon as Ruby said they were done for the night, they closed down the circle and headed up to the house in weary clumps. Miriam hung back, however.

"You did something extra to it, before, didn't you?"

Ruby cocked her head. "I don't know. Did I?"

"It felt like a different energy than our usual casting, an additional protection, of sorts. I thought it might have been something Mr. Stormwind left, but it felt like you."

Ruby almost smiled. Mr. Stormwind, indeed. "Yes, I did

an additional protection before you arrived. You have good instincts. Keep working on that."

Miriam nodded. When she didn't move, Ruby realized the young woman was intending to walk with Ruby toward the house. Linda's kitchen had a bank of spacious windows, throwing warm light onto the lawn. Open French doors brought the clink of glasses as wine was taken out and poured. The beginnings of soft chatter and tired laughter wafted down the slope. Just as she'd anticipated, the women were doing what women did so well, particularly when they shared a common purpose.

"Oh, I'll . . ." She bit back the urge to escape. They had a lot to accomplish in the next two weeks. Tonight was barely a warm-up. Bonding with the teacher would be essential for them to trust her lead, let her abuse them in all the necessary ways.

She knew how to appear intimate, confiding, without actually telling someone anything about herself. It had been necessary in dealing with her mother's clients *and* her mother. Cultivating that talent had helped her launch a successful gun shop, which depended on a loyal clientele who needed that reassuring combination of professional firmness and warmth from the proprietor. Yeah, she was primed and ready to scribble out one of those management success books. *How to Turn Dysfunction into Dollars.* She'd add it to her to-do list. Not.

Pulling the scrunchie out of her hair, she shook down her brown locks and scrubbed at her scalp to relax the tense nerves. "I'm starving."

"Then we better get up there. It's going to go fast. Hope Linda made extra tonight. So when did you start practicing . . ."

THE SUCCESS OF THOSE TENTATIVE BONDS BETWEEN teacher and students proved themselves over the next three days. On day four, she felt they were ready to move into scarier territory. She called Christine into the center of the circle with her.

Next to Linda, Christine was the strongest member of the coven. For that reason, Ruby now had her holding the Fire Quarter, opposite Linda's Earth Quarter, a good balance. "All right, everyone. How do we shield ourselves from magical attack?"

She looked toward Christine. "I'm going to throw a spell at you. It's going to be uncomfortable, but I promise you it won't be painful. All right? I want you to feel it first, so apprehension won't distract you from what I'm about to teach you."

Christine nodded, a little warily, but she was game. "How do I—"

Ruby thrust out her arms, as if she were snapping out a towel with both hands. Calling fire energy was barely more than flipping a switch and pulling it in. Christine started, gave a short yelp and clapped her hand over her stomach. "Ouch. That felt like . . . like electricity."

"Yes, at that level, that's what it feels like." At a higher level, it felt like an explosion that rocketed through the skeletal system and took over the body, making it jitter like a puppet on strings. Or picked it up and threw it onto the windshield of a car.

"Ruby?"

She tuned in to Linda's voice, realized the woman had called her name a couple times. She shook herself out of it. "Sorry; I was thinking of the next step," she lied.

"I saw the energy arc," Miriam said, her eyes wide. "It was like . . ."

"The air shimmered, and sparked," Robin finished.

Ruby kept them on track by sharpening her tone. "All right, now. Christine, you remember the protections I had you practicing for your Quarter? Good. When I throw it at you this time, I want you to make a similar motion toward me, but focus that protection through your hands. Imagine it's suddenly become a big, life-sized shield in front of you, and put everything you have behind it. Remember, just like me, you're drawing from the elements for the energy source.

You pull it into yourself, bind it with your own power signature so the shield anchors itself to you, then project. It will feel cumbersome right now, but with practice, you'll do it as instinctively as you throw up a hand to ward off something coming at your face."

It didn't work the first or second times, but it was a new skill for Christine, and for the rest. Few of them had seen magic manifest in a physical form from a witch, versus feeling its abstract movement through their bodies. No matter how well tuned a person was to ritual and the terminology, seeing active magic like in the storybooks could be unsettling.

The fourth time, Christine was tired of getting zapped, and her resolve and focus firmed. Her shielding held for a handful of seconds before Ruby got through. The praise she gave Christine, as well as the approbation of the group, bolstered the woman. She'd also been able to detect those shimmers around her own hands, not just Ruby's.

Students gave a hundred extra miles for even the most minute success from their hard work. It spurred the teacher as well, such that Ruby found herself grinning, genuinely proud of them.

Several more times and Christine found the groove. She anchored the shield and held it for a solid minute until Ruby let it go.

"*Yeah.*" Ruby gave her a high five, which Christine returned with a pleased smile and a shaky hand. "Now, in a few moments, we'll break out into pairs and let you all practice that."

"But we don't know how to do the zapping part," Sally said.

"Yes. That's a more complicated skill, and one we'll discuss after you get this down. Right now, you guys are like rookie cops. No chief in his right mind would give you a Taser until he was sure you have the control skills to curb a quick trigger finger. Sally, you were getting a little heated in your political discussion with Georgia last night. You might decide to zap her to prove your point about Middle East policy decisions."

As the women laughed, Ruby moved back to the center of the circle, to the laundry sack she'd laid there earlier with tools for today's lesson. "Here you go. One for each pairing." She pulled out an assortment of colored Nerf balls, tossed them to every other woman in the circle. "You can do this at home as well, with a trusted family member or friend. If your shield is working, the ball will veer off when it's thrown at you, as if a stray wind caught it. It's best to use Nerfs, particularly for the homework. Far easier to explain to nosy neighbors than you slingshotting the hundred balls your husband shoots out of his pitching machine at you. Though if you get that good, you get to graduate Hogwarts."

More laughter. She could see each woman was eager to try it. "All right." Ruby sobered. "Get to practicing."

Day Six.

"All right, this lesson is how we're going to spend most of our Saturday. By the end of it, I guarantee you'll all hate me. If you don't, I haven't drilled you enough."

"If we say we hate you now, can we go ahead and break for Danish?" Sally joked.

Ruby snorted. "Obviously too much energy in this crowd, if I have a smart-ass before I've finished my coffee."

The ladies were now coming "to class" like Amazons in training. It was the most dangerous time, when they had more knowledge of their capabilities than they'd known was possible, but little practical experience. However, like fighter pilots, they just needed a certain amount of cocky enthusiasm to get into that cockpit. Ruby was glad to see their spirits were holding. It had been a tough week, and today was going to be even tougher. It was good for them to get this lesson when they were less fresh, though.

She was tired, too, but for different reasons. Each night, when Linda was asleep and the women were safely away from the property, she walked that line. She wasn't foolish enough to call him outright, but if Asmodeus was making incursions here, she was sure she'd feel something, some sense of him stirring or moving in the area. She felt the incursions, but not from him. From that nebulous, unknown threat that Derek had detected. If the demon ever did show, though, she'd show him what her capabilities were *now*. They'd settle what lay between them, with no one else in harm's way.

At least the pleasure and challenge of teaching this group was keeping her occupied, diluting the frustration. Sort of. The thorny possibility of him not coming in range at all while she was here was starting to dig into her consciousness.

"Okay. What if this circle was broken and one of you was dragged out of it? How do you get that person back inside and the circle recast, the fault line reinforced? Say Smart-ass Sally over there got knocked out, so the line is broken. I'm right next to her, so I pivot, move forward and anchor that perimeter with me." Ruby stepped with purpose outside the circle, touching Sally lightly as she did so. "I *am* the circle. It's not separate from me, so when I step out, that circle comes with me. I know you've all seen *Gladiator*. Seriously, who can resist Russell Crowe in a short tunic?" There was a quick titter, but thirteen pairs of serious eyes remained fastened on her.

"Remember those diamond formations during the staged Battle of Carthage? It's the same theory." She pointed toward the ground. "This is the starting point of a new circle. Get away from the idea of a circle as a shape. In this kind of magic use, it's a concept. When you adjust your position, you will align with me left and right from this protective point, like that triangular diamond shape. The attacker's energy will flow along the sides like a current. A spell or energy casting, once released by the user, can't change course. It has to unfold as intended. So I plant my 'shield' in front of the fallen member"—she pantomimed it—"and someone else drags her back into the perimeter. You close ranks, bring all those shields together even more tightly, back into a closed shape. Then you hold."

Her voice sharpened. "When Underworld creatures assume corporeal forms aboveground, it takes a lot of energy. Because of that, most have blissfully short life spans in that form, and they don't like Light energy. If you have the stamina, you'll force them to give up. The army trains their soldiers over and over in the same methods, establishing muscle memory, helping them to act under extreme circumstances, where that training is the only thing that can keep them from either panic or overthinking a situation, both of which can get them killed or defeat their objective.

"Now, once the Underworld creatures give up and appear to vanish, do *not* assume they're gone. You will move as one unit to the fault line, stretch out over it like I showed you earlier this week, and reinforce it. The same way you'll do daily to hopefully prevent any such attack from ever happening."

She stepped back into the circle perimeter. "All week long, I've been teaching you the individual steps of the full dance I just described. So today, we're going to practice the entire sequence, over and over again. You get this down, you have the building blocks you can break down or chain together to use for defense, protection and enhancement of not only the fault line, but yourselves and your sisters. Just like Mr. Miyagi, putting together wash-on, wash-off."

The women chuckled. However, as hands briefly clasped, squeezed, Ruby saw them acknowledge the serious nature of what they were doing. As the week had progressed, it had become more real to them, the idea that a time might come when it would be about more than reinforcing the fault line. Lives might be at stake. Those clasped hands were solidarity, sending the message: *We can do this.*

And Ruby was the one making sure they'd be ready. Their lives might depend on her teachings. She swallowed.

"Let's get started."

* 8 *

BY THE END OF THE DAY, LINDA WAS SO WORN-OUT RUBY fed her dogs, ordered her to go to bed and sleep in Sunday morning. She'd given them all the time off, knowing they needed the break at this point.

As for her, she was still wired. Earlier in the week, she'd asked Linda about a good place to practice her shooting. Apparently, on the north end of the property there was a clearing and natural embankment she could use as a firing range and backdrop for the bullets, respectively, so they wouldn't zing through the woods and be a hazard. The nearest neighbor was a couple miles down the road.

She took her Sig, the Desert Eagle and a pump-action riot gun, Derek's purported favorite. Most of it she carried in a large mountain backpack, working out her muscles with the heavy load. By the time she reached the location, she was out of breath. As she set up her targets, she decided to work with the pump action first.

She'd left Theo and the shepherds locked up in the guesthouse. While Theo was used to the sound of firearms, hearing the muffled reports behind the steel-reinforced door of her indoor firing range was a bit different from being right next to her when firing. She'd brought her ears, a sound-muffling headset, to dampen the high-decibel range. At home, she had a pair with a built-in connection to her music player, so she could play some heavy metal as she did her target practice. It kept her mind from wandering into disturbing areas. But here, where the surroundings were less familiar, she wasn't going to block her senses to that level.

She rapid-fired the riot gun's six slugs, reloading smoothly when needed, checking her target work as she went along. Just like the shielding, shooting for defense was something that had to be accurate based on repeated practice, not dependent on careful sighting every time. She was pleased to see her bullets grouped in a lethal cluster in the center mass of the paper target. After putting the shotgun through its paces, she moved on to the Sig 226, her preferred weapon for concealed carry, though it was bigger than more recent models. While the grip was a bit larger for her hands than recommended, she liked the solid feel of it. The vendor who'd sold it to her had grinned when she said that.

That's the way most women are about their first gun. They tend to think the bigger one does the best job.

He was right, but it didn't change the instinct. Even now, having so much more knowledge of firearms than she'd had then, such that she knew a smaller grip gave her better control, she'd still take that Sig over the sleeker Walther she'd left at home.

After she did about fifty rounds with each weapon, she policed her brass, then took a seat on a stump. Slipping her feet out of her shoes now that there was no danger of hot shells falling on her toes, she propped them on the edge of the cut tree, rocking on the point of her buttocks as she popped open her soda, took a sip from it. One hundred percent Dr Pepper, no additives today. Being immersed in all this the past week, and being away from Raina, Derek, all of them, she'd had no need for deception.

That thought should have made her miss them less, but of course that wasn't the case.

She studied the way the leaves fluttered on the trees above, a canopy stirred by the wind, showing bits of the late-afternoon sky. Shards of dying sunlight found their way through, touching her face. Now that she'd stopped shooting, she heard birdcalls, the rustling of squirrels foraging on the forest floor. She stopped rocking, because filtering through those noises was something else. Human movement. A human moving on booted feet.

He could move like a ghost, but he was smart enough not to sneak up on a woman with loaded guns. As she let her feet slip to the ground, she realized she hadn't showered after the grueling coven practice. Her hair was scratched up into a tail, and her hike through the woods with munitions and multiple firearms had left her sweat-stained in her T-shirt and jeans. She told herself she didn't care she looked like she'd been working with a railroad gang.

He was following the same trail she'd taken, though there were several from Linda's house that led to this place. Had he woken Linda and asked her where Ruby had gone, or had he just tracked her? She was guessing the latter.

He wore his hat with his jeans and boots, of course. Since it was still winter, technically, and the early evening was bringing back a touch of that chill, the battered long coat and long-sleeved shirt under that wasn't out of place, but she wondered from what cold environment he'd come that he needed more than he'd usually wear in a Southern climate like this. When he lifted his gaze so that the hat brim revealed his face, she tried hard to remain unmoved, but it was pretty much pointless. She hadn't taken any Deception, hadn't expected him here, so she was defenseless.

She'd spent the week teaching the coven to be prepared in every instance, but she'd lowered her own guard.

There was something in his eyes, something different. More cautious, as if he was holding something in, something pretty strong. Coming to a halt a few feet away from her, he swept her with that appraising gaze. Stayed silent an uncomfortably long time.

"You should have called Linda to let her know you were coming." She cleared her throat. "She would have made you dinner."

He dug into the pocket of the coat, came out with a package of beef jerky and a cold beer. She expected he'd swiped the latter from Linda's fridge. "Care to share your seat?"

She obliged, moving the Sig from the stump to the top of its case, making room for him. Opening the jerky, he offered some to her. She made a face at the smoky smell, but took a piece. When he popped the beer, also inviting her to take some of that, she gestured with the Dr Pepper. "Is beer and jerky all you're having for dinner?"

"Had a late lunch. Twelve-pack of beef tacos at Taco Bell. This will hold me awhile."

She shook her head. "When you die of heart disease, if the Pearly Gates are guarded by cows, you're going to be in deep shit."

"My cholesterol's pretty good for a man my age."

She pressed her lips together, chewed the tough jerky. His hip was pressed against hers, his shoulder sliding along hers in casual familiarity. Every place he touched was warm, and though she was trying to be discreet about it, she was inhaling his scent with the desperation of a coke junkie. He was staring into the forest in kind of an absentminded way. Though he didn't feel distant, there was something pretty weighted between them.

"They're doing well," she ventured. "The coven."

"I expected nothing less, especially with you as their teacher."

"You chose good students."

He looked down at the arsenal at her feet. "Can I ask you a question?"

"I don't know. Can you?"

At his expression, she shrugged. "You so rarely ask permission for anything. Were you attacked by a Miss Manners demon on the way here?"

"I vanquished it, but the residual effect is lingering." His gaze lifted to her face. "Why did you choose to do this, Ruby? The gun shop? I'm not picking a fight. I want to know."

It was a fair question, and one she could probably answer without getting into some sticky areas, because she'd had to answer the same thing for Raina and Ramona.

"You remember Mad Max?"

Warmth and wry amusement crossed his expression. "I had a feeling he was behind this."

"Other than you, I guess you could say he was my only friend, for all that he was a bit crazy and I had to be careful not to go see him on one of his bad days." He was one of their Monterey neighbors, an eccentric who rarely came out of his home. She met him when she was eleven, during one of the rare occasions when they were at the Monterey home for longer than a few weeks. Escaping Mary's never ending list of demands one afternoon, she'd wandered onto his extensive property by accident. He'd caught her, and instead of being terrified by him, she'd been intrigued by the bushy eyebrows, the fact he had a patch over one missing eye, and that he was a World War II vet. He'd liked that she was quiet and listened, and before long she'd discovered his passion. He was a gun collector, and he shared that love with her, showing her that guns were intricate and amazingly engineered little machines. He didn't particularly like cleaning them after target practice due to his arthritis, so in exchange for learning about each of them and getting to shoot them under his supervision, she'd helped him out with that.

When he'd died, he'd shocked her to the core by leaving

the whole collection to her, along with a note. *If you ever decide what you want to do to set yourself apart from your mother, sell these to finance it.* She'd kept the gun he'd carried during the war, but she'd used the rest to finance Arcane Shot.

She explained that to Derek, but she could tell he was already up to speed. "You went to see him."

"When you first mentioned him to me, I paid him a visit. Made sure he was okay. He was. Messed up some by the war, but he loved you to death. You have that effect on older men."

She made a face at him, but couldn't help shoving at him with her shoulder, coloring a little. It shouldn't surprise her that Derek had done what Mary should have done, safeguarding her welfare with a solitary male stranger. He nudged her back.

"I understand the background and why you'd be good at running Arcane Shot. My question is, why this instead of Witches R Us? Last time I saw you, magical study was what you wanted to do more than anything."

She shrugged. "You know the whole 'people suck' thing? Well, I figured out love, peace and understanding only go so far. You have to keep a choke collar on some people. Everything is about balance. So this helps me do that, in a different way."

He took a swallow of the beer. She smelled that appealing combination, high-testosterone male mixed with fragrant hops. "Give me specifics," he said. "Help me understand."

She pursed her lips. "The focus of my shop is self-defense and protection of the things that matter. A lot of my clientele are military. I have a group of Vietnam vet retirees who come out once a week to use the firing range as an excuse to just hang together, connect. At least thirty percent of my customers are women, who want to take care of themselves and their families. Sometimes that includes the ones dealing with those joke restraining orders against abusive spouses. I get some hunters, but only those who hunt to feed their families, not to put some rack on their wall. That's the kind of vibe I put in the wards on my shop. I don't want the guys who consider killing a sport, or the skinheads and gangbangers, the testosterone junkies. I want my guns in the hands of people like Mad Max, those who are willing to help keep that choke-collar balance out there. I run gun safety courses for anyone who wants to learn, any age, even minors accompanied by parents. Kids are better off knowing how to handle and respect a firearm, not having them hidden away from them like skin mags they'll obsess over."

She paused. "I guess it's a different passion, but related. And I get on a soapbox about some of it. Sorry."

"I noticed. You grew about a foot taller during that speech. Figured you were standing on something. So you still serve the Light."

"Did you doubt it?" She arched a brow. "Dark and Light magic can both serve the Light, Derek. You just can't give a shit about your soul when you use them both to do it."

Oh, hell. *Fuck, double fuck and damn.* She shouldn't have said that. Even though she averted her gaze to stare out in the woods the same way he'd done, she could feel those intense blue eyes on her face. She tensed as he set his beer aside, the jerky, too. However, he merely stood up, took her hand, drew her up as well. In bare feet, the height difference was quite a bit, so she stared at his throat, the pulse thudding there.

"You have a choice now," he rumbled, sliding his arm around her waist. "Kiss me good enough, I won't make you tell me right now what the hell that means. You might put it off another day."

She set her jaw. "I'm not going to kiss you, Derek Stormwind. Or tell you anything."

He touched her chin. Guiding it up with his large hand despite her resistance, he made her meet his gaze. Not the gaze of her former lover, but something more powerful and ancient than that, something that guarded the gates.

Sudden panic had her wrenching away, though she couldn't get away from the arm around her waist. She put both hands on his chest, straight-armed him. "Derek, if you try to read me to figure out whatever it is you're trying to figure out, we're done. I mean it. You'll never darken my door again. You won't rape my mind to get what you want."

Betrayal and frightened fury underscored the words. *Please don't cross that line.* The shadows of the past were quick to surge up. Wind cut the ground at their feet, sending a spray of dried leaves swirling around their bodies. The trees groaned above. Angry heat throbbed beneath her soles.

"Shit." He took care of her strong-arming, cinching his arm around her shoulder blades like a lasso, folding her against his chest. It burrowed her in the scent of old leather, shirt and Derek. "Fine. Easy, girl. Settle down. I wasn't going to."

"Were, too," she muttered, trying to settle her heart back down, trying to shove those shadows back down with a mental plunger. The wind died, the ground becoming dormant again.

"Maybe a little. But I'd never push it past your will, Ruby." He cupped the back of her skull now, fingers tangling in her hair, mussing the hold of her ponytail further. "I wouldn't do that to you. Okay? Can you trust me that much?"

It broke her heart, the rough note in his voice. It told her he knew he'd lost her trust, and he didn't know where or how. But he wanted it back.

"I've always trusted you more than I trust anyone." She wasn't enough of a bitch to deny him that. Curling her hands in his coat, she pressed her face harder against him, his strength. Fuck, she couldn't do this. She was slipping, slipping toward something dangerous. She wanted to wilt in his arms.

Instead, she lifted her head, stretched up on her toes and pressed her mouth against his. It was tentative only in that first second. Another blink, and it was hard, angry, needy. She told herself to cloud his intent with lust, push away her personal need to surrender. She could take control with hammering desire, because it would serve both their purposes.

He held her head in those large hands that could cover her ears, tease her nape with his fingertips. His thumbs stroked along the hollows of her cheeks, the corners of her mouth. They dipped down to her jaw, his touch so close to her sensitive throat, the pulse thudding there.

Taking her anger, he responded with a fierce tenderness that was far more dangerous and overwhelming. She could feel he had his own anger, his own scores to settle with her, but he wasn't holding back on the yearning, the emotions, that made those things so important to him. She latched onto that yearning, tried to ignore the rest, the elephant in the room. Maybe she could pretend, go back to the way it felt before, and it would be all right. As a child, magic was make-believe, not Dark or Light forces, arcane studies and such. It was supposed to be easy, flowing, coming when you called it. Like this. Maybe that was why sex was so easy to mistake for it . . . or to accept *as* it.

She made a noise in her throat, and his fingers tightened, one hand dropping to pull her even closer. His body was solid oak, yet she melded into its hollows and valleys, a perfect fit. Her hands, now folded in against him, could spread out like a bird's wings over his chest, feel the man beneath the cloth. As she gave herself over to the heat of his firm mouth, they slid up to his neck, dug in to hold, because when Derek Stormwind put his mind to kissing a woman senseless, she needed all the support she could get.

He hadn't needed to tease her lips apart because she'd come to him open and heated. His tongue tangled with hers, his lips caressing and stroking her mouth the same way on the outside, a primal yet complex foreplay that had her whole body humming, coming alive wherever it was touching his.

God, she wanted him to take her down right now, right here, on the forest floor, that serrated edge of need tearing at her. "Fuck me," she muttered against his mouth. "Now. Right here."

Though her urgency with Derek in the past had been

expressed in similar yet less crudely blatant ways, it was a definite tell of the kind of company she'd been keeping. She cursed herself anew as he picked up on it, stiffened. Still holding her tight, he lifted his head.

"Sex without the heart involved? Is that what you've found with your friend?"

"He's not my friend."

Fast as a striking snake, Derek whipped her around. Her breath sucked in on a gasp, but he already had her pressed against a tree. One large hand locked around her wrists, pulling her arms up above her head. When he pushed his body against the back of hers, his aroused cock pressed snug against her buttocks, almost making her moan in need. "Is this what he gave you, Ruby? Rough, taking total control? Like I'd do it, only instead of for your pleasure, he did it to cause you pain?"

Her muscles contracted, remembering such play between her and Derek, a delicious version of the dark cruelty that Mikhael would inflict. She needed it Mikhael's way to make sure it stayed physical, no emotional demons able to rise and take her.

"Yes," she whispered. "He *gives* me that." She goaded him with present tense, needing to keep it angry. She couldn't afford to remember the other.

He stayed still against her, violence vibrating between them for several long moments. Shit. She'd overplayed her hand. Derek might shove her away like garbage and leave her alone here, with nothing but the unspent need.

While that was her main concern, her mind sensibly had a few others. Her heart was beating like a rabbit's. He had her pinned, was twice her weight, and she knew she'd seriously pissed him off. Though that was the Darkness coming through; the person she'd once been still knew Derek would never touch her in anger, never harm her that way.

As he shifted his grip on her wrists, she imagined a variety of scenarios. Tearing open her jeans, using the toe of his boot to shove them all the way to her ankles and then ramming into her in the straight-legged position. Her moist tissues contracted at the thought, nipples hardening against the bark. Goddess, do *something*.

He answered her plea, but only to torment her. Bending, he put his mouth on the back of her shoulder, where the T-shirt had gaped open during their struggle. It was the place in their fantasy where he'd branded her. A lingering itch, like a healing scar, had remained, though there was no visible mark. If she were speaking to Raina, she'd ask about it, but it was the least of her current priorities. Particularly right now.

He kissed her there, long, lingering, the tip of his tongue caressing that area. Then he moved up to her collarbone, taking his time there as well, tracing the curved line of the bone, making his way up the side of her throat.

"Stop it," she whispered. She was trembling, her stomach tightening, her thigh muscles doing the same.

"No. You still can't do it on your own, can you? Your mind gets too involved. Your fears, the guilt and insecurity. And now . . . the Darkness drives that need even harder, but it won't let you put those capable fingers between your legs to do it for yourself. I can smell that wetness, so strong, like an animal in heat."

"Please . . ."

"Not this time, girl. You want to play rough. I'm going to hear you beg."

He did slip the button of her jeans, took the zipper down with the force of his hand pushing into the loose front, finding the elastic edge of her panties and nipping beneath those. He didn't hesitate, knowing her body so well. She cried out as his knuckles snugged on either side of her clit, his fingers reaching her slick labia. When she struggled and bucked against him, that made it worse, adding to the clever stroking of his fingers.

"No. I don't want it this way."

"Tough. All you want is to be gotten off? Since your boy toy's not here to oblige, that's what I'll give you."

She pressed her forehead hard against the bark, couldn't stop herself from shamelessly working herself against his hand. Mikhael would make her do that, croon cruel comparisons to a dog when he really got her going.

"Stop. Please stop. Derek, I'm sorry. I can't . . . Please, I can't bear to do it like this with you."

He gave a harsh chuckle, punctuated it with a scissoring of his fingers that made hers dig painfully into the bark. She was gasping, so close. He was going to make her go over anyway, be just as ruthless as Mikhael but in a way that was far crueler than the gunrunner, because Derek cared. He understood that the pain and pleasure was mixed up with raw emotion, heart. He could make more than her body surrender, and her soul wouldn't take being ripped open like that.

With a heartfelt oath, he stopped, holding her on that edge. "He's past tense now, Ruby. We're not in that room at Raina's. No playing. Say it. And I'll know if you're lying."

"Past tense." Tears had squeezed out of her eyes, and when he turned her now, lifted her chin, she couldn't stop the quivering of her lips, her hands clutching at his waist.

"Ruby." His eyes were full of pain, his mouth a hard line. He was going to say something, open that can of worms that would force her to push him back again. Her body was just too damn greedy to allow that. She put her trembling fingers on his mouth, eyes pleading, needing him to understand.

The muscle in his jaw flexed. "Take off your clothes. All of them."

The temp was dropping with the waning sun, but it was Florida. Of course, she wouldn't have hesitated if she was in Alaska. She stripped off the jeans and shirt. Unhooked her bra as he watched, eyes sliding over her curves, following the track of the garment as it left her, fell to the ground. Then, as he waited, she shimmied out of the panties. She was unsteady, but when she teetered, his hand was under her elbow. As she straightened, she shivered, unable to help herself.

He shrugged out of the long coat, threaded her arms into

it, left it hanging open in the front so he could see her bare body cloaked by it. It fell to her ankles, brushed her heels. He unbuckled his belt, opened his jeans, then caught her around the waist, palming her bottom with one big hand as he lifted her up against the tree. She caught his shoulders with both hands, her fingers curling against his throat, the soft chest hair at the base.

"Look at me. And don't look away," he added in a husky voice. "Whatever happened, Ruby, we're going to work through it. Maybe not today or tomorrow, but you're not running from me anymore. You're not alone."

Yes, she was. Because he couldn't go down the path she'd chosen. So she curled her arms around his broad shoulders, buried her face in his neck. He sighed against her but put his hips between her thighs, pushing them out wider to take him. As much as he wanted to resist her, she could feel that he couldn't. He was as hard and large as she'd ever felt him, and Derek had never been a small man, in any way. He didn't have to grip himself. Another flood of emotions made her bite her lip as he angled his hips and slid into her with unerring accuracy, knowing her well enough to find his target on the first try. He sank himself in that pocket like a champion pool player.

Three years without him, without this. *Oh, God and Goddess.* As Derek had pointed out, Mikhael just gave her the shamefully needed release. Whereas even angry, hurried, in-the-outdoor-cold sex with Derek was bliss, to feel that connection after so long. Clutching his shoulders harder, she made whimpering noises into his neck as he worked his hips, his buttocks flexing under her calves as she clamped her heels against his thighs. The climax shuddered through her lower belly, through her tight nipples and aching breasts, rubbing against his shirt. She inhaled him, aftershave, soap and Derek's own male scent, and wanted to be here in this moment forever.

"Derek . . ."

"Go on over, baby," he whispered into her ear. "I'm right

behind you. I want to feel you clamp down on me. Fuck, you're heaven."

Girl was for when he teased or flirted, or sometimes in the heat of lust, like in the barn fantasy. *Baby* was when he thought her emotions were going to get the best of her, or when he himself was particularly moved by something. This moment was both.

Her body simply exploded with the pleasure of it, from the soles of her feet to the crown of her head. Somewhere along the way she realized the duster was not merely for warmth, but to protect her skin from the bark of the tree. She could still feel the sharp edges through it, enough to relish that abrasive discomfort with the overwhelming power of the climax. The bitter with the sweet, bad with the good. She hoped that wasn't what she and Derek represented right now, the Dark and the Light, a doomed coupling in this corner of quiet wood.

But she'd take what she could get. She didn't care. She came apart in his arms, screaming out like a feral animal, her fingernails clawing his back, holding on to his shirt hard enough to rip it if she'd pulled with opposing force. But she wasn't pulling the cloth away from him. She was digging her fingers through it, wanting the man beneath.

He released then as well, all the sculpted muscle under her legs and arms hardening into steel as the hot flood of seed gave her an aftershock that shuddered her against him, made her even more glad for the strength of his arms to hold her together.

When he pressed his mouth against her shoulder, she felt him bite, clamp down on her there. She wanted the mark, tossed her head back to encourage him to go even deeper. As his release was spent, it became a firm, fierce kiss against her flesh. His fingers, underneath the duster to make contact with her bare skin, brushed over that phantom brand once again. It made her shiver.

The forest was quiet once more, except for the occasional birdcalls, the rustle of creatures foraging. Now those shards of higher sunlight were all gone, the sun setting. In a few moments, it would be behind the embankment she'd been using for her target practice backdrop and things would start to gray, get dim. Even colder.

Derek slid from her, still erect enough to make her murmur incoherently, contract on him. His eyes held hers as he pulled out. He maintained a good grip on her as he did so, keeping her against the tree. Looking at her for long moments, he framed her face, sliding down to collar her throat, then spread his fingers out over her shoulders, pushing the duster back so he could see her breasts, the nipples still tight from arousal and now from the touch of cool air. He caressed them with his thumbs, making her quiver, her inner thigh muscles rippling against his hips. Then his hands went down farther, below her breasts to the rib cage, thumbs passing gently over her abdomen. He stopped there, his head bent, studying. Ruby felt a trickle of uneasiness.

"I'm cold," she whispered.

He nodded, kept looking. Just as panic was about to take her, he let her feet slide to the ground. He'd been looking at the flushed petals of her sex, she told herself, the way she looked as he pulled out of her. Derek was usually a breast man, big-time, though he'd told her more than once he liked seeing her from either side, coming or going, such that a woman's ass was a close second for him. Or maybe it was just hers. Her breasts, her ass, her . . . everything. He'd told her that, too.

She wanted to move away, get her clothes back on, get past this moment, which she already knew was a mistake, but he thwarted her there. He'd picked up her panties. Dropping to one knee, he directed her to hold his shoulder.

"Derek, I can dress myself."

"But you're not going to." He put his hand on her leg, found the pocket of the duster with the other one, withdrew a cloth. As she held her breath, he pressed it between her legs, cleaned and dried her. Then he re-pocketed the cloth and picked up the panties where he'd left them folded over his thigh.

"Step in."

He dressed her from head to toe. Panties, jeans, socks and shoes. Threading her arms back into her bra straps, he hooked it and adjusted the cups, his large palms fitted around the breasts to shift their weight to their proper placement, as deftly as she did it herself. Then the shirt, a quick brush of his thumbs over her nipples again, evident through the thin cloth. Pulling her hair out of the collar for her, he reclaimed his coat, turned and moved back toward the stump.

She was quivering again, this time for another reason. He'd been silent the whole time he'd cared for her, and she, still overwhelmed by that climax, hadn't known what to say, either. She kept thinking about the way he'd stared at her stomach for so long. If he'd lifted his gaze then, met her eyes, she would have said the hard, terrible words. And that would have been only half of it. He was never going to learn the other half. But he'd started dressing her, giving her a reprieve. As if he didn't want to know the truth he'd already guessed. For some perverse reason, suspecting that about him hurt almost as badly as having him say it outright.

"Come here." Sitting down on the stump, he took out his pocketknife. Flipping it open, he held out his other hand. She came to him numbly, pushing a hand through her disheveled hair. She needed to redo her ponytail.

He pulled her in the area between his splayed thighs and lifted her hand to the fading light, examining it. He began to gently clean the bark debris she'd gotten beneath her nails when he was arousing her so violently. She hadn't even noticed it until now, but it was uncomfortable enough that his deft extraction of the material in smooth, crescent strokes of the blade was welcome.

If someone didn't say something completely irrelevant to break the tension, she was going to lose it. She glanced down at the array of guns. "I brought the shotgun. Want to pop off a few rounds on it before we go back? Or one of the handguns?"

"Nope." He kept his attention on her nails. "Never had a use for a handgun."

"You've never had a use for one, or you never used one? I have seen *Quigley Down Under*, you know."

"I know. We watched it together." There was a small quirk at the corner of his serious mouth. "Good movie." Folding the knife now, he stood, sliding it back into his pocket in that inadvertently sexy way a good-looking man could, with a shift of his hips and slight adjustment of his thigh. Picking up the Sig, he handed it to her, butt first. "Point it at me."

She raised a brow. "First rule of gun safety. You never point a gun at someone unless you intend to use it on them. Doesn't matter if it's loaded or not." She ignored the memory of sighting on him with the sniper rifle. She couldn't have hit him at that distance, anyway. Maybe.

"I'll trust you to exercise restraint," he said dryly. "If not, I'll catch the bullet in my teeth."

"Yeah, I'm seeing that happening." Actually, she wouldn't put it past him. He backed up several paces. When she lifted the Sig, she found she couldn't do it, couldn't point it right at him. He closed the distance between them as she aimed it off to the left. Gripping her wrist, he moved her resisting arm so the barrel was squarely aimed at his chest.

"Derek—"

"Bang," he said mildly. She jumped, regardless of the fact she'd kept her trigger finger on the barrel. Looking down, she saw a tiny spray of wildflowers tumble from the muzzle and land on the ground between them, just as the magazine thudded right next to them. She hadn't pressed the release. Leaning down as she lowered the weapon, he picked up the tiny bouquet. It was growing out of the bullet that had been in the chamber. Plucking one of the flowers free, he put it in her hair, lingering over the shell of her ear.

"So very sixties," she commented. His wry smile tugged at her battered heart. Reaching up, she painted a faint peace sign on his forehead with the gun soot. Catching her wrist again, he pressed a kiss on the palm, holding it there.

"Want to learn how to fire one, just in case?" she asked desperately.

"Will you stand behind me and press your breasts into my back, rub against my ass while you show me the proper stance?"

"No."

"Then I'll pass."

"I wouldn't be able to see around your massive body, you big bear."

He grinned at her then. Surprisingly, the gesture eased the tightness in her stomach, so much it was a palpable relief. Taking out the handkerchief again, he wet it with the extra water bottle she had, took a seat on the stump once more. Pulling her back between his knees, he cleaned her fingers. Things got quiet again as she looked down at him, but it was an easier quiet this time. He'd put his hat back on, but she took it off, letting it drop to the side so she could touch his hair. She closed her eyes at the feel of the strands moving between her fingers. So many simple things, simple pleasures that were unappreciated until the right and ability to do them were long gone.

He was done with cleaning her fingers, the handkerchief tucked away, but he was still caressing her knuckles, keeping her a willing captive in his grasp as he massaged the palm with broad, callused fingers.

"Did you ever remember wanting to be anything else?" she asked softly. "Other than a sorcerer?"

"I was born to be what I am, Ruby. I forgot the way my mother's breath felt on my face long before I forgot the way it felt to be smacked by my teacher when I wasn't paying attention." When he lifted his blue gaze to her, she glimpsed those things about him that she knew so little about. Before their relationship ended, he'd started letting her in, letting her get to know that side of him, so maybe she wasn't the only one who'd been working through trust issues.

"You got smacked by your teacher?"

"Teachers. I had a variety of them through the ages. And boy howdy, did I. The worst thrashing I ever got was during my awkward years, when I was all uncoordinated arms and legs." He grimaced. "I stepped on Taliesin's harp and broke it."

"You did not."

"Scout's honor."

"You were never a Boy Scout."

"Just an expression."

"So 'Scout's honor' means less than nothing when you say it."

His eyes twinkled, but he kept his gaze on his task. She was curious now, though. "So were you instructed by Merlin, too?"

He grunted. "We were on different paths while he was alive. I had the good fortune to study with some great teachers, though, through every century. Some of the best ones were quiet monks, unremarked by history." He blew on her fingertips, making them warmer, then pulled her in closer to tuck both of her hands under his armpits, letting her take advantage of his warmth. "Before Gutenberg came along, monks copied all the great manuscripts for the libraries of the Church and the wealthy. And not all of those monks did it as a tedious exercise. Many really read what they were transcribing. The works of great Greek philosophers, Renaissance scientists, obscure texts by Samurai warriors, you name it. Monks were keepers of the word, and they studied them, to the point that even today wizards go to certain monasteries to seek counsel. One of my favorites, and most recent, was a Brother Thomas I met in the early eighteen hundreds. He eventually left his order to become servant to a vampire queen."

"You made that up."

"Did not. I actually did some work to protect her from the Fae world when she was a child, though when I met her again later I let her believe that was an ancestor of mine, my own little deception. I don't think she bought it. Women are smart that way." That mischievous light played with the somber cast of his eyes, so she wasn't sure what was truth and what wasn't. "Like that monk, you have a love of knowledge, the ability to question that which most people don't. And you've used it to take your abilities much further."

He tightened his grip, anticipating her. "No, now, don't get all fuzzed up like a cat. Hear me out. The path you're walking, the forces you're messing with . . . You may think you have to handle all that alone, and you probably have your reasons for believing that. But I'm here. If there's something you need to talk over, you can talk to me. I can't promise to be perfect about it, but I'll do my best to listen as another magic user, not as your lover. Okay?"

She studied him. "You a miracle worker now?"

"I'll give it my best shot." Then he sighed, glancing at the sky. "Damn it. I need to go now. Just for a few hours. I'll be back by morning, and then I'm here all this coming week, so you can use me for the more advanced demonstrations. All right?"

She tried to quell her disappointment, the resentment that he'd just arrived only to disappear again, like a candy held out and then jerked out of reach, a child's taunt. *Psyche.* Why'd he come here first, anyway, knowing he had to take off again?

Then she thought of the urgency with which they'd come together. She'd been immersed in how much she'd wanted *him.* She hadn't thought about his perspective, the fierce insistence of his kisses, the hard need of his body. She swallowed.

"Got a date?" She put an acid bite in her voice so she didn't give away her reaction to the fanciful idea that he hadn't wanted to wait another minute to see her.

"Nope. Just some loose ends on something up in Atlanta."
He curled a strand of her mussed hair around her ear. "Keep
my side of the bed warm, girl."

"Sorry; that's where I keep my Sig. And my Taser."

"Thanks for the warning. I'll be sure and move them over
when I slip under the covers. Might be nice if you were
wearing nothing."

"And freeze to death until you get there? No, thanks."

He gave her that grin. "Tell Theo to keep you warm."

"I think that's illegal in this state." She paused, struggled
with it, but forced it out. "Derek, what just happened . . . it
doesn't change anything."

"Think that all you want, baby." He tipped her chin up,
his hand briefly on her throat, a firm squeeze that got her
attention, the suddenly far less casual look in his eyes sending a ripple of butterflies through her stomach. "Nothing's
going to keep me out of your bed again. I don't care if you're
cuddling up to a damn bazooka when I get there."

Then he was gone, striding off through the woods, setting
his hat back on his head. He'd reclaimed the duster, and she
already missed it, the smell of him enveloping her. He was
right. Nothing was going to keep him out of her bed, especially not her. Not right now. She wouldn't deprive herself,
now that she'd had a taste again. But it really didn't change
anything. Her bed was one thing; her heart was another. The
fact she'd be going to bed without him tonight, with him off
to Atlanta, just underscored it. She was alone. Always alone.

As well as he knew her, she knew him pretty well, too.
That was why she'd sent him away three years ago, and why
she wouldn't be confiding in him anytime soon.

She picked up the Sig. She could get in another hundred
rounds before full dark. Before she couldn't see to get back
home.

* 9 *

HE'D WALKED OFF, BUT AT A CERTAIN POINT RUBY SAW him fade into the gray dusk and disappear. Derek rarely used modern modes of transport. He took himself to different places using the fault lines as railways. He did know how to drive, and somewhere he had a pickup truck, one of those sleek Dodge Rams with an eighty-cylinder engine that could pull a mountain, but like most magic users, mechanical things weren't always reliable around him. *It's not just Harry Dresden who has that problem,* he'd mentioned with an ironic smile, the first time he'd burned up her toaster in the morning. When she questioned why, his answer had been straightforward, typically Derek. "You know when your computer does things, and you're not really sure why? Natural forces are always interacting with man-made things. Sometimes Nature wins."

It wasn't that he didn't like traveling those other ways. He'd told her when time wasn't critical, or the journey itself was important, he drove or even hitchhiked. It gave him time to think, reflect, absorb. He'd admitted he missed travel by horse most of all. *It gave you someone to talk to about*

*things, an impartial audience, so to speak. Seeing those
ears swiveled back toward you was comforting, somehow.*
In times past, he'd also chosen an animal form, like a wolf
or stag, to move in wooded areas unnoticed. However, in
the crowded twenty-first century, with more chances to
encounter problems with humans in those forms, he rarely
chose animal shapes to travel.

She shook her head, finding her footing on the path, heft-
ing the backpack. Old fossil. Gorgeous, stubborn male,
determined to find his way back into her soul.

Oh, hell, Ruby. He never left it. That's the whole problem.

She came to a halt, a prickling chill shooting up her
spine. In the blink it took for the sound of leaves rustling
around her feet to cease, the forest fell grave silent, a stillness as ominous as the moment before a tornado hit. *Shit.*

Thrusting the backpack off her shoulders so it thudded
to the ground, she bolted forward. *"Illumina,"* she snapped.
A small spotlight generated from the energy of her own
body cast light forward so she could see the path. She ran
full out, lengthening her stride, pushing herself hard. Toward
Linda's house and the threat gathering there.

Her heart was back to rabbiting in her throat, but this
time for a far more frightening reason. She'd imagined facing Asmodeus a hundred different ways, yet this would be
her first time fighting anything from the Underworld
toe-to-toe. Anything since that terrible night.

She cleared a fallen log, dodged an uneven drop in the
trail. She hadn't been prepared then, she reminded herself
between gulps of air. She was now. Despite that, the weak,
traitorous thought couldn't help but cross her mind. *Goddamn
it, Derek, why did you have to take off again? We need you.*

She wouldn't say, *I need you.* She wouldn't.

As she burst into the clearing, she saw Linda already out
of the house, hurrying toward the circle. Miriam and Christine, both of whom lived within a mile of Linda, were running
to join her from where they'd left their cars at haphazard

angles when they screeched into the driveway. Ruby was proud as hell they'd picked up on it themselves, but damn it, she should have had the coven members staying on the property. All the work they'd been doing these past few days had probably stirred things up. Those tunneling rats had decided a preemptive strike was in order.

Ruby veered off toward the circle, such that she and the other three arrived within its boundaries at the same time. "Take a Quarter, call it quick, get the circle in place," she ordered. "We need to reinforce the fault line before they can shake themselves completely loose of it. Deep breath—a quick one—then go."

"What's coming out of it?" Miriam asked.

"Something we don't want to get out. You'll see it soon enough. Follow my lead to the letter. *Air. Now.*"

Miriam scrambled for the Air Quarter. Linda took Earth. With a gesture to Christine, Ruby moved her to Water while she took the Fire counterpoint. Christine understood without argument. For this first real battle, it was best to have the two most experienced members in the circle at the north and south anchor points. The chants were done fast, in quick succession. All the drills had paid off—with her staying calm and brusque, just like she'd been in class, they automatically snapped into the groove of what they were supposed to do.

While they were calling Quarters, she concentrated, reinforced the circle's perimeter with an extra boost. The heat was building beneath them, intensely enough she could feel it through the thin soles of her sneakers, and the ground gave the illusion of shifting. Miriam's eyes were wide as saucers, Christine's mouth tight and strained. Linda was focusing for all she was worth.

"Hold fast," Ruby ordered. "Concentrate. Remember, just follow my lead."

So many of the ancient spells, potions and rituals of witchcraft had been built on the domestic craft of women, things of hearth and home. The Weaving Chant was one of those. As she began to call out the words in Old English, she made the shuttle movement with her hands, a sign language to bring the coven members quickly into the focus with her, without having to do a lot of explaining. Body language also intensified the magic.

Her hands rose and fell rapidly, aiming that focus and intent at the weak point of the fault line, the darkness she could feel expanding from it like a swelling boil. Their hands flashed, the three women emulating her, growing more confident with it, as women did when they had something tangible to do. As that confidence grew, she could see energy building, swirling around the three of them as they transitioned from simple imitation into channeling that weaving energy together, feeding it to her so she could aim it where it was needed.

Damn it. That boil had gotten too big, too fast. Miriam screamed as the ground erupted at her Quarter. It was outside the circle, but so close the girl recoiled instinctively, stumbling back several steps. A cloud of smoke spewed forth, billowing up like a dragon spreading its wings, wings that surrounded the circle in a heartbeat, doming over it to seal them in darkness. Crimson light was the only illumination, flickering in the swirling wall like eyes of hellhounds. There was the flash of fangs, low growls.

"Illumina," Ruby snapped again, throwing light across the interior of the circle before their panic became part of the choking, foul energy closing in on them like a coffin. Miriam was frozen and pale as new snow. Christine and Linda held their positions, but the energy they were raising was now all defensive. What they'd drawn up to reinforce the fault line faltered, sensibly diverting to reinforce the circle and their own protection. Hissing and low growls started to emanate from that blackness, rattling the women further.

The widening of that fault line rift felt as if it were happening beneath Ruby's very feet, though it was a stone's throw away. The beings wouldn't come out right beneath the circle; that held too much residual Light energy. But they could use intimidation tactics to turn strength into fear, use the converted energy to feed their own purposes instead. They'd keep the witches inert in their own circle, cowering in their shelter while they freed themselves. Well, the hell with that. She'd worked with the coven a week and knew these women wouldn't stand for that. Not if they got past this moment.

"Miriam." Ruby caught her arm, used the pinch of her short nails to yank her attention from that pitch-black cover over them and glimpses of what was milling in it. "It's all smoke and mirrors. *Focus.*" Jerking her to the circle's edge, Ruby positioned her halfway between the Fire and Air Quarters, and gestured Christine to take a similar position between Fire and Water. "You know the peace symbol?"

At Miriam's blank look, Ruby caught the necklace right beneath the girl's whimsical cat pentacle, tugged, held it up. It was a piece of costume jewelry, the metal tie-dyed to reflect the sixties period, but the power of a symbol wasn't merely in its material; it was the belief in its pure purpose.

"It's not a random design. Not just about nuclear disarmament or Goya's peasant before the firing squad. There's a deeper meaning. You can hold the circle at these three points, you understand? But you have to be strong. You have to get in the game and send energy to that hole. There is only this moment, and what you do with it. You understand?"

She'd closed Miriam's hand over the symbol, her own hand clamped over it. She kept her feet planted, her body rigid, as she held the integrity of the circle. Thank Heaven Christine and Linda were still at least 70 percent in the game, because Ruby couldn't do it alone, not and put this much intent and focus in the conversation. Flame flickered through the darkness, the flash of glistening fangs. She held Miriam's gaze, though, waiting precious seconds for Miriam to regroup. *Come on, sweetheart. You can do it.*

Miriam's jaw tightened, and her gaze swept to the other two women, then back to Ruby. The perimeter reinforcement increased exponentially.

"That's it." Ruby squeezed her, firm approval. Miriam adjusted her stance, fully anchoring herself to the spot in the circle Ruby had indicated. The power flow from Christine and Linda connected to her, and Ruby felt them take over control of the circle boundary.

"Good. Close your eyes," Ruby ordered all of them. "None of what's happening around you matters. Hold the circle's perimeter, but focus on that fault line. Do the chant; keep it going; keep weaving it closed. Doesn't matter how often it breaks; keep doing it. Don't let *anything* distract you."

Moving to Linda, she put her hand on her shoulder to lean in, speak low in her ear. "I'm stepping out of the circle to push these bastards back. They're not all the way free, but they're aboveground. When I get them below the fault line, you need to be ready to seal the lid. Got it? Do you feel it? Know where it is?"

Linda nodded, a quick jerk, though Ruby sensed her doubt that leaving the circle was the right thing. However, Linda's concerns weren't her major worry right now. If anything made it all the way out of the fault line, became fully corporeal, they'd have a much bigger fight on their hands, and Ruby wasn't sure they could hold the circle against a fully concentrated Underworld attack. Not for their very first time.

Despite all her resolve and knowledge, she was scared, too. And what they were dealing with right now was up there with Freddy Krueger, Jason and Michael, all wrapped up into one.

She didn't look back. Shoring up her own personal defenses, strengthening her shields, she stepped out of the circle between Christine and Linda. The black smoke swallowed her immediately.

LIGHT ENERGY WAS A FORMIDABLE WEAPON IN THE hands of those who knew how to use it. Even in the hands of advanced students, such as Linda, it could do a lot when there was time and focus to build it. In the hands of confident, advanced magic users, ones like Derek, it could turn bullets to flowers before they even left the chamber.

Right now, though, Derek wasn't here, and they needed zero to one hundred speed reaction time. She could provide that, but she couldn't avail herself of the protection of their circle, couldn't pull them into that. What she was about to do would disrupt and unbalance their energy, and her first priority was getting them out of this alive and unharmed. To do that, she had to make sure that threat was contained, by whatever methods necessary. Being on the outside, there was the added plus that she was drawing the demons' fire, and the circle could focus on strengthening the fault line.

Damn it, she wasn't supposed to be doing the fighting. *Derek, next time I see you, I'm going to punch you in the mouth.*

Shit, there were three of them. Outside the circle, she could feel their form and substance, the way they swirled around her, creatures of ash and fire. Soul-eaters, the carrion of the Underworld. Not so powerful, when all was said and done, but they made up for that in numbers, deception ability and their sheer bogeyman-in-the-closet fear factor. Many lower-echelon creatures of the Underworld appeared as an odd assortment of parts—horse heads, goat legs, body of a man, engorged privates, large fangs. Their sole purpose was fear, and they fed on it. They could be strengthened and sometimes even spawned by people's fear of the dark and shadows, but once created, could not be dispelled, a self-fulfilling prophecy. One could create the monster in one's closet, a frightening thought.

It was part of why she'd often used the Sarah Williams quote to go to sleep at night: *Though my soul may set in darkness, it will rise in perfect light. I have loved the stars too fondly to be fearful of the night.* And of course the poem from which it came, "The Old Astronomer," had been an inspiration for her own studies in and of itself. It inspired her now. She had the knowledge to do this, the will and the power, damn it.

The soul-eaters were all pumped up, sure of their victory now, because they were nearly free. But they were too eager, like rats tunneling out of holes in truth. The opening was still too small for them and yet they were trying to squeeze free, which left their attention divided, making them more vulnerable. She had a precious few more moments, but she told herself that was all she needed. Particularly when she caught a whiff of something that put everything else away— fear for the coven, fear of failure, any concerns about anything beyond this.

Asmodeus. Not him directly, no, but these creatures were part of his army, his minions. She knew the smell of that energy, had nightmares about it. At the trade shows, which didn't have the same spells she maintained on her gun shop to repel certain types of visitors, she sometimes sensed it from some of the fringe participants. Evil had a base smell, an ingredient that infected all its recipes. That was fine. Right now, she wanted to smell that smell, wanted to be fully aware of the shape and substance of that energy. Use her rage against it to dispel her fear.

Chanting the words, she began drawing in deep breaths, oxygenating her muscles and internal organs, preparing them for the load they were about to bear. Sensing the impending threat, the darkness closed around her, the soul-eaters trying to press their searing heat so close they would cook her inside the barrier of her own defenses if she let them seep in through the pores.

She didn't. When she opened her eyes, one was staring at her, red eyes inches from her face. Her stomach was tied in knots, but her feet were anchored in the earth.

"*Boo*, you son of a bitch," she said, baring her teeth. Lifting her arms out to her sides, slow, deliberate, like a kung fu master drawing in energy, she curled her fingers and began to rotate her left wrist, slow, a winding dial to gather energy to her. The energy of the creatures trying their best to crush her.

While she did that, she began to rotate the right wrist. With that hand, she pulled in energy from the circle and from the fault line. Light energy. Once again, the domestic arts took precedence. As she brought the two strands together, she started braiding them, turning her body clockwise to wind it around her, using herself as a spool. The heat was getting intense, burning her skin despite the protection around her. She could smell the putrid scent of rotting souls, of death, hopelessness and decay, of everything that life was beneath the surface, and sometimes not beneath the surface at all.

As if trying to get ahead of her winding movement, they were swirling around her faster now, like a tornado, hoping to twist and disorient her, upset the human top and watch it fall. The weight made her body shudder. She felt their desire to take her. She was a creature with Darkness within her, one they could use and overpower.

She put the final twist in the braid, and then thrust out with both hands, a sharp, blunt movement. They squealed, recoiling as two braided whips of Light and Dark energy slashed through the smoke, finding its target. The Dark held them to her, didn't allow them to get free, and the Light burned them like holy water on a vampire. She ripped the energy free, taking Underworld flesh with it, then went with a dual overhand strike like she was wielding two single tail whips. Slashing down, across, bisecting their energy, snapping her wrists so the tails didn't come back to hit her in recoil.

The smoke was burning off as they spent more energy fighting her than creating distractions. She saw their skeletal bodies, the long talons and burning eyes. They belonged to *him*. At this close range, the truth of it was even more potent. They were an advance guard, sent to test the perimeters, see what Asmodeus would be up against. The desire to protect and reinforce disappeared beneath the weight of her need to obliterate, destroy, cause pain.

They were circling, trying to dodge that weapon, but she was moving just as fast. Or so she thought. One of them punched through her anger, made contact. It sent her somersaulting. She hit the ground hard, plowing up the dirt with her shoulder. She thought she heard a scream. Miriam, maybe, close enough to see some of what was going on now that the beasts were more form than fog. The girl lunged out of the circle, grabbing at Ruby's arms to get her back into it.

"Miriam, no!" Linda's cry, but it was too late. In that blink, one of the soul-eaters had grabbed the young woman. They were tossing her among them like a rabid rock concert crowd who'd captured the lead singer. Pulling at her hair, her flesh, her clothes. It would take them fewer than two seconds to rip her limbs from her torso. Scrambling back to her feet, Ruby lashed out full force, no doubt or restraint.

The explosion illuminated the clearing like a warhead, showing her ugly, hungry expressions, Linda's white, determined face, and Miriam's terrified one.

The soul-eaters screamed as the burning, braided weapon cut deep, deep enough to truncate. The recoil sang back up Ruby's arm, rocketing pain through her body, but they dropped Miriam. She dove on her, covering her with her own shields. Then Christine was there, shouting. "*Back*. Back, you bastards."

She was using the strength of female anger to bolster herself, but she was holding that shield in front of them just as Ruby had taught her. But they needed more coven members to make that diamond formation strong enough. Christine couldn't hold it alone. Not for more than a second. Then Linda was there, grabbing at Ruby. Ruby shoved Miriam into her grasp, pushing them back toward the circle. Miriam's blood was on her arms, her shirt. She had no idea how badly the girl was hurt, but at least all limbs appeared to be attached. Linda dragged her back over the perimeter.

"Go, Christine, she's in. Back to the circle. Hold the circle."

Christine obeyed, though her expression, a quick flick toward Ruby, suggested she thought she'd lost her mind, staying out here. She probably had, but the demons were still not contained.

She wasn't sure whose blood was whose, but she'd use it. Bringing her hands together, she screamed out another chant. The braided line of power coiled back up in her hands like an obedient serpent, then melded into an oblong shape. Like bread dough, she kneaded and spread it, a quick alteration of the magic. As she did that, she called out the words to reinforce her shields and recharge the energy, using her blood and the darkness, the scattered shards of Light sparking off the circle. A potluck of things like a magical dirty bomb, many different unpredictable elements combined. Unpredictable was exactly what she needed here.

She flung it outward, like a master pizza chef expertly launching his dough. As it left her hands, it became the snake again, whipping out into a rippling, seething line of Dark and Light fires, a deadly white squall line. Reinforced by the circle's strength behind her, she moved forward with it, driving it, driving the soul-eaters back toward their rift point.

They snarled, lunged. Then screamed their rage and pain as that line tore shreds out of them, as if they'd stepped into a minefield. They backed off. She kept coming, driving them back like a lion tamer. Two steps forward, one step back as they lunged, dodged, and she parried, ducked shots of flame back at her, thrown punches. They were at close quarters now, less than two or three feet between them, but they were getting more stubborn and brave, the closer they got to that hole. She tasted her own blood on her lips, knew they were getting in some strikes as well. It didn't matter.

Pain slashed across her back. A cry broke from her lips as she went down hard, but the pain wasn't the danger. She was trapped beneath the suffocating weight of a fourth soul-eater, one who'd gotten past her guard. How had she missed him in the smoke? Maybe he'd come out behind them. More important, he was completely independent of the rift, no longer tethered to it at all, the chains broken. Corporeal.

Struggling to her back, she punched wet, slimy flesh like sticky Jell-O, a thought that would keep her from eating Bill

Cosby's favorite dessert ever again. Damn, she really liked those pudding cups, too.

She'd become two creatures, one standing back with oddly rational mind, cracking wiseass remarks and thinking about the next step. Then there was the part of her that was screaming her rage, wanting him off. She was outnumbered. But it didn't matter. The fight was what mattered. She'd been preparing for this for so long, and suddenly it was here. After that initial moment of fear and hesitation, all she'd thought about was protecting the coven; then rage took away even that much thought. It was all reaction now.

Energy gathered in the pit of her stomach. Up until now, her power had been coming from a combination of will and mind, but this bastard was about to find out what it would feel like to be fried by what she could summon from the darkest part of her psyche. It was darker there than anything these pieces of Underworld garbage knew.

As if sensing the imminent danger, and realizing he was free to leave the party, the soul-eater let her go, tried to make a break for the sky.

She caught him around the throat with that lariat of streaming energy—*Go, Wonder Woman*—and tossed a few more volleys at the others, but the problem with tethering one enemy when others were around was that it made her just as vulnerable, as anchored in one place as he was. And they knew it. She threw up a protection spell as they bore down on her. The weight, the pressure, was incredible, making her snarl out as the air around her decompressed like a plane cabin. She couldn't hold it. Couldn't. Damn it, she wasn't going to let go. He was the only one who was corporeal. She had to have him. Had to take her shot.

A blast shuddered through the ground and blinded her like lightning at close range, a strike that could have come from the hand of God Himself. It crackled through the three soul-eaters, seared them down to their very essence. Shrieks of pain and a god-awful smell filled the clearing, the electrical energy searing across her nerve endings so she convulsed in its backwash.

It was impossible not to feel a surge of fierce exultation and love. He was here, with her. He'd come back.

The darkness was slashed to ribbons, cut by the enchanted flash of a broadsword's blade, wielded in Derek's capable hands. He could change anything to a different weapon, as long as it kept the same properties. She suspected what she was seeing was his switchblade, transmuted for a different purpose. She turned her attention swiftly to their enemy.

They weren't gone, of course, but they'd been blasted off her. Two were pushed back toward the rift, but they were scrambling to re-form ranks. The fourth soul-eater was still held by her line, and now she sure as hell wasn't letting go. Managing to struggle to her knees and then to her feet, she started to reel him in. *You're going to be my guinea pig, you monster.* This was her chance, to test the deadliest weapon she had in her arsenal.

Derek was by her shoulder. At a screech behind them, he shoved her down so they both ducked. The missing third soul-eater swooped over them. It bowled into the other two like a pterodactyl whose radar had gone haywire. It was the deciding moment. They crawled, flapped, and clawed their way to their rift opening, flinging themselves back down into it, conceding defeat.

Unfortunately, that shove had lost her purchase on the fourth one, and he'd come to the same conclusion his companions had. Best to live and fight another day. He dove for the rift, a straight shot down like a pelican dropping out of the sky.

No. Not that easy, pal. Muttering the proper chant, feeling the Dark energy uncoil eagerly, she tossed out that powerful lash one more time, but this time it had barbed ends. Those ends caught the fourth soul-eater, latched onto him just as he had his foot in the rift door. Because he was corporeal, it wound around him, using his own Dark energy against him, but also feeding it back to her. She felt it pumping inside of her, like an answering heartbeat. She knew what he was, what he was made of. She knew the composition of his soul in that connection.

"Ruby." Derek's voice, urgent, a command. "Let him go. They're retreating. We need to seal the rift."

"No." Her voice was hoarse, unrecognizable. She'd managed to get to her feet and now took a step away from him, toward the soul-eater, coming out of fire and smoke. She saw fear in the demon's eyes, and she loved it. *Be afraid, you bastard.*

He writhed, the poison and power in those barbs sweeping through him, twisting his body and lifting it in the air, making it contort. His essence was turning sickly green, traces of flame. He screeched. It was an unearthly sound of torment, one she recognized because she'd made it herself, the night everything had changed.

Face the nightmare of what the world truly is, what it will always be for you. Desolation and emptiness. No purpose, no worth.

The energy she was using spilled out a bloodred light that illuminated the night, cast the moon with a red tinge, made the fountain nearby look as if it were a pool of blood. The soul-eater's body was visible, the winged form, the forearms and legs roped with muscle. Unlike the skeletal shapes of the others, he was a heavyset gargoyle, a thug of the Underworld. However, under the power of her spell, his skin began to break like cracked mud in a desert long after the rain had dried up. Bits of him rained down onto the ground, each one moving, whimpering of its own accord.

Revenge was not bitter. It was glorious, the sweetest thing she'd ever tasted, and all she wanted was more.

∗ 10 ∗

SHE COULD PLUNGE INTO THAT FAULT LINE, KILL THE other three. Follow the trail to Asmodeus, and she'd bring the fight to him, literally. She could bring this to him. In the Underworld, they were corporeal. So it would work there. She just had to find her way to him.

Then Derek knocked her to the ground, breaking her focus. She snarled at him, fully intending to give him a dose of what she could do against brute physical strength. However, he'd shoved her to her stomach, had a knee in her back as he knelt over her.

"Obliterate." The thundered command made the ground shake once more. Forcing her face up, she saw all those little pieces of demon crackle up like paper, roll toward the rift opening and slither back in, like garbage collected and thrown away.

"Now," Derek shouted. The energy from the circle swept over them. It had Christine's and Linda's distinct signatures, and now Derek's added to it. The purity of it made her body cringe, salt burning in raw wounds. They covered the fault line like bricklaying, Christine and Linda laying the stone while Derek provided the mortar to strengthen them. Witchcraft used women's arts; sorcery apparently used men's. Build, nail, hammer, bind.

But in the end, it was like tossing dirt into a sinkhole, trying to fill up something that was bottomless. As long as Asmodeus, soul-eaters and the whole foul army were still under there, containing them was pointless. It needed to be a grave, not a cage.

"Let me go," she snarled, fighting him. Since his booted foot was at her shoulder, she hammered at his calf with her fist. "Let me up."

Derek obliged, yanking her up by the arm hard enough it jarred her shoulder. "Help," he commanded, his tone brooking no disobedience. He wasn't her lover right now, but a much more powerful sorcerer who would kick her ass into next week if she didn't do her job. But she couldn't. Those two forces warred within her. She was furious at him for interfering, for not letting her finish it. Damn it, he didn't understand. He couldn't. And he was keeping her from what she needed to do. Darkness swirled around her, thick and choking as the soul-eaters' smoke. When he shoved her toward the circle, she whirled on him, energy sparking off her fingertips.

It was a lucky strike, for he hadn't expected a hit from his own camp. As a result, black exultance surged through her when she knocked him to his knees, but she didn't linger over it. She ran back toward that weak rift point. She'd stand on top of it, send that barbed energy down like fishing line, get the blood she craved. Go in after it if needed. She wasn't afraid to go into the Underworld. She belonged there.

It was like being hit by a battering ram. As she hit the ground, she tasted dirt, but that wasn't what made bitter bile in her throat. Derek had the flat of the sword against her, and she screamed in protest as it stole her strength, drawing it into the metal so that she was limp, helpless. Grimly, he ignored her weak snarls of defiance, keeping his attention on the job of reinforcing the rift. The Light energy streamed over her.

Yet he was also letting it stream through him, into the hard palm he had against her neck, the knee he had in her back. It flooded her, made the Darkness recoil, made other parts of her writhe in pain, just like that fourth soul-eater. That was the key to it, why her barbed magic had worked. To know how to hurt something, you had to know its pain. The key to destroying evil was stepping into its soul and blowing it up from the inside.

She'd sacrificed parts of *her* soul for that kind of knowledge. So now the Light energy coming from Derek's hand, soaking into her pores, was scalding acid. She shrieked, clutching at the ground. The fire of it was unbearable. She cursed and fought, aware of nothing but that her blood appeared to be boiling inside her body.

She didn't know how long it went on, but she was vaguely aware of the rift being sealed, of Linda's and Christine's energy levels depleting and Derek taking more of the load. Ruby should be helping. It was that thought that told her she was coming back to herself. That, and the fact the extraordinary pain was ebbing, one last rinse from the Light washing through her, balancing things again. But in a fragile way, like a glass figurine sitting too close to the edge of a shelf.

Things got quieter, the roar of the power flow dying. The worst of the hurricane had passed, down to a few lingering gusts, puffs of random energy. Linda and Christine were still weaving, additional stitching. It was the spell she'd started, now reinforced by their Light and Derek's as they sealed that rift hole. But she could already tell sealing wasn't enough. It was like placing a piece of plywood on top of a hole. It wouldn't change the fact that below that rift point was an empty space, where that boil, what the soul-eaters had dug out, had weakened the fault line, the energy there no longer dense as it needed to be.

The solidity could be restored only by a powerful infusion of Light, something comparable to a nuclear bomb. That level of power couldn't be accessed without pulling it from other things that also needed it. The usual way to restore a fault line was to restore it a little at a time, drawing on the necessary power in increments. But in this case, given that this might have been a test run for attack, they might not have that kind of time.

Of course, one way to keep them from coming back in the interim to test what was being rebuilt was to instill terror of what would happen to them if they tried it. She'd had that capability, and Derek had stopped her.

He moved off of her now. The sword was gone, probably folded and back in his jeans pocket, once again the knife. Adrenaline pounding, she scrambled to her feet, throwing herself at him. "You bastard," she raged. "You had no right to do that. To interfere. You—"

His face hard as granite, he ducked under her swing and slung her over his shoulder like a sack of grain. His long arm clamped over her legs and hips, holding her in place as he strode away from the circle. She tore at his back, but was miserably unable to inflict damage. She wanted to bite him, claw the flesh from his bones, make him suffer—

She was airborne for half a second. Then she landed in Linda's man-made pond with a resounding splash. The temperature was cold enough to drive the breath from her, make her shriek. As she was sure he intended, it knocked her flat on her ass, took her mind away from the heat of battle, from everything but the fact she needed to get the hell out of the water. She struggled to paddle over to the edge of the pond, fear of hypothermia playing tug-of-war with her anger. He was waiting for her on the bank, sitting on his boot heels in a patient squat.

She didn't want his help, but there was no way she was getting up that steep embankment without him. While some part of her might be willing to drown, it was too fucking cold. She took his hand. Another time, she might have tried to pull him in, a grim and probably futile retaliation, since the bastard was like a granite mountain, but not this time. Fuck, this was cold.

When he hauled her out as if she weighed no more than a spitting cat, she was shaking so badly from cold, fury and the aftermath of her first real demon fight, she couldn't stand. Despite her less than voluble protest, he picked her up, slinging her over his shoulder again. He called out something to Linda as he passed the circle; then he was headed for the guesthouse. She was so cold. So cold, on so many levels, the frigid waters seeping in to other things. But she'd done it. It had worked.

Catching his belt to anchor herself, she used that hold to turn her head, see the moon. Instead of the pink she'd seen earlier in the week, a tranquil color that had brought her a rare moment of peace when preparing the circle, it now had that bloodred tinge. The pink had made her imagine her baby's soft skin as she lolled in a hazy, misty world . . . as she swam inside the moon. But this, the color of blood . . . That reflected Ruby's true world and true self, far more than that pink.

Derek shoved open the door of the guesthouse, said a sharp, quelling word that sent an anxious Theo folding back down on his bed. Striding to the spacious bathroom, Derek set her on her feet, spun her and shoved her against the sink, forcing her face inches from the mirror. "Look at yourself, Ruby. *Look*."

She didn't want to, but the tone of his voice warned her that the cost of disobeying would be dear. Cursing her cowardice, she lifted her wet lashes, stared into the glass.

Her gray-green eyes were completely dominated by pupil, her face sallow and drawn. She could see the shape of her skull. The feral intensity of her expression was frightening. Blood was on her shirt, her throat, though she didn't know if it was hers or someone else's. She looked like something that had crawled out of the Underworld with the soul-eaters. Something that belonged in their ranks, not Derek's.

She tried to look away, and his hands clamped down on her face like a vise. "Look at what you're becoming. What you're letting yourself become."

She couldn't let it matter, couldn't let the rapid pounding of her heart be translated into panic, into recognizing what it meant, that she was losing this fight, just when she was on the cusp of winning it. She'd known from the first it was a game of chicken, to see if her body would succumb to Darkness before she could destroy Darkness itself. And she was still too damn willing to play the game, even if she looked like a soul-eater herself.

Using that thought, she lacquered her insides with a dead calm, stared at that image. Accepted it. She could do that, mostly, but she couldn't shift her gaze, handle the revulsion she knew would be in his face. "Guess you'll be sleeping somewhere else now." Her voice was raw, shaking. Looking down, she saw her palms were black from soul-eater residue and what she'd channeled to fight them. Where had all the blood on her clothes come from? She closed her eyes. Blood hemorrhaging out from between her thighs, blood on her hands as she closed her fingers on inert flesh . . .

Her knees buckled. She slid down to her butt on the cold floor, still staring at those hands. She wasn't surprised he didn't catch her. Wouldn't be surprised to look up and not find him there at all. He was probably packing her bags, would stick her in the van and send her on her way as soon as she was clean.

But she'd done it. However, she couldn't feel it. It really wasn't a yee-haw, throw-your-fist-in-the-air kind of victory, anyway, right? The image of her face was a brand on her mind, but more than that she felt Derek's silence. His eternal absence. The hollow emptiness of it all. Thinking of her exultance when she'd gloried in the creature's pain, she felt a little sick. A lot sick.

She barely made it to the commode, and then she was coughing, retching it all up. Breakfast, lunch . . . Actually, she hadn't eaten lunch, so just breakfast and bile, dark, putrid bile that smelled a lot like the soul-eaters. She'd taken the Darkness into her, made it work for her, used it to drive them back. Kept Miriam . . . *Oh Goddess, Miriam.*

She straightened from the commode with a snap, reaching for a hand towel with shaking fingers. As she scrubbed it over her mouth, she made it to her feet. She needed to go see if Miriam was okay, if they needed help.

When she stumbled to the bathroom door, she ran into Derek's chest, as he was coming back in. "I told you to stay here," he said evenly, taking her arm and leading her back to the commode. She winced in embarrassment because she hadn't flushed yet, but before she could close the lid, he stayed her, stared down at the leavings from her stomach. After a weighted moment, he used the toe of his dragonskin boot to close the lid and depress the handle as he maintained his less-than-gentle grip on her arm.

"I didn't . . . I didn't hear you say that. Is Miriam . . ."

"She's on her way to the hospital. Linda and Christine are taking her. She's got a broken arm and some nasty cuts, nothing that required an ambulance, but she does need medical attention. The two of them will do a cleansing on her there. The soul-eaters got hold of her long enough that she'll need that to prevent soul infection. As it is, she's going to have some pretty serious nightmares for a while."

She was shivering in her soaked clothes. Looking down at the tile, she saw mud, blood, soot and water tracking up the floor. "At some point, you're going to have to look me in the eye, Ruby," he said quietly.

"I don't want to."

"I know you don't. What do you think you're going to see there?"

"Things I don't want to see." She didn't want to play games. She was miserably cold, and everything felt wrong, broken, unfixable. Her shields were too thin. "Leave me alone, Derek. I'll get cleaned up and get out of here. I've taught them enough. We only had a few days left anyhow, and you can handle that." Her teeth were chattering, making her voice quake. She'd figure out how to get at Asmodeus another way. Where innocent bystanders couldn't be hurt. She had the key to getting in now. She didn't need to be here anymore.

"Lift your arms."

She stared at his chest, feeling his eyes on her face. "No. Go away."

"Ruby, I'm a lot bigger and stronger than you are. You'll either help me undress you, or I'll rip the fucking clothes off you, but it's going to happen. You're going to take a shower, get warm, and then we're going to talk."

"You can talk. I'm not going to."

He pushed her arms up over her head, worked the shirt up with a quick, impatient jerk, discarded it with a wet plop on the ground. Then the undershirt, unhooking the bra with neutral efficiency. He pulled off the jeans with a bit more force, since wet jeans were never easy, and once he got them down her hips, he pushed her back onto the closed commode to get them and her sneakers all the way off. He'd turned on the water, and blissful steam was curling out now. Her trembling increased. Why was it that cold became even colder, almost unbearable, on the outskirts of such a blissful, heated spray?

"I swear to God," he muttered, "I'm going to blister your ass before this night is done."

"I had it handled."

"Yeah, you against four soul-eaters. I could see that."

"Took your ass long enough to get here," she managed.

"I didn't anticipate that Asmodeus would try a test strike."

She pressed her lips together. "Neither of us did. Really, is Miriam . . . all right?"

He cupped her face, his thumb tracing her lips. Ruby closed her eyes at the touch. When a shudder went through her, she realized she hadn't expected him to touch her in more than a functional way. Ever again.

Letting out a sigh, he put his forehead against hers. "She's pretty shook up. She'll need to talk to you, understand what happened to help her deal with it."

"You'd be better at it."

"No, I wouldn't. It needs to be a woman, someone she respects. You're her teacher. She was pulled out because she tried to help you, Ruby. Because she thought you needed help. You taught them well, though. Christine and Linda were nearly flawless in that advance-and-retreat circle formation to get her back. What they lacked in strength they made up for in sheer guts and will."

"Mom always said I was a good teacher."

"Fuck your mother, may she rot in Hell." His fingers slid around to her nape. She could feel how much he wanted her to lift her gaze, but she wouldn't. He let out that sigh again, a part growl in it this time. "Since at some point I'm going to be yelling at you, a lot, I'll say something else now. I always knew you had the capability you showed tonight. You're a hell of a witch. You knew they'd overwhelm the circle, and you handled yourself pretty damn well outside of it to draw the soul-eaters' fire and keep the fault line from having a bigger split. Miriam is alive because of you. As far as the rest . . . we'll hold it for now. Jesus, your skin's like ice."

In her entire life, no one had ever commended her on her magical abilities. Granted, until tonight, no one had known she'd discovered and embraced them to the extent she had, but it was still an unexpected, incredibly warm feeling, no matter how brief, amid all the other wretched things she was feeling right now.

He guided her into the shower. When she hit the hot water, she sucked in a breath, experienced a deep, almost convulsive quake. Leaning against the tile wall, she wished Linda had a bench in here, because she wasn't sure she had enough strength to clean herself up and stand at the same time. Magic use at this level was more draining than she'd expected, and now that the adrenaline was leaving her, things were starting to hurt. Throb. She was so cold, she wasn't sure even the hot water could penetrate her numbness.

She was about to slide down the wall, grab the soap on the way down, when he got in with her. Closing his arms around her, he brought her full against his heated, naked length, keeping her back to the spray, her front against him. Laying her cheek against the sleek, firm skin and light covering of chest hair, she pressed her lips together to taste the water drops running down her face. Simple, straightforward things. She didn't have to think about anything else right now. He'd said so. Later. All of it could be later. Her and Scarlett O'Hara, thinking about it tomorrow. Though Scarlett hadn't had the advantage of Rhett joining her in the claw-footed tub to help scrub her back and make that temporary amnesia possible.

Derek worked the band out of her snarled ponytail, set it on the soap tray, then combed his fingers through the strands, loosening knots, helping the thick mass become saturated with water. She tilted her head back at the pleasurable sensation, keeping her eyes closed. He met her parted lips with his own, sealing the heated water drops between them, his fingers tightening on her scalp.

He was giving her more than heat in that kiss. She felt the tendrils of power unfurl in her chest, her stomach, her legs, all originating from that point where their lips touched. It was pure elemental magic, spreading out to all corners. A cleansing. He was giving her a cleansing, not with the usual chants and meditation, but through touch and the gentle exercise of his own reservoirs of pure Light energy, letting it sweep through her, cleansing her inside the way the shower was cleansing her on the outside.

It was always amazing to feel Derek's power. In the heat of battle, fueled by psychotic rage, she hadn't been able to appreciate it, but here she could, on so many levels. As a passive, grateful recipient. As a magic user, awed by how effortless it was, how it felt. He didn't need to speak chants, use wands or staffs. The magic *was* Derek, making it difficult to say whether the man was a conduit for it, or the magic was a conduit for the man.

It did have one negative effect. It unsettled the Darkness, made her shift uneasily under his hands, but maybe because the woman wanted what he offered, that feminine energy overcame the resistance. She eagerly embraced it, grabbed onto it like an outstretched hand before she could be swept away on a dark tide.

He folded her in to his body, and the warmth of it, even better than the hot water, caused a moan in her throat. His bare thighs pressed against hers, his cock and testicles an intriguing nest of flesh against her mound and lower abdomen. She slid her hands over his slippery skin, the muscular sides, the valley of his ribs, until they came to rest on his hip bones. His hands slipped to her jaw, fingers on the sides of her throat, teasing strands of her hair as he kept kissing her, kept that focus happening. She quivered, becoming even more limp, letting go of all of it, letting exhaustion move in.

When he finally broke the kiss, she lay against him in vertical repose as he washed her hair, moved and turned her as needed to soap her skin. He propped her in the corner to do her front, to kneel and wash her legs. She watched his hands move over her with such intimate familiarity. Unlike the way he'd been in the forest, he was taking his time. Part of it was the cleansing. Though he was aware of her, a man in the shower with a naked, wet female, she could see the focus in his eyes, the serious set of his mouth. He was cosseting her in the way only a sorcerer could, ensuring every inch of her felt the touch of that cleansing, healing Light, drawn from the Earth and Water, the elements that had the strongest connection to the female spirit, driving out the taint the fight with the Underworld might have left upon her.

He was thorough, going into every crevice and corner, inside and out, making things stir to life under his arcane and physical touch. He was spiraling around the Darkness, and as he did, it burrowed deeper, drew in on itself, the turtle in its shell. He was going to hit it dead-on eventually, because now that gentle, inexorable flood of power was in her chest, around her heart, and deeper. The place where the soul resided, that closed fist. A fortress.

A dangerous part of her wanted to open it up, let him cleanse there. And he couldn't. She couldn't let him.

Leaning forward, he placed a kiss on her thigh as the water ran down, rinsing the soap. When he turned his head, his wet hair brushed her mound, the sensitive flesh between her legs. He settled the weight of his skull there as he probed the shape of that clamshell behind her heart.

"Derek . . ."

"Hush," he said mildly, but in an unexpectedly stern tone, given his intimate position. "Be still, Ruby."

"You can't . . . I don't want you there."

"I won't force myself past your will, Ruby. I told you that. Though God's truth, you've pushed that to the limits of my integrity. So be still and don't push it further. Let me help the way I can help."

She pressed her lips together, tense and uncertain as he wound the energy around her closed soul, stroked it, gave it touches of warmth and heat that made it ease, that made it feel like it could be unguarded. She could trust him to cleanse the area around that sealed, infected wound, not try to pry it open and drain the pus inside. Of course, they both knew that, without a full cleansing, the Darkness would rise up and wipe away his impact, as soon as he withdrew.

"A soul is a full container," he rumbled against her flesh. "The only way there's room for anything more to be inside of it is if pieces of it have been let go, leaving pockets for Darkness to grow, like tumors."

"That's my business." She was ready to get out of the shower now. But he was blocking her way. The steam swirled around them, a pale mist. He rose now, holding her in that corner.

"The hell it is." His voice was so mild, the words so at odd with the tone, that she finally looked up into his eyes. That was a mistake. The blue was such a fierce, vibrant color, she knew it had to be a residual effect from the fight, but the emotions she saw there were even more alarming. Her throat tightened.

"No. I need to go."

"You promised to do a job for me. You've never been a chicken, even when you *didn't* have the confidence to stand toe-to-toe with the Underworld and fight like a she-tiger. I'm not believing you'll start now."

"This is who I am," she said, having trouble breathing. "I can't . . . I can't fight with you about this, Derek. I need to get out. I need to go."

In answer, he slid his arm around her waist, his other under her knees, scooping her up. Shutting down the shower tap with his elbow, he pushed out of the stall, using her feet to open the door. He carried her back into the bedroom, where Theo looked at her with that worry wrinkling his brow. She tried for a reassuring expression, but it gave way to alarm as, instead of putting her on her feet, Derek laid her on the bed. She knew that intent look.

"No." She tried to roll away, but he was far quicker than she was. He had her trapped beneath the full length of his body in a heartbeat, his hips pushed between her thighs, holding her open. His cock brushed her sex, making her shudder again, though for the moment he was just holding her like this, pinned down, open to him, nowhere to look but up into those relentless blue eyes. "No," she begged.

"Hell, yeah," he said shortly. When he pushed against her, her traitorous body was already moist for him. It let him break through that initial gateway, seat himself inside that opening. A quiver went all the way through her, head to curling toes. Toes that were curling against his calves.

"Doesn't matter what you do to try and shake me, Ruby. I won't let you do it again. I don't care if you tell me you hate me every day of your life and that you never want to see me again. I'm not going anywhere."

"Until someone calls you from Atlanta, or Rangoon, or fucking Disneyworld," she shot back. "I can't do that anymore, Derek."

"Me being a Guardian isn't why you're like this. Something happened, and you're eventually going to trust me to help you with it. I'm not letting you give yourself to Darkness, Ruby."

"I'm not giving myself to it."

"Yeah, you are. And it ticks me off, because I know you know better." He slid forward several more inches and she mewled, arching up to him as he came to a maddening halt once more. Her muscles were clutched around him, blood pulsing against his length in a rapid beat of need. "We're going to figure this out. But for now . . ."

Catching her face in both hands, he made her look at him. "Look at me while I send you over, so I see you feel what it means, the two of us joined like this."

He slid all the way in then, deep and filling her. She gasped, tears leaking out over his fingers. "There you are, baby," he rumbled softly. "Keep feeling it. This is part of the cleansing, unique to you and me."

He withdrew, then slid back in. The rest of his body stayed still and firm upon her, giving her his heat and life, his relentless presence, as he flexed his hips and thighs to slowly push in, draw out. Over and over, as he rubbed tissues that caught fire, that had her panting and her hands clawing at his sides, his hips and buttocks, wanting him to go faster, shove harder.

"This is the way it's going to be, girl. My pace, my way. You just take it, go along for the ride. I want to see your eyes all wide and glazed. You open up to me; give yourself to me. I could break open the lock on your soul any damn time I want to do it, but I'll wait, because I love you too much to be smart about it."

The tears increased, but so did the arousal. He wouldn't let her run from him, from the explosive cliff edge to which he was taking her, one long, dragging stroke at a time.

"Can't . . ."

"Yeah, you can. You'll come for me, scream for me. You'll do it now."

He knew her body too well, could already feel that telltale ripple in her lower belly, in her sex. Her lips parted, stretched, throat gulping air. He held that firm clamp on her head, made her stare at him as it took her, swept over her. As the first cry broke from her lips, and then the next, her nails raked his buttocks, drew blood while looking for a purchase. He was the only anchor, though, those blue eyes. His expression became savage, the irises going to seraphim fire.

"Yes," she whispered. "Come for me, too . . ."

It was the sealing touch, a heat that could sweep everything else away, that would surround that locked Pandora's box. Even if she couldn't let him into that Dark part of her soul, he'd be the dragon guarding it on the outside.

Her legs and arms tried to hold on to him throughout his finish, but as her climax left her, her strength went with it. She could only cling weakly to his arms, melt back into the bed like candle wax as he completed. Soft cries came from her with every hard thrust. As he became more brutal and punishing, she relished it, relished him being in her body, finding release there.

When he finished, he lay down on her for a bit because, even though he was heavy, he remembered. He knew how much she loved that, needed that feeling of being encompassed by his strength, his weight, the stroke of his fingers along her face, her body, as he stayed within her, joined.

Perfect, at least for this one moment.

* 11 *

SHE CRIED IN HER SLEEP.

Derek watched the tears seep out, slide down to pool on the bend of his elbow, crooked around her. Her chest quivered, her mouth twitching with silent sobs, her soul alone with her grief. Even though, lost in dreams, she trusted him like a cub hibernating against its mother. If she could have pulled him over her like a blanket, he thought she would have. He gave her as much of that feeling as he could, keeping his arms folded over her chest, cradling her hips in the lap of his, his legs pressed up against the backs of hers, feet tangled together. He had his head on the pillow just above her, his breath warming her fragile neck, her delicate, shell-shaped ear.

What he'd seen out there in the clearing had been far from fragile. She'd been an enraged yet purposeful force of nature. Thank the Lord and Lady that he'd lied. He hadn't gone to Atlanta; his feelings were just too close to the surface, and he'd had to get away from her for a little while before he blew it by shaking her until her teeth rattled and then confronting her about all of it, the known and unknown. He'd gone only a few miles, to a quiet stretch of the Gulf. Unfortunately, it had still taken precious extra minutes for him to register the disturbance in the fault system, and pinpoint that it was back where he'd left her.

When he'd materialized in Linda's backyard, the unique blend of Light and Dark energy had hit him, lightning forking through a thick wash of black, putrid smoke, the signature of the soul-eaters. They enclosed their victims, disoriented and trapped them, then moved in to feed. They were scavengers that roved in packs, and if not for Ruby being right in their midst, he would have exterminated them into harmless dust and swept them back into their hole with a healthy gust.

Yet more than that had given him pause. He'd taken that extra vital minute to feel the shape of the power being wielded against them, because it was like nothing he'd experienced before. And it was coming from Ruby, his shy Ruby.

It was the barbed weapon she'd used at the last that disturbed him the most. It took tremendous skill and in-depth knowledge of magical properties to concoct such a thing, let alone use it. While that was damned impressive, he knew enough about Dark power to know that type of magic came at a terrible price to the magic user. The stories of sorcerers who'd sold their souls for power, who'd been tricked by demons and torn to shreds outside their own circles, weren't just cautionary tales. They were history.

He bit back a quiet oath. What she was messing with had bigger implications. His job was staying on top of such hazardous forays into Dark sorcery, but he was pretty certain that "staying on top" didn't mean what they'd just done. Damn it all, though, he'd beaten the problem in his head for more than an hour now, watching her sleep, and he had no easy answer of where to go with it.

At least her battle with the soul-eaters hadn't resulted in serious injury. Miriam had gotten the worst of it; Ruby mostly had scrapes and bruises. What would make her sore as hell tomorrow was the high-adrenaline muscle-locking that came from a fight of this intensity. But it wasn't the physical that concerned him. When he'd done her cleansing in the shower, that Dark spot in her soul had been like a stillborn fetus, a hard shell grown around it. Even moving gently, he'd found it as tight and clenched as she'd been the first time he'd taken her, a virgin in her early twenties.

He latched onto that, a memory to bolster his own soul, because he needed something to loosen the hard fist in his gut.

In today's modern world where the decision to have sex was treated as casually as the choice of candy in a vending machine, he'd been surprised and humbled to find she was still a virgin at twenty-two. When he realized that, he'd made sure it was special. He'd taken her to one of his favorite places, a small private cabin perched on a breathtaking overlook in the Smoky Mountains. The bedroom had a wall of windows to watch the sunset, and an oversized king bed that could accommodate his frame and give him plenty of room to show her all sorts of wonderful things. Maybe he did that; he couldn't really remember that part. What he most remembered was how many wonderful things she showed *him*, things he hadn't really ever felt for another human being before. He'd been in love here and there, but never this all-consuming need to bond he felt with her.

She'd been tense, anxious. But then he'd realized it was not because of the act, but because she was afraid she'd disappoint him. The absurdity of that had broken his heart wide-open.

He'd been gentle, patient, overwhelmed by her trust in him, the wonder in her eyes after the initial pain was out of the way. He'd told her beforehand he could keep her from feeling it, but she'd taken him to task.

"You're just being silly, Derek Stormwind." Those graygreen eyes glistened with passion and more poignant emotions at once. "It's just a moment, but it's a really important moment. I want to have it to hold, to remember. The pain as well as the good stuff."

To have and to hold, until death do us part . . . He should have married her that very weekend. Marriage had never crossed his mind until he met her. Mainly because he had no idea how long he would live, and she was mortal. In all his centuries, he'd never aged past the appearance of a rugged forty-something. But looking down at her now, he knew, despite the craziness of the idea, he wanted to marry her. Hell, he'd probably known it then. He wanted that sacred bond, wanted to put a ring on her finger, give her another baby.

He did a Rejuvenation Ritual every hundred years, an essential step to keep his mind and heart from getting jaded, an unfortunate side effect of his kind of immortality. However, even with that, he'd never felt the urge to make that kind of commitment. He'd thought it was because it was unrealistic, unfair, whatever. But with Ruby, even when her bones were dust and the world had left her memory far behind, he wanted to be wearing the ring that said she'd been his wife. And he'd been her husband.

Maybe in terms of his life span, he'd have her for only a moment, but it was as she said. *It's a really important moment. I want to have it to hold, to remember. The pain as well as the good stuff.* Because that was what made life so damn precious.

The thought twisted in his heart. Moving so slowly, not wanting to wake her, he cupped his palm over her abdomen. That twist became a damn railroad spike.

Oh, Ruby.

When she'd sent him away, he'd sensed pain and grief, but beyond that, a desperate desire not to feel anything, as if she couldn't afford the emotions he raised in her. He couldn't penetrate or understand her pain, and so he'd made a mistake. Soul magic aside, he'd been an arrogant fool, thinking he knew everything. She was young, something was bugging her, he'd come back in a few months, stay in touch with her throughout, see if he could help ease it out of her, bullshit, bullshit, bullshit.

It was often said that Fate made everything happen in its own time. Thinking about what she'd endured without him, what she'd given up of herself, he didn't accept that. He'd fucked up, and it just plain infuriated him that he hadn't been with her when she needed him. As Raina had said, it was Ruby's time now. And he sensed she needed him more now than she'd ever needed anyone.

What was she crying over in her dreams? He was going to get to the bottom of this and help her, before she lost herself permanently. Because no matter how amazing and terrible she'd been today, no matter how it confirmed what he'd always suspected, that she had a reservoir of power that could eclipse the most capable witches he'd ever met, he would rather see her a mundane, sassy gun-shop owner than swallowed by the brutal claws of the Underworld. He'd love her as witch or woman. And maybe somehow he'd finally help her learn to love herself the way she deserved. The way he loved her. Help her repair the damage her mother and a childhood of living in the lonely shadows had done.

For all the things he'd done to help the world, he thought he'd never been given anything so important to do. It was as if the fate of the world hung on her one soul. Given the things he'd seen in his long life, it wasn't as far-fetched as it sounded.

He'd better catch a few minutes' sleep, though he didn't want to do so. He didn't want to waste a second of the time she was lying in his arms. However, when she woke up, they'd have difficult things to discuss. Since discussing difficult things with Ruby was like fighting a cornered coyote with one hand tied behind his back, he'd best be rested up for the challenge.

Unfortunately, his stomach was rumbling, telling him he'd have to go look for food soon.

Maybe later. As she made a quiet, plaintive noise, a soft plea, he tightened his arms around her. "I love you, baby," he murmured. "I'm right here. I'm going to take care of you, going to take care of all of it. Just trust me, and I won't let you down again."

RUBY WOKE FEELING BRUISED AND ALTOGETHER OUT OF sorts, particularly when she found she was alone. Derek had left a note on the side table.

Wanted you to sleep as long as possible, and my stomach wouldn't shut up. Went to scare up some food. We need to talk. Don't try running. I'm damn good at hog-tying.

She indulged a vision of hanging him with his own rope, but it was a little discomfiting, how graphically that gruesome image came to mind, as if the residual effects of her magic use last night were lingering like a hard-to-shake flu.

She'd try to avoid him as long as possible, she decided. An entirely unrealistic thought, but it was the lie she was going to use to get out of bed today. Thank the Goddess they'd given the coven the morning off, though she was sure she needed to touch base with Linda and Christine and find out about Miriam. Possibly go see her and have that talk Derek said should come from her. The fact he was right just made it, and him, more irritating.

With the help of a few Advil, she got dressed, fed Theo and then spent some time on the floor with him. She rubbed ears, scratched the good spots on his belly and hips, until the creases in his face went back to the normal crumpled paper look, rather than the drawn look of a worried old man. Linda's dogs were probably as freaked-out by the energy storms, but of course Theo had had a front-row seat to the fallout, seeing Derek carting her in here, and the subsequent fireworks from that.

Laying her head on Theo's side, she closed her eyes to hear his heartbeat. He nuzzled her hair and then sighed deeply, dropping his head off the edge of the dog bed. She wanted to go home, back to her shop. She shouldn't have agreed to do this. Her foundation, already too tenuous, was about to crumble.

Nonsense. She straightened, scrubbed a hand over her face. Tightening her hands in her hair, she gave it a harsh tug, then rose from the bed. She forced herself to step in front of the mirror, check that she didn't have that freakish look she'd had last night. Fortunately, the scariest things she saw were her mussed hair and tired face. She hadn't brought any makeup, but it was the first time in a while she'd had a serious vanity twinge over it. Since she couldn't seem to keep herself from crying a couple times a day, it was point- less to put on any. Revlon might make waterproof mascara, but they meant waterproof in terms of gym sweat, not Niag- ara bursting out of a woman's tear ducts.

Given how often most women needed to cry, she expected if they did come up with a mascara that met the challenge, it would be a million-dollar best seller. Marketing would have a dilemma on that one, though. *Overwhelmed by tears once, twice, even three times a day? Never fear. Even if you're so depressed you're considering suicide, our mas- cara won't come off. You'll look* great *at your funeral.*

She sighed. At least her face no longer had that scary angu- lar look, and her pupils were normal pinpoints from the sun- light coming in the window. Though she felt like she'd been hit by a truck, it was the soreness of her inner thighs that cap- tured her attention, the lovely ache that came from cradling a man's body. She didn't experience that postcoital side effect with Mikhael much; he wasn't the missionary-position sort.

She pushed that away, instead thinking of the first time Derek had ever made love to her. A storm over the moun- tain, rain coming down against the windowpanes, his body on hers, moving easily, sinking deep after he got her good and wet, too aroused to be nervous—much. Her very first time, with her very first love. The only man she'd ever loved.

An odd memory to have at this moment, but it helped. As she stepped outside the door, she took a deep breath of the forest air, the morning sunlight washing over her. It gave her some bracing hope. Despite the debris left inside her from last night's storm, she could clean it up, handle whatever the day would bring. She didn't have to tell Derek Stormwind one damn thing. She didn't owe him anything.

Even if she left today, she'd done the job as he'd laid it out to her. She'd intended to use the next few days to explore more in-depth the things they'd learned, different nuances that would help them self-teach into deeper areas, the more they practiced. But they'd figure that out themselves, with Derek giving them pointers. And she could of course always leave her shop number with Linda if she wanted to do any phone consults.

She bit her lip. She could admit it, if only to herself. If Derek didn't start riding her ass and making her miserable, she kind of wouldn't mind staying here several more days. Leaning in the doorway, she looked at the sun coming up over the trees, watched Theo meet up with Linda's dogs at the edge of the wood, do the usual sniff greetings and tail waggings.

It wasn't until she pulled herself away from that view that she tightened up. Because when she turned back toward the house, she saw Linda and Derek standing together at the gazebo pavilion. While she'd been studying the day's beautiful blue sky, the green marsh, a contrast to the dark and frightening events hours before, they were watching her.

Suppressing the desire to run, she crossed the lawn to join them, trying to look unconcerned, indifferent. Amicably so, for Linda's benefit at least. The priestess's gaze was unreadable, but Derek was giving Ruby his frog-dissection look, noticing everything from the circles under her eyes to how she was moving. To stop him from saying something that would immediately make her want to slap him, she spoke as soon as she was in earshot.

"I thought you were off at some pancake house, stuffing your face at the all-you-can-eat buffet? You know they get suspicious when you single-handedly empty out those bins of bacon and sausage."

"That's why I usually go to two or three of them in a morning, spread myself thin. You're hurting."

"I took Advil. Don't start nagging. Old woman."

"Shrew."

Ignoring him, Ruby nodded toward the dogs, who were now moving in a determined patrol of the clearing perimeter, as if they would ferret out what had happened last night and set it all to rights with a few strategically placed leg lifts over shrubbery. "Maybe we should have let them handle things last night."

"Since I've seen them herd my nieces and nephews, a pack of Underworld soul-eaters would have been a piece of cake." Linda managed a wan smile.

The joke eased a tightness in Ruby's chest. "So Miriam's okay?"

"Very shook up. She won't be coming back to join us anytime soon, though I told her she handled herself very well. She said . . . once things got settled, maybe she would, but she just couldn't handle it right now."

"She's young, and she's had a bad trauma. She showed real guts, though. I think she'll be back."

"Young." Linda pursed her lips. "She's twenty-four. Maybe three years younger than you?"

"Well, there's young, and there's young." Ruby lifted a shoulder, uncomfortable with the topic.

"Ruby matured at age ten," Derek said lightly. "I'm going to go finish up my breakfast, give you two a chance to talk."

He gave Ruby a look that clearly said he was saving their conversation for a more private moment but, like the dawn, it was coming whether she wanted it to or not. She gave him a fuck-off look right back. His brow arched, a challenging glint in his eye. "I'll save you a biscuit or two if you want to come join me when you're done," he added. "But you better hurry. Theo may get it."

"He likes blackberry jelly on his."

That feral grin flashed over his face, but he addressed his next words to Linda. "Thanks for making me a meal. You're a great cook." He touched the woman's shoulder, a brief squeeze, and then he was gone, striding back to the house. No help for it, Ruby had to watch, and she saw Linda doing the same.

"No man should look that good in a pair of jeans," Linda noted.

"Temptation and sin never come in ugly packaging," Ruby returned, but she watched right along with her until he disappeared into the house.

"Well, it's clear my little crush is all it's meant to be."

Ruby glanced at her. "I told you, if you want to try and make a move—"

"Ruby." Linda gave her a look that Ruby suspected quelled her dogs *and* nieces and nephews, when either species became too rambunctious. "I'm not clueless. It's obvious his heart already belongs to you and—"

"That's his business and his problem."

"And," Linda repeated, "*your* heart belongs to him as well." A wistful smile touched her lips. "You watch him like he's the sun, the moon and the stars, even when you're angry with him, as you are now."

Ruby thought of a hundred ways to deny it, but gave it up as a botched job. "Doesn't matter," she said. "And I'm not angry at him. I just don't know how to deal with him."

"That's usually how you know he's the right one."

Linda sobered then, shifting so she was squared with Ruby. "I have a great deal of respect for Derek," the priestess said carefully. "A great deal of trust. He sent you to teach us, and you're doing that, for certain. My ladies have learned more about magic use in a few days with you than we've discovered in three years of practice together."

"I'm glad I could help," Ruby said in a neutral tone. "I think you all will get better and better, building on the information we've given you."

Linda nodded. "Ruby, the way you talked about Dark and Light that first day . . . I'm very grateful you're here, and for all your skill and expertise, but I have my own skills, and my own connection to the Lady's energy. What you were doing . . . it made me extremely uncomfortable. I don't want to offend you, but it was more than a sense of danger." She took a deep breath. "Something felt very *wrong* about the magic you were using. Can you explain that to me, so I can understand better?"

"It got the job done," Ruby said shortly, turning toward the house. Linda reached out, touched her arm.

"Yes, it did. But that's why Derek and you are fighting, isn't it? I'm not trying to pry into your business. I don't have the right to that, I understand. But this coven, I feel a responsibility to protect them. To understand, to not hide from knowledge that can hurt as well as help them."

It was fair; Ruby knew it was. Even so, she still had to fight the defensiveness, the ugly feelings that surged up. *None of your goddamned business, stay off this lawn, no trespassing past this point . . .*

She shoved down the anger, managed to answer in a civil tone. "I have some magical skills that are fairly . . . different. I stepped out of the circle specifically so they wouldn't be exorcised within it, so it wouldn't touch you or your people. Miriam was brave, and her intentions were the best kind, but you and I both know her stepping out of the circle was a judgment error."

"You were down, and the soul-eaters were closing in."

"I was fine."

"If *fine* means you don't care if you live or die anymore."

"Don't think you know me," Ruby snapped. "Bottom line, it saved your asses. If you don't want me here, I don't have to be here."

Linda recoiled. "I wasn't trying to—"

"Yeah, you were. Ninety-nine percent of what comes out of people's mouths is lubricant, trying to make shit go down smoother. Anyone paying attention knows what's really being said. You've been taught Dark magic is bad, wrong, and anyone who uses it is either evil or misguided, destined for a tragic end. It's my choice, my business. Not yours. What is your business is this: I didn't teach you or them anything that wasn't based on the principles of Light magic. So you don't have to worry that I've infected you or your coven."

All the good feeling she'd felt from the sistership of the coven, the things she'd recouped in the past few days, seemed to vanish. She *really* wanted to be back at her shop.

Linda looked as if Ruby had punched her in the face. And Ruby wasn't as unaffected by it as she wished she was. Spending a week with a coven, working together on stuff this tough and scary, couldn't help but create a sense of camaraderie and nascent friendship. Ruby just couldn't afford any more friends. But she couldn't afford to make enemies, either.

Plus, she wasn't so far gone that she couldn't be ashamed of her behavior. Linda hadn't done anything to deserve it, except innocently step into the target line of Ruby's loaded emotional state.

In fact, Linda deserved credit for saying something that took guts to confront with another witch, and doing it with kindness and tact. It wasn't her fault that Ruby had turned a flamethrower on her.

Incinerating her into a pile of human fat grease and hair, the smell of charred flesh . . .

It was just like earlier, when the graphic image of Derek hanging from a rope was way too immediate and detailed, refusing to be blocked. Ruby backed up three steps, fighting down that violent image that jumped out of her head like a skeleton waiting in the closet. Rubbing a hand over her face, she averted her gaze toward the tree line, the rising sun that had seemed so comforting a moment ago. Now it heralded another day of harsh light shining down on her shortcomings, the people she was failing.

"Linda, I'm hungry, worn-out and cranky. Later, let's talk some more, and I'll answer the questions I can. Okay? I'm sorry." She took a deep breath. "I stepped out of the circle to protect your coven," she repeated. "While I'm teaching you, your safety and theirs is my top priority. Always."

Unless Asmodeus comes, and then you'll burn down the whole world to tear one scream from his throat.

"You're right." Linda relaxed some, though her expression remained tense and a little closed up, a woman shielded against further attack. "I did hit you with this out of the blue. Go eat some breakfast. I made enough for two, even considering Derek's appetite."

"Really? You have an industrial kitchen and enough food stores to feed a marching army, plus me?"

Linda's gaze warmed. "He does have a very healthy appetite."

Ruby snorted. "He needs a southern-cooking granny who equates love with food and stuffs him to the gills every time he visits."

"I'm not a grandmother, but I'll see what I can do while he's here." Linda allowed herself a small smile, but made a tentative gesture to hold Ruby an additional second. "One last thing. I was talking to Derek, and he agrees we should reinforce the fault line, thicken the energy at the place where it was weakened. A Great Rite would be appropriate."

"Makes sense." Ruby's fingers curled into balls inside her hooded sweatshirt pockets. *I don't want to see that. I can't watch Derek lie upon another woman, raise energy with her . . .*

"So you concur?"

"Yeah, why not?"

Linda arched a dubious brow, telling Ruby she should

have started the day by chugging a pint of Deception. "Sheila, another of our coven members, is Miriam's best friend. She's understandably staying with Miriam for the next few nights. Might even move in with her for a little while, until the residual effects of the soul-eater contact die back. So without Derek and you, we're down to eleven. With you both, it will be thirteen, the best number for a strong energy raising."

No way was she going to stand there during a Great Rite featuring Derek and Linda. If the intent was a strong energy raising, they'd get it. Ruby would probably turn the circle into a crater.

"I think you two should perform the Rite," Linda said. "I'll coordinate as head priestess."

"What?" Ruby didn't realize she'd taken another two steps back until Linda followed her, probably because Ruby looked ready to put something the width of a football field between them.

"Is that a problem? I don't discount my own abilities, but I admit things have me a little rattled. I'd do better in a support role this time. The two of you are the most capable magic users here. We need the energy flow to be as strong as possible. And since you and Derek already have an obviously strong bond—"

"Bonding doesn't mean anything. Grant and Lee had a bond. They didn't become golfing buddies."

Linda pressed her lips together. "I'm sorry; I misunderstood. I was just thinking of what might be best for mending this rift, and it seems the two of you would be the best avenue to that."

"Coffee. I'm going to drink coffee. Then we'll deal with this."

* 12 *

RUBY PIVOTED AND MARCHED TOWARD THE HOUSE. *A Great Rite?* Sure, why not? She'd just had visions of hanging Derek with his own rope and turning Linda into a lard stew. Why not put her in the center of a powerful energy raising, where she could become a bomb, capable of exploding into shrapnel inside a closed circle?

She stopped outside the side door to the kitchen, breathing hard. Okay, yeah, she was a bit volatile right now, but it was boiling to the top quicker and more often because she'd taken herself out of a routine, a controlled environment. She needed to get the hell out of here. When she got home, she could contain it.

However, even fighting her own reaction, something Linda said filtered through. *Derek agreed . . . ?* He thought this was a good idea?

Yanking open the door, she stomped inside, determined to tear a strip off his ass for planting such a ludicrous idea without even discussing it with her first. Now Linda was involved, and she was going to be disappointed or confused—more than she was already.

As Ruby stepped into a laundry room that led to the kitchen, her arm was caught and she was flipped around. Before she could do more than yelp in surprise, she was lifted onto the top of the washer. Derek put himself between her knees, caught her face and put his mouth on hers.

It was an entirely unexpected assault on her still-foggy morning senses, but it brought back last night with vivid clarity, particularly when one broad hand clamped down on her ass and snugged her up against him. Her legs faithlessly curved around his hips, her canvas sneakers sliding down hard thighs, the tender insides of her knees remembering the way his backside felt without denim covering it.

He had the other hand on her jaw. Every man who'd ever been smart enough to watch Richard Gere kiss a woman knew that was a devastating assault on her senses, the way those fingers could stroke temple, cheek, throat, ear, all those little erogenous nerve centers. An overwhelming level of emotional stimuli was communicated by a hand on the face. It made the focus on *her*, not just her assorted pink parts.

Of course, since Derek had been alive way before Richard Gere, maybe Richard had picked it up from *him*. She didn't care, couldn't care, and was lost in the demanding heat of those firm lips on hers, reminding her he'd possessed her body fully last night, that he considered her his in every way. And that he had implied, rather strongly, that he considered himself hers.

He pulled back when fluttering moths had inundated her empty stomach, her heart was pounding, and she was wet between her legs. She looked up at him, trying not to appear as dazed and off-balance as she felt. "You bastard," she said weakly.

"I figured I'd get this out of the way before you start taking shots at me." He braced his hands on either side of her hips, kept his face steady and square in the field of hers. "What's got you riled up already?"

"Great Rite? You told Linda—"

"I agreed a strong energy raising would be good after last night. She decided the Great Rite would be most appropriate. I didn't suggest it, but you and I both know she's right. It's one of the most powerful means of delivering Light, particularly with a coven that's still learning its way. The magic of a Great Rite is connected to the root energy center of our souls, so when needed it can be more instinctive than learned."

His brow creased at her look, and he flicked a curl over her ear, giving it a little tug. "Ruby, you of all people know what a Great Rite's about. There's no need to be jealous. Linda's a fine priestess, but I don't—"

"She doesn't want you to do it with *her*, you arrogant ass. She wants you to do it with me. Thinks it makes more sense." She glared at him, shoved him back, which of course was like trying to move a brick wall. "I want to get down."

"In a minute. I do better at getting answers when I can keep you cornered."

"A cornered animal will bite," she advised.

His blue gaze twinkled at her, despite the hard set of his mouth. "Thanks for the warning." When she made a noise of frustration that sounded remarkably like a trapped and infuriated badger, he sobered. "Seriously, I didn't make the suggestion, Ruby. I don't lie."

The bite to his voice suggested which of the two of them was guilty of that sin. But before she could get her hackles up over the entirely valid accusation, he pressed on. "But it *does* make the most sense."

"For who?" This time she managed an awkward but determined hop off the appliance and ducked under his arm, pivoting to face him, her arms akimbo. "Derek, I can't. And I won't. So you'll just . . . have to do it with her. And I won't help. Twelve will be fine for a circle. We held it last night with three; for a Great Rite, twelve will be plenty. It's time for me to go. I need to go."

"Ruby, this is about more than your secrets, or you and me. Something's going on here. Things that aren't making sense. I know you've asked yourself the same questions. Why has Asmodeus chosen this place? Why did he send forerunners to scope out our defenses? If it was a simple breakout, he'd have done it fast and dirty, done his worst and tried to vanish again before I could catch him aboveground and do enough damage he'd have to stay in the Underworld for the next twenty years to recuperate."

She could do enough damage he'd have to stay down there ten times that length. Long after she was dead and gone.

"Because I don't have those answers yet," Derek pressed onward, "I want this line strengthened as much as we can make it. Seeing your capabilities last night, the power reserves you have, your participating in the Great Rite is vital to what we'll face going forward. Hell, we might even be able to reinforce this fault line enough that we set them back to square one, so that they lose heart and go look for another access point."

When she said nothing, he sighed. "You want to go back to North Carolina after that, fine. While I think the ladies could benefit from at least a few more days with you, we'll call it square if you can do that much. The truth is, if you refuse to participate in this, based on what happened last night, I'm going to need to pull in another magic user of similar strength. There aren't that many available on short notice."

Another magic user of similar strength. No matter how much she accused him of it, Derek wasn't into bullshitting, and definitely didn't do idle praise. While the compliment last night had been validating, hearing that he truly considered her a strong magic user, a peer, rocked her on her axis.

"I don't know," she said sullenly. "I haven't had coffee."

"Come eat." Giving her a considering look, he tugged her by the hand into the kitchen. She saw a plate full of pancakes on the kitchen counter. Next to it was a platter that she suspected had once held quite a few more of them. Setting hands to her waist, Derek boosted her up on a stool next to him and that plate of pancakes. He pushed it toward her, handing her a second fork. "Maple syrup's right there. I didn't soak them up yet, because I know you like to eat them before they become soggy with it. I'll take this end and we'll work our way to the middle."

A choice of words she knew wasn't idle. "I'm not doing it, Derek."

"I think you've already decided you will."

"You think so? A snowball fight in Hell says you're wrong."

Forking up some pancake, he aimed it toward her mouth. "Eat."

"I don't need you to—ooph." She gave him a narrow look as he poked the food past her bared teeth. She was hungry, and the pancakes were very good. "Linda didn't make these. *You* did." He was the only man she knew who made pancakes like fluffy sweet manna instead of the bitter, thin pancakes most people consumed.

"She made the meat, fruit and grits. I wanted to make you pancakes." He speared one on the platter, dropped it on her side of the plate. "That one has butterscotch chips in it, like you like. The other two have chocolate chips, so you can tuck them away for a snack later, since I know you prefer that type cold, when the yeast settles and makes them really dense. The two in the middle are plain, for your maple syrup. You're bound to have an appetite after last night."

In fact, the use of black magic acted contrary to white magic, robbing one of an appetite. But with Heaven melting in her mouth, the Light won out. She'd tuck away as much as she could—to keep him from nagging, of course. From the look in his eyes, she was pretty sure he already knew her appetite wasn't what it should be. So she'd eat all of them, even if she had to go throw some up later. Though it was probably a criminal act to throw up pancakes made by his skilled hands.

"I can feed myself." She snatched the fork away from him and stuffed another mouthful in, reaching for the syrup.

"Lovely table manners." Putting a napkin by her elbow, he picked up his own fork and repeated the command. "Eat. We won't talk for a bit."

That part almost made her smile. Derek took food consumption very seriously, actually preferring to eat in silence. Since she really didn't want to talk about a lot of subjects, it suited her as well. However, while they ate, she shot surreptitious looks his way. Mostly he was studying the scenery outside as he chewed, though occasionally he glanced toward her. His knee pressed against hers because of the length of his long legs. She didn't scoot away.

The warm kitchen, the good breakfast smells, the sunlight bathing them, made things feel lazy and slow. After she ate as much as she could, it therefore seemed pretty natural to sigh and lay her head on his broad shoulder. She closed her eyes to take another quick five-minute doze, letting the rhythm of his body's minute shifts as he chewed, swallowed, cut and speared each bite, take her to that resting state.

Breakfast was the most aromatically comforting meal of all, and when Derek's scent was part of that concoction, coffee and leather, laundry detergent and the sandalwood shaving soap he used—it just enhanced the effect.

It intrigued her, thinking of him doing his laundry. From the times he'd stayed with her, she knew he didn't handle mundane chores with sorcery unless it was a teaching exercise to hone skills. In his opinion, doing otherwise was a misuse of power and also negated the importance of doing tasks in the way they were intended to be done.

Only a man who'd lived hundreds of years could feel that

way about vacuuming. She'd be happy to break all the rules of sorcery to do the Mickey Mouse Sorcerer's Apprentice thing and have her vacuum roll out on its own.

However, from what she could tell, he liked doing such things. The world was full of men who hated chores and house maintenance. Derek acted like it was a vacation to wash dishes, fold laundry, measure and hammer a shelf in place for her. Standing back from everything, all her fears and insecurities, she remembered how he'd captured her heart. He was a unique spirit who seemed to understand the precious value of every simple moment, and when he was with her like this, she understood it, too. Things seemed clearer, more in focus. Steadier. Less painful.

Like now. She could rest her head on his shoulder, know he'd let her be, let it stay quiet, no matter what they'd be fighting about later.

After a time, he shifted, used one hand to scrape her stool even closer to him. Then he slid his arm around her so she could pillow her cheek on the inside of his arm, the firm curve of pectoral. His hand lay on her hip, fingers stroking there, over the soft give of her buttock. When he lifted his coffee to his lips, she smelled the pleasantly bitter aroma, for he drank it black and strong. Then there was the clink of the fork, the smell of maple syrup, his jaw moving against her hair as he ate another pancake.

Probably twenty minutes passed that way. She didn't think she'd been this . . . still, in a very long time. She dozed some, but mainly she just let herself be hypnotized into a tranquil zone by his rhythm, the calm energy around him. When the screen door creaked, suggesting Linda was returning, she opened her eyes to see the platter of pancakes was empty except for her two chocolate chip ones. He was mopping up the maple syrup on his plate with the last few bites of his sausage.

As she straightened, blinking, a wet nose touched her hand. It wasn't Linda but Theo, who'd simply nosed open the warped screen door and come on in. "Did those young'uns leave you behind, Theo?" Derek asked, reaching down from her hip to scratch his ears. "Or have you had enough of that nonsense and thought you'd come get some leftovers?"

He picked up a sausage link she now saw he'd deliberately set to the side and offered it to the dog. Theo took it with polite stateliness and then moved to the corner of the kitchen to collapse into a sun spot, propping his chin on a one-foot stool that was left next to the pantry. A piece of furniture every short woman needed, Ruby knew, because home builders assumed everyone was Abraham Lincoln's height. When Derek stayed with her, she hadn't needed such a thing. In fact, he usually tucked her short stepladder under her kitchen counter so he wouldn't trip over it. A small, familiar ritual of his comings and goings in her life.

She slipped off the stool. "However this Great Rite is going to happen, I need to go and do some things to prepare for it. Thanks for breakfast."

Wiping his mouth with his napkin, he turned and leaned an elbow on the counter, hand lying loosely on his splayed knee. "We talk first, Ruby. *Particularly* if we're going to do this thing tonight."

"Is this the superpower cop talking to me, or Derek?"

"Whichever gets the job done." He gave her an even look. "You used soul magic to drive me away from you."

It wasn't as much of a shock to hear him say it out loud as she'd anticipated. After all, if Raina knew it, that meant she'd probably learned it from Derek. But the angry feeling that sprouted in her chest like a thorny vine of Mother-in-Law's Tongue was sharper than she expected. It didn't feel like herself, scared her a little bit. But telling him the truth scared her more.

You let *it drive you away.*

That was entirely unfair and unreasonable, which was the only thing that kept her from lashing out with it. But her cursedly transparent face must have shown it, for his expression tightened.

"You've been experimenting with spell and energy use that pulls from both the Light and Dark sides of the fence. Dipping into the Underworld's well. Who've you been paying for that? And, more importantly, how much?"

"No one."

His expression clearly said he wasn't buying it, and she knew he wasn't going to let it go. Derek didn't follow the rules that civilized men did, and he wasn't just hitting her with the demand of a lover and friend, but a cop who was in charge of this kind of shit as well. And no one took his job as seriously as Derek. A white knight in truth. *Shit*.

Maybe she could give him parts of it, and that would be enough. Circling to the other side of the island, she took a stool there with the barrier of the counter between them. Of course, it put him square in front of her, those relentless eyes seeking the total truth.

"You know I've always studied magical theory, the unique way each magic user twines their internal energy with collective and divine energies."

He nodded. She laced her fingers together, unlaced them. Though she took some moments gathering her thoughts, it wasn't to prevaricate. This was complicated. And she appreciated that he said nothing, waiting. He was prepared to listen. In truth, this was the first time she'd ever been able to tell anyone about it. Despite what could happen when he forced her to discuss application instead of theory, she couldn't help but feel some eagerness to explain it to someone who would understand the significance.

"I discovered that I could draw power from places recently . . . visited by Underworld energies. Or places closely aligned with them. Harvest the residual rather than visit the store and pay the direct price for it. It's like taking crumbs falling from a table, Derek. I figured out a way to gather it up, meld Light with Dark magic. Like adding another metal into silver to make it into a stronger frame."

"No one's ever done that before."

"No." And it pleased her in an altogether dangerous way, that he acknowledged the accomplishment while showing little surprise that she was the one who'd figured it out. *Careful, Ruby. In this, he's not your friend. He can't be.*

The insidious reminder made her hunch her shoulders, took away some of the pleasure of it. When she rubbed her hands over her arms, getting rid of the goose bumps, she was way too cognizant of how he caught the motion, how he interpreted it.

"All that study." She gave a bitter laugh, lifted a shoulder. "Turns out I can't cook a grilled cheese sandwich, but I'm a fucking gourmet genius when it comes to dishes that combine unexpected ingredients."

"What changed?"

"One day, I started understanding the underlying spirit in the matter. I could see it, like puzzle pieces. I knew how to file and fit them, whether they were Light or Dark."

It was amazing how great trauma, a life-and-death, soul-shattering event, could open the eyes. Some people saw the white tunnel, relatives waiting. She'd seen knowledge, like the tree in Eden, just waiting for her to grasp that apple, the serpent whispering to her to take the power.

She snapped back into the present again. She knew she really hadn't answered the question he asked. But like a patient lawyer, he rephrased to get at the information. While, like a witness trapped in the box, she watched him change the angle of his attack and couldn't move, a deer in the headlights.

"Why not focus on white Light magic, apply that genius there?"

Because it couldn't do what I needed done. "It's like what I said about my shop, Derek. All that bullshit about not being able to use Dark magic without it exacting a price? Yeah, they're right. But if you're willing to pay it, you can do good things with it."

"You're messing with the rules of the Universe."

"Whose rules? Yours?" Her temper, and the storm that lay waiting behind it, sharpened her voice. "The Powers that Be? Those nameless forces who are so all-powerful and wise that they'll let the weak and innocent go down because they just happen to see this great cosmic plan and how it all fits together? Well, fuck them. What I hate the most is that when I meditated, when I drew Light energy in myself, I understood that. I could feel the wisdom of it, and I knew it as Truth. But Truth doesn't mean a good goddamn to those of us in the trenches. We're not floating in the fucking clouds of enlightenment. It's all bullshit."

She'd said too much. She was breathing too fast, her face hot. Things felt light, floaty. She was going to break open in a minute, and she couldn't. Derek rose from the stool, his expression grave. "Ruby, what happened?"

His lips pressed together, hard. She saw the knowledge flicker in his gaze. Panic clustered in her chest, and she wanted to do anything to keep him from saying what he was about to say next. But those words came out anyway, hitting her like a solid punch in the face. "What happened to our daughter?"

Raina. Raina had told him. Of course. Treacherous, loving bitch of a friend that she was. But all Raina could tell him was that the baby had died because of a car accident.

The warmth of the sun-soaked kitchen died out of her, leaving everything cold and still. She remembered that stilted moment in the woods, the sense of something large and unstable he was holding back. He'd been carrying it around with him, and the strain of it was now in the hoarse note in his voice, his heartbreak capable of breaking hers anew.

She knew this man. Knew what it would have meant to him. She wasn't one of those heartless women who thought that because the mother carried the baby, the father had no right to make decisions about its life, its well-being. They bore an equal weight in the creation; the responsibility was shared. But that knowledge just made the guilt and pain worse.

She closed her fingers into tight, tight balls, as tight as the rock sitting in the center of her chest. "She died, Derek. And everything else died with her. You want me to do this tonight . . . the Great Rite, I'll do it." She could do it, would do it, like any other ritual. Then she'd walk away. "Tomorrow, I go home, and I don't ever want to see you again. Please, give me that. I can't handle . . . how you make me feel."

She couldn't handle feeling.

* 13 *

He wouldn't have let her get away with that, she was sure, but with fortunate timing, Linda came into the kitchen then to let her know some of the coven were arriving early to prepare for tonight. She left a white-faced Derek with her, and escaped to her guest cottage, Theo trotting along behind her. He wouldn't have left that sunny spot, but that old-man worry wrinkle was back on his homely expression. He knew she was a mess right now, rattled down to the bone.

Dushing ice-cold water on her face, she threw up the pancakes, put a Deception potion together at double strength, took it down like a frat boy downing shots, and stood in front of the mirror, deep breathing until everything went back to where it should be. Calm, still, like a sludge-filled lake, everything trapped and suffocating beneath the surface.

What in the hell was she thinking? Why had she said she'd do the Great Rite when she knew it was a bad idea? Because the secrets in her life demanded ironclad control. She had to be able to sever the friendships with Raina and Ramona, turn her back fully on Derek, not by running, but by standing by what she said in the kitchen. If she could do this tonight, she'd prove all of that was possible. She had to prove to herself she could contain everything inside of her without breaking.

There was a weariness in the bedrock of her soul, though, something that told her she'd taken this far beyond where it should have gone, but she'd faced that before. There was no turning back now. She just needed to get home. It would be all right once she got there.

A rap on the door made her wince as she realized she'd left the door to the cottage open, but then she snarled at herself. *You will do this, Ruby. Pull your shit together.* If there was one thing her mother had taught her, it was the power of enduring the unbearable.

When she stepped into the sitting area, she saw the last person she expected. And it pulled the rug right out from beneath her. Not that she was going to be competing for Weeble of the Year at this point. She was getting knocked on her ass left and right, and it was getting harder and harder to come back up.

Mikhael was studying his surroundings, his hands in the pockets of his tailored black slacks. He was wearing his sunglasses, the artful strands of hair playing across his forehead. Having shed his suit coat in his car, apparently, he had the sleeves of his white dress shirt rolled up, the neckline open to show his strong throat. Her heart started pounding, the headache behind her eyes weakening her knees.

"I was in the area," he commented, as if it was entirely normal for him to show up in the backwoods of Florida. He tilted his head to look at her. "You did not answer my call."

"No."

He sauntered forward a couple steps, and she jumped, she couldn't help herself. Removing the sunglasses, he considered her from head to toe with dark brown eyes. "Frightened, little rabbit? Perhaps you should be."

She swallowed. "I can't do this here. It's time for us to walk away. Like we said at the beginning."

"Like *I* said at the beginning. I do the walking, not you. I can see the need written all over you. You are hurting for it."

The fact it was true only made it more awful, because she knew she hurt for it so she wouldn't have to face what she really wanted. Derek's scent was in her nose. The impression of his shoulder, the faint crease from the fold of his shirt, were still there on her cheek. But she had to prove she could do that Great Rite, had to have the balance for it. Right? The solution might be standing in front of her. Or the road to Hell.

Hadn't Mikhael said that this was already Hell?

He was moving toward her. "No," she said, the word catching in her throat. This was wrong, but that Dark part of her was reaching eagerly for him, craving what he could give her. Pulling her back from the unacceptable temptation of pancakes and the illusion of safety, of healing. Of love.

The moan as he clamped his mouth down on hers was part despair, part sharp-edged lust, that constant need surging up to meet him. With Mikhael, kissing was more like branding, but of course that made her think of that barn fantasy, Derek lifting the branding iron. She actually felt a tingle go through her shoulder. As if he knew he was fighting an unseen foe, Mikhael's teeth scraped hers and his fingers bit into her arms, bruising with his strong grip. When she struggled to get closer, he shoved her back against the wall, sliding his fingers down into her loose jeans, under the panties. She was wet, helpless and trembling. Catching her belt loops, he stared at her with those cold eyes. "You will stand still."

She put her head back against the plaster, her palms flat against it. Tears were gathering in her eyes, but it was all right. She needed this. She had to have it.

He struck her across her right cheek, rocking her head to the left so her neck tendons popped at the sudden jerk. Catching her shirtfront, he ripped it down the middle and off her shoulders, yanking her bra straps so she was exposed to him. His eyes flamed at the sight of her breasts, full, the nipples tight, tight as the ache in her gut. When he lifted his hand again, she forced herself to keep her eyes on it, knowing he would strike her on the left cheek as well. Mikhael was all about balance, after all.

She closed her eyes at the last second. The blow landed, pain exploding in her cheek, but at the same moment, there was a snarl like an enraged bear. Her eyes flew open in time to see Derek catch Mikhael's arm, spin him around, and slam a fist in his jaw.

The gunrunner was actually lifted off his feet by the blow, no small feat since the men were the same impressive size. Mikhael hit her small kitchenette, sending table and chairs spinning, crashing with a cacophony against the walls and floor. As Mikhael landed with them, she registered another snarl, a large body hurtling past Derek.

Mikhael made his living through violence. He was already rolling to his feet, and when he saw the dog, in the same motion he'd pulled his Walther. The gun fired.

"*No.*" Ruby screamed it, lunging forward. She wasn't cognizant of what happened in those next two seconds, but when her mind cleared, she was being held hard around the waist by Derek, her flailing feet off the ground, his body turned so she was not in Mikhael's direct line of fire. Theo was lying on the floor, motionless.

"No, no, *no.*" She struggled against him, such that Derek had to snarl her name to draw her attention.

"Ruby. *Ruby.*" He gave her a shake painful enough to bring her gaze up to his fierce eyes. "He's asleep. Sandman spell."

Her attention flitted back to the dog. An absurd snore broke from Theo, powerful enough to make the loose upper lip quiver, giving her a hint of the teeth that had been fully bared a moment before.

"He fired . . ."

Derek nodded. Showed her his other hand. He had a burn mark where the hot projectile had marked him, but the bullet was firmly in his grasp. "I rerouted it," he murmured.

Mikhael rose to his feet, holstering the Walther under his shoulder again. His expression was remarkably indifferent as he studied the two of them.

"So, this is the one you have been running from. He caught up to you, did he?"

Derek glanced at Ruby. "You *know* him? But he was . . ." His attention slid down her face, which she was sure showed the mark of Mikhael's skillful backhand, to the tattered front of her shirt. Realizing she was exposed, she wrapped it around her best as she could, but her cheeks were burning shamefully.

"No need to hide what we've both seen and enjoyed," Mikhael remarked.

"Shut. Up." Derek was staring at Ruby hard. When he at last shifted his gaze to the other male, she wasn't sure who the contempt in his gaze was for. "Mikhael Roman."

"Derek." The gunrunner lifted a brow. "Had I known I was feeding at your trough, I might have had second thoughts. Or maybe not. Sometimes the forbidden is too tempting, hmm? And she seemed to want something from me you could not provide."

"What she wants and what she needs are two different things."

"Forever making choices for others, are we? Be careful, Derek. When you make those decisions, you are trying to own her soul. Can you handle the responsibility of owning someone's soul?"

"A hell of a lot better than you can."

Ruby watched the byplay between the two men, with no idea where to interject or how. The fact they knew each other, the situation itself, had her speechless. She wanted to go to Theo. Thinking he might have been shot before her eyes made her need to touch him. But Derek was holding her wrist like a steel manacle.

"Ah, the dilemma of what kind of master it takes to hold a strong woman's heart. For a woman like her needs a master." Mikhael shrugged. "But this is not my concern. My interest was in her cunt, and how far her desires would drive her to sate it. She was a pleasure to me, but the pleasure appears to be at an end."

"Yeah. That's a wise decision."

Mikhael gave him a speculative look. "She bears my marks, sorcerer. Sometimes scars are left on the outside as well as inside. One in particular, on her very delectable ass. You may have noticed it if you've taken her from behind since you've gotten back into her bed."

"Get out. Now." Derek's voice was capable of dropping the temperature in the cottage by ten degrees. Mikhael met his eyes in challenge, but then he inclined his head. He looked toward Ruby.

"*Do svidaniya,* Ruby. If you have need of me, our paths will cross again. I'm sure I will enter your dark dreams on occasion, as I am sure you will mine."

"Out," Derek said. "Or I'll shove that gun up your ass and pull the trigger."

"You can try, sorcerer." Mikhael gave him a cool nod. Stepping over Theo without a glance at the dog, he moved past them and out the door.

"Derek—" She let out a gasp as he let go of her, but only to shove her down against the still-standing kitchenette table. Catching the waistband of her jeans, he yanked at them to expose the upper curve of her buttock. "Stop."

She closed her eyes as he touched it. His heat and anger were at her back like a storm boiling up on the horizon. There was a mirror on the wall behind the table, now cracked from where one of the chairs had hit it. Even though she told herself not to look, she did. He was staring down at the mark, but then his eyes lifted, met hers. She managed, just barely, not to flinch, because the expression in his eyes was as if he were looking at someone he didn't even know. And no matter how true that was, it hurt like hell to see it.

"You're right. You don't need to be here anymore. I'll do

the Great Rite with Linda. We'll deal with this later, but I don't need this shit right now. Get your things and get out of here. You're no use to us on this."

He let her go so abruptly she sagged against the wood surface. Turning on his heel, he strode out of the cottage, leaving her bent over the table, her feet braced against Theo's back. The pain in her gut was so intense it cramped, made it hard for her to straighten. She didn't want to straighten. She just wanted to lie here with her cheek on the wood and not ever move again. Then she heard Linda's shout, and the other women crying out in alarm.

Shoving off the table, she tripped over the prone Theo, and stumbled toward the door. On her way, she discarded the tattered shirt and snatched up the hoodie. When she got it zipped, she bolted out onto the lawn.

Mikhael had reached his car, his black Ferrari with silver trim, but Derek had caught up with him there. She didn't know if any words were exchanged. Somehow she doubted it. Derek reached the car, took off his hat, tossed it on the hood, and just hurled himself on the Russian.

No magic use, no guns. The two of them were using what appeared to be quite considerable and fairly well-matched hand-to-hand skills to beat the crap out of each other. Only Derek apparently had the advantage of stone-cold fury. A punch was answered with a kick; then they were grappling on the ground. Then Mikhael was flipped over Derek's head and they were back on their feet. Blood was coming from Mikhael's nose, but it looked like he'd planted a solid fist in Derek's right eye.

Ruby caught up with Linda, who stood at a safe distance with Christine, Jocelyn and Marie. Linda gave her a what-the-hell look, but then took in Ruby's disheveled appearance. The hoodie might hide her state of dress, but there was no way to conceal the swelling marks on her face. Linda's eyes narrowed and she turned that look onto Mikhael.

"No." Ruby forced it out through stiff lips. "It's not like that, Linda. Let me handle this."

Linda put a quelling hand on her arm. "That's nothing any of us need to be in the middle of." Fortunately, her grip was a lot less powerful than Derek's, for Ruby twisted out of it with a shake of her head, and moved forward. "Stop it," she shouted. "Both of you. Cut it *out*."

The energy she used was like a Taser, the electric voltage hitting the ground between their feet, powerful enough to sing up the legs and grab their attention. When Mikhael gave her a startled look, Derek's fist slammed into his jaw like a battering ram. The gunrunner hit the side of his car hard enough his elbow punched a spiderweb crack in the driver's side window.

Ruby swore, took two steps and jumped on Derek's back, locking her arms around his shoulders, her legs around his waist. "Stop it," she hissed in his ear. "Quit it, or I'll get a hose and cool you down with it, cowboy."

The tone worked on him where the voltage had not. Derek stopped, his chest heaving with temper and exertion, fists still clenched. Mikhael straightened from the car, wiping a hand carelessly at the blood under his nose. He glanced at the Ferrari's window. "Beating on me is one thing. But the car is blasphemy."

"Would you like to see what I can do to its paint job?" Ruby felt the energy gathering in Derek's body. Quickly, she slid off his back and put herself in front of him, her back to Mikhael. Reaching up, she put both hands on the sorcerer's face, bringing his eyes down to her.

"Enough," she said, low. "Please. This is my fault. Not his."

"You bear responsibility for your choices. He bears responsibility for his actions."

"You owe me a favor, *cowboy*." Mikhael spat blood into the dirt, his eyes sparking fire. "She stands against the angels. If not for me, Hell would already have claimed her."

Ruby spun around, met his gaze. Though she saw nothing in his fathomless eyes but his usual indifference, there was more. A lot more. She felt it in a vibration of power that pushed her back against Derek's body like a sudden gust of noiseless wind, a heat that was not comfortable or reassuring, more like the brief sense of standing far too close to a furnace.

"But there is one shard of hope, Ruby. When Hell takes you, I will be there waiting."

"Mikhael, get the hell out of here." Derek spoke through stiff lips. "Or I swear by the Lord and Lady I will turn you into a greasy spot . . . and take that car for my own."

"Just be sure to have it painted white, Marshal Dillon. Remember, Hell loves shades of gray. So many things can happen amid the clouds of an approaching storm." Those dangerous eyes fixed on Derek, and for a moment, something else was in them. No sarcasm, just deadly purpose. "Keep her close, sorcerer."

Linda began to slide around Derek and Ruby, probably to give Mikhael a quiet and firm request to leave, to respect what was happening right now and go. Of one accord, Derek and Ruby reached out, latched onto her arm to hold her behind them.

With a brief, sensual smile that, remarkably, was capable of making that frisson of nerves still tingle through Ruby's lower belly, Mikhael gave them a mocking nod. Opening the car door, he slid into the driver's seat. As the door shut, he kept his eyes on her face. It made her remember every dark, overwhelming moment, every lick of pain and pleasure, and all the twisting range of emotions that had gone into those interludes. The spiderweb crack disappeared, as if a shimmer of water had run over it, taking it away and leaving the window whole again.

The car turned in the driveway; then Mikhael skillfully fishtailed it, accelerating so he disappeared up Linda's long, winding driveway like a raven taking flight.

She stands against the angels . . . Who *was* Mikhael?

* 14 *

SILENCE DESCENDED. RUBY WAS VAGUELY AWARE OF THE
women retreating into the house, giving them their privacy.
When she dared to look up and behind her, she saw savage
violence on Derek's face. It made her want to pull away, but
he caught her wrist before she could, turned her to face him.
By the time she did so, the look was gone, but there was a
fierce discontent she knew she had no desire to confront
right now.

She swallowed. "You know him. You know each other."

"If I had known you were tangled up with him, I would
have been here a lot sooner. There's more to Mikhael Roman
than meets the eye. If he didn't just make that crystal clear."

Her chest tightened. "You would have been here a lot
sooner if you'd known he was tangled up with me? So that's
what it would take for you to get your ass back to me when
I need you? Some other guy fucking me?"

His gaze snapped down to her. "That's not what I meant
and you know it. Ruby, you left me. You vanished."

"Yeah, I did. But you found me. You eventually found

me. When you really started looking, how long did it actually take? I know you haven't been conducting an exhaustive manhunt . . . womanhunt . . . for three years."

"You used a soul spell on me. You told me to stay out of your life. When I figured out the damn spell, I did look for you, *kept* looking for you, but I had to keep doing my job."

"And it was your job that finally brought you back to me. This." She made a vague gesture toward the circle.

"I had to have a reason to pull you back into my life. If I'd showed up and said, 'Hey, Ruby, I just want to take up where we left off, even though you seemed kinda pissed the last time I saw you,' how would that have worked?"

He was right, but he was also wrong, the same way she was both right and wrong. She struggled with her wildly vacillating emotions, which seemed as hard to pin down as the range of his emotions over the past few minutes. "You acted like you hated me, back in the cottage. But then you come out here and knock him around. What was that, marking territory? I can't stand the bitch, but she's *my* bitch?"

"*Ruby.*" He caught her shoulders, hauled her up to her toes. "Stop it. Love and hate, it doesn't matter. They're all in the mix when it comes to the way I feel about you. Yeah, I'm old as dirt. I know a lot of things about magic and the way the Earth works, but when it comes to you, I'm a man. And when I saw him touching you, *hurting* you, that was all that mattered."

Her anger deflated at his weary, frustrated honesty. His grip dropped, slid around her waist. After a hesitation, he dipped his fingers back in under denim to stroke over that marked spot again. When she moved her hand to his arm, trying to stop him, he made a noise, shaking his head, so she put her hand uncertainly on his chest as he traced the scar. "What did he use?"

She didn't want to tell him, but she couldn't give him the truth on what really mattered, so she'd give him this, no matter how shameful the words felt in the light of day. "A knife blade, heated by flame. Then he . . . he used his belt buckle over it."

Derek's eyes darkened. Ruby wanted to look away, but couldn't. "You wanted him to hurt you," he said.

"Yes. I . . . I begged him for it, most times. Derek . . . I'm sorry. I told you, it's just . . . It's too late. I can't go back to being what you want me to be."

"It's not about that, Ruby. If you were what *you* wanted to be, I'd feel it, know it, because I know who you are. I know your heart, girl; don't you realize that? Your soul, too. I know what you like and don't like, what makes you afraid, what makes you laugh . . ." His lips tightened. "There's an important chunk of something I don't know, but what I don't know are the specifics. I know the important part. You made a choice, and in your heart, you know it was the wrong one, but you couldn't turn away from it, and now you're losing a little bit more of yourself to the Darkness every day.

"Whatever that choice was, it was so important that you can't turn your back on it, so all you can do is try to slow it down, keep the Darkness appeased and from clawing more of the guts out of your soul at an even faster pace. You're hanging from a cliff edge, Ruby, and you don't know whether it's best to let go and have done with it, or keep hanging on."

He was so accurate, so dead-on right, words stuck in her throat. But he wasn't finished. His blue gaze held hers, burning her down to her soul.

"The reason I'm here now, why I'm not going anywhere, is because I'm the one kneeling on that ledge. All you have to do is reach up, and I'll take your hand and help you back up."

He gave her an admonishing squeeze, let her go so abruptly she swayed from the lack of support. Stepping back, he gave her a hard look. "That's your friend talking, the man who loves you. But here's a message from the man who knows you *are* his bitch. His sharp-tongued, stubborn, amazingly strong and talented, wildly fragile . . ." He shook his head, unable to say it again.

"He's right about one thing. You do need a guy with a strong hand, one who makes things clear and doesn't fuck around with being PC or leave it in shades of gray. So here it is, crystal-clear."

He jerked his head toward the driveway, where Mikhael had disappeared. "You let him come anywhere near you again, I'll kill him, Ruby. Same goes for any man you let touch what's mine. As long as I can tell from the look in your eyes, in your response to my touch, that your heart, soul, mind and body are mine, I don't share."

On that astounding and chilling statement, one she didn't doubt at all, he turned and left her.

HE DIDN'T EVEN BOTHER STRIDING OUT OF SIGHT. ONE moment he was there, and then the next he was gone. Ruby had no idea where he'd gone, but based on the emotions vibrating off him, she expected he was going somewhere he could pound on something for a while. Hopefully something inert, like a punching bag.

Wearily, she moved away from the tire tracks and disturbed gravel in the circle drive. She made it as far as one of the natural areas; then her knees buckled. Sinking down on a whimsical concrete pig that had the breadth of a sea chest, she stared at a quaint grouping of azalea bushes around a cheerfully bubbling fountain. Linda liked lawn art, for there was an array of stone woodland creatures placed throughout the heavy layer of pine-straw mulch. Squirrels, birds and one hedgehog. More concrete pigs.

She rubbed a hand over her face. She was too tired to cry. All that was left to do was pack. Derek said he wanted her gone, and though he might feel differently after he settled down, he was right. As much as she hated to think of him with Linda, maybe that was tit for tat, right?

No, not really, since performing the Great Rite was far different from him going off and screwing some woman for release when Ruby wasn't handy, but maybe she could think of it that way and the sting would be less. *Yeah, right.*

She struggled for that lullaby in her mind, found the words. Closing her eyes, she folded her arms against herself, rocked back and forth on the pig's broad back as she hummed, trying to find that spot of peace, the groove that made everything okay.

A soothing hand on her shoulder, and Linda was there. Ruby didn't open her eyes, not even when Christine put the ice pack on her swelling cheek and Linda stroked the hair away from the other one. They picked up the lullaby, though, humming it with her, recognizing it as the catharsis it was. She did open her eyes when she felt hands on her feet, sliding off her sneakers. Jocelyn was there with a basin of fragrant, steaming water. As Ruby watched, unresisting, Jocelyn guided her feet into it, began to massage them beneath the water. Oh Goddess, what a sensation. What . . . what were they doing?

"Before the Great Rite, we cosset the coven member who will be fulfilling the Goddess's role," Christine explained in a calm tone. "We'll give you a full bath and massage, leave you to meditate in a sacred place on Linda's property with the proper aromatics to help you get to an elevated state, but we thought you—Ruby, the woman—needed this right now."

"It's something we do, when one of our coven members is sick at heart," Linda said quietly. "When she needs to know that the Lord and Lady understand all things, and that if we just open ourselves to Them, it will all work out. And that it's never too late to do that. You don't even need the will to do it. Just the desire can form a crack inside of you, a crack They can widen, if you can give Them time, help you find the will."

Ruby swallowed. Once, soon after her mother died, she'd

gone to a masseuse who did laying-on-hands as part of her offering. She would offer up the impressions she received only if the participant wished her to do so; otherwise, she simply gave the massage. But Ruby had asked, curious.

I see you, only you look different. You are in a beautiful, serene place. A body of water, green grass, a cave lit by firelight. There are other women there, like you. And that version of you looks up at yourself now through the Veil, and says 'It's going to be all right. We'll be here. It will all work out.'

"What if you can't afford even the crack?" Ruby said, swallowing the tremor in her voice. "He doesn't want me here, Linda. He wants to do the Rite with you. My work here is done."

"No. No, it's not." Linda shook her head. "You and Derek may know a great deal more about flashing lights, bells and whistles when it comes to magic, but there's no denying what I've been feeling since yesterday. The Lord and Lady want the two of you to do this Great Rite. And I don't care what you or Derek Stormwind says. You can argue with each other or me all you wish, but you don't argue with Them. So you both do that Rite tonight, or it doesn't get done, and the fault stays dangerously weakened. That worries me, but not as much as going against what I know is meant to be."

Jocelyn's capable fingers were massaging her arches. Ruby wasn't sure what to do as Linda slid her arm around her back, giving her support as Christine adjusted the ice. "So you just relax. We're going to pamper you this afternoon. And maybe if you can relax some, get some real rest, the answers will come to you."

This was the type of thing coven sisters did for one another, whether they were a coven of three or a coven of twelve. It made her miss Raina and Ramona so much. When Mikhael had walked into the cottage, she'd been focused on how to get through the Rite without exposing too much of herself. But Linda reminded her now that the Rite was a conduit for the Lord and Lady, and the Lord and Lady already knew all her secrets. She would serve Them capably, as she knew she could, without having to reveal herself to others. But perhaps, as Linda said, the answers would still come.

The pain and grief had clouded everything for so long. She hadn't wanted to feel anything, which she realized was a big part of why she'd sent Derek away. And now she couldn't stop feeling.

"We need to check on Theo. Can we do that first?"

"Absolutely. Maybe we'll give him a bath and massage, too." This from Marie, with a hint of a teasing smile.

"Heck, maybe when Derek gets back, we'll strip him down and see what we can do for him." Linda elbowed Ruby.

"I'm sure he could do with a healthy ear scrubbing," Ruby said with a wan smile. "Especially after that fight. Lord knows, he acts like he has wax plugs in them most of the time."

Actually, that wasn't the truth. Derek heard everything, didn't miss anything. He just had his own very definite opinions and judgments about things. Pigheaded man.

"We need to do a cleansing of this area." Christine wrinkled her nose. "The lingering testosterone is so strong it'll probably wilt your flowers, Linda."

"Or fertilize them so they'll proliferate." Jocelyn laughed. "Like little rabbits."

The women continued their gentle teasing, but once Ruby gave herself over to her massaging hands, her attention wandering, Christine glanced at Linda.

"I've never thought about having boxing gloves as part of the preparations for a Great Rite," she muttered. "But we may need them."

Linda had her own concerns, but she'd seen Derek's face when Ruby left the kitchen after breakfast. Whatever was between them, it was a deep wound, and it needed healing. As she'd told Ruby, she might not understand all that was needed to face demons coming through a rift. But she knew when magic was needed to help bring connection back between two souls who couldn't do without each other.

DEREK MATERIALIZED ON TOP OF A SNOW-COVERED mountain, where the wind could whistle through and drive the breath from a man's lungs, freeze them before he realized he was facing his own death. It was a far cry from the tropical Florida climate of Linda's property, and it was that sharp contrast he wanted.

He'd meant every bloodcurdling word, still felt the homicidal urge boiling through his veins. He'd walked in just as Mikhael's knuckles had struck her fair cheek. Even now, in hindsight, it didn't matter what sick game they'd been playing. He'd seen Mikhael kill before, a sharp, powerful blow with his closed fist that had snapped his opponent's neck with a pop like a carrot stick. A woman's neck was fragile, not structured to sustain a strike from a man's hand, because men were never supposed to hit women like that, period.

His patience was at an end. He'd known she was going down some dark roads, but seeing that feral edge in her gaze, craving the blow a split second before it landed, pushed him past what he could tolerate.

He could recognize trouble building like a white squall line on the horizon, bearing down on an unprotected small craft. Ruby was that craft, and she not only wasn't going to survive that line; whatever was driving her from inside seemed to want her to embrace it.

She stands against the angels . . . I did you a favor.

As ruthless as Mikhael was, it was nothing next to what Derek could be when pushed past this line. Love at the visceral level he felt for her had no boundaries or rules. He'd known he loved her for a long time, but perversely it was learning she'd used the soul magic on him, and everything that had happened since, that had hammered it home.

She was everything to him. He wouldn't tolerate this happening to her, even if she was the agent of her own destruction, making all the choices. If she was too far gone, he wouldn't hesitate to embrace Darkness himself, do whatever was necessary to protect her, keep her safe.

And there was the key. The road she'd chosen had something to do with their daughter, driven by a love so deep, so grievous, she hadn't cared about consequences. She still didn't. Which meant she was fast slipping beyond his reach.

Fuck that. He snarled, dropping to his haunches like a lion prepared to spring. Fighting what was within him, an enraged bear in a cage of matchsticks, he took the necessary second to clear the field, make sure there was nothing in harm's way. Then he let it loose. He thrust his hands up toward the sky, as if delivering a fiery message straight to Heaven's gate.

His power compressed the air into folds around him, and then it launched, shuddering through the air, resulting in a cosmic thunder that boomed out over the vast mountain. A rainbow of fire like the Aurora Borealis gone full Disney Technicolor seared the sky. He split it, caught it in nets he conjured straight out of the clouds, channeled it into forms. Giant dragons shot through those clouds, roared their rage, then spun into funnels of energy that whipped up the air, darkened the sky further.

Those black holes could suck the Earth into them, if he let it go that way. He was a man, but because he was also more than a man, when sorely tested, he had Darkness inside of him as well. Only unlike Mikhael Fucking Roman, Derek could back it up with a destructive force that could take out half the planet.

So many years, so much power. From the moment he'd been born, he'd had a connection to the invincible power of the elements, a child of Earth. He understood histories and cycles, could stand inside a forest and touch each individual spirit inside every tree. Or level the entire landscape with a thought.

Just as the wind that flirted across a field could also send huge banks of clouds scudding across the sky, a never-ending panorama of movement, so, too, could the energy inside him light a candle or ignite an inferno. Years of discipline. He'd studied with so many masters, those with far less power than him but far more knowledge. He'd made the mistakes of ego and arrogance, lived to learn from them, to regret, to move on and do better, to make those mistakes worth it.

He was a man who could afford to lose his temper only to a point, but he'd learned to divide himself between Derek the man and Derek the sorcerer. It was okay for Derek the man to beat the shit out of Mikhael. But it had been many, many years since he'd felt this kind of rage, the kind that could bleed into the sorcerer's realm, the side far more dangerous when angered.

But it was all too much. He'd had a daughter, a daughter he hadn't even been allowed to touch. The woman he loved was in grave peril, her very soul at risk. And all of it had gone down while he was out doing what the Powers that Be required of him. In short, he was seriously pissed, resentful as hell, and he was going to make sure somebody knew it, even if it was merely with an awe-inspiring pyrotechnics show.

I am what You created me to be, and I serve You, but there are limits.

Darkness could hover on the edges when such challenges were issued. He felt its attention and presence. He snarled, dared it to get closer. He'd obliterate it in a heartbeat, because this was between him and the Light. The Darkness had no part of it, no matter what it felt spiraling out from his soul.

The dragons were now a flight of phoenixes, cutting great swaths of fire across the darkened sky, leaving trails of multicolored sparks. The earth trembled beneath his feet. The stars were shining brighter through the scudding clouds, everything closer. He could pull the moon into the earth, the stars down with it, hold all of it in his hands and crush them with the anger he was feeling.

But Ruby liked it when the sky was full of stars. A true witch, she reveled in the light of a full moon, would slide off her gown and stand out beneath it, letting that silver sheen glow over her skin. And if he crushed the earth, there wouldn't be those lavender flowers she liked. Or long, hot baths with her, where she fell asleep against his chest, their toes overlapping beneath the water's surface, wrinkling into prunes.

The energy responded to the shift, the sliver of feeling that wasn't rage, that widened the crack between destruction and reason. And because his love for her was powerful, that was the only leverage it needed to slowly turn the tide, ease him back toward balance again.

She had driven him out here, but ultimately, she was what helped him remember what he was. She was damnation and salvation both. The definition of every woman worth a man's heart.

His lips twisted into a wry smile. He wasn't a child having a tantrum, ignorant of consequences. He knew there were ways to let pressure off the boiler without requiring it to explode. So, giving himself time to do just that, he transformed the phoenixes to dragons again, had them engage in battle, a spinning of wings and a flash of talons, tumbling through the sky. Kids, playing their computer games, would look up in the sky and think their dreams had come to life. Anyone who tried to capture it on their camera phone would discover technology had no hold on such images; they could linger only in the viewer's mind.

He created thunderstorms that could wreak havoc, but contained them in spheres that hovered in the sky, oscillating fast, then slow. He was conscious of his breathing, of every cell in his body, in his brain, all of them engaged in what he was doing, all a part of it. He purposefully pushed himself, spending all that rage, turning it into this.

Of course, in time, the need for it started to ease. He wondered if reengineering asphalt so a black Ferrari had a harmless spinout would be okay. It could land in a nice cushiony mud wallow in the swamps. It was a sweet car, though. He'd rather have Mikhael thrown in that wallow, the expensive clothes and pricey haircut covered in sludge. But damaging the vehicle would really piss the gunrunner off.

The dragons now danced instead of fought, spiraled around one another in breathtaking display. Like mating dances. He wished Ruby were here to see it. He wished he'd known the first moment Ruby had crossed Mikhael's path. He'd have stopped it. He wished he could have stopped a lot of things.

Gunrunner. Yeah, right. What better cover for a Dark Guardian? Mikhael was his mirror image. A cop for the Light, a cop for the Dark, both serving the cause of balance, but Mikhael's side of it was incomprehensible to Derek. To his way of thinking, there was never enough Light force in the world, always too much Dark. Mikhael's opinion was entirely opposite. The only thing they apparently shared was the same taste in women.

Of course, if Ruby was tipping toward the Dark, that meant the bastard *had* actually done him a favor. He could have let her embrace the Darkness fully, but instead Mikhael had fed it rationed amounts, kept its hunger at bay to buy her more time. Time to get herself out of this mess. Time for Derek to get to her, to help.

Yeah, maybe Mikhael had been right, but if he was going to be looking for an FTD thank-you bouquet from Derek, he was more likely to lop off his testicles with a machete first.

The grim but wry thought told him the steam pressure was truly falling off now. He let the power ebb accordingly. It was then he realized he wasn't alone.

It wasn't a surprise. He hadn't expected he would be for

long, because there were forces in the universe that went on full alert when power like that was exercised, even in a chaotically controlled way as he'd just done it.

All the angels he'd met in his life had been male, and warriors. He didn't know if they were all like that, or those were just the kind his work involved. When he lifted his head, he saw a phalanx of about a dozen of them hovering in a semicircle above the dying funnel of his power, the shimmer around its lingering presence suggesting they'd added some reinforcement to containing it.

Crap. He dropped to a knee in automatic respect, bowing his head. "My apologies, my lords. Didn't mean to set off the fire alarms."

He knew the guy in front. Silver-white wings, solid dark eyes and dark hair, praises to the Goddess etched on his greaves and wrist guards. Derek suspected he was pretty high up in the echelon, a commander. At his raised brow, a silent request for more information, Derek straightened. He wasn't a diplomat, and didn't see the need to complicate it anyhow. "Woman trouble."

A slight quirk moved that firm mouth, and the angel lifted his left arm, drawing his attention to something below the wrist guard. A bracelet of braided golden-brown hair. So angels did know about love, and maybe how crazy it could drive a male. An intriguing thought.

She stands against the angels . . .

His lips pressed in a firm line, Derek gave the angel the image of Ruby, of Mikhael, and Mikhael's words.

You didn't ask angels for anything. They either helped or didn't, depending on their purpose in your business. But when the angel saw the image, his brow creased, making Derek's gut tighten. The commander glanced at the angel to his right, a burly, powerful-looking male carrying a long sword in a back harness, neatly fitted in the channel between his wings.

There was apparently some type of communication; then

the head angel looked back at Derek. His expression got even more serious as he gave Derek three chilling words, delivered direct to his mind.

Help her soon.

Nodding to Derek, he made a gesture to the others, and they turned, winging back up in the sky.

Derek watched them go. At different times in his life, they'd been there like this. Watching him, for sure, but more than that. Sometimes, like now, they felt like backup. Reinforcement and reassurance. Being so close to something so directly in the Lord and Lady's service was an even more leveling experience than the power surge. It cleared his mind, strengthened his resolve.

It was time to handle this, once and for all. He'd get this Great Rite out of the way, pick up Ruby's trail and deal with this. She was too damn important to him, but not only that. With the strength she had, both as a woman and a witch, he knew she could send that Darkness shrieking out of her like a scalded cat. So he was going to help her deal with whatever had put her between the rock and hard place and be whatever she needed him to be so she could blast out of it.

Help her soon.

I'm on it.

* 15 *

THE SUN SET OVER THE MARSH WITH A PAINTER'S dream of rose and gold hues, deep violet blue slashes of sky throughout. The breeze slid through the long grasses, creating hushed whispers. It was as if all the elements knew the coven's intent and, given the destabilizing forces of earlier in the day, they were pitching in to help restore order.

At least that was what Derek hoped. He adjusted the belt of his ritual robe, probably for the sixth time. The thing was designed to slide off easily, of course. He'd done Great Rites plenty of times, was completely clear on what it was and wasn't, so why he was having difficulty getting his head in the right place on this, he didn't know. Linda was an exemplary priestess. They'd channel Light to the fault line, reinforce it, get the job done.

But maybe because of the earlier revelations of the day, he hungered for it to be Ruby. He needed to touch her, needed to integrate their personal magic with the Joining as Lord and Lady. It would be more powerful that way; he knew it. Better for the fault line, better for her, better for all of them. He shouldn't have sent her away.

When the door opened behind him, he assumed it was Jocelyn, come to see if he was ready. Instead he faced Linda in her priestess garb, the pearl coronet representing the moon on her forehead, her black dress beaded with tiny bits of starlight. The garment fell in a simple line to her bare feet, but showed her as woman, clinging to unbound, generous breasts, the line of hip.

"Blessings of the Lord and Lady upon you this night," she said formally, giving him a bow.

"And you, my lady," he returned. It was unusual for the head priestess, the one who would be serving as the Lady in the Great Rite, to be here, talking to him beforehand, but since he could tell she had a specific purpose, he waited for her to gather her thoughts. She'd bowed her head, thinking, but now she lifted it, met his gaze again.

"I try to follow Their guidance in all things, Derek. And though your power and grasp of Their Will is greater than mine, on this night, I believe my path to be the correct one. I hope you will forgive me, if forgiveness is needed. Tonight I am ceding my position to another more appropriate for this Great Rite. She will await you in the circle."

Derek swallowed. "She was leaving."

"No. She merely thought you wanted her to leave."

"I don't."

"Which is why she is still here." A faint smile touched Linda's lips.

On impulse, he held out his hand. When Linda took it, he pulled her closer, wrapping his arms around her. "Thank you," he murmured.

"Oh." Surprised, Linda gave a little laugh, then returned the hug in full measure. "I like you quite a bit, Derek Stormwind. And though Ruby worries me, she worries me in my heart. That means she's good people. She needs you. She needs this. I think you both do."

When he released her, she took a seat in one of the chairs in the small sitting room, gestured him to do the same. "We have some time. Would you indulge me a question?"

"Linda, at this moment, you could probably ask me for anything."

"Well, instant weight loss and a rapid metabolism that allows me to eat all the chocolate cake I want springs to mind, but I think it's best you not reveal whether you have that power. You'd be mobbed by hordes of women."

He grinned, enjoying her. "You're soft in all the right places, Linda. I think you should give Sheriff Wassler a chance to find that out."

"And now I know a secret's not safe with Ruby. At least not from you." She smiled again, though. "From the beginning, I sensed there might be something between you and Ruby. But when I saw you together, it was obvious. The two of you are . . . timeless. That's the word that's stuck with me, so now I'm curious and nosy. Since we have a few minutes, and it might help you to get your mind in a different place, would you tell me about her, how you met?"

She was right. It would help. Now that he knew he'd be facing Ruby in that circle, he needed some time to adjust his thinking, be sure he was going there in the right frame of mind. Thinking how they started was probably a great way to do that.

"I met her when she was a little thing, five years old. I interacted with her mother on various matters, maybe three or four times a year, and after I met Ruby, I made sure that happened more often."

He was used to leaning forward, splaying his knees and clasping his hands loosely between them, the pose more in keeping with his restless energy level. Despite the fact the Great Rite was done sky-clad, without clothes, he didn't think it was good manners to flash Linda in the short robe. So he settled for rising and moving to the window, feeling better on his feet.

"That first visit, I conjured her a stuffed toy, a possum.

She smiled, this tiny expression, like a flower growing out of the crevice of a concrete sidewalk. Mary had another client there that day, and she said, right out, 'Mary, that's the first time I've ever seen her smile. How pretty she is.'" His expression darkened. "By the time I'd turned back around, Ruby had disappeared. She lived in Mary's shadow, and that's the way Mary liked it. The woman had as much business raising a child as a praying mantis. But I felt Ruby's potential in that first meeting, and something else."

He paused, deciding not to go there yet, wanting to give Linda a better order of things. "She almost never went to a regular school, was always schooled on the road as Mary was traveling." His lips curved. "But when she was eleven, she got the chance to go for a couple months. During one of my visits, she told me about a boy she liked. Billy Morris."

When Linda chuckled, Derek glanced at her. "What?"

"You remember his name."

Derek gave a wry smile. "Yeah, I do. I kept track of my competition, even when he was twelve years old and could knock a softball out of the park. Oh, and he climbed trees as well. But he jumped right out of his tree when Ruby fell on the playground, helped her up, asked her if she was okay. And she was in love."

Derek remembered how Ruby had told him about it. At first shy and hesitant, then more enthusiastically. When Mary had called out for her in that querulous voice that said she thought her daughter was getting too much attention, Ruby had cut herself off short. Derek recalled how she'd stopped at the door, looked back.

I don't love him like I love you. But I do like him a lot. That's okay, right?

"What did you say?"

Realizing he'd spoken aloud, he tuned back in to Linda. "I told her of course it was okay. And that if Billy didn't keep treating her right, to let me know because I'd kick his ass. She almost giggled, but not quite."

Derek turned to look at the priestess. "I know you've guessed I don't have an age line like most humans, so it's different for me, Linda. I didn't have any inappropriate feelings for her at that time. She was a child, and I thought of her as a child, saw her as a child. But my heart knew. In this quiet, understated way, it knew. And the thing is in what she said, so serious, too serious for an eleven-year-old, I knew the same subconscious part of her knew as well."

"Soul mates," Linda murmured the words, weighting them with reverent amazement.

He sighed. "It changed when she turned twenty. For various reasons, I hadn't been able to come see her for a couple years. At that time, it was the second longest stretch of time we'd been apart since we'd met. But at that point, it all just clicked. We were both aware of the change, but I didn't act on it, didn't push it. Those first couple years, I moved slow and cautious, because twenty is a time of a lot of changes, choices, and I never wanted to take anything away from her. Mary had done enough of that."

The bite of it was in his voice, but he quelled it. Tonight wasn't about that. "But she never . . . the way she looks at me, her heart in her eyes, it's that thing. *There you are. You're it.* And I feel the same way when I look at her. Always have. Even when I first met her. In a very non-creepy way, I promise."

Linda laughed, rose to lay her hand on his arm. "I get it. Nothing about you strikes me as the child molesting type."

At twenty-two, Ruby had lost patience with his gallantry. She met him at the door, stepped right into him, went up on her toes, and put her mouth against his. Their very first real lovers' kiss. He'd ended up taking it over, his arm banded around her waist, pushing her up against the doorframe, her toes practically off the ground. Everything he wanted to feel was in that kiss. When he finally lifted his head, she'd been breathless, flushed. A smile reached all the way into her eyes, made them shine. "Wow. That left Billy in the dust."

He'd realized something earth-shattering then, long past the age when he'd expected such life-altering surprises. When she smiled like that, it was a reaction she had toward him alone. Trust, faith. Joy. It swept him with humility and eternal gratitude. He'd found someone who touched his soul. He was no longer isolated and alone.

Coming back to the present, he knew that was what he'd missed most these past several years. He was going to get it back, because life wasn't worth going on without it.

"Better?" Linda asked.

He laid his hand over hers on his arm, squeezed. "Yeah. Better. Thanks."

When she stepped back, the mantle of priestess dropped over her again, though her gaze remained warm. "It's about time to go. The Lord and Lady wait. Best not to keep them. Come out when you're ready."

When she left him, Derek closed his eyes. The elemental energies were gathering, both Light and Dark. They knew what was happening here tonight and, as Linda had pointed out, best not to keep them waiting, either.

He left the cottage, a small bungalow in the woods near the main house, one a little more remote than the other guesthouses. After returning from his mountain, he'd materialized within it, spending the rest of his day there in meditation, gathering energy. It was why he hadn't realized Ruby was still on the property. He'd simply assumed she was gone because he'd been such a bastard about it.

As he emerged, half of the coven was there to precede him down to the ritual site. When Jocelyn came forward, he bent to accommodate her as she placed the antlered crown on his head, symbolizing the Horned God. Since it had been blessed, the energy settled over him like a mantle. As above, so below. Like the Lord Himself, Derek knew there was just one essential component missing.

Her. The Goddess.

As he walked down the path to the circle, the coven

members scattered flower petals ahead of him, singing chants praising the Lord, asking for His power and strength as a hunter, as a protector, to safeguard the fault line. When they emerged from the woods, he saw a similar procession making its way from Ruby's cottage. The petals they were scattering for her were shades of white, the color of the moon, whereas his were yellow, orange and red, the colors of the sun.

Linda and Christine waited at the North and South points of the circle. An altar had been set up in the center, a sturdy oak table with a wide blue cloth on it, the veil for the Goddess. He'd used a small bit of magic earlier in the day, after breakfast and before Mikhael, to move the heavy ritual object for the ladies. The metal of the wine chalice and jewels in the hilt of the athame blade caught the setting sunlight. The ritual flogger was spread out in a fan shape between them.

He'd given it all a cursory glance to make sure everything was in place, but then his gaze went back to Ruby. As he drew closer, he lingered on her hair, loose on her shoulders. The naturally streaked brown hair always reminded him of an animal's soft pelt. Then there were her eyes, the gray-green color with a thick dark ring around the iris. The impossibly delicate jawline and small, pink mouth. The generous bosom and slim legs, the toned body that was stronger than it looked.

She'd never stopped being beautiful to him, but since they'd reunited, her beauty had been overshadowed by weariness, anger, lies, betrayal. Tonight, the coven had truly prepared her, inside and out. She was balanced, calm, that inner power radiating through a cleansed aura, however temporary that was. Divine power enhanced a woman's beauty, but it also brought out what was already inside, since the Goddess was present in every female soul. He was looking not only at a vessel for the Goddess, but the woman he loved. He could sense the calm mixed with an accelerated heartbeat, anticipation of what they would do tonight, drawing energy down into their bodies for the ritual's purpose.

He held her gaze in his as she and her contingent approached the northern end of the circle, and he and his approached the south. As he stepped into the boundary, his group fanned out, taking their places, and Ruby's mirrored them. When the circle closed around them, he obeyed instinct, dropped to one knee and bowed his head to her.

She humbled him by doing the same. Lifting the hem of her silken robe so she wouldn't catch it beneath her bare knees, she pressed both of them into the ground, held herself there a moment before rising to her feet again. He helped her up, his fingers closing on her slim ones.

It was an effort to let her go, but Linda had initiated the calling of Quarters. As she reached the Fire point, two coven members came forward. He straightened his arms, allowing them to unbelt the robe and take it off his shoulders. Two coven members did the same to Ruby so they faced each other naked. Following the parameters of the ritual, they stepped forward, closing the distance until there was only a pace between them.

Jocelyn spread the oil over his shoulders then. The scent of jasmine, representing the Lady, came to his nostrils. Because it was associated with Artemis, as much warrior as woman, he had to press his lips against a smile. They couldn't have picked a more appropriate flower to represent the woman before him. They were using a blending of sandalwood oil on Ruby, a scent associated with the Great Lord.

"As the Lord and Lady are marked to belong to one another, so we mark you with those scents now, underscoring that their binding is what brings balance to all things," Linda said.

Ruby's face was open, the message in her expression clear. Tonight was for what they were meant to be. Vessels conducting energy, using the deep, soul-level bond between them to enhance and strengthen that effort, setting aside any of the obstacles that stood in the way of that bond outside the circle.

Was it possible to divide the two that way? He expected they were going to find out.

As the hands of the coven members moved over them, coating their skin with the slick oils, the chants building in rhythm and strength, he concentrated on the energies gathering in the circle, on the energies in her, his Lady, directly before him. Her lips parted as if she was feeling it, too. He barely paid attention as hands handled his genitals, oiled them as well, slid over his buttocks. The Great Rite wasn't about that. It was more intense than simple lust. Desire was sacred here, an offering to Them.

The aroma of the oil was dizzying, capable of taking them to a different plane of thought together. The attendants had returned to the circle, and now Derek knelt once more before Ruby, closing that last distance between them. Bending, he began the Five Fold kiss. Though Linda could offer the chant, Derek spoke, telling the priestess he was taking the option of saying it himself.

"Blessed be Thy feet, which brought you to this Circle." When his lips brushed the tops of Ruby's bare feet, he smelled jasmine and soap.

"Blessed be Thy knees, which kneel at the Sacred Altar of the Lord and Lady, a vessel of Their Will." When she quivered, he remembered her knees were a little ticklish.

"Blessed be Thy womb, without which Life is not possible." He stopped there a moment, his throat thickening. At this point, Ruby was supposed to straighten her arms out to her sides, like a bird taking flight, but she touched his head, her fingers whispering through his hair. He felt the hitch in her abdomen, the great emotion binding them together.

He straightened onto his knees, brushed his mouth over each of her breasts. "Blessed be Thy breasts, which nourish us all."

As he rose, his feet aligned on the outside of hers. Her

eyes followed him, gray-green color still vibrant. He spoke the next words against her lips. "Blessed be Thy mouth, which will utter the Truth we need to do Your Will."

Normally, she would be laid back on the altar at this juncture. Instead, she made a gesture to hold back the coven attendants. She knelt, and began to give him the Five Fold kiss as well.

"Great Lord, Blessed be Thy feet, which bring and keep you at My side, through storm and lull." He closed his eyes as her mouth touched his feet. Power vibrated through her voice, shuddering through him. It was the Lady, as well as Ruby, and the rest of the circle felt it as well. The Lord's energy within him stirred and strengthened, responding to it. He could feel it coming, that point where he wouldn't know where he ended and the Lord began, and it would be all one and the same, regardless.

"Blessed be Thy knees, which kneel to Me, unashamed of Your Love and Devotion.

"Blessed be Thy seed, which makes new life and rebirth possible." Just as he had with her, she paused at this point, her mouth holding against his semierect shaft, not a provocative tease, but a reverent homage to the Lord's virility it represented. The life it had given her.

"Blessed be Thy heart, which never fails, even in utter Darkness." She was standing now, her lips pressed to his chest. When she tilted her head up for the final kiss, he bent to her, because of the difference in their heights.

"Blessed be Thy mouth, which gives comfort and strength in its Truths."

A brief, gentle touch. Then Ruby stepped back, her gaze focused and intent on his. As two coven members came forward again, she lifted her arms straight out to her sides. They used them to lower her to her back on the altar table.

Linda had removed the blue cloth and now she laid it on Ruby, the translucent fabric settling over her with the weight of a feather. Ruby stretched out her arms and legs, forming the Pentacle symbol as Derek knelt between her legs once again. Linda blessed the athame and Christine the chalice. Christine gave Ruby the chalice, and Derek leaned over her, placing the blade in the cup.

"As the Lord and Lady are joined, so, too, are this cup and athame, representing what is necessary for Life and the Light to continue."

The coven members returned to their spaces. Several of them held small drums, and began to play them, tapping out a primal, slow beat. Linda started a new round of chanting, this one to raise energy, condense it in the circle.

"Woman is the altar," Linda said, her voice rising. "She is the sacred point in the Universe, the sacred hearth and home, while the Lord is the hunter, motion and change. We thank them for their presence here tonight, within these vessels of High Priest and Priestess, to strengthen the forces of Light that maintain balance, that allow us to do Your Will."

Christine had taken a position behind Derek, and he closed his eyes as the scourge hit his bare back, the oil enhancing the sting, giving it a wet slap. Christine had a strong arm, and while some pain was part of it, it wasn't the main purpose. It was the focus, the repetition, in line with the drumbeats. Ruby's scourging would have happened earlier, for the High Priestess stepped into the circle already prepared as a willing receptacle for the Goddess.

Ruby's gaze never wavered, but Derek saw the shimmer of power, felt it coil around her, and around him. When the scourging stopped, he wasn't even aware of it. Taking the edge of the blue cloth, he watched the transparent cloth slide below her eyes, over her lips, the valley of throat and rise of breast. He handed it to a waiting attendant. The Lord's power was within him, his cock hard and ready. Kneeling between her spread knees on the cool rock, he laid his hands on her thighs. He could see deep into the Universe in that gray-green gaze, and knew she could do the same in his.

The energy was rising, spiraling. He slid into her slow, gradual, the magic of it taking hold of them both. The Great Rite was like being in the direct, pure flow of the Lady's Love, the Lord's Strength, held by both of them even as they acted as their divine instruments. Sometimes, like now, it was hard to remember they were anything else, anything separate. The coven would do the energy focus and release. Their only job was to get lost in it, go where the Lord and Lady wanted them to go. They were still here, Derek and Ruby, but they were more than that as well, a part of something so large, they were swept away by it, floating in a sphere of gold, gray and rose, where it was just them.

He thrust, withdrew, feeling the energy cycle and spiral tighter, the focus of the coven pulling it toward that fault line. He cupped Ruby's face in both hands, seeing her and the Divine twined together. Her body responded to each thrust, her focus within just like his, feeling that energy, both knowing what was needed as High Priest and Priestess. However, the bond that was between the two of them, that rose up pure and strong now, was part of it, undeniable.

Ruby's body lifted to him, power rolling through her, the continuity and strength. Her eyes . . . He could get lost in those eyes forever. All the answers were there, and the answers were in stillness. He knew that, hadn't found that answer on his mountain, but he found it here in Ruby's eyes, in the Lady's eyes. As his climax built, and hers did as well, he gave himself over to that, let his mind go, surrendered, as he felt Ruby do the same.

At the top of the spiral, bodies close to offering their final power release, the climax, they were unable to resist their innate response to each other any longer. Then they felt the coven set the energy loose, sweeping them away in the same tide.

Ruby's throat arched as she cried out, her fingers pressing hard into the stone as she tried to maintain the position prescribed by the ritual. Instinct told him to go about it differently. Catching her legs up on his hips, he encouraged her to wrap her arms on his shoulders, increased his thrusts, driven by his own powerful orgasm.

As a sorcerer, he felt his energy and hers join the coven's, all of that power targeted toward the fault line, a concentrated flood of power. As the channel for the great Lord, as Derek, he was all sensation. The drumbeat vibrated through him; the backwash of the spiral's release rushed over him.

And then, everything disappeared except the woman beneath him, a tornado wind sweeping them away from the current plane.

THIS WAS WHAT THE GREAT RITE WAS LIKE, WHEN DONE with one's soul mate. He'd heard that said, only he'd never experienced it before. He and Ruby were in a world of their own, their souls unfolded to each other, a vital part of the magic they'd done.

He was aware of Ruby as part of the Lady, though he couldn't see her solid form anymore. He thought he might be drifting in the Lady's consciousness, but then he saw a small sphere of light. Like a will-o'-the-wisp, that sense of a passing soul. Moving toward it with only his mind's desire to do so, he circled it, drew closer.

There was something within the sphere. And as it became aware of him, it turned, a hazy form. A hand reached out, touching the convex side, like the inhabitant of a snow globe reaching out to the world outside its perfect shelter.

Deep shock jolted through him as he touched the other side. He couldn't feel that hand, but it didn't matter. He was rocked down to the foundation of his soul.

Great Lord and Lady.

The Truth he was seeing overwhelmed him. He was rendered mindless, speechless, purposeless. He could only stare at that tiny, utterly miraculous, utterly horrifying magic. The magic Ruby held deep in her subconscious.

DURING THE CLOSING RITE, LINDA DIPPED THE ATHAME once more in the cup of wine, blessed the cakes she'd had ready and passed both around for grounding and to reinforce the ritual. Thanks to Ruby's tutelage, she was fairly sure the Great Rite had worked. The fault line was fair pulsing with energy now, no hint of weakness or the Dark coming through. She'd never experienced such a wave of power, the strength of what had come from Derek and Ruby's Joining. Was it too much to hope that they might have squelched the threat entirely?

Looking between Derek and Ruby, she knew she'd have to ask that question another time. Some covens turned their backs during the actual intercourse of the Great Rite, or cut an opening in the circle and departed until that part was over. That hadn't been an issue for Derek or Ruby. It was what was between them now that she could tell required privacy.

Since Miriam was in the hospital, Linda had Alice, who represented the Maiden for this ritual, to cut a symbolic hole in the circle, then close it after the departing coven. They left Ruby and Derek facing each other.

From some of the backward glances, Linda could tell she wasn't the only coven member who detected something momentous hovering in the air between them. Since whatever that thing was seemed potentially catastrophic, Linda added another prayer to the circle's power before she followed the other women up to the kitchen area.

May the Lord and Lady guide you both.

* 16 *

DEREK BENT, RETRIEVED THEIR ROBES FROM WHERE they'd been carefully folded under the table. He draped them over his arm. "Want to go rinse off in Linda's freshwater pool? It's heated."

Ruby nodded. Every inch of her skin felt alive, tingling. She was still a little dazed. Parts of her that had been sealed up for so long had opened for a short time, albeit cautiously. She didn't want to think about anything, so splashing around with Derek sounded good. And he was being so gentle and easy with her, offering her his arm so they walked together, naked as Adam and Eve. When they got to the gravel path that led to the pool, he simply bent and scooped her up, cradling her in his arms.

"The gravel doesn't bother your feet?"

"Nope." And it didn't appear to, the way he was crunching over it, as matter-of-fact as if he wore his boots.

She slid a finger through the oil lingering on his shoulder. It felt good, to touch him that way. Nothing more, nothing less. Just quiet and good. "You were right. That worked really well. I think anything's going to have a hard time getting through the fault line. Maybe we should have done this the first day. Would have saved me a lot of teaching."

Though she wondered if she would have trusted him as much at the beginning of the week, when she was still dealing with the potential threat of him coming back into her life. She still worried about that, but like always, for good or bad, her nerves just seemed to settle when Derek Stormwind was around regularly.

"They'll still need your lessons to keep it that way. Things tend to happen at certain times for a reason." Still carrying her, he took the steps down into the pool. When they reached the deeper portion, beyond where her feet could touch, he let her legs down. She kept her arm crooked over his neck, while he kept his at her waist. Since he was looking down at her with those serious blue eyes, the firm mouth, she couldn't help but trace his lips. He kissed her, biting the finger lightly and making her smile.

"You're being awfully quiet," she noted. "Just the ritual fallout?"

"Hmm." Picking up a washcloth in a basket left at the poolside, he wet it. Then he began to wipe the oil from her skin in easy, massaging strokes. "No talking right now. Let's just do this."

No objection there, though a frisson of uneasiness stirred at his laconic reply. Taking up another cloth, she began to wipe his shoulders and chest. Of course they got in each other's way, all tangled, and it made her smile. It even made him smile, though he kept that intently thoughtful look. Rituals brought a lot of things out. Usually good things, but still things requiring a deeper level of contemplation, so she tried to leave it at that.

Tossing the washcloth to the side, he cupped the back of her head, tilted it back and settled his lips over hers, his body pressed flush against her much as it had been during the Five Fold kiss and afterward, when he lay upon her. She made a noise in her throat. In the wake of the Great Rite, desire was a lazy, slow river, organic and deep, something to take at a steady, pleasurable pace.

His hands gripped her face, held her as she held his shoulders. She twined her legs about him anew, and his cock was brushing her sex, the seam of her buttocks. Before she could angle him into her body with a flexible undulation of her hips, he cinched the arm he had at her waist, holding her close to him. His cock teased those tissues with a slow rub as he kissed her, so thoroughly and long that she was drugged with it, lost and hazy in the sheer, deep pleasure.

When he pulled back, he loosened her hands on his shoulders, made her lie back, float in the water with her arms out to the sides, much like she'd been on the altar, only here she had to tighten her stomach muscles to keep herself level. He studied her body, gaze coursing over her throat and mouth, her breasts, down the slope of her abdomen.

"Close your eyes," he said.

When she did, he took them both under, dropping to his knees and bringing her down with him, sliding his hand up her back so she was straddling him on the pool bottom. It was there he penetrated her, taking her all the way to the hilt. Because of the pool lights, she was able to look at him beneath the water, that wavering impression of his face, jaw muscles tight as he experienced the same pleasure she did, in this silent, still environment.

When he brought them up again, she clutched his shoulders, wanting him to thrust, but instead he pulled out. Turned her around, and with an effortless move that took her breath, he lifted her and slid back in at the proper angle from behind. Bringing her back against her body with a hand on her throat and his other hand low, just above her mound, he kept himself deep inside despite the precarious angle. She wanted to lean forward, wanted him to be able to drive into her, but he held her there, making small, incremental movements that caused her to squirm, tiny, pleasurable shocks going through her.

"Derek."

"Sshhh. Just feel it, Ruby. Feel what I am to you. Trust me. Relax."

She couldn't relax, not with him doing that, but she relaxed her need to try to direct things, instead experiencing the incredible sensations he was giving her. There were definite advantages to being with a guy who was centuries old, because he'd had lots of time to practice. The male libido never faded away, God bless it, as long as the body was strong enough to sustain it. And Derek was all power in this moment.

His fingers slipped over her clit, massaged, and she cried out. Her back arched, her breasts thrusting out, needing attention as well. The water lapped over them, increasing the sensation of friction over her nipples. She struggled instinctively, wanting more, wanting to go over, but abruptly he stilled again, his fingers a maddening pressure on her tender tissues, his hand locked in a gentle squeeze on her throat, holding her in place.

"Ruby . . . take me to our daughter."

She'd been on the cusp of one of those long climaxes like the endless stretch and twist of a rubber band. Now it came back with a snap, stinging her with reality. She wanted to move, but of course Derek had her pinned like a butterfly, his cock deep inside of her, that immovable hand upon her throat. A vivid reminder that she could run from him, but she could never resist him.

"No." She shook her head, almost violently. "No. You promised not to read me."

"It happened during the Great Rite. There was nothing I could do about it. The knowledge just unfolded in front of me."

"Then pretend you didn't see it, because no. I won't."
With a burst of manic strength, she shoved away, breaking
their connection, and backed across the pool. He turned to
face her but didn't move, those blue eyes dangerously still
on her face.

"You have to, Ruby. She's my daughter, too."

"You won't understand." She made it to the pool edge,
lifted herself out. Wanting her robe, she snatched at the
bundle he'd left there. When she threw it on, she realized
she'd picked up Derek's. The robe came past her knees, the
sleeves flopping over her wrists. She didn't care. She began
to retreat. Damn gravel path. She picked herself over it, tried
to bolt when he came up behind her. When he caught her
wrist, her reaction was instinct, power sizzling through her
skin, sparking off his palm. Instead of letting her go, he
countered. She cried out as the shock jolted through her
nerve centers, forcing her to one knee.

With a curse, he caught her up, carried her back to the
smoother concrete collar around the pool. When he let her
back down, he held on to her wrist, his expression dark.
"You try that again, I will wear your ass out," he said. "I
can get a lot rougher, and you can't stand against me, Ruby.
Now that I know you have a taste for rougher, I'm not concerned about being gentle."

It wasn't like Derek to be cruel, but she had enough sense
to understand why he was struggling with his temper. She'd
been lying to him. He'd known that for a while, obviously,
but now he'd seen the truth behind the lie. She didn't blame
him for being angry with her. Hell, she wouldn't blame him
for kicking the shit out of her if she pushed him to it. She
thought she might prefer that to the alternative, so she stubbornly locked her jaw, closing her arms around herself.

"You want me to rip it from your mind?" When he bent
close, she closed her eyes tight, locking her arms even harder
around herself. His breath was hot on her face. "Ruby, cat's
out of the bag. It's time to come clean."

"You do what you have to do. If you're that much of a bastard."

"Ruby, for God's sake, she's my child, too."

"She's safe," she burst out in a near scream, startling him. "She's happy. Leave her be. Just leave her be. Let her stay that way. *You left*. You left. You didn't care."

"You told me to go," he shouted back. "In every way, you made it clear you didn't want me around. You used a fucking soul spell on me."

"You weren't supposed to listen! You never listen. You always railroad over everything I say or do, and that one time, I needed you to be that sexist bastard, to be stronger than the magic I used, and you weren't. You didn't."

Derek didn't know whether to laugh bitterly or scream himself, but then she tried to bolt again. When he snagged her sleeve, she came out of the robe, but it hung her up enough that she tripped in her attempt to get away from him. She went down with a cry.

The gravel would cut her knees, so he reacted on instinct, lunging forward. He controlled the descent, so that her knee landed on the top of his foot. As he knelt behind her, holding her between his thighs, he wanted to be furious. But all of a sudden, he couldn't think of whipping her around to face him, shaking her to make her listen. Instead, that small sphere of light was in the forefront of his mind, the tiny hand pressed against it.

He wrapped his arms around her, wouldn't let her shake him off. He found himself murmuring to her despite his helpless rage, his frustration with her, him and all of it.

"Okay. I'm here, baby. I'm here. I should have been here and I wasn't. Please tell me. Tell me what happened."

She was crying, having trouble breathing. He thought she was trying to speak, but then he realized she was trying to sing. That same little lullaby he'd heard her croon to herself a couple times now. She was trying to calm herself down with it. He picked it up, hummed it with her, stroking her hair, cursing his ineptitude for dealing with this, but in truth, he didn't know if there was a proper way to handle it. He couldn't remain detached, in control, and he didn't think she needed that at the moment anyway.

He set his jaw, thinking about what she needed, what was required. It might be the wrong way to go, but if he was wrong, it could be rectified fairly quickly. Holding tight to her and the robe, he concentrated, and took them somewhere else.

THEY MATERIALIZED IN HER GUN SHOP, DARK AND locked up for her absence. He'd had them appear in her back stockroom and repair workshop, not wanting to take the chance some late-night pedestrians might be walking by the storefront. Seeing two naked people kneeling on the floor would be unsettling, like the opening of a Terminator movie.

A glance around showed him it was a good choice, because the back workshop was also the way to the upper level, where she kept her living quarters. Lifting her in his arms, he tried not to be concerned that she was still humming that lullaby in broken tones. It was as if she hadn't noticed them disappearing from one place and reappearing in another, hundreds of miles away. He carried her up that staircase, a quick focus and tiny frisson of sparks unlocking the door to her apartment.

When he kicked it closed behind him, he saw a one-bedroom with a kitchenette, bathroom and small sitting room. The Ruby he'd known had loved flowers, knick-knacks, had crystals hanging in her windows for both their aesthetic as well as their magical properties. The girl loved a sparkly. Colorful pillows and throws had always punctuated her living space.

Except for some small detritus—a coffee cup left in the dish drainer, the half-open door of the closet revealing an amazingly small amount of clothing and shoes for a woman, there was nothing of Ruby here. By the bed were a couple paperbacks on magical theory, some gun catalogs, and a no-frills radio.

It was like looking at a halfway house for a released convict. The convict didn't accumulate much because she didn't really believe she was out of prison.

He let her feet down. She'd quieted, and though she was still trembling, she seemed calmer. As he shrugged into his robe, belted it, he moved to the closet. A thin ritual robe wouldn't be warm enough for her. His throat constricted as he found the most accessible article of clothing, hung on a hook instead of a rack amid the others. It was one of his long-sleeved shirts, obviously worn often.

Bringing it back to her, he threaded her arms into it. It fell to her knees and had long sleeves he rolled up for her so they were between elbow and wrist. She stared at his chest, her tawny brown hair falling forward over her pale cheek as he dressed her. It made her look young, whereas when she lifted her eyes, they were impossibly old, even more ancient than himself.

Taking her hands, he guided her over to the bed. Laid her down on it and himself behind her. He opened his robe, draped it over her and pulled her into the warmth of his naked body. He crooked his knees up behind her. As he did, his still-firm cock nudged her buttocks. Following instinct, he gripped her thigh, a mute command. With a tiny sigh, she let her thighs loosen and he slid back into her, lodging himself deep, holding her there on him while she quaked at the intimacy of that connection, what it symbolized.

"I'm here," he said softly. "I'm a part of you. Tell me, Ruby. Close your eyes and tell me. Tell both of us."

It took a long time, and he had to ask a couple more times, but he made sure he did it gently, a quiet sound in the dark room, like a request from her own mind.

"Eight months," she whispered at last. He had his arm under her head, and her hand crept into his palm, her fingers tangling with his own. "She was eight months old. I could feel her, moving inside of me. Sometimes I think she laughed. I didn't think a baby could laugh in the womb, but with every month, my joy having her there just grew. I don't know if I made her laugh, or she gave me the joy, or if they fed each other, but it didn't matter. I could feel her soul, Derek. She was inside of mine. Still is."

That uneasiness stirred again, but he left it alone for now. His fingers tightened on hers, a silent appeal to go on. He didn't want to get too demanding about it, didn't want to do anything to make her falter now that she'd begun. Though in truth there was a part of him that didn't want to hear, didn't want to know.

"Her energy sparked mine. All those years where the magic was a dull flicker, an unpredictable flash . . . all those years of Mother telling me I wasn't gifted with any power at all. Then, all of a sudden, I had this *flood*. It frightened me, the strength of it, because I could tell it wasn't hers. She somehow brought mine to life."

The emotionally abused child became a mother, and the mother discovered a tiger in herself to protect her own child. It made perfect sense to Derek.

"But I screwed up. Because I was scared, I didn't do anything with it. I kept a lid on it, didn't tell anyone. I was too intimidated to understand how to manage it."

"Oh, Ruby."

"My mother told me, Derek." Ruby twisted her head to look up into his face, so close to her own. "She said if I ever discovered any natural ability, I needed to hide it, ignore it, keep it dormant. Otherwise it would come to tragedy. She said she saw it."

"You know why I didn't like your mother, Ruby?" He managed it in measured tones, but he gave her the edge of his anger because it was on her behalf. "She was like a cop who abuses power. There's nothing worse, when the person who's all about protection, justice, someone you should be able to trust implicitly, betrays that trust and cloaks it behind the badge."

"But she knew things—"

"Yes, she was a great Seer. She was never wrong. And because she was never wrong, she lied to you, told you things that weren't true because what she truly saw was that you would surpass her."

Ruby stared up at him. Derek touched her face, caressed the line of her cheek, still tracked with drying tears. "Your mother was a great Seer, but she was a competitive, selfish bitch who feared being eclipsed by her own daughter. Most parents, they hope their children will go further and be even more than they are, because that's part of a parent's love. She couldn't get there. She was too afraid of being forgotten." He bared his teeth in a humorless smile. "It's one of the reasons I do my best never to think of her. It's my small spite, but there you are. I love you too much to ever think well of her."

She swallowed against his hold. "You aren't going to love who I am after this."

He made a tiny movement that lodged him deeper inside her, made her bite her lip, her fingers tighten on his arm. "Ruby, if I was dead as a post and dismembered and ingested by a Grat demon, I would still love you. Keep talking."

The combination of devotion and impatient tone almost made her smile. He felt the tentative curve of her lips against his biceps as she turned her head away again. But he also felt her fear, and something far darker, ready to fight against whatever his reaction was. So he kept it easy, realizing he might be dealing with a wild animal. A wild animal with unpredictable powers.

"The magic was so powerful, I didn't realize it would be noticed, even if I kept it locked up inside me. I was bringing home groceries one night . . ."

Cold gathered in his vitals, remembering Raina's words. *She was thrown on his windshield, with fireworks . . .* He tightened his arm around her, cupping her breast to stroke the outer curve, soothing and pleasuring, reminding her he was here.

"I was carrying two sacks of groceries. Fresh fruit. The market had mangoes, and I was excited about that. I was remembering when you and I had mangoes and wine, a picnic on the floor of my very first apartment."

"I remember." Though Mary had left her nothing, Ruby had been thrilled when she was making just enough on her Witches R Us salary to set herself up in her own place. He would have helped her out financially in a heartbeat, but he'd understood the significance of the moment for her, a value that couldn't be measured in dollars.

"I wanted to re-create that night. I wasn't drinking wine, of course, but I'd gotten one of those sparkling grape juices. I was going to spread a blanket out on the floor of my place, light candles, pretend you were there."

Ruby slid her other hand over his on her breast, gripped it. It pressed her nipple farther into his heated palm, increased the sensation of her bare body against his, the fact he was still inside her. He could tell she didn't want to go forward with the memory, so instead she gave them both the gift of her imaginings that night. Before everything changed.

"I was so big then, but I knew you'd want to see me all naked. And I'd be reluctant about it, uncertain, and then you'd make me feel so beautiful, because you always do. And Derek, at that point, you're just so . . . I wanted you so badly. I was imagining you stroking my body, altered as it was, your hands between my legs."

She paused another moment, then continued. "I was walking along the sidewalk, having this great fantasy, mixing it with reality. Since you weren't there, I'd be doing the stroking, but I'd close my eyes, pour the wine over my breasts, feel the tingling over my nipples . . . Though I missed you so, in that moment, it was like I was completely alive. I knew you were coming back; it was just a matter of time. That's what I kept telling myself."

Another swallow, and tears clogged her words. "I knew you were probably somewhere you couldn't talk to me. You'd done that before, and I always tried not to worry, because even with bumps and bruises, you always came back to me. So I imagined your face when you saw me. I knew you'd be so happy. I could just see it. I'd set up a nursery, but I knew you'd want to help me decorate it even more when you got back. We'd put all these amazing things in it, color wheels and crystals, chimes like birdcalls . . . Great big stuffed animals and blankets so soft Theo would tug them out of the crib and steal them. We'd curl up on them with her. Even though we'd never talked about having kids, I knew you'd be so happy about her."

She'd overcome herself, he could tell, her throat thick on those final words. He wasn't sure he could have spoken louder than a husky whisper himself. So he spoke against her ear, giving her something back, something that might give her the strength to continue, to share the secret that she feared.

"You know me better than anyone, Ruby. In all my centuries of living, I've never . . . gotten someone pregnant. Eventually I figured it was the price of what I was, the power I carried." He pressed his lips to her temple. "I know there are men who don't think about it, don't care about it. But sometimes I watched kids playing in the park with their dads . . . and I'd ache for it."

A tear rolled over his hand. "Never . . . in centuries?" Her voice was so soft.

"Never." And he let the import of that sink in. He'd never bothered with protection once he'd figured it out, centuries ago. He was immune to STDs; nor could he convey them. So it said something pretty significant, that it had been with her that he'd finally conceived.

The woman who meant more to him than any other ever had.

"Have courage, girl," he said roughly, bringing her closer, inside and out. "I'm here."

"And the whole Grat demon thing . . ."

"I meant it. Though I might throw you over for Marilyn Monroe. If she was alive. I always had kind of a thing for her."

"Ass," she said, her voice muffled because she'd turned it into his forearm. He lifted a brow.

"Did you just wipe your nose on my arm?"

"I was sniffling."

He growled at her, rocked her back and forth, making her catch her breath at that sensation, but then he slid free, tucked himself intimately between her buttocks, recognizing they were about to get into a darker area. He didn't push her, but he sensed when she quieted again. He stilled as well, waiting on her.

"I could feel her laughing inside me, seeing what I was imagining, that great big dog playing tug-of-war with her and her blanket. Then . . . he came. Asmodeus."

His hands reflexively clenched on her, hard enough that she quivered. He made himself ease the touch, though Derek remembered the way she'd reacted when he spoke the demon's name in the gun shop, that first day. It had made something in her blacken into a rage so strong, a hatred so visceral, it was an actual hunger.

"He sensed I was . . . unprotected, inexperienced. I was a veritable vat of brimming power, lacking any confidence or skills. I might as well have slapped a tag on myself that said 'Christmas came early.' He wanted that power, wanted to drain it from me. But then something happened. Rage.

"I felt so much rage, Derek. She was afraid. It was as if she knew . . ." Her voice faltered, then strengthened. "And I was her mother. I was supposed to protect her. That rage overflowed and I fought him on instinct, no idea what the hell I was doing. I got lucky."

Her tone suggested just the opposite. "It knocked him on

his heels. In hindsight, I realize he hadn't expected any resistance at all, so he hadn't projected with any real strength. I vanquished him back through the opening he'd come from. I fought him, Derek. I fought a demon."

It terrified him, just imagining her standing alone against something like Asmodeus, whether he'd done a lazy, half-assed projection or not. But she'd done it. His girl had done it. At a terrible, terrible cost.

"He hurt me . . . injured me. The trauma . . . She died inside me, Derek." Her voice trembled anew. "I was connected to her soul, hers inside of mine, and I felt her die."

Holy Goddess. A mother might feel a fetus die in the womb, which was terrible enough, but a witch, with her enhanced powers and connection to the Earth . . . It would have felt like her very soul was being ripped out. Especially since it seemed the child had possessed nascent abilities, abilities that had very likely twined their essences together, in a manner similar to twins, but different. The baby had been nourished not only on her mother's body, but on her soul as well.

"He'd thrown me into the street before I sent him back to the Underworld. When I rolled off the windshield of a car, I was lying on the pavement, holding my stomach. Crying, feeling that life slipping away. She'd been laughing, Derek, and now she was afraid. She could feel herself slipping away, and she was reaching for me, crying for me. I couldn't let her go. I had to protect her," she repeated.

She'd studied so much, growing up in her mother's shadow. He'd been in and out of her life enough during those years to remember how her academic interests had blossomed on their own, until she'd become a veritable encyclopedia of all things arcane. Not just for dutiful recitation. She comprehended it at an amazing level, made connections far beyond her years. She'd have impressed Roger Bacon. In fact, he saw quite a few similarities between Ruby Night Divine and the learned monk who'd explored the scientific aspects of sorcery.

Early wizards, such as himself, had come before order and science was applied to nature. He'd been part of both worlds, the instinct and chaos that was felt intuitively, that required genetic acumen, and the later world, where magic became about understanding the patterns and lines, the order in Nature.

Her unborn child had helped her unlock her inherited acuity, and her years of study had already been there, ready to marry it. Apparently that night, that union had occurred. Her vast knowledge had unfolded like a sky of constellations in her head, while her intuition had been the navigator, knowing exactly which course to take among the hazards.

"I pulled from the elements around me. I'm sorry to say that night I didn't care if I was draining them. That didn't matter to me."

Raina had said that was mentioned in the police report, how the trees lining the streets were dead, birds limp and fallen as if they'd hit windows. A water main busted, a storefront on fire. She'd assumed whatever had attacked Ruby had done it. They hadn't considered it was Ruby herself.

"I put her somewhere secure. And just like that . . . I wasn't pregnant. Not a mark on me. No stretched skin, my breasts suddenly just back to the way they were before I was pregnant . . ." Her voice broke. "It was horrific, wrenching, like it had never happened."

Which was why the medical report didn't indicate a pregnant woman, Derek realized. It was a remarkable piece of magic. One that would have required as much Dark magic as Light to pull off, because reverting a near-term pregnant woman back to her pre-impregnated state was about as adverse to Nature as any magical act could be. He held the thought, even though the significance of that told him she was about to head into even more troubled waters.

"I simply shifted her into a different kind of womb," she said softly. "I wove a temporary illusion so she thought she was still there. I hummed a lullaby, wove it in with her, so she'd hear it whenever she needed it. I hoped that would hold her until I got out of the hospital, and it did. Once I got out, I went to work. That's when I brought it all together, figured it all out. How to embrace my powers, how to twist together Dark and Light in a unique way. And I used it not only to give her a permanent Paradise, but to find my potential at last."

She looked up at him again. "My mother, you, Raina . . . You all had the fireworks *and* the knowledge for so long. When I started embracing that power, it was the first time I'd ever felt the fireworks."

He knew what she was talking about. It had been a long, long time for him, but he still remembered, as an apprentice, those glorious moments when experience and academic knowledge came together and became something tangible, useful, building until it became expertise.

"I've made sure she's in Heaven, Derek," she concluded softly. "Not the kind where there's doubt whether or not it truly exists, or a temporary way station to a new life. She's in a place where she'll never be afraid, never know anything but love and beauty. Every day is something different, but it's always sunshine, happiness. Laughter."

Holy Goddess. He repeated the mantra to himself, even more fervently. Ruby had created a soul prison.

* 17 *

DARK SORCERERS KNEW HOW TO CREATE SOUL PRISONS, the ultimate torment to any living thing caught in them, and they fed off the energy of that fear. Ruby had done something impossible, and just as dangerous. She'd reversed it. Her daughter's soul was in a soul prison, but one created to give her never-ending happiness and peace. The price of twisting the magic was that it was feeding off Ruby's soul.

The knowledge required to do such a thing was extraordinary, unprecedented. His heart was breaking, for several different reasons. When he turned her, she anticipated him, resisting, clinging to his arm. "No."

He forced her to face him, with gentle but ruthless hands. "Ruby, the baby would have returned to the Hall of Souls. She would have been loved."

"No." She shook her head. "That's what they always want us to believe."

"You know it's possible that Asmodeus's touch infected you with this kind of despair, that it's still clouding your viewpoint."

"There is nothing of him in me," she shot back. "My child died, Derek. That's enough despair for the whole world. That bastard doesn't need to do a thing to add to it. And what if they do care for her in the Hall of Souls? Eventually, they have to let her be born, to another set of parents. Can they protect her? Will they love her? This is my baby. Mine to care for. Because of me, she will always experience happiness, contentment and no fear—"

"But it's not real, Ruby. It's not living. Her soul never has the chance to rejoin the flow of divine energy and try life again."

"Who cares? Why is that so important? Because some divine power says so? Well, fuck them. They weren't there when I needed them, and neither were you. No one has ever been there for me; no one has ever been willing to give up or sacrifice a single bit of themselves for me. Maybe I've done nothing to deserve it, but a child always does, and my child is going to have that. Forever."

She was out of the bed, facing him with hands clenched, her eyes wild and feral, mouth curled in an ugly, determined line. He rose from the bed then. Fuck it. He didn't usually take advantage of such a mundane magic, but he concentrated, brought his clothes to him from where he'd left them in the cottage. Yanking on his jeans, he shrugged into his shirt, facing her in a better position than bare-ass naked.

"This magic is a death wish. No one can interact with Dark forces for long without being pulled into full servitude to it. You've been avoiding that fate by using your soul as bargaining chips. And bravo—you've turned yourself into a formidable witch, possessed of great abilities. Abilities that will serve no one and nothing in the end, because they'll be consumed in the fires of the Underworld like popcorn."

"You need to leave. This is no longer your concern." But the desperation in her voice said she knew that wasn't going to happen.

"Ruby, I can't let you do this. You know I can't."

"So the sorcerer steps forward. The *cop*." She spat it out. "It's always that side of you that takes precedence, isn't it? You'll never simply be the man who loves and supports me. Fine. You want to try, you try. But you will have to kill me to do it. If you have the balls to do it, to kill the woman you claim to love, then do it."

"Damn it." He seized her shoulders before she could evade him. "Ruby, you can't see; you're too mired in it. This is wrong. And if telling you that, forcing you to face it, makes you hate me, then that's the price I'll pay for loving you . . . and for loving her. Because I would have loved decorating a nursery with you. I would have loved knowing the very second you were carrying her. I hate like hell I was trapped in a Fae world, unable to be there for you. I hate it enough that I'm willing to change everything in my life, right now, to make sure I'm always there for you going forward, but there is no moving forward unless you let her go. You're killing yourself, Ruby, destroying your soul. Worse, you're keeping her from having the life she should have."

"Who. Fucking. Cares." She screamed it, loud enough that she could probably be heard on the street, if it wasn't deserted this time of night. He saw it rise again in her eyes, that Darkness, the fear and despair that fed it. "What does life bring you except pain, rejection, hatred, loneliness—"

"Love." He brought her to her toes, eye to eye with him. He wasn't losing her to that darkness. He hadn't lost her yet. He hoped. "I love you, Ruby. Everything, down to your broken soul. And we can do this together. If I'd been here, we could have gotten through it together. You trusted me enough then. Can you trust me again?"

She shook her head, lancing his heart, which was already feeling like a pincushion for a legion of spear-wielding gladiators. "No. I won't let her go, Derek. I won't."

He had to swallow down more arguments like jagged glass, because she broke into those painful sobs again. Her tense body sparked with energy, ready to fight to the death in a battle she knew she'd lose, because she thought she had nothing but the fight left to her.

Damn it. He pulled her back into him, struggled with her, then firmly mashed her against his chest until she went limp, cried there. Suppressing a sigh, he stroked her hair, kept stroking until she hiccupped a few times, settled down.

The plain truth of it was she was brilliant. And young, so very young. Ruby was a twenty-six-year-old woman who'd been treated like worthless chattel by her insidious mother all her life. All that intelligence and baggage rolled together, the trauma of losing a child all by herself . . . He knew she had strength—Lord and Lady, in some ways, she had more endurance and adaptability than anyone he knew. But he also knew just how fragile certain parts of her were. He honestly wasn't sure how to go about fixing this without shattering her like blown glass.

Firming his jaw, he lifted his head at last, cupping her chin so she had to turn her head, look up and back at him. "Here's what we're going to do. I promise I will not take any action about this yet. Not until you and I can talk this through. A lot. Okay? You have my word. But I want to see her."

She studied him a long, long moment. It hurt, that she doubted him, but he waited her out. "You promise. Swear to me."

"I swear it, on my love for you and my oath as a Guardian. The two most serious commitments of my life."

Ruby bit her lip. He recognized her struggle, had to keep silent not to reassure her further. It wasn't just about protecting the baby. She was realizing that if he betrayed her, she wouldn't survive that blow to her heart.

"All right. We need to go to the basement."

THE DOOR FROM THE SHOP TO THE BASEMENT STAIR-well was heavy steel and double dead-bolted, but that was nothing next to the magical protections on it. He had to marvel at Ruby's skill again, because while they were multilayered, complex, they were barely noticeable until she started to unwind them, sketching symbols in the air, shimmers of heat energy collecting around her fingers she dispelled with a quick snap of her wrists.

The protections had been designed not only to distract the attention of mundane thieves, but to evade notice by magic users, no matter their level. On top of that, the protection had the strength needed to slow them down or keep them out if they *did* notice. Usually it was a trade-off. A magic user could cast a spell that made something of value invisible, or could pile protections on it like Fort Knox— impregnable, but highly visible. She'd managed to do both.

Throughout this world and others, Light as well as Dark Guardians had access to hidden arcane libraries, repositories of organic as well as literary sources of great knowledge, skills, how-to manuals for all the most unlikely things. When opened, those books possessed illuminated, fiery script that allowed the tomes to be read in places where no other light was allowed. And that fire would consume the reader, if he or she wasn't worthy to be holding it.

Whether she realized it or not, Ruby was well on her way to being added to that resource list. On top of that, he imagined what she could accomplish if she was given *access* to those repositories. He was sure she'd be found more than worthy. There was no telling how much more she could expand the archives. She could become an invaluable aid to Guardians like himself, who were always facing new challenges to their magic.

As long as she didn't lose her soul to Darkness and turn that knowledge on them to destroy the world. Other than that, it was a great idea.

She was quiet, tense. Though it was tempting to reach out to steady her, intuition told him to stay silent, keep his hands to himself. The truce between them was so fragile, one wrong word or sudden movement could shatter it. That sharp tongue and smart-assed attitude she used to parry with him, that could arouse, frustrate or amuse him by turns, wasn't in evidence now. She was a strained-looking waif in the shadows, gray-green eyes luminous and intent.

As they descended, he saw the typical basement of every horror movie. Narrow, unfinished stairs, open slats for ankle grabbing by the monsters. A furnace hummed. The area was illuminated by the single bare bulb. She'd put their daughter here? Cell-like cinder-block walls and dim light, the dank smell of past floodings.

She'd preceded him down the steps after pulling the chain on the bulb. He wondered if it had ever gone out while she was down here, leaving her in utter darkness so she had to feel her way back up the stairs. At the lower level, she answered his unspoken question by pulling another chain, lighting a second dismal bulb. "This way," she said in a monotone.

There was another door under the stairs, behind a tower of boxes, a bicycle and a stack of metal pipes impossible to move without setting up an obnoxious din. He helped her shift it all out of the way, a process that took five minutes. Five minutes of silence. As he straightened, she laid her hand on the door, closed her eyes. Her head bowed.

"You promise?" She whispered it.

"Yes." *And, Lord and Lady, please let me not regret that promise.* Or worse, have to break it. Because Ruby would never forgive him. She'd trusted him once, more than she'd trusted anyone, but he wasn't content to merely be on the top of that heap. He wanted to be the one she trusted wholly and fully at last, a treasure he could keep forever, like her heart.

She spoke a quick incantation in Greek, an interesting choice. The point usually wasn't the words, but the focus they provided. Most times, it was possible to do the same magic in complete silence, but for a trained magic user the words provided a shortcut, a conduit. Like Harry Potter's wand. He allowed himself a tight smile at the thought, because he was feeling the need for something to reduce the constricting pressure across his chest. It didn't help.

A brief flash of green light under her hand, and the old-style skeleton-key lock disengaged. Tumblers whirred, and then she pulled the door open.

"Illumina," she ordered. She deposited the tiny spout of flame from the palm of her hand onto a torch mounted in . . . rock. It was a fissure, and as she led him on and downward, stopping periodically to light torches along treacherous steps rough-hewn into the stone, he smelled old Earth. Then he saw it, for the shape of the tunnel changed, the dividing point between what was carved out by man and what had been hollowed out by Nature. A place of the ancients, unaltered by human hands. A sacred space.

His brow creased. This place was not on a fault line, but he sensed the power and strength of fault-line power supporting it. "Ruby?"

She stopped, glancing up at him. She'd taken the last torch out of its sconce, was carrying it, because of course from here forward there were no brackets desecrating the walls. That paleness in her face was getting more pronounced, the farther they descended, and he knew it wasn't just a trick of the shadows. "How is this place being powered?"

"I created veins leading from the closest fault lines, and feed their power here. A lot of small veins, so they weren't easily noticed, and randomly scattered, so if they were noticed, it would look like their typical extensions over an area and not a targeted effect."

She'd created a magical irrigation system, using a fault line as her water source. Though he still had no love in his heart for her mother, he was reminded again of how Fate often saw threads where others saw dead ends. She'd been neglected by her mother, an isolated child who desired her approval. Her mother had said study, become a good assistant, and to please, Ruby had thrown herself into it wholeheartedly. In driving her in that direction, Mary had helped Ruby discover her natural passion and talent, in a love of learning all things arcane. She was a fucking genius. A genius who'd thought she had no natural ability and doubted herself because her mother had taught her she wasn't worth loving.

"How did you find this place?"

"The previous owner of the shop was elderly, and it had been in his family for several generations. He showed it to me. Said he and his cousins found it when they were little, would go down and play here, until their parents found out and padlocked the door, afraid that it wasn't structurally sound. But it is." She laid her hand on the wall, as if absorbing the vibrations there, a natural inclination for a magic user.

"I did a little history search about it. Though I could never find a direct reference, I think it's been used for a variety of clandestine things. Meetings during the Revolutionary War, even a little bit of home witchcraft. A meditation group in the sixties."

A vague smile crossed her face. "Took a lot of digging to find those references, and most of them were just implications, not really fixed to this place, but to the local area. This location has been protected, either subconsciously or intentionally. The owner himself . . . When I came to look at the shop, he said he'd had very few who'd shown interest in buying. And he told me I was the first person he'd shown that door under the basement stairs, because he didn't want word getting around that it was a feature of the place, attracting drug dealers and such. But he said he felt good things from me and if . . ." She paused, swallowing. "If I ever had children, he wanted me to know about it, so they wouldn't find it first and get into trouble."

She turned away, led him onward. They kept descending,

until he was sure they were a good hundred feet below-ground. When it leveled, there was a series of openings that went in different directions, some big enough for him to walk upright, some so tight his shoulders might not get through. Fortunately, she turned off toward one that allowed him to walk upright. When things crunched beneath his boots, he looked down. The glitter and scent told him, but he dropped to his heels, scooped up some of the white, grainy material. Salt. A bed of salt. Hearth magic to supplement the more complex protection renderings.

He straightened. Standing in an archway, she gestured to him to join her. When he moved toward her, she had her other hand on the arch, her grip white. As he reached her, he could look right and see whatever it was that had ratcheted up her tension a hundredfold. But first, he leaned down, pressed his mouth to hers, a gentle kiss. Put his hand against her face, his fingertips in her hair.

He'd learned to pay attention to those moments when everything was about to change, to be sure he did what he wanted to do on the deciding side of that line. Because once he stepped over, most times that chance was lost. He wanted to kiss her, give her all the passion and meaning in his heart in that gesture.

She made a noise in her throat, reached up and gripped his shoulder with her free hand like a person floundering on a cliff edge. He brought her against him with an arm around her waist, a low hum rumbling in his throat, and deepened the kiss. The torch quivered in her hand, the heat coming close to his skin, such that he closed his grip over her wrist without looking, steadied it. Her every curve was against him, the rapid beat of her heart, her thigh pressed against his leg. His woman. For better or worse. No matter what lay behind this door. He conveyed that and more, and hoped it was strong enough to weather them through this.

Giving her one last look, he turned to face what was in that cave.

It was small, probably no larger than her one-bedroom apartment. Like the latter part of their descent, the folds and lines of the walls were created by water and heat, not chisel and blast. Her torch showed him nothing but an empty space, but he sensed far more. He took a second look, gaze coursing over the walls, his senses reaching out. Nothing . . . *No.* Picking up on something at a spot where there was nothing visible, he nodded toward it. The signature was similar to what was upstairs. However, he wasn't entirely sure he would have found it unless he'd felt it from the unwinding she'd done on the door lock.

Something shifted in her countenance. He'd passed some kind of test, but her expression suggested she preferred failure. Still, she drew him into the small cave, moving to the back wall where he'd indicated. When she made an unexpected right, he realized it was an optical illusion. There was another chamber, through an even narrower fissure that required a tight squeeze for a man his size, though Ruby shimmied through it with practiced ease. She doused the torch, left it on the ground next to the opening. He was in total darkness as he navigated the snakelike passage.

When he made it through, he realized why she'd done it. Where they were going, a dim light was already provided. Because of that dimness, and the angle of entry, this chamber didn't throw its light out into the next one. The serpentine approach doubled back and was blocked by another rock outcropping, adding to that optical illusion.

He registered the cleverness of it, but it wasn't the most remarkable thing about the chamber. Coming to a halt just inside its entrance, he fixated on the thing that was.

Vaguely, he noted Ruby had moved to the center of the room, putting herself between him and the source of the dim light. That constriction in his chest increased to the point he couldn't speak.

It was the vision he'd seen during the Great Rite, only even more vivid. A sphere, no more than two feet across, possessing the most densely compressed and complex magic he'd ever detected. He'd thought what she'd done to protect and reinforce this chamber was incredible. This was beyond it, a miracle. A wondrous, terrible miracle.

The sphere floated with apparent aimlessness across the room, like a child's balloon. When he'd pulled himself into the room with a grunt and deep inhale to get the breadth of his chest through, Derek sensed a mild shimmer of energy. It was a gate of sorts, to keep the sphere here. A child gate.

Soft green, blue, lavender and pink colors swirled in the light of that sphere. What emanated from it was peace, a child's laughter . . . quiet.

Looking around the cave, he saw the sphere wasn't the only thing here. He found the things he would have expected in Ruby's room above. Crystals and favorite pieces of jewelry were tucked into natural hollows in the rock. Unlit candles were clustered here and there with a variety of compatible scents. Vases of dried flowers and herbs added color. These weren't random choices, but items placed in key positions. Items with great sentimental value that could be infused with power and intent, a continuous feed for that sphere. Seeing a faded stuffed dog with a wrinkled face, he recognized the second toy he'd ever given her, for her seventh birthday.

Studying the layout, he detected the five points, the bisecting lines. The pentagram was anchored with a blend of complex magics, but what each had in common was a rare, one-of-a-kind ingredient. This was where Ruby had woven the power she'd gained from trading pieces of her soul.

She'd brought together Dark and Light, and created a mother's womb.

He drew closer to the sphere, his throat aching. The colors swirled, melded, separated, like an animated Impressionist painting. However, the pale pink, the color of innocent, new flesh, stayed the same, though it bobbed around in the sphere, a tiny astronaut holding her toes to do slow somersaults in what appeared, to her, as limitless space.

He was looking at the soul of their daughter. She still held the last shape she'd had in the womb, such that he could see the fragile skull, the fingers and impossibly small toes. If he'd had any doubt, the spirit shimmered, telling him it was of course not the physical body. However, to help the magic, maintain the focus, Ruby had likely visualized her as she'd been when she'd died. Which meant . . .

"You saw her," he realized.

"I held her."

Derek's eyes closed as Ruby's voice, punctuated by a tremor, whispered through the chamber. "As I said, when I was lying in the street, and summoned all that power, I sent the fetus here, held her in a stasis, so the soul wouldn't leave. When the hospital released me, I came here, worked the magic, finished it.

"I buried her in a pretty place. That place we went to, in the mountains, you and me. I thought she'd like having her remains there. And one day . . . I thought I might tell you, so you could visit her. I knew you'd want to, and that you'd like knowing she was there."

Derek drew in a breath as the fetus rolled. "Her eyes are open."

"Yes. It's kind of misleading, seeing her this way, when what we're really seeing is a soul."

He nodded, not sure what to say to that. Putting out his hand, he touched the sphere, knowing the magic would allow that. He felt it. Felt her. The soul that was a combination of both his and Ruby's DNA, of their hearts, minds and spirits.

Her face lifted, those eyes blinking. With his own expanded senses, he knew their daughter detected him. As if, through his touch, he became part of the dream she was in, a pleasant, unquestioned addition, but there was no awareness of this place, of where he actually was.

"What world did you give her?"

"All the best of everything." Ruby had drawn to his side, but there were six inches between them, six inches charged with almost as much energy as had gone into making that sphere. "She's in a place where she feels loved, accepted. She laughs and smiles and plays. There are meadows and sunlight, ponies and dress-up. When she wants to sleep, she lies down on soft grass and sleeps while the moon rises above her with a million stars in the sky. It's Paradise. It's Heaven, for a baby. For a little girl."

He nodded. That fetus was so close to his hand, bumping the side of the sphere. There was no impression of contact, only the sense of light over his fingers, but it was still startling, seeing her so close, seeing how, as she turned, her head would have been dwarfed by his hand. She would have had Ruby's ears, her fingers. Goddess help her, she looked like she got his big feet, but maybe she would have grown into those. Or he could have come up with a spell to shrink them for her.

A tremor went through his hand.

RUBY HAD KNOWN DEREK STORMWIND SINCE SHE WAS a little girl, had fallen in love with him from the moment she'd liked boys. He'd been her friend, her mentor, her staunch supporter, and eventually her lover. She was so used to him being a know-it-all, had actually relied on it, hyperaware he was centuries old, always so wise and strong. Though in a sexy, appealing way, not an ancient, bearded-wizard way. She'd teased him about that when she wanted to yank his chain about their age differences.

She thought she knew him pretty well. Even so, she wasn't at all prepared to see the emotions that crossed his face. Maybe later he'd be angry by what she'd done. Or, worse, repulsed. But right now, she was looking at a father meeting his daughter for the first time, at the same moment he had to face the bittersweet knowledge that the flesh-and-blood person she would have been was dead and gone.

She'd known him to get pissed off, frustrated, and even grieve in a silent, strongman type of way. She'd never seen Derek Stormwind with tears gathering in his eyes, or fingers shaking as he tried to stroke the wisps of energy that flowed around the sphere like fog. The way he might have stroked the wisps of his baby's hair.

She'd felt shame for what she'd done, even knowing she was going to keep doing it anyway. But she'd never felt that shame as keenly as she felt it at this moment, so sharp it could cut out her heart, if she hadn't already diced it up to preserve what was in this room.

She'd thought of him as the enemy, the one from whom she had to keep her secret or he'd take it away. Yet he was a male who'd lived for so long without any family. In those first stunning months of pregnancy without him, she'd alternated between yearning for his presence and euphoric rejoicing, imagining his face a hundred times over when he learned he had become a father. She'd nursed the indisputable belief that she was the *one*, the very special person, the only woman given the gift of offering that to him, though she hadn't been entirely sure of that until he told her a few minutes ago, in the bedroom above. Before that, the idea of it, the hope of it, had made her believe in his love for her all the more.

Now she couldn't dispute it.

She'd forgotten so much of that in the intervening months, but, watching his reaction, it came back in full flood. It surged up in her even more strongly when he finally spoke, his husky tone taking her breath.

"What's her name?"

"I wanted to call her Rose. Because she was perfect, just like a rose."

He swallowed, his voice thickening. "Ruby and Rose. My girls."

She was crying now, too, silent tears coursing down her cheeks as one meager but powerful teardrop made its way down his. Lifting her fingers, she took it away, a treasure so full of power that it was as much magic as what she'd spun in here. When he looked down at her, something shifted inside her. Something painful, like a boulder rolling off a vital organ, letting it function for the first time in a long while, difficult and rusty though she might be at using the squashed thing. She couldn't deny the Dark part of her was still on maximum-security lockdown, but for this she couldn't keep the regret and pain out of her voice.

"You weren't here when I needed you. I couldn't forgive you that, Derek. That's what I told myself. I wanted to punish you. I blamed you. But the truth is none of it's your fault. I just wanted it to be. I wanted it to be someone's fault, because otherwise I had to face the truth. That it was mine."

"What?" His brow furrowed. "Ruby, there's no—"

"Yeah, there is. First thing you ever taught me was that any level of power, even if it's just the power over self, over the choices you make, is a responsibility you can't abdicate to anyone else. Or blame anyone for. If I hadn't been afraid of the power, if I'd embraced learning how to use it from day one, she'd be alive. I should have reached out to Raina and Ramona for help, even if I couldn't reach you."

•

* 18 *

THOUGH IT HAD BEEN DIFFICULT TO TURN HIS GAZE from that orb, her pain was palpable, and that pain echoed in his own chest. Derek faced her fully, laid his hands on her fragile shoulders, shoulders that had borne so much. His thumbs stroked over her collarbone, drawing her gaze up to his face.

"Ruby, I've fought the Dark for centuries. And every time I wasn't clever enough, strong enough, intuitive enough, I blamed myself. It's an irrational truth that has a very vital purpose. It makes us strive to be stronger, more clever, to defeat our obstacles as often as we can. But the rational truth is this: No matter how strong or clever I am, I will continue to lose people, because sometimes, some days, evil and Darkness win. It's a balance of its own. Yes, you should have reached out. That was a mistake."

He touched her chin as her eyes darkened with pain. "It's a difficult one to face, but it doesn't surprise me at all to hear you found the courage to see that truth." Now his voice hardened, and from her expression, he was sure there was a dangerous flash in his eyes. "However, Asmodeus bears all the blame for taking the life of your child, an innocent who should not have been part of this fight at all. It is his sin, Ruby, not yours."

Her lips gave a tremulous quirk. "You're using your teacher voice."

"Does it help?"

"Some." Her gaze was wary, but something else was there, too. A tender, vulnerable wisp of trust. Shifting his grip, he ran his knuckles down the side of her face. It was an effort, with everything that was in this room—the past, the present, the hovering specter of the future he knew she didn't want to face—but he tried to ease things up for both of them, give them a little breathing space.

"With you, I wear a variety of hats. Your skills are some of the best I've seen, Ruby, and you have a great deal of raw power. If you need and want a teacher to help you use it, the type of teacher your mother should have been for you, I can be that. But it doesn't mean I'll stop being the guy who occasionally wants to strangle you, or who gets hard as a rock when I see you pull a colander out of the bottom cabinet."

"I remember that night." Her eyes gleamed with cautious amusement. "You changed your mind. Said you didn't need the colander. I had to put it back."

It didn't surprise him at all she remembered, given what had happened later that night. He'd never eaten Mexican in quite that way. Now he stayed silent, his brow lifted as he waited for that clever mind to put it together. Her mouth bowed into a delectable pursed shape.

"You didn't need the colander at all."

"Smart girl. The jeans you were wearing that night needed a workout. I was just helping put the stretch in the denim."

She stroked her fingertips through the strands of hair over his brow, shifted her weight. "I've only ever seen you wear one hat. How old is that thing?"

"It doesn't like revealing its age. And it's a figurative statement."

"Yes, Professor." She'd pulled on a pair of jeans under his shirt, so now she found the back pockets beneath the long tail and tucked her fingers into them. She considered him another long moment. He held her gaze, watched the thoughts gather, sift. The sphere floated behind her, then toward the opening, bounced gently off the barrier, came back, passed between them. It wasn't matter that could be grasped, but he could feel a warm touch of that Paradise, hear childish laughter, as it passed by.

Ruby was a young woman who'd lost her baby, who'd dealt with it alone. He was asking the impossible; he knew it. The field of her heart was so scarred. All she'd ever wanted was to be loved, and nothing loved so purely and completely as a baby in the womb loved its mother.

Lord and Lady, help her. Help us both.

"The lullaby?" he asked.

"It was part of the magic. I use it now sometimes to connect to her. It reinforces the sphere at the same time."

Music was part of the trinity for powerful spellwork. Math and poetry were the other two, but music was probably the most potent, when done right. It required a synchronization of lyrics, harmony, an aesthetic and intuitive balance. Its binding was almost irresistible, such that the end intent would gravitate toward it. She'd held the baby in the sphere with a lullaby. If it wouldn't have made his heart hurt too much, he would have smiled.

At length, she withdrew her hands, crossed her arms, gathering his shirt into folds against her body. She fastened her gaze to his chest, so many emotions in her eyes it was hard not to reach out and touch her. "I know what you want me to do. I just . . . I need to think about it. Can you give me time to think?"

It was so much more than he'd expected after seeing all this, after realizing what he was asking her to give up. Letting out a breath he didn't realize he'd been holding, he looked toward the sphere with her; then he found her hand. Tugging it free from that locked position across her body, he squeezed her fingers.

"Yeah. If you quit pretending otherwise and tell me you love me."

HER LIPS PRESSED TOGETHER. "I THOUGHT ONLY GIRLS needed to hear it said out loud."

He didn't say anything further, just tipped up her chin with a finger to meet his gaze before his mouth took hers again. Slow, long, devastatingly sweet. A touch of his tongue, tracing the seam of her lips and then inside, a languid dance with her tongue that brought her in closer to him, made her lean full into his body. When he lifted his head, she kept her eyes closed, until his fingers flexed on her hips and he spoke, low. "Ruby."

She opened her eyes, saw the sphere had moved. It was now right next to them, shining its light on them like a moon. Though the occupant wasn't supposed to have any conscious awareness of this room or who was in it, Ruby had noted the sphere gravitated toward her when she spent time with it. Not so much like Theo following on her heels, but a definite drift to be near her. And now, here it was, right with the two of them. Derek reached up, laid his hand against the energy, his large palm curving around the side as if it were corporeal, following that arc. She lifted her own and did the same, holding it between them. It stayed still, fixed between their two points. Her heart overflowed, as if the soul inside had validated Derek's presence here, the two of them together.

It gave her own battered soul something it hadn't had in a while. A tendril of hope, the potential for happiness again.

"She was perfect, Derek. So perfect."

"Like her mother." She was amazed to again see that

faint glistening in his eyes, so moved by her words he couldn't rein back the emotion. "Perfect in her imperfections. The only woman I've truly loved with every part of my soul. I would have loved our daughter the same way. I do love her the same way." His gaze darkened. "We have to let her go, Ruby."

A quiet statement of fact, not a threat. The pain in his gaze told her he understood, didn't want to say it. That he'd do anything not to have to say it, because of what it could do to her. "Give her the chance to grow up, meet boys, read books, think her own thoughts against all the good and bad of this world. Embrace every ounce of her potential. One day, we'll see her again."

Knowing he understood helped. Sort of. It at least helped her to respond honestly, no shields up.

"I don't know if I can bear it, letting her go."

"I'll be right beside you. Behind you. Wherever you need me to be. You can use my strength, Ruby, every bit of it. It's all yours." Putting his hand on the side of her neck, he curved his strong fingers on her nape. "Though you won't need as much of it as you think, because you're the strongest woman I've ever met. There's been something inside you all your life, waiting for you to embrace your own potential, take it and own it. You can do what so few people are ever able to do. Leave the past behind, make it your foundation and build your own worth on top of it, rather than letting it drive you into the ground. You're so close to it. I know you'll get there. And I'm going to love seeing it happen."

His fingers tightened then, his expression becoming irritable. "But, damn it, girl, you still haven't said you love me."

"I didn't think it was needed. You pretty much demand everything, so I wouldn't dare not to." Her smile created a little pain in her chest, so many things happening in this room, so many possibilities shifting. But she framed his face with both hands, stared up at him.

"I love you, Derek Stormwind. With all my heart and

soul. If you ever go away like that again, I will turn you into a house cat. Theo will slobber all over you and carry you around in his mouth like a chew toy."

She knew it was a confusing statement. He couldn't help having been in the Fae world, and afterward, *she'd* sent him away. Plus, sooner or later, because of his job, Derek would have to leave again. She understood that. But she was counting on him to understand the feelings that drove the statement, versus the unlikely reality of it.

"You're a cruel woman." Sliding his fingers over her hips now, he cupped her backside. The sphere continued to float in their proximity, but gave them more space. "What would you think about coming with me?"

Ruby blinked. "What do you mean?"

"Exactly what I said. I want you to travel with me. Let me help you learn how to use your power, and you help me do what I do."

At the intensity in his gaze, her heart thudded up higher into her throat. "When you're given power, it's given for a reason. You aren't intended to sit on it. While there are a hell of a lot more personal reasons you and I are fated to be together, the Powers that Be may have drawn us together specifically because of what you're becoming, and what I already am.

"You have free will," he added carefully, at her uncertain look. "You always have a choice of what to do with it. But I'm offering. Light Guardians aren't all that plentiful, and I wouldn't be the first to apprentice a strong magic user to aid his work."

She was floored. From his look of concern, the tightening of his grip, she suspected she'd gone about two shades paler. She made an effort to pull it together. "Well, I guess you are getting kind of old. Probably need younger eyes, and all that."

The lines near those appealing blue eyes crinkled. "You're probably right about that. And, thank all the gods, young as you are, you're already potty trained. I won't have to worry about that."

He took her blow to the solar plexus with good grace, not even moving to defend himself. But he stilled her when his expression changed, his touch gentling, coming up high on her waist. His thumbs brushed her rib cage. "If you get pregnant again, then we both take the time off. However many years are needed. Protecting our child is as important as anything else I've done. I'll dedicate myself to it, and you, the same way. I've given the Light centuries; they can give me a few decades to see my children grown. I should have been here the first time around. I'll never make that mistake again. Okay? Not even the fires of Hell or treacherous Fae mages will keep me away from you. I'll incinerate the entire Fae world if they try."

It was a bolstering thought, having her centuries-old boyfriend offer to destroy an entire world for her. She wanted to give him a smile, but there were so many thoughts going through her head, so many conflicting feelings, she wasn't sure how to react. And then he really sent her into a tailspin.

He took a deep breath. "Later, I'll think of a better way to do this, in a more memorable way, but given how our lives are, I don't want to wait another minute to say it. If you want to go with me, I have a condition. I want to marry you, Ruby. I want you to be my wife."

SHE DIDN'T GIVE HIM AN ANSWER ON ANY OF IT, of course, and was relieved he hadn't expected it, not right now. He appeared content to have said it, to know she understood— though with the incredulity of Moses seeing the burning bush—that he meant every word, that it wasn't some spur-of-the-moment thing driven by fear of losing her again.

Well, okay, yeah, a little, but not in the wrong kind of way. More in the totally flattering, can't-believe-I've-waited-this-long kind of way.

However, he seemed to understand her answers were on hold until certain things were resolved, the most important of which was in this cave. There was a cot in the corner, and of mutual accord, they gravitated toward it, because neither one wanted to leave just yet. They sat on the edge of it, watched their daughter, talked quietly of this and that, hands loosely linked. Derek's arm was around her, his other palm curved over her hip so she was in the shelter of his body. At one point, the sphere descended to rest in their laps, then drifted off again.

Ruby laid her head on his shoulder, realizing how late it had gotten, and that she was getting sleepy. Rather than suggest they leave, Derek stretched out on the cot, bending his knees since it was about a foot shorter than his frame, and pulled her back into his body. She rested her head on his biceps as they continued to watch their daughter's soul randomly drift among the circle of magically imbued objects. Ruby kept her fingers tangled with his under her head. His other hand stayed on her hip. They fell silent, staying that way a long time. Not sleeping, but resting all the same, dreaming along with Rose of what might have been.

"I thought there was no Heaven," Ruby spoke softly. "No place where there's peace, stillness. Where there's only Light, no shadows. I gave that to her, gave her Heaven, because I couldn't bear the thought of letting her go where there was nothing, and that was all she'd ever know. When she was ripped from me, she was afraid. The first thing my daughter ever felt from the world."

"No, baby. The first thing she felt, the first and last, was your love." He considered the sphere. "I'm going to say something, but it's not to initiate a decision, all right? I don't want you to tense up. Want to keep you loose and relaxed like a snake on a warm rock, just like you are right now."

She smiled against his arm, and tried to comply, tried not to feel the trickle of uneasiness. He rubbed her back in slow circles, helping.

"A mother's love is an incredible, huge thing. But there may be another factor in play here. If you'd had a normal grieving process, over time you would have made peace, let her go. However, because you used a combination of Dark and Light to keep her here, it grew in you, has made you more possessive. The main reason you can't let her go now may be the hold of the Darkness, rather than the love. I'm not saying you don't love her," he added, giving her a squeeze, anticipating that strong reaction. "I'm saying it's like when scam artists troll obituaries to prey on grieving widows."

"You think the Darkness is using me."

"That's what it does. It latches on and feeds. Much the same way the Light does, building itself."

"You're teaching again."

"You've always respected knowledge, Ruby. It's why you were able to do magic the likes of which I've never seen before. Your heart's involved in this, but I know your mind is as well. I wanted to give you that to think about." He paused, capturing her attention.

"What is it?"

"After I kicked Mikhael's ass, I went to let off some steam. I ran into a cadre of angels."

"Of course you did. That happens to me all the time. Were they playing darts at the local pub?"

"Smart-ass." He gave her a light pinch. She squirmed against him, enjoying his grunt and the glint in his eye from the sensation. Then he sobered. "They said, 'Help her soon.' At the time, I thought they meant you, but now I think they meant Rose."

That drove away any playfulness. Ruby lifted up on her elbow, looked at him squarely. "Why?"

"You did a wrong deed, but you did it out of love. It's that love, and other factors"—somehow, she knew Derek was grudgingly giving Mikhael his due; she also thought it had been a mutual ass kicking, but kept her tongue, loyal to her man—"that are helping you straddle the line between Light and Dark." He let a finger glide under her eyes, the shadows there. "But you're sliding down that slope faster now. I know you feel it. What happens to her, when you do? When the Darkness takes over? This room, everything feeding that sphere, the sphere itself, is an incredible power source. It can be used for a lot of different things."

Derek saw various levels of distress cross her face, those factions warring within her. He could see the ugly shape of the Darkness, whispering its fears and lies to her, just as he could see her mind working it, the mind and heart he knew and trusted. He hated that all he could offer was words right now, but part of this battle had to be hers, much as he wanted to fight it all for her.

"I'm not going to talk about it anymore," he soothed. "Not right now. But I want you to think about it, all right?" When he brought her back down, he gave her hair a tug, repeated it. "All right?"

"All right." Her tone was uncertain, her hand curling into the open collar of his shirt, which she was still wearing.

"Let's do something else," he suggested. "What games did you imagine playing with her?"

She was quiet for a bit, but he waited her out. At length, she sighed. Lifting her hand, she made a tracing in the air. At the shimmer of power, he bit back a fierce smile of pride, an odd sting of tears, as she created the simple, beautiful magic. Up until now, he hadn't had the opportunity to enjoy what she could do, to celebrate that with her. Now he did.

The pretty white dragon, no bigger than a house cat, flapped its wings and sneezed, turning in a somersault. It was an illusion, but in a child's room, it could perch on the edge of a crib, circle her bed like a mobile, or spout tiny gouts of flame. He concentrated, and a black male dragon appeared in her shadow, initiating an indignant chirp and an impromptu aerial duel as they tangled and danced through the air, then settled into soaring about the small space like birds, swooping high, then low, passing through the sphere to give Rose a glimpse of dragons.

"I think she had special abilities of her own," Ruby murmured, watching the dragons as they dissipated, became a shower of starlight that orbited the sphere. "I think that's why she was able to jump-start my own abilities. With your blood . . ."

"And yours." He squeezed her.

"I think she would have been remarkable."

"She is remarkable. A soul can't be killed, Ruby. The energy just goes elsewhere when the mortal form can no longer contain it."

"But I want her here."

"I know." Crossing his arms over her chest, he held her close as she wept. She was grieving, letting go. Leaning on his strength to do it. Pressing his face into her hair, he shared that sorrow with her. "Do you think she would have been a princess, wanting bows in her hair and her room all in pink?"

"Probably. Since pink always makes me think of Pepto Bismol."

As a teenager, Ruby had been a tomboy, his shy girl with alert eyes, always wearing jeans and T-shirts on her slim, boyish form.

"Nope." Ruby changed her mind. "I'm thinking cowgirl. She'd love horses, and I'd have to fuss at her to take off her boots before coming in the house. We'd live somewhere with lots of land so she could have her horse. She'd probably want to rescue horses, and before we knew it, we'd have a herd. And her daddy could ride horses everywhere, since that's what he likes. He'd put her on the horse in front of him and trot off to Walmart when I needed some groceries. They'd put in a hitching post for him."

He grinned. "I like the sound of that. Of course, when she hit her teens, her Aunt Raina would get hold of her and turn her into a Goth, just to torment me."

"All girls go through their rebellious stage."

"Any chance Raina will get out of hers before she collects Social Security?"

"You like her. You know you do." Ruby stroked his forearm, her chin angling up as he placed a kiss on her throat. When she stayed in that position, unconsciously seeking more, he accommodated her, taking a nip that caused a sexy little tremor.

"I think you like *that*." His hand slid under her shirt, found soft skin and stroked. "And this."

She swallowed under his mouth, and he set his teeth there again. "Derek."

"I want to put another baby inside of you, Ruby. I want to see you and her grow together."

She closed her eyes. "I'm afraid of it. I couldn't stand to lose one again."

"I know. But that won't happen. I won't let it."

There was a question she wanted to ask him, even knowing it could shatter this fragile truce between them. But she had to ask. "Derek . . . you have the power to resurrect, don't you?"

Years ago, she'd overheard Mary, talking to a fellow witch about Derek. *He's a man with the powers of a god, but he's inflicted a code on himself so he never considers himself a god. Of all the extraordinarily unnerving—and irritating—things about him, that rates at the top.*

That was the first hint of it. But there was something else that had happened as she was growing up, something that made her almost certain of his answer now. Almost.

Long before any of this was relevant, what Mary had said had made Ruby's heart swell with pride, thinking of the great and noble character of the man she loved. When she'd had her encounter with Asmodeus, that pride had turned into bitter resentment, near hatred, thinking that if he'd been here, he could have saved their child. She'd cursed his absence in the Fae world, his inability to be reached when she needed him most, on so many levels.

He'd gone silent and still behind her. Somehow she knew his eyes were locked on that floating sphere. "Yes, I do, Ruby," he spoke at last. "But not for this. It's a very limited, very restricted magic."

"If I'd gotten to you sooner, would it have made a difference?"

"Ruby, don't do this to yourself. To us." He tightened his arms around her. "I'm begging you, don't sabotage us with your grief over what might have been."

She closed her eyes. "I need to hear the honest answer, Derek. I know it doesn't change anything, and I know about Fate and natural cycles, and all that, but I just need to hear it."

"In order to be what I am, I have to live by a code. There are lines I can't cross, no matter what. I can do certain things to help, but other things I can't, even when I'm capable of them." He was giving her the answer the best way he could, she knew. It didn't make it hurt less.

"So, yes," she said quietly. "You could bring her back to life."

"At a cost too dear to you, to her, to all the world."

"What about my kitten?"

He sighed. "That's how you figured it out."

"I wasn't sure, until now. But yes."

When she was ten, she'd acquired her first pet, a stray orange tabby kitten. Mary had let her keep it as long as it wasn't underfoot, and for the first time in her life Ruby had something that loved her, slept in a ball against her chest, the little purr matching her heart's thump. In a moment of carelessness, Mary had left the side screen door of their Washington brownstone open, the place they'd been living at the time. The little tabby, whom Ruby had named Sirius, had gone outside to chase butterflies, right under the wheels of a car on the busy city street.

She hadn't brought the kitten to her mother, of course. She'd learned not to expect any nurturing from that source. So she'd gone to the dining room, hidden underneath the table with its long tablecloth that gave her some privacy, cradling the lifeless body in her lap. It had been a glancing blow, so Sirius wasn't bloody or mangled. He was just a limp body, the neck broken. He'd of course voided his bladder, so she had him wrapped in a towel.

Derek had arrived an hour before, had been meeting with her mother. As if he'd felt her distress, she'd barely settled in her shelter before she'd heard his approach from the upstairs rooms. His boots stopped by the table, and then he crouched down to see her. Ever since the big man had been visiting her mother, getting insights into this or that future event, he'd always looked at her with such kindness and understanding in his eyes, as if he knew how lonely she was. That day, she didn't hesitate. She'd crawled right into his lap, crying her heart out with that little body cooling in her hands. And then suddenly, it wasn't cool at all. Sirius had stirred groggily, making a soft, distressed mewl, and Derek had smiled, patting away her tears.

"See, girl? He was just knocked out for a bit. He'll be just fine."

And he had been, living for a wonderful additional nine years, until he died suddenly of an aneurysm.

Ruby vividly remembered that limp body, the lolling neck. "You brought Sirius back to life. Why was that different?"

"I have to weigh the cost and impact of a resurrection. That one . . . the cost was one I could pay, and the impact was something the world could handle and adjust to." He nodded at the sphere. "This is not. Though I hate to tell you that. I wish like hell I could give you what you want."

"You can give me what I want. You just . . . won't."

Derek remained quiet. After a long moment, she sighed, deep and long. "Maybe, right after . . . I would have hated you for that. I did hate you, because I guess I knew. But I also know why. And maybe . . . I probably won't ever say it again . . . it was good you weren't here."

Derek turned her so she was looking up in his face. It was the last thing he'd ever expected to hear her say, because he was damn certain he'd never stop castigating himself for not being there. "Why, baby?"

"Because . . ." She tangled her fingers with his on her hip, looking down at them. He didn't know why she couldn't look at him until she spoke. Acknowledging her own value was hard for her. Even that day with the kitten, she'd cried so silently, not wanting to disturb her mother.

"Because if you love me the way you say you do, in that moment, when everything was so terrible and final-feeling, I don't think you could have stopped yourself. Whatever the repercussions." She looked up at him then, tears in her eyes. "*Gift of the Magi*–type stuff, right?"

At his cautious nod, she continued, "And I guess, the same way the world could handle a kitten coming back to life instead of our child, it was better for me to give part of myself to Darkness than you."

Truth could be stark and heartbreaking. But he refused to accept it. As he wrapped his other arm across her chest, he held their joined hands against her breast. "No, baby. That kitten and Rose, they were both valuable to the world, for different reasons. I thought . . . No, I *knew*, if you didn't have that kitten, when you were on the cusp of womanhood, with no sense of love or value, we might have lost you altogether. The world agreed. With our baby . . ." He hesitated, his throat thickening. "Yeah, I would have. I would have done anything, given you anything, to keep you from feeling that horrible loss. But we've always been better, stronger, together, Ruby. And you have to take that into account. I think before I did it, you would have stopped me. Because you have a better grasp of the natural order than any witch I've ever met. That's why you knew how to twine Light and Dark together—because you understand them both so well."

He sighed. "There are dangers to altering order, always. Knowledge of that is one of the things a wizard spends most of his time learning."

"Under that kind of thinking, our baby was meant to die."

"No. Not necessarily. It simply means sometimes what's done mustn't be undone. No matter how much we wish otherwise."

She looked back down at their hands, her fingers still twisting with his, agitated. Her brow furrowed. "I need to cry a little more now. Is that okay?"

In answer, he tucked her head beneath his jaw and wrapped himself around her, bracing her body as the tears came.

WHEN SHE WAS DONE, THEY LAY LIKE THAT FOR ANOTHER hour or so. She dozed. Derek watched the sphere, dozed some himself. He woke to find her studying his face, and he cupped her jaw, stroking her hair along her temples. After a time, he laid his forehead down on hers, and they both closed their eyes, feeling truth and loss, love and hope, slowly twine around them, keeping them silent and still, but more aware of each other than they'd ever been.

Putting her hand between them at length, she touched his mouth. He kissed her fingers, then let her trace his lips. "Make love to me," she whispered. "Make me feel whole."

He nodded, bent to her throat as she lifted her chin, offering it to him, a quiet, pleasurable surrender. He nuzzled her there, placed his mouth on the beating pulse, reveled in the way it felt when her hands found him under his shirt, slid up along her rib cage, fingers digging into his back.

Sliding off the cot reluctantly, he put his arms beneath her, lifting her. As she linked her arms around his neck, he returned her quizzical look with a wry smile. "Aware of us or not, I'm not sure I want to do this in front of our daughter."

She smiled, but he wondered if she realized her eyes were

wet. Wrapping her arms farther around his shoulders, she buried her face in his neck. He had to put her down so he could squeeze his bulk through the S-shaped fissure, but he held her hand throughout, and when they emerged, he lifted her again to carry her up the narrow stairs.

"I can walk if you need me to."

"I like carrying you. It's nice to have you depend on me to get around sometimes."

"I didn't think men liked needy, clingy women."

"Girl, you are the least clingy and needy thing I've ever met. I've never known you to ask for help in all your life. That's something you need to start fixing, because I'm going to give you all sorts of help from here on out."

"You always have, even when I don't ask." Her fingers tangled in the hair at his nape. "This is getting a little long. I could cut it for you."

"I'd like that." He took her to that cheerless apartment upstairs, but at least there was a window that showed the early-evening star-filled sky, and the somewhat romantic view of streetlights and a band of asphalt winding away to places unseen. There'd been rain while they'd been below-ground, so there was a black shine to the street, the streaked reflection of the streetlights. Laying her down on the bed, Derek slid off her shoes as she watched him with those beautiful hazel eyes. "Take down your hair, baby. Spread it over your shoulders."

She'd pulled it up in a tail before they'd gone downstairs. Now she complied with his desire as he slid her jeans off her hips, then her panties, leaving her in his shirt. Before they'd gone downstairs, she'd put on a bra under it. Now he worked his hands up under the shirt, caressing her breasts through the cups, tracing the nipples when they came up hard against the padded foam. She undulated into his touch, her eyes getting hotter, mouth more taut with need. When he reached under her, she arched her back as he unhooked the undergarment with one deft hand. Pushing up the shirt then, he bent and found her breast, began to suckle a stimulated nipple. She made a sweet sigh of pleasure, curving her leg up over his denim-clad ass, and tightened there, trying to draw him closer. He complied, rubbing his cock against her wet core, making her gasp. He liked having her like this, half-naked, her hair swirling in disheveled array around her intent face, the pink mouth pursed, her tongue touching her lips.

"My wanton," he said softly, looking at her, making sure she saw all she was doing to him, inside and out. "Roll over onto your hands and knees."

Desire flared in her gaze. He'd rarely done that with her, but now he wanted the deep penetration of that angle. He wanted to cover her like a stallion on a mare, because they both sure as hell understood how it had become a stereotype.

She slid over to her belly, then pushed herself up, canting up her ass so it rubbed right against his groin, the little tease. She tossed her hair over her shoulders in a mouthwatering display. He wanted to tangle it in his hands, pull on it when he drove into her.

He unbuckled his belt, unzipped his jeans and got them pushed down and out of the way. When he guided his broad head into her, he had the additional pleasure of seeing the soaked pink flesh contracting, pulling him in. When he went to the hilt and his testicles rocked in a slap against her clit, she let out another gasp, her fingers digging into the bed.

"That feel the way you want it to feel?"

"Big . . . you're so big. Can feel you all the way . . . in my womb. But it feels so good, too. Don't stop."

"Good. 'Cause I wasn't going to."

She shivered at the blatant dominance, and it fired him up further. He wasn't giving that one to Mikhael. Maybe the Dark Guardian had exploited it, but it was as Derek had told her, when she was worried about that side of things. It had always been there between them, ever since she became sexually mature. Because of her age, he'd just taken it easy on her with it, little hints here and there. He'd given her her head, letting her feel that bit in her teeth, determine how much she wanted him to pull on the reins.

But now he was ready to take over the reins, see how far she wanted to go with it, tangled with the emotional depth that existed between them. She was the most stubbornly independent woman he'd ever met, and one of the most damaged, two things that often went together. In her case, the combination begged for a lover with a strong hand to help her drop those shields, find out how much more she could be if she trusted.

He wanted her trust. Hell, he wasn't waiting anymore. He was demanding it. Pulling off his T-shirt, he came down on top of her, his long arms over her shoulders, pushing her down to her elbows, which shoved her ass farther back into the cradle of his hips, taking him deeper. "Jesus." She was milking him, too, helpless little contractions around him, driving him crazy.

Sliding his hand underneath the loosened bra, he cupped her firm breast, her position making it a nice weight pressing into his hand, all that blessed gravity. Squeezing the generous curve, he flicked the nipple with his fingers, giving it a pinch. Her hips jolted up like electricity had struck, her internal muscles clutching on him. He set his teeth to her nape, nipping, teasing with his tongue as he withdrew his hips, then slammed them back in, hard enough to knock her elbows deeper into the bed.

"Oh Goddess . . ." Her plea drove him on. He kept it slow, small movements; then he'd surprise her with another series of those hard plows that had her body rocking, trembling on that cusp, so close . . .

"Derek . . . please . . ."

"Beg some more," he rasped in her ear, withdrawing so he was almost out of her, then slowly, slowly pushing back in. A long, guttural moan broke from her lips as he did it again. And again.

"Please . . . let me come, Derek. I want to come for you."

"Only me," he said, biting the lobe of that perfect ear with sharp teeth, making her contract on him. "Now and always. You're going to be my wife. Say it."

"Now . . . and always. Your . . . wife. Yours." A shudder went through her, and through the pleasure, he was aware of tears falling onto the pillow, tiny splotches. Pushing her hair out of the way, he pressed his mouth to her cheekbone now, making her eyes close, the lashes fanning his flesh. He was in her deep now, at all levels, and passion was subsumed in raw vulnerability. "I love you more than anything, baby. More than anything I've loved in my whole long life."

He moved against her, slow, steady, built her up through tears and cries, and when he felt the perilous ripple of flesh against his cock, when she was about to go over, he whispered the command against her. "Come for me, girl. Come for me now."

It started with a low series of cries that built into screams, into a hard clench on his cock as it plunged in and out of her slickness. He lifted up, his hand clamped on her shoulder, the other tangled in her hair, holding her steady as he slammed into her, over and over, that primal male desire to let her feel him, be marked by him, stretched to delicious soreness she'd feel in her thighs and sex for the next couple of days. And then the most primal marking of all, he released, spilling his seed inside her, driving her to another mini-climax with the sensation, goading him with her moans, the flush across her skin.

He'd never felt so content.

* 19 *

RUBY SLIPPED OUT OF BED, WASHED HER FACE, PULLED her hair in a ponytail. Sliding on Derek's shirt and one of her ankle length Sacred Thread skirts, she found some cash. The Dunkin' Donuts around the corner, with its cake doughnuts and strong black coffee, would be just the thing to wake Derek up. The man had a sweet tooth. Hell, he had a salt tooth as well. The man just loved food, and the starchier, the better. It could make a woman hate him, seeing it all packed in that lean, muscular form, but since she'd had the pleasure of her mouth on about every inch of it last night, several times, she was feeling particularly magnanimous about that.

He slept light as a cat, such that he snagged her wrist when she came back to the bed, though his eyes remained closed.

"I'm going to go get you breakfast," she murmured in his ear. "You worked hard for it. I'm feeling nice."

"Well, I wouldn't want to interfere with a miracle," he grunted. He made a half chuckle, half protest as she pressed a pillow over his face. Wrestling it off, he caught the back of her head for a morning kiss, taking her punches to his chest and shoulders, focusing on plundering her mouth instead. She smiled, feeling it all the way to her toes as he pulled her back into him, his arm around her waist, sprawling her half across his body.

It was hard to ignore the sizeable erection pressing against her thigh. God, they must have made love four, maybe five times, through the night, and she was still dampening for him, wanting that extra morning thickness to fill her once more.

Yeah, some of it might have been that needy edge that Mikhael had exploited, her body's urges enhanced by Darkness. But this was all her, wanting him. Derek. She wanted to eat him alive, have him over and over again, and it was glorious, knowing that it was because she plain wanted him that much. While some of her needs and fantasies about him were dark and wicked, they weren't of the Darkness. She was sure of it. She'd just missed the man and she'd been without him three damn years. She wanted him *now*.

He wasn't waiting for her to change her mind. Whether or not he was half-asleep, Derek knew his way around her body. He'd already shoved the covers impatiently down to his thighs, using those long, strong arms to lift her into a straddle. She could only hang on as he found his way under her skirt. She'd pulled on a silky pair of panties, but he simply caught his forefinger in the crotch panel, moved it aside, and pushed that thick hardness inside her. She was sore from last night, and he knew just how gentle and rough to be, inexorable in his demand, but tender in his care of her.

"I love you," she whispered, realizing how many aspects of their relationship had experienced that special, magical combination.

His eyes opened then, the blue color full of emotion and that morning languidness that was a pleasure all its own. Bringing her down for another kiss, he constricted his other arm around her waist so she was full hilt on him. He allowed her very little movement, instead working his hips in and out so all her tissues were stroked and brought to combustible level in an astonishingly fast amount of time. When the kiss broke, he kept holding her that way, and so she pressed her face into his throat, gasped out her climax, her fingers clutching his shoulders wildly, toes curled tight where her legs were folded on the outside of his legs.

He released a few minutes after her, drawing out that unbearable yet wonderful sensitivity of her post-climactic tissues. The spurt of hot seed created an aftershock like a subtly intense second climax.

"Doughnuts," he said against her ear after a very long few moments. "I saw a Dunkin' Donuts around the corner, the first day I came to see you."

"Really? You don't seem the type to go for that crap. I was thinking the health-food store a couple blocks down. They have falafel sausage patties, kelp juice and tofu scrambled eggs."

"Harpy." The slap on her buttock made her yelp and other things tingle. His half-lidded eyes said he registered both reactions. His slow, easy grin said that he was willing to follow up on it . . . as soon as she brought doughnuts.

She slid off him with a smile, and he held her hand to the full length of their arms, until she had to let go of his fingers. "I'll be back soon," she whispered.

"You better be."

It was the first time in three years she'd felt happy.

KEEP HER CLOSE, SORCERER.

Derek came out of his doze with Mikhael's words replaying in his mind. He'd thought it an acid taunt. But the memory was caught in still frame. He woke with the picture front and center. The sneer had disappeared from Mikhael's lips, the eager light for battle dropping from his eyes as if it had never been there. He'd been delivering a serious message. *Keep her close.*

Derek thought it through, looked for anything that didn't feel right. He did a speed-read through everything that had happened since the Great Rite. Then he hit something that made the small hairs lift off his neck, cold fingers stabbing his gut.

The chamber where Rose was. Last night, when he was there with Ruby, there were so many things happening, he'd attributed the funny "off" feeling to the Dark energies she'd used to create that magic. However, he'd talked to her about the magic, mostly high-level discussion during lazy pillow talk, but now he recalled one point vividly.

"The Darkness part is like using wine in a recipe," she'd explained. "It burns off as part of the process, evaporates. It affects me, goes inside of me. It's not part of that chamber. Nothing but Light near Rose, ever."

So why had he felt Darkness in that chamber? It hadn't been from Ruby. No, it wasn't in the chamber. It was *beneath* it.

Why had Asmodeus attacked the Florida fault line? Why had he given up so quickly? Because it had been bait, to get Ruby away from here.

"Holy fucking Goddess." Derek bolted up out of the bed, grabbing for his jeans.

Not knowing the whole picture until last night, he hadn't put it together. But now it all made terrible sense. Whether they realized it or not, terrorists learned their strategy of sleeper cells from the Underworld. No one was as good at waiting as a demon. Three years would be less than a moment to Asmodeus.

He couldn't maintain corporeal form in the world unless he worked the right spells, which often attracted attention, since it meant a lot of dead bodies. However, he could drift in spirit wherever he wished, apparently harmless, but a spy was never harmless. He watched and learned. Asmodeus was a lord of chaos in a variety of ways, but he was also known for taking lust, twisting it into darker realms. So Asmodeus had likely been watching her all along, goading her in some of the paths she'd chosen, taking what was a natural compulsion and turning it into the violent hunger that Mikhael had mitigated, but which had still clouded her radar.

The demon probably knew every damn thing about Derek and Ruby, down to how many pancakes they'd had the other morning.

He'd known the fault line would bring Derek. It was also geographically too close to Ruby not to use it as an excuse to see her, involve her. And the moment the name Asmodeus left Derek's lips, Ruby would be on board.

Fuck it all, he'd been played by a demon. He'd drawn Ruby out, to Florida, giving Asmodeus time to craft a portal below the cave, the shortest escape route back to the Underworld. Blessing Raina, he reached out, looking for that tracking mark. Ruby was still a few blocks off. Maybe he could lock things down before she got back and into harm's way.

If Asmodeus got his claws on that sphere, he'd have access to an extremely complex magic he could unravel and reverse engineer. On top of that, once he had it, the bastard knew he had Ruby, because she would do anything to protect its contents. Including finish the job, sell her soul to him and make the Underworld her new forwarding address.

With the magical abilities she had, they'd force her to serve them with all that knowledge. She'd be the first to figure out how to stabilize demons' corporeal forms outside the Underworld. Giving them time to create all sorts of chaos and mayhem on the Earth, and still have time to shop at Walmart and hit up Hooters for a basket of wings.

Ruby'd had three years not only to hone her power, but

to tether it to Darkness, so hell, she'd put salt on his pizza for him. Asmodeus could just grab hold and reel her in.

SINCE IT WAS BEFORE DAWN, THE STREETS DARK, SHE'D been a prudent girl. She'd tucked her Sig in a belted holster beneath Derek's roomy shirt. It was a lot of gun for carrying, but she still had a thing about walking the streets in darkness, a phobia she refused to let deter her from a morning coffee run. Besides, the shirt went to mid-thigh over the voluminous skirt, so she wouldn't be scaring any early-morning dog walkers.

Logically, she knew she wasn't going to have any problems. The sleepy coastal town wasn't known for its plethora of predators, but a woman walking in a downtown area while the streets were still mostly deserted and it was dark didn't take any chances—other than the walking in the dark in the first place. But she had a different arsenal of weapons, above and beyond the gun, so a mere mortal wasn't much of a threat, really.

She was first in line for the fresh, hot doughnuts, and bought Derek a dozen, as well as his quart of black coffee. She chose two powdered sugar doughnuts for herself. Later today, once they checked in with Linda and told her when they'd come back to get Theo, maybe she and Derek could take a little time, stroll along the streets, and she could show him some of the shops here.

When she'd fled to this town, it had been an escape, not a planned destination, but over time she realized she liked the little coastal village, even the seedier elements that sometimes clustered near a military base. It was well integrated, a community of Light and Dark.

That thought sobered her some, thinking of the things Derek had said. He hadn't talked much about it for the rest of the night, holding to his promise. Which of course left her room to start thinking about it in her own way.

He'd probably known that, like he knew most things, the

arrogant bastard. But as she took her time now, walking down the street, watching the dark sky become streaked with those smoky blues that heralded the dawn, she sifted through his words. She knew he was right. She'd probably always known it, but she hadn't had the strength or inclination to face it, until now. Until he was back at her side.

She faced that truth, accepted it. Accepted that it wasn't because she couldn't stand on her own, but because there were things in this world too much for anyone to handle on their own. Having the person who loved you unconditionally stand at your back, be there to give strength, was vital. She'd needed Rose's father to be there with her, to give her the strength to say her final good-bye to her little girl.

Tears came as they always did, but this time they were like Easter rain, gentle and less painful. Less harsh. They were sorrow, regret, but there was hope in them as well. She imagined Rose growing up, having the chance to find a love as she had found one, learning the things she'd discovered.

Please, let her have parents who love her so much, it hurts. And they won't be afraid to show her how much they love her. She'll know she really, truly matters.

She closed her eyes, holding the thought. Drew a deep breath. He'd said the decision would be hers, that he could give her time. That—

Her eyes sprang open. A flight of birds was passing over, a rush of wings against a dark sky. They weren't flying as a flock, but in a haphazard manner, bumping into one another, their internal radar and navigation skewed, like a plane with instruments fried by lightning.

Her heart and stomach bumped into each other in the same chaotic response. She was attached to that sphere deep in the earth, blood and bone, and something was terribly wrong. In that first moment, she couldn't believe what she was feeling. Someone was messing with it. *No.* He'd promised. But she'd left him there . . .

Dropping the doughnuts and coffee, she bolted into a

run. Then she was airborne, hit by a blast as if an IED had gone off just beneath her feet.

Yeah, it might be nightmarish déjà vu, but she wasn't that same helpless girl. She twisted, called the winds to her and bounced off a cushion of air that slowed her momentum. She landed on her feet, spinning around to face her attacker.

That night long ago, she'd had only brief impressions of him. He moved so fast, he seemed more like wind than a corporeal being, which explained why she'd dispatched him in that lucky strike. He hadn't thought he'd need to be fully planted on the earthly plane to defeat her. Tonight he was as real as a nuclear device, ticking toward zero. She wondered how much blood had been spilled to make that possible.

He was leaning in a position of casual indolence against the light post. The town liked those traditional ones with the globe on top, the turned spindle posts. It suited him. Horror movies liked to depict creatures of darkness with mutated faces and gross, powerful, monstrous bodies, but the reality was they often looked like the front-row audience at a New York fashion show.

He had long silver hair. Not gray, not white, but actual gleaming, polished spoon silver. Bloodred eyes, ringed with a silver band prominent enough to be noticed and complement the hair in a disturbingly coordinated fashion. His clothing choice definitely wasn't a blend with the coastal environment. Tunic, leggings and boots, as well as long black fingernails that shimmered occasionally to give the impression of talons. They went well with his fangs, and she wondered how they got hold of Colgate whitener strips in Hell.

A ruby pendant hung on his neck, secured to his body with additional silver chains that ran to the belt of the tunic and down his back. They ran around the joining point of his wings. Large, dark leathery-looking things with tattered edges at the trailing ends and taloned scallops higher up that looked like sharp teeth. The talons oozed something venomous and blood-like, staining the leather.

He was beautiful and terrible. Like the children at the end of the hallway in *The Shining*, no one would mistake his beauty for anything but a pretty nightmare waiting to happen.

"He outthought me by a matter of seconds. That is very annoying."

She didn't care what he meant or why. She mainlined the Darkness in herself, pulled on the elements around her, and shot power at him like Nolan Ryan, a blinding arc of fire and speed.

He countered with his own volley, one that made the earth shudder beneath her. She dove into the alley between the hometown bank and the Western Union, conveniently located together. The fire rolled by as if ejected from a flamethrower, only the light of the explosion was as red as that ruby around his neck. She shielded herself against the heat, feeling it blast over her. Then all was darkness, silence.

She scrambled to the corner, listened. Nothing. She eased out, just a sliver of her face, then all of it. The street was empty. She looked up quickly, knowing those wings would make gravity a nonissue, unlike her biped self. Nothing. The residual was there, but the substance wasn't.

He'd been solid. She'd felt it. So how had he dematerialized like that?

Because he *was* solid, only not right here. Close by. Way close by.

He outthought me by a matter of seconds.

Her breath clogged in her throat, and she bolted out of the alley. *Derek.* Derek had gone into the chamber without her, but not to betray her. He'd felt Asmodeus coming and went to protect Rose. Even as her heart nearly burst with love for him, it was gripped with terror. He would be facing Asmodeus alone, with Rose to defend and hamper what he could do, because he didn't know enough about the magic that protected her to risk doing things that might harm the soul within it.

She'd left him blind, handicapped. She could very well lose them both.

* 20 *

THE METAL DOOR TO THE BASEMENT HAD BEEN BLASTED
on its hinges, charred frame still smoking and flickering
with sparks. It was Derek's work, in too much of a hurry to
attempt an unlock spell. His urgency only increased her
own. At one time, she and Derek had been so close, they
could almost read each other's thoughts, sense the other's
pain and distress, but she wasn't getting anything right now.
Maybe there was too much going on, Derek too involved to
project anything. Or, noble bastard that he was, he hadn't
wanted to draw her back here. She was betting on the latter.

That explained why Asmodeus had projected his phan-
tasmic self, to goad her into coming as fast as possible. He'd
tossed her around a bit to rattle her, of course, but the demon
wanted her present. She was supposed to distract Derek,
give him one more thing to worry about. Asmodeus wasn't
counting her as a real threat, which, while insulting, might
be the most important mistake the demon was making.

Even knowing she'd been pulled here deliberately, it

didn't slow her down. The man she loved and her daughter's soul were in danger. That was all she needed to know.

She flew down the steps, not bothering with those dim bulbs. The one at the top of the steps had been shattered, anyhow. She knew her way, and there was no need to announce the exact moment of her arrival by turning on all the lights.

Now she did feel Derek. In spades. She felt his urgency, his hyperalertness toward the foe he was facing, and his sharp, directed command for her to get the hell out of here. Not in words, of course, but the feeling was so pointedly strong there was no mistaking it for anything else. He didn't want her there. He thought she didn't realize that Asmodeus was bringing her deliberately. If she wasn't so worried about him, she'd have been insulted. And how the hell did he know she was this close?

Derek needed to learn she wasn't that same uncertain girl whom Asmodeus had attacked three years ago. Hell, she wasn't the same girl she was twelve hours ago, when she'd been beset by the fears and insecurities that came from shutting him out, lying and not trusting him. Things were different now, and if he wanted her to travel with him, she was fine with that, with him being her teacher, but he was going to learn she could stand and fight on her own two feet.

If they lived through this, she'd be sure to tell him so.

Moving swiftly down the stone steps of the cave tunnel, she sank quickly to a sitting position, hugging the wall as a rumble rocked the foundation under the stairs. Intuition gave her a blink of warning and she threw up a shield, just as the dust and heat from the explosion billowed up the stairs like a pyroclastic cloud. The scalding touch of sheer power roared over her. Without the shield, it would have peeled her skin from her body and left her a melted, gooey skeleton. Even sitting, she rocked precariously as it rolled over her like a freight train. Bits of rock showered down on her, but, thank Heaven, the walls held. She didn't relish being buried alive. Not that it was the biggest issue on her mind right now.

Derek. Rose. Scrambling back up, she fought her way through the smoke, holding the wall, following the steps from long familiarity instead of sight. She kept that shield in place until she reached a lower point where she had visibility again. Like the Starship *Enterprise*, she couldn't shield and attack at the same time. Otherwise what she threw would bounce off her shields from the inside and ricochet right back onto her. Embarrassing *and* terminal, a sucky combination.

She was going to figure out how to fix that glitch. Again—important caveat—*if* she lived through this.

The outer chamber was empty, of course. Derek would choose to protect Rose in the area that had the most protections for the sphere. Ruby slipped to the illusory opening, wormed her way carefully through its *S* shape, then flattened herself against the wall, trying to determine tactical advantage from the throw of shadows and voices.

"Give me the soul, and I will accept half of what I came for," Asmodeus rasped.

Derek let out a short but notably strained chuckle. He was hurt. The fear around her heart constricted, her adrenaline spiked by uncertainty. If the demon could do that to Derek, what could Asmodeus do to her? Was she just kidding herself? Or was she still that girl with too much power and too little knowledge to use it?

If you use your power, it will only come to tragedy. Hide it; never use it . . .

God, she wasn't sure what was worse at this moment. Facing a demon or being haunted by her mother's syrupy voice. Derek had not responded further, the chuckle an answer in itself. He wisely didn't believe in making chitchat. She was sure he was looking for an opening, because their voices were moving, circling. Daring a glance into the chamber, she came back against the wall, her heart thumping high in her throat once again.

Derek was bleeding from his temple, so much blood that it was blinding his right eye. He was also holding his side, as if his ribs had been damaged. The sphere was behind him. Somehow he'd anchored Rose so she was moving with him. As she'd feared, he didn't know the magic well enough to risk anything more than shielding it. And that was tying his hands.

Asmodeus was done chatting up Derek as well. An ominous chant started, heat swelling in the room as fast as if a furnace door had been opened. Derek countered before the demon could complete the chant.

Ruby yelped, jumping to the right as a battering ram of power exploded past her, taking out a large chunk of the wall, creating a new, more spacious doorway into the other chamber. More dust and smoke rolled over her. The cave rocked from the impact, rumbling for a much longer period. Somewhere, things were falling, crumbling. She hoped it wasn't the stairwell.

Asmodeus had moved past her right before it hit, narrowly escaping being caught in the volley. He yowled, though, suggesting he hadn't come off unscathed. She needed to move. Derek might know her position, but he might not. That had been awfully close, and he'd be pretty aggravated with her if he blew her to pieces before he did the same to Asmodeus.

Before she could do anything, however, another percussion hit. Goddess, it was like the soldiers said, those who discussed firefights when they were in her shop. No time to breathe, nothing but the noise, noise, noise, explosions vibrating through the chest and feet and head, every survival instinct screaming to run, though training kicked in and made you do otherwise. She'd dropped to her heels, her hands over her ears. The chamber shook as if in the fist of an angry giant. The sense of crumbling, disintegration, the roar of rock, grew louder.

"No." Ruby scrambled to her feet, but instead of retreating, she plunged forward through the crumbling opening. If Derek had tried that deliberately to keep her out, she was so going to kick his ass.

It wasn't Derek. She came up short, a shriek catching in her throat. A yawning hole had replaced the cave floor. Jagged edges gave the macabre impression of teeth around the maw of a monster. She stared down into a dizzying abyss, saw dark flame waiting, far below. Waiting to accept a body after it ricocheted and smashed against the rock like a pinball.

Derek. She gazed wildly into that opening, seeking him.

"Ruby, down."

She dropped as the net of green flame passed over her. It snagged her flailing arm, snapping the net back like a rubber band. It wound around her biceps, growing outward to cover and pin her to that ledge, drag her over it.

"Serrate," she snarled, swallowing the pain as the spell's detonation, so close to her, flashed over her skin. Hell, she hadn't even put on her SPF 40 moisturizer this morning. For some crazy reason, the macabre image of a makeup party she'd attended with Ramona years before flashed in her head. The perfectly made-up hostess explaining, *Every night you don't take off your makeup before bed ages your skin three days.*

Wonder what she recommends for a thousand degrees centigrade at a ten-foot distance?

The green net parted as if sliced down the middle. Scrambling free, she leaped to another ledge of rock, an incisor over that gaping hole. She spun in time to see Derek engage Asmodeus again. He was wielding what appeared to be a thick staff, about a yard long. She recognized the rainstick she'd used when she integrated a gentle rain noise into the rotating array of illusions in Rose's world. Just like selecting the music options on an MP3 player, Rose's mind could choose whatever gave her pleasure from moment to moment. Ruby hoped this moment wasn't penetrating, unless it was like a soothing, distant roll of thunder behind that gentle rainstorm.

Derek could use anything to focus his energy, but it was incongruous to see him lifting the relatively fragile object as a weapon. Until it transformed, and he held a white ash staff instead, nearly as long as he was. But oddly, as he used it to absorb the shards of fire from Asmodeus's random attacks, she could still hear the rainstick. Both males grunted with exertion to dodge, deflect and absorb the whistling projectiles they were hurling, and those noises of battle were mixed with that rain noise, like the tiny chuckle of fairies.

As Derek pivoted, Ruby could see the aura of the tether he'd used for the sphere, like tying a balloon to one's wrist to keep it from floating away. With a direct line of sight, of feeling, she could tell nothing was disturbed in the sphere. Rose was still dreaming, unaware a demon had come to suck away that charged amniotic fluid, leaving her soul a defenseless husk, adrift forever if he was successful.

She couldn't get a clear shot to help. Derek and Asmodeus were moving too fast, astoundingly, awesomely fast, ducking, lunging, attacking. Sharp rock was flying, such that she'd had to put her shields up again. Some were finding their target on both demon and sorcerer as they danced around the ledge. They didn't stay on the ledge, though. Asmodeus used his wings, and when Derek moved into open space, it held him, as if he'd conjured a platform for himself out of air, and he likely had. The magic of all elements was available to him, after all, and he was not afraid to draw from them. He had the ability, the understanding.

You can't use your power. It will only lead to tragedy.

She was standing here, impotent. She couldn't do anything like what they were doing. How could she be anything but a hindrance? It was the first rule of gun use. If you weren't sure what you were doing, you were better off retreating, running or getting out of the way. Else pulling your gun would likely get other people or yourself killed.

Asmodeus howled and threw his body forward. Derek backpedaled, for a demon's touch was as venomous and deadly. In that brief second, Ruby saw the shadows gather above and leap.

Fuck, soul-eaters. Goddamn demon was cheating, calling in reinforcements. They landed on Derek as he backed right into them. Because of the protections on Rose, they stayed clear of the sphere, but they covered him, blinded him. His heels hit the ledge behind his air platform and he stumbled. Normally, he'd blast them right off. But he couldn't, not while shielding Rose.

Asmodeus snarled, moving in, those long talons now glowing red like iron, reaching for Derek. He clamped down on Derek's wrist through that dark blanket of shadows, and Ruby felt the reverberation of agony from the sorcerer as the soul-eaters, eager to drain him, sank their fangs into him.

Fuck you, Mother.

The power unfurled inside of her, Dark, Light and all shades in between. While this battle might be happening underground, lightning didn't exist only in the sky. Unlike Derek, she wasn't hampered by what she could draw from below. Reaching down, she called for a storm of energy from the bowels of the Underworld itself. Belatedly, she realized she'd stepped right out into that open space, but she'd conjured herself a platform of air, just as Derek had. Years of study had dovetailed into automatic instinct.

Asmodeus's crimson eyes flickered toward her, surprise and alarm there. The cold wind spiraled up, straight from the mouth of the Underworld Asmodeus had opened himself, helpful bastard that he was.

Unfortunately, his shock was short-lived. His lips pulled back from his fangs, his hissing voice filling the chamber like a thousand snakes. "You will unleash Hell on Earth, little girl, and you will not know how to put it back."

"Pandora didn't have him." Jerking her head at Derek, Ruby let the power go like hitting the lever of a catapult. As she released it, she shouted the command at the top of her lungs. *"Derek, shield yourself. Now."*

Lightning cracked through the chamber, shooting up from that opening. The soul-eaters screamed, their bodies flashing transparent, like a macabre cartoon where the skeleton could be seen. They let go of Derek. Asmodeus snarled as the charge reverberated through his soles, grabbing him. His bat-like wings snapped open, holding him up, even as he jittered in the grip of the voltage.

Ruby got a quick glimpse of Derek's pale face behind a shimmer of power, a major relief, since she wasn't sure if he'd managed to protect himself. He looked pissed off in a major way, even beneath the blood, which meant he couldn't be mortally wounded—right? Of course, he was the type of guy who would react to being mortally wounded just that way. Trying not to think about that, she stepped farther out over the abyss, advancing on Asmodeus. Her hair was flying around her face, lightning shards crackling over her palms in a disturbing tingle as she lifted both hands. Her skirt whipped around her.

The Darkness reared its head, summoned by her anger, her desire for revenge. *You took my baby. You made me afraid. You attacked my guy, you son of a bitch.* As the barbed magic lashed out from her, she recalled the scene from *Lord of the Rings* she'd always associated with Derek. Khazad-dum . . . *You shall not pass.* Only instead of Gandalf, now she saw the Balrog, striking with that fiery whip at the last moment, taking him down. She was the Balrog, coated in darkness, and she'd take it all down with her. All of it. She could make Asmodeus suffer, writhe in pain, scream with the agony of it.

But Darkness was all about pain and agony. The more

Mikhael had given her, the more she'd wanted, the hunger only abated for short periods, not gone. Her gaze snapped to the sphere, where Rose lived in a world with no darkness, no pain. Even though her mother had dealt with Darkness to protect her, there'd been no Darkness in that spell, nothing in that chamber to touch Rose with fear or pain. There'd been a reason for that.

Twelve hours of love, of trust and healing . . . Her heart might be fragile as glass, but it had made a key difference, given her back vital parts of herself. She saw Derek register what she was doing, his alarm and calculation, but she didn't give him time to go beyond that, to decide what heroic and unacceptably dangerous measure he needed to take to protect her. She let go of the barbed magic, vanquished it with a sweep of her hands, a thrust of energy to send it spiraling off into the air, inert. It wasn't the weapon she needed for this.

"Derek, let her go." She shouted it over the din of the funneling elements. "Let her go."

He locked gazes with her, verifying she'd said what she said. It was barely a blink, but if she survived this, she knew she'd recall it later as something much longer. Because in that split second she saw he understood what it meant to her to make that decision. And she wanted to tell him it was because of that comprehension, his love, that she had the strength to say it, mean it.

He let Rose go. Asmodeus, recovering way too fast from that strike, zeroed in on it like a torpedo's tracking system. Before he could leap, Derek tossed a handful of sand in the air. In an instant, the grains became a hundred orbs the same size as Rose's, spinning and moving through the chamber, confusing the eye and thwarting any attempt by the demon to interfere with the real sphere's path.

When the illusion cleared, she'd called the sphere straight to her, anchored it in her hands. The power of it pulsed between her palms, the complex world she'd created. She'd become a Goddess, shaping this small world the way the bigger one should be, not the way it was. And she'd told Linda that wasn't the way the world was supposed to work, no matter the heartbreak that such a truth brought.

The meaning of that Goddess's power, the choices, the good and bad of such energy, coursed through her as Ruby stared over her daughter at Asmodeus.

She was cognizant of Derek watching her, ready, alert, locked on the way she stood over the abyss, her magic holding her up, its strength continuing to blow her hair back in wild disarray. What held her up was solid. A foundation that could never be shattered. Her faith in herself.

I decide who and what I am, Mother. Not you. You doubted your own worth so much that you had to steal mine. But I forgive you for your weakness.

"Is this what you want, Asmodeus?" She rotated it in her hands, and the mist that wisped around it began to lengthen, twine around her wrists. All of it was here, the magic traded with the pieces of her soul. Given out of love, as Derek had said. "Then open wide, because here it comes."

With a sharp word, she cracked it like an egg between her palms.

The contents zinged forth like a chaotic explosion of fireworks. She'd woven the magic with clever, painstaking care, but, like all power concentrations, if the wrong string was pulled, it could detonate like a bomb.

The meadows and ponies, butterflies and rainbows, candy and long naps on green grass . . . all that, plus the incredible array of elemental and Underworld magics. The brilliant tapestry illuminated the room, filled it to bursting. She was plastered against the wall, the weight of it compressing her shields such that if they gave way, she'd be crushed.

She'd held off on her shields as long as she could so as not to warn the demon. It might be minutes or seconds; time lost meaning. She couldn't see whether Asmodeus had managed to protect himself, whether Derek was all right. Though he'd probably give her hell about it later, she'd found the power in that last blink to throw a net over him as well, not knowing how hurt he was at this point or whether he had the strength to protect himself from something of this magnitude so quickly.

Pieces of her soul had paid for that magic. Now that it was released, her soul weakened, the connection lost. She focused all her will on holding her own shields, holding Derek's. And with fierce resolve, holding that one tiny spark against her breast, all that remained of the sphere.

As the light cleared, she blinked, oriented herself. It was hard. She was dazed, as if she'd been caught in a bomb blast in truth. But she had to see; it was critical, because the job wasn't done. She wished it was, but she was sure it wasn't.

There. Asmodeus was still holding himself up, still corporeal, but he was struggling. The pieces, charged by love and Light, had embedded themselves in him like shrapnel, and they were eating at his skin. He was losing ground, but unless she could weaken that corporeal form further, he might rebound. Unfortunately, she was too weak, no magical energy left, and she didn't see Derek. Just a pile of rock where he'd been, another chunk torn out of the wall. *Derek.*

Goddamn it all. Her lip curling back from her teeth, she reached beneath her shirt, drew the Sig and fired.

Fifteen shots in the mag. Despite her weakening body and the recoil of the powerful gun, she did it steady and one-handed, emptying every bit of it into Asmodeus, blowing chunks of his torso away, tearing those nice clothes. No, she couldn't kill a demon. But an unexpected attack on the shell? Maybe that would be her ace in the hole. Goddess knew, it was the last card she had to play. She was slipping off the edge of the too-narrow ledge, had no strength left to hold her up. But that was irrelevant. She just had to stay high enough, long enough, for this.

The demon was howling, snarling, his body twisting. The precious bit of Rose pulsed against Ruby's heart, even as her mother's breath got more labored. She was going to slip, needed to let go of Rose. Free, the baby's soul would float, get where she needed to go. She hoped. If that happened, nothing else mattered. She had to believe Derek was alive, would make sure of it. He was invincible, her cowboy.

Then she felt him. His magic reached out to her, twining around her, holding her up. She sobbed at the sheer physical relief, like a climber who'd been hanging on to a ledge for so long that being hauled up was a pleasurable agony.

His hands were on her now, pulling her back into the widened opening to the anteroom chamber, which, thanks to the Asmodeus & Derek Demolition Company, had a spacious front-row view to the chasm of Hell. Managing a quick look up into his bloodstained face, she immediately picked up on his lead. Reaching out with her free hand, holding that spark against her breast with the other, she clasped his wrist so the reserve of power she found now, bolstered by his presence, came surging through her and joined his.

His body pressed against hers, arms out to either side, all that energy coalescing and firing through his palms as if he were a two-pistoled gunfighter. Every shard of power that shot from him like lightning from a cloud was focused as a laser, the circle of protective power and energy around him as solid as a wall. They let Asmodeus have it, a combined volley of Derek's energy and Ruby's will.

Twining together their magic with effortless artistry, he used it with ruthless power to send her enemy back to Hell where he belonged. And at every point their bodies touched, that power coursed through her as well.

Melded together in their intent, it was the most incredible thing she'd ever felt.

Then the feeling was gone, fading. She watched blearily as Asmodeus fell with his soul-eaters, disappearing in a chaotic spiral of wings. He bounced off those rocks, just as she'd imagined herself doing. *Boing, boing, bang. And don't come back, asshole. I'm not weak. I'm not your victim. I'm nobody's victim.*

She was suddenly having a hard time breathing. As Derek lowered her to the floor, she noticed the rainstick next to them, a rainstick once more, and touched it. It almost made her smile. He'd used it as a weapon, but it had also been used to soothe a little girl. That was the way power worked. As she moved it, it made its little metallic shower of comforting sound. Derek was there, crouched over her, cradling her face. "Ruby? Ruby, girl, look at me."

She gazed up at him. He was too pale under his tan. She could smell his blood, feel it in the tremor in his hands. "I'm sorry. It hurts. It hurts so badly."

"I know." His countenance darkened. "Hold on."

But her attention shifted, and Derek looked over his shoulder to track it. He spun, rising to his feet to block her, but she caught the leg of his jeans, shaking her head. "No . . . he's come before."

Derek glanced down at her, saw the truth of it, then looked back to the silent visitor, gauging who and what he was. When he figured it out, she saw his broad shoulders ease, even as his mouth tightened, understanding.

Ruby swallowed. Every time this being had come, she'd defied the apparition, blocked him, refused to give him what he wanted, as fiercely as she'd just denied Asmodeus. But she couldn't deny him this time. Derek had helped her see. She had to do it. She knew that, just as she knew she'd never reach a point when she was truly ready to do it.

The death angel spread his wings to half fold, his expression somber, waiting. He wasn't unkind. In fact, there was a deep compassion beneath his ruthless inevitability. He didn't reach out, didn't push her. He simply waited, a force as undeniable as the ocean.

"Can you help her?" Derek asked. He'd dropped back on his heels, his hand on Ruby's shoulder. She was shaking, too, she realized vaguely. It didn't matter.

The angel shook his head, nodded toward what she had at her breast. She made herself look up at Derek, held on to the strength in his blue eyes. The grief he showed her openly, sharing it with her.

"I would have loved her so much, Derek."

"You did love her, baby. You do. You always will. Be her mother. Let her go. Just like you told me."

She bent her head, touched her lips to that bundle of light, now no longer in a heaven of her making. But she'd made sure the soul had stayed close to her breast, had given her that tiny, thin cocoon as the rest of the magic was pulled away. The baby's soul was aware things had changed, but she wasn't afraid. She was with her mother. She would take her mother's love with her, and she would be happy, because Ruby couldn't bear to think anything else.

Lifting her head, she cupped both hands around that soul, and extended it to Derek. "You hold her. Give her . . . to him."

Derek nodded. His expression was full of emotion too painful for her to see as he cradled the much smaller sphere in his hands. As she had, he bent his head over it, laid his lips on it, his eyes closing. She imagined he was saying a prayer for their daughter. Knowing Derek, it included the stern admonition that the angels had better take care of her, or he'd come kick some major ass. She'd have smiled over it, if her smiles didn't feel far away, in some part of her she'd given away.

He handed over the spark. The angel took it, in the same gentle manner, nodded to them both. Then he was simply gone, and the chamber was empty, silent, except for the whistle of air coming up through that chasm in front of them. Or maybe it was the chasm inside of her, where a whole soul used to be.

HER BREATHING WAS GETTING MORE LABORED. "I GUESS you'll need to repair that," she said at length, gazing at the abyss.

"One thing at a time. You first."

"Any good ideas on that?" She managed a wry smile that he didn't answer, his gaze concerned, worried. "My body won't die, but without those soul pieces . . ."

She was a broken porcelain figure, holes and cracks. She couldn't move without risk of further breakage. She didn't want to move. "What do you think we should do?"

"You marry me; we have two point five kids, a picket fence and a golden retriever that will bite Raina when she comes to visit us."

"Theo may have something to say about that."

"I know—he'd rather have the pleasure of biting Raina. We'll make sure the golden's a girl for him."

"He's been neutered."

"A guy can still flirt."

He was lifting her, though she felt the strain of it in his body. "You broke ribs. How are you . . ."

"Not broken. Just extremely bruised. He got in a lucky strike."

"Yeah, right." She laid her head on his shoulder as he carried her back up the stairs to the basement area. Once there, he laid her on the floor, took the piece of broken rock he'd brought with him and began to etch a circle around her in the dirt. "What—"

"Lie still, baby. I'm going to make it all better."

He drew the circle, cast it with a deftness that would have impressed her with its immediate solidity and weight if she wasn't drifting, purposeless. It was so hard to care about anything, but it still hurt like hell. How weird was that? She came back to the present fast when he used his pocket knife to cut open the shirt she was wearing. He drew the blade across his wrist, the blood welling up, bright and red. The drops pattered onto her sternum.

"Derek, no . . ." She knew this magic, knew it was never done. Rarely done. People gave kidneys to loved ones, because that was the nature of those organs; they had two of them, after all. She tried to lift her hands, but he simply pressed them down, out of his way, as he began the chant. Laying his hand over that blood on her chest, he charged it with his intent.

Even if she could accept that he was about to do this, it required a full coven. He couldn't do it alone. Not and have any strength left when it was over. No matter how well he'd done at the end, she knew he wasn't at full peak.

"Then I guess you'll be the one carrying me up those stairs."

She must have said it aloud. She wet her lips, stared up at him. "Don't do this."

"It's happening. Deal with it. You promised to marry me. You're not going to get out of it so easily."

"Yeah, well, I promised you coffee and doughnuts this morning. See how that turned out?" Her voice was fainter. His brow creased and the pressure of his hand on her chest increased.

"Be still, baby. Just close your eyes and let it happen."

He built the power in that circle so fast and strong, it was overwhelming. This was what he knew how to do, what came as easily to him as breathing. It didn't matter that he was hurt, that he'd lost blood. Nothing disrupted his focus. She had to open her eyes to watch him, because as a magic user she couldn't *not* watch him pull off one of the most awe-inspiring pieces of magic there was. She'd had to do it with complicated potions, chants, working with elemental energies and dipping into the Dark well of the Underworld. He simply focused the power on himself, reached into that well of . . . essence, for lack of a better word, and split a chunk off for her. A piece of his soul.

He stiffened, a lance of obvious excruciating pain doubling him over. "Derek—"

She cried out then, alarmed, because suddenly she was pinned, held down by an incredible weight, as if something enormous was being pushed under her rib cage, something that would never fit, never go right . . . but then, like a dislocated shoulder, it popped into place.

She was gasping, her vision blurry. Twisting to her side, she retched out black, vile-smelling liquid. The stench of it, the feel of it, told her she was seeing the Darkness she'd taken into herself, the change from those pieces of soul she'd sold for Rose's Heaven. She knew what to do here, didn't need to make Derek do more than he had already. She cleansed it with white fire as soon as she could prop herself on her arms. Then she turned to find him collapsed, the blood still trickling from the cut on his arm.

Scrambling drunkenly over to him, she turned him with a grunt of exertion and had a harrowing moment, trying to find his pulse. There, steady, strong. He opened his eyes.

"Going to lie here a bit. Then we'll get that coffee."

IT WAS AN INEXPRESSIBLE FEELING. HER SOUL, BUT something more than her soul, too, cobbled with his. That intuition they'd always shared was somehow enhanced, as if they didn't even really need to talk at all. She was as aware of his proximity and the emotions he carried as she was of her own. Was this what twins were like? One overly large soul split apart at birth? Of course, they were already soul mates, weren't they? She'd denied it for over three years, but as a young girl, it seemed like she'd known it before she even knew what it meant. This just enhanced the truth of it.

He did lie there for quite a while. When she could manage it, she went above, got some blankets, pillows. She wished she had some fresh flowers to bring down and add color and life to the dank basement room while he convalesced there. Funny, it had been a while since she'd thought of something like that as important. Though he grumbled about it, she brought her first-aid kit and at least cleaned the gash on his skull, which fortunately hadn't fractured the bone, as far as she could tell.

"So not even a demon straight from Hell can crack your hard head," she noted. "Color me shocked. This could use some stitches, you know." She was trying to hide her worry. Her body felt revitalized, whereas he was still pale and obviously sapped. Had Derek given her too much? What if he'd simply exchanged his own life for hers? It would be like him to do that. He might be ageless, but it didn't mean he couldn't be killed. She'd never asked him about that.

"Are you going to die or go soulless zombie on me?" she snapped abruptly. "Did you do something that pigheaded and stupid?"

His blue eyes opened, firm mouth quirking in that way she loved, that made her heart hurt. "As much as you would obviously appreciate that sacrifice, no. What I did . . . It's like giving you a piece of lung, and the cells regenerate to create more of a lung, build on it. I gave you an extra piece of soul to adhere to your own, and as you practice the Light magic, stay away from Dark, it should strengthen it, restore you fully as time goes on."

"And what about you?" she asked shrewdly. "How does this impact you?"

"I'll feel its loss awhile. But as long as you're near, I have my whole soul, don't I?" Lifting a hand, he brushed it across her cheek. "I'm sorry about Rose."

"No." She shook her head, even as her voice broke a little over it. "You were right. She's where she needs to be. It was time. I'm not sure I can ever regret holding on to her as long as I did, even though it might have been the wrong thing to do. I can't ever regret a single second she got to be mine."

"She'll always be yours. Just like me." He gave her a shadow of his usual heart-stopping smile, then paused, considering. "If we could turn back time, I wouldn't want you to do it the way you did it . . . but I'm glad I got the chance to see her, touch her." He met her eyes, opened himself to her in a way that was new for her experience of Derek, a way that warmed the cold crevices of her heart. "I never had a child. Someone who would miss me if I wasn't around, in a blood-related kind of way."

She ducked her head so he wouldn't see the tears gathering in her eyes. "If you're as insufferable to our next child as you are to me, she'll probably want you gone."

"Especially if it's a girl."

"You are a natural irritant to females," Ruby agreed.

"Did you just put me in the same category as feminine itching?"

"If the shoe fits . . ."

"I'll get even with you for that later," he promised.

"I needed your strength to do it, to let go," she admitted. "You've come in and out of my life so much, ever since I was a little girl. Giving me room to become who I am, to make my own decisions. But you've always been there when I truly need you, to help me get through things. I've told you why I pushed you away, but I didn't tell you that, and I . . . I just want you to know."

He cupped her cheek, his thumb caressing her lips. He was so attentive, so loving, so essential to her, she wasn't sure now just how she'd managed three years without him. Well, yeah, she did. *Badly.* And wouldn't it just feed that overbearing male ego to hear her admit that? She had a responsibility to womankind everywhere to pull it back together.

Sniffling, she pushed his touch away to wipe her nose gracelessly. "But I swear, if you did something that causes you to be permanently . . . maimed, or whatever, I won't talk to you again. Besides which, you knocked my gun off the ledge when you were scrambling over me. That was one of my favorite guns."

"Shooting him was an effective tactic. A very unexpected one against a demon. Fighting two magic users, he never saw that coming. You weakened him enough to put the nail in his coffin." Derek's tone was admiring, pleasing her, even though she took pains not to show it.

"Well." She shrugged. "It's like I said. Magic doesn't always work, but superior firepower has never failed me."

"I might have to consider adding to my arsenal, then."

"I might give you a discount, with the proper incentive."

His chuckle eased her tension, but she wouldn't be fooled any longer. She touched his face. "You need a healing ritual by a full coven. And you need it now. Do you think you have one more transport in you? I'd do it, but that's a sorcerer trick, not a witch one. At least, not one I know. Yet."

"Trick?" He gave her an offended look. "I'll—"

"Please." She gripped his shoulder. "I'm worried, Derek. You don't look good."

He squeezed her leg. "Don't get all worried, girl. I've been worse off than this plenty of times. Hold on to me. I'll take us right to the circle. You can go get Linda and her ladies. Just don't let Theo trample and slobber all over me while I'm on my back, helpless as a turned turtle."

"You sure you have the strength to do this?" She stretched out at his side to put both her arms around him, trying not to hang on to anything that might be hurting. "I could call Raina and Ramona."

"Be at Raina's mercy? Not in this lifetime." He snorted. "Besides, it's no big deal. If I don't have the strength to transport us, we'll end up in a million intertwined atoms, scattered across the universe. Kind of romantic, don't you think?"

"Derek, you ass—"

The world disappeared.

* 21 *

THE HEALING RITUAL DID HELP HIM. HE INSISTED ON walking out of the circle, but the fact he allowed her to hold him up on one side and the sturdy Christine on the other told her he needed some recuperation time. A shower would have to wait. She put him in her bed in the guesthouse, pulled off his boots. By the time she'd done that, he was already out, slumped back on the bed. He was wearing only jeans, because of course that and the boots were the only things he'd taken the time to yank on before he went to the cave to protect Rose from Asmodeus.

Christine helped her get the rest of the clothes off in a fussy, no-nonsense manner that would have told Ruby she was a nurse, even if her taking a quick check of his vitals now didn't do so. "He's all right," the older woman said reassuringly, with an understanding look at the hand Ruby kept on him, as if he'd disappear if she stopped touching him. "Just worn-out, poor man. Let him rest; keep him company. I think that's what he needs. And get some rest yourself."

While the more cognitive levels of her brain were completely tapped out, physically she actually felt better than she'd felt in months. She hadn't realized the sapping energy of that Darkness within her, but she knew it was not only that. She'd made some important decisions. About herself, Rose and Derek. Though there were sorrow and regret, she knew whatever direction she chose from here would be better.

Of course, that brought a fleeting shadow of a thought, about her and Derek, but she pushed it away for now. There'd be time to deal with that. Instead of feeling helpless about the inevitability of it, she had a quiet, resolute calm, underscored with the painful knowledge that it was the right decision.

For now, though, first things first. She found a basin in the kitchen, filled it with warm water and soap, got a washcloth out of the bathroom and gave him a sponge bath, knowing he liked to be clean, that he'd grumble about messing up her sheets. She didn't care. He was here, and alive. As she passed her cloth over those fine long limbs, the muscled chest, his handsome face, she didn't realize she was crying again until he shifted, his eyes half opening. His hand came up, cupped her face, and then he was groping for her waist, tugging her onto the bed with him.

"Come here, girl. Sleep with me. Be with me."

She put the basin aside. "Tell me if I'm hurting anything."

In answer he grunted, pulled her closer so she was draped over him. Putting a hand over her temple, he absently stroked her there. "Sleep, baby."

So she did, stretching her other arm out over him. Theo climbed up on the bed with painstaking effort, but once there he managed to lie down on Derek's other side without trampling the sorcerer. Now they had him sandwiched between them. She laid a palm on Theo's side, her forearm across Derek's chest so she could feel both their hearts beat, and let her eyes close.

SHE CODDLED DEREK AS LONG AS HE LET HER, WHICH of course wasn't long. She brought him food in bed, kept him company, opened the doors and windows wide in the cottage during the sunny day. By the second morning, he wanted up. They joined Linda for dinner each night after that, and sometimes the coven came as well. Ruby handled the final teaching points with Derek watching and offering input from the bench in the gazebo they insisted he use.

During the days, she managed to coax him into mostly sitting on the cottage or main house porch, particularly when she sat between his feet, leaning against his leg and scratching Theo's stomach. Sometimes the coven members joined him there, and he showed them things. Simple things for him, but amazing to the array of witches. Like creating wind knots from a length of rope.

With mesmerizing skill and grace, he'd focus his power, speak the phrases, and twist and thread the rope into the necessary three knots. Depending on which knot was untied, a fisherman would be given a pleasant breeze, a stiffer wind to pull him out of a tricky area, or an all-out gale. Perhaps for the days when he'd prefer to stay in the marina to drink beer, he explained gravely, amusing the women.

Occasionally, during their morning breakfast times out on that porch, she tried to tickle Derek's bare soles while he drank his coffee and read his newspaper. One morning, he rolled up the latter and threatened to swat her with it like the dog. But it was the day he came out of the chair, managing to chase her a few paces, all without gripping his side or showing much discomfort, she knew he was getting better. Things eased in her stomach, even while they tightened up in her chest, that shadow returning.

TODAY HE'D CAUGHT HER. SHE WIGGLED AWAY FROM THE slap of the newspaper with an indignant shriek, taking a boxer's defensive stance once she got free.

"You better be careful when I'm drinking hot coffee," he advised. "I might burn something you have a use for."

She sniffed, unimpressed. "You better be careful how you use that newspaper. Don't forget what happened with Merlin and Nimue, tough guy. She locked him in a cave for a bazillion years."

"Yeah, but when he got out, payback was hell."

As he settled back in his chair, giving her a gimlet eye, she put herself in the chair across from him. Folding her knees up against herself, her feet curled over the edge, she knew she was taking a defensive stance, cradling that cold ball of apprehension that had formed in her stomach. It was time for the idyllic pause to end; she knew it. He'd given her part of his soul. Forgiven her, as she'd forgiven him. She had to be brave enough to broach the subject.

"I guess I better be getting home, and you need to go do . . . whatever it is you do next."

Derek glanced at her over his paper. With his usual infallible intuition, he folded it precisely, set it aside and leveled his full attention on her. "I expect what I do next is up to you, Ruby. You have a decision to make."

She nodded. It didn't surprise her that he'd neatly and directly turned the muzzle of that gun right at her, but it didn't make it easier. She was determined not to get what she wanted and what was right messed up again. If she could learn how to do it on a regular basis, maybe one of these days she'd get both in the same package, right? Folding her arms on her knees, she laid her head there, looking toward him. Her hair spilled down her arm.

"You need to do what you do, Derek. I understand that. And I appreciate the gesture, the things you said. But . . . I can accept the way it is for us. I like North Carolina. I'll stay there for now, and, you know, you come to me when you can. As you always have. I can accept that."

"You can, hmm? Is that what you want?"

She lifted a shoulder. "It isn't about that."

"Yeah, as a matter of fact, it is." He leaned forward, his knees splayed, forearms braced loosely on them. It brought his regard closer to her, hemming her into the space with the intent look in his eyes. "I'm all for selflessness, sacrifice, service. The world needs those things in good measure from all of us. But remember the whole balance thing? What happened, you having to deal with all that alone, not thinking you had the right—*the goddamned right*—to ask for more . . . Thinking you had to figure it out all by yourself, that's when things get out of balance."

She rose from the chair, moved out of his unsettling proximity. "I realize that. I would handle things differently now. I mean, birth control might be a good idea, because obviously, we should plan better in the future, now that you can, you know, have kids. At least with me." She cleared her throat, aware of his narrowed glance. "But you can't not save the world when it needs saving, Derek. Neither of us could handle the weight of that. We'll make this work the way it needs to work, but I'm not going to let you be less than you are. You wouldn't let me do that, so I'm sure as hell not going to let you get away with it just because you're worried I'll do something dumb to compromise my soul again. And I'm not going to let you—"

Derek rose from the chair. In two steps he closed the distance between them, putting his hands on her arms. "You think you run everything in this relationship? You can tell me what I will and won't do? You won't be doing that again, with or without soul magic."

She flushed. "You're going to be harping on that forever, aren't you? I wouldn't try to tell you to do anything, because you're stubborn as a brick wall."

"Says the kettle."

She struggled to hold on to her temper. She was trying to do the right thing, the noble thing. He wasn't getting it. She also tried to move out of his grasp, unsuccessfully. His grip just tightened. In fact, he pulled her closer, so she was almost up against his chest, staring angrily up into his blue eyes. He looked a little riled himself.

She fought for calm, rationality. She'd thought this through, during the long hours he slept, the nights she'd sat out here alone and looked up at the stars and the moon. At that time, she'd felt at peace with the decision, calm with it. In hindsight, she should have just hit him on the head with a skillet, told him this was the best way, and see if an extra wallop with the cast iron might be more effective than the pointless exercise of adult conversation. Actually, there was a skillet in the kitchenette. She could try it just for the personal satisfaction.

"All I'm trying to say," she said evenly, "is we don't have to change things right away. We can take some time, make sure that decisions . . . weren't made in the heat of the moment, things we might not have meant, not right away. You don't need me hanging around your neck, hampering you when—"

"Ruby." He cut across her, biting off each syllable. "I'm older than some of the Seven Wonders. How often do you think I say what I don't mean these days? Don't be pulling this 'we' bullshit. If you're scared of me being a bigger part of your life, you say so. We'll deal with it. If you don't want me as a bigger part of your life, you go ahead and spit that out. I'll call you a liar and we'll be done with it."

"You son of a bitch." She shoved at his chest, managing to put space between them this time. "You're not listening. You—"

"No. You're the one not listening," Derek exploded. "Damn it, I'm not giving you a choice. Either you come with me, or I stay here with you. Either way, we will be together, and you will be my wife. That's the end of it."

She stared at him. "Derek, you can't stay with me."

"Doesn't matter if I can or can't. I'm not going to be without you anymore. If you're too damn stubborn to come along with me, work with me, have a life with me, then I'll put down roots and it will be right here. Or in North Carolina," he amended, as if she was too addled to understand he didn't mean *here* here.

"I'll get old. You won't."

"That's the body, Ruby. As fine as yours is, I don't care about that. I'll love you as much or more at ninety than I love you at twenty-six."

"That's what you say now. But—"

Reaching out, he snagged her wrist and yanked her back against him, so hard she hit his chest with an *oof*. Jerking up her chin, he kissed her, angry, hot and deep, gripping her hair to hold her still, his hand low on her hip and then down, a firm clamp on her ass to keep her in place, let her feel every hungry inch of his body. She struggled, but he wouldn't let go. In fact, he just hiked her up around the waist, made her wrap her legs around him and carried her inside, shouldering open the screen door easily enough to tell her he was, in fact, pretty much all Derek again.

He took her straight to the bed, laying her down and putting himself on top of her, holding her there with his far greater weight, size and strength.

She thought about blasting him with electricity, but of course she might electrocute herself as well, and she'd just done her hair. She didn't care to have it teased up like a hedge by static. She told herself that as he moved his mouth, went to work on her throat, turning her world fuzzy on the edges as he pulled open her shirt with an impressive, breath-stealing jerk. He took possession of her breasts, cupping their weight, thumbs sliding over the nipples under her thin bra as he went down under the waistband of the skirt she'd pulled on, found her mound and slid over it. The moment he sealed the heat of his palm over her clit, she nearly came off the bed, arching into him and grabbing his biceps. "Derek."

"Got your attention?" he asked.

She was set to be mad at him for overwhelming her with testosterone, a way that proved nothing, but then she met his gaze. She saw anger there, frustration, and something else. Something she didn't expect. Raw need.

"Derek." She said it softer this time, but the question stuck in her throat. It was fine, because he voiced it anyway.

"Why is it so hard for you to realize I need someone, too? And you're that person, Ruby. The only one. For the rest of your life, that's going to come first to me. And when I have to say good-bye to you, because that's the kind of bitch mortality can be, every time I save the world after that, it will be so people like you and me have a chance to love one another. Have a life together. And I'll watch after every generation that comes from the kids we make. You'll never have to worry about anything happening to them, because I'm going to be there, watching their backs."

She couldn't wrap her mind around it, so she went for something else. "Seven Wonders? Really?"

"Really."

"Wow. You really *were* around to compare knights to cowboys."

"Cowboys had more comfortable clothing. But, yeah." He framed her face, his urgency conveyed through the touch. "Ruby. Say yes. Take a chance on me, on us, on us being way more than we've been. No more half measures. Full commitment. Biblical stuff. Whither thou goest . . . I go."

"You know, people always think of that in a romantic way, and Ruth actually said it to her mother-in-law. It was a mother-daughter bonding thing."

"I *will* thrash you within an inch of your life."

She smiled up at him. "You aren't supposed to beat your wife."

"Unless she enjoys it. Ruby, you're killing me here."

She sobered. "Would you really want that, Derek? Me going with you?"

"Would you want it?"

"I need you to answer me first."

His jaw flexed. "Fair enough. I'd rather keep my family as far out of the range of danger as possible. But with respect to your abilities, I'd rather help you learn to use them to the furthest extent you can, than be like your mother and tell you not to use them for my own selfish reasons."

"You could never be like her."

"My motives might be out of love, but it wouldn't make them less wrong."

Like what she'd done for the baby. His words came back to her, but they didn't hurt so much, particularly when she saw how he was in fact struggling with accepting what the two of them being together, the way they wished, could mean. It would be difficult for him. But he truly wanted her with him. And that meant more to her than any gift he could ever give her.

"All right, then. Yes. I would love to go with you, see the things you see, fight at your side. Know I could be a help to you, and to those who need help. And I'd love to learn from you . . . if you don't get all overbearing and Mr. Know-It-All about everything."

He grinned then, though his eyes remained serious. "But we could play stern schoolmaster and naughty student. I could conjure a ruler, or a paddle . . ."

"Who says we'd be playing?" Stretching her arms up around his neck, she met his mouth. Bringing her body up tight against his, she mashed her breasts against that hard chest. She wished he wasn't wearing a shirt, so she could feel the pleasant rasp of his hair there against her smoothness. She had a feeling she wouldn't have to wait long for that. He growled against her mouth, delved deep again, until he was hard and she was damp, both ready and wanting.

But at length, he raised his head. Derek was a man who didn't lose sight of his objective. She was sure he was related to those large, slobbering hounds that tracked prisoners through swamps.

"How about this?" He nuzzled her throat. "We make ourselves a home, wherever you want it to be. North Carolina, the mountain cabin, it doesn't matter. A place that's ours, where we go to be us, a family. And we stay there for a bit, give ourselves a real honeymoon. Then we'll take it one step at a time. But you still have to say yes first. After that"—his head lifted, his gaze making her shiver deep inside in all the right places—"I'm not of a mind to give you many other choices about getting rid of me."

A montage of memories passed through her mind. The way he'd squatted down to look under a table at a hurting little girl, holding a dead kitten. His quick, reassuring smile for an awkward teenager as she told him about that first boy crush. Bringing her a rare book on arcane theory she'd thought was out of print. Sending her postcards from different places, just short, funny notes, giving her a lifeline in a dark world.

When he visited her, he'd told her stories of his adventures. She knew he hadn't truly been lying about the monk and the vampire queen, because it wasn't the first story he'd told her about vampires. He'd provided magical teachings to another vampire, a solitary male who lived in the Sahara desert, apart from his own kind. The love of his life had been murdered, and Derek had helped the grief-stricken man preserve the body of the woman he loved, so he could visit her in her tomb and see her perfect and unchanged, year after year, until his heart could heal.

When he'd told her stories like that, he said she was the only one he'd ever shared them with. And she believed him, because he'd never lied to her.

As memorable as those times were, there were others that eclipsed them. Like that first moment his eyes had warmed on her and she knew he saw the woman she'd become, and wanted what he saw. Even when she'd been too uncertain of herself to realize just how much, to recognize a man falling in love. A man who wanted to spend his life with the woman he held in his eyes, his heart and soul.

She might not ever get over her incredulity that this complex, powerful man loved her, actually admitted to needing her in a way he'd never needed anyone, but she knew her own feelings would never be in doubt. And she was done with being afraid of grabbing hold of the things she wanted most.

"Yes. Derek Stormwind, I will marry you. I will be your wife, as long as the Lord and Lady give us. And I promise to try and be someone you can depend upon, the way you've always tried to be there for me."

"And no soul magic," he said sternly. "Ever. I'm putting it in the vows."

"Unless you refuse to be considerate. Leaving toilet lids up, forgetting to pick up your socks. Then I'll hypnotize you and turn you into the male version of Martha Stewart."

He raised a brow. "If I recall, you're the one who leaves your clothes everywhere when you go to bed."

"When you rip them off me," she returned archly, her lips moving into a pout that quivered at the corners with laughter. "Who left a coffee ring on my side table because he couldn't be bothered to get the coaster that was sitting less than ten feet from his big old booted feet? Which were *propped* on the coffee table, I might add—"

He kissed her again. She gave herself to it, flooded with the warmth and joy he offered, that she saw in his face from her decision. He loved her. He really, really, loved her, and wanted to be with her. She pushed his shirt off his broad shoulders, wanting to clutch that bare skin, tangle her fingers in his chest hair, kiss his neck when he was moving inside of her, over her, press her face there, hard. He tugged her skirt off her, their arms getting in each other's way as she opened his jeans, tried to push them off his hips. Her arms weren't long enough to reach beyond his taut ass, and that was a distraction she couldn't resist, anyway, her palms sliding along the firm muscle to palm him there. He muttered an oath of need and got the rest of his clothes and hers out of their way so he could lie back down upon her.

"Now," she breathed. "I'm ready for you now. Don't wait. I need to feel you inside me, Derek."

"You're wet as you can be for me, girl," he agreed, his eyes intent, his hand sliding through her folds, making her shudder and give a soft cry. "Wrap your legs high on my back. I want you to feel me deep."

She obeyed, and held his gaze as he thrust, slowing himself only enough to make sure he didn't bump into her too rough in the more open position. He always remembered things like that. Knew when to give her roughness, when to be gentle. Always. She realized then how much, in how many ways, she already trusted him. And the past few days had only expanded that feeling into even more vital areas.

"So, who do you want to be at our wedding?" She managed it in a breathless whisper as he bent to kiss her throat again. Working his way down toward her breast, he used one large hand to cup and tilt it up to his mouth. She gasped as he suckled the nipple, hungry for her. He lifted his head, though, his mouth wet with it. Met her gaze with eyes on fire with desire, the need to ride her to the finish.

"As long as you're there, I don't give a damn." He put his head back down, then came back up, a breath away from taking possession of the nipple again. He gave her a narrow glance. "As long as Mikhael Roman isn't on the guest list."

"There go my plans to have him give me away."

That earned her a sharp nip that made her squeal and wiggle beneath him, but then she sobered.

"What happened in the barn, Raina's fantasy room, it wasn't the Darkness." She wanted it to be true, though she knew she really couldn't say if it was or not. It was going to take her a while to trust her gut again.

Before that uncertainty could take hold, spoil the moment, Derek gave her the truth, reinforced it. He touched her face. "I know that, girl. It's something . . . I've got the need to rope and brand, and you've got the need for the taming. It helps you to let go, to drop all the shields and fears and surrender to trust. You need some help getting there, and that's part of what it's all about. No shame to it.

"I've got all sorts of rope tricks I could show you." He gave her a grin, then sighed. "And I'll give Raina her due. She said it was something that had always been between us, part of who we are, and the fantasy just gave us the chance to explore it a little more."

"And that brand?"

"A tracer mark. Raina's idea, but in the end, I wasn't sorry for it. It helped me keep track of where you were when you were out on the street, then on the way down to us."

"I'm lucky your aim was good," she retorted, a gleam in her eye. "That one explosion, the one that turned two chambers into one? It would have taken me out if I'd so much as twitched the wrong way."

"You aren't the only one who practices marksmanship. My weapon's just quite a bit bigger, baby."

She snorted at that, made another halfhearted effort to wrestle him off her. She succeeded only in being pinned more decidedly. Then he settled down to taming her in earnest, ironically by making her so wild she was clawing at his back and mindless with need in no time. Thrusting, teasing her with his mouth. His hands were everywhere, stroking, leaving her all open and aching for him. She came around him, once, twice, before he let himself go, and then he started all over again, proving that her sorcerer's strength was back in full glory, their souls invincible, bound as closely together as their hearts, minds and bodies.

LINDA USUALLY STOPPED IN DURING THE MORNINGS TO chat, but apparently the vibes coming out from their guesthouse were unmistakable. Except for Theo padding in and out occasionally to give them a reproachful look for hanging about the bed all day, they were left alone. As the sun started to set, Derek pulled on his jeans. He didn't want Ruby to get dressed, so he wrapped her up in the blanket, despite her weak protest. Carrying her out to the porch so they could watch that sunset together, he brought a beer for him, a soda for her, and a biscuit treat for Theo. She sat in the cradle of his legs on the lounge chair, bare feet peeping out of the bottom of the blanket, playing with his toes, because for once he'd left the boots behind. She had her head on his chest.

"I'd like Raina and Ramona there."

"I expected that. I'll be nice."

"No, you won't. Raina would die of shock if you were, and I need her to be my maid of honor. You sure you're up for this? A lifetime with me?"

He shrugged, tugged her hair. "I don't have a lot of choice. You know that dog of yours isn't getting any younger, and Theo told me when he has to go to Dog Heaven, you're going to fall apart."

"You both have an overinflated opinion of yourselves. A typical alpha male trait. I won't miss cleaning his slobber off everything. Oh wait. He says that's your slobber. You just blame it on him."

"Probably. Drooling over you, the way you turn every little gesture into something that makes me want to get you on your back. Or on your knees, or—"

"Do not."

"Do you still scrub your tub on Saturdays? You know, where you bend way over, knees braced on the edge of the tub, your ass high in the air—"

She pinched him, hard, and he squeezed her, grinning. As they got quiet again, though, she spoke against his chest.

"You remember what you said that day . . . about the soul being a full container?"

He nodded, his jaw brushing her hair.

"You said the only way there's room for more inside of it is if pieces of it have been let go, leaving pockets for Darkness to grow, like tumors in the flesh."

"I know. But that's . . ."

"Sshh." She touched his mouth. "I think there's another

way. There's room for more if pieces have been given freely to another, to make room for pieces of his soul to come inside of yours, filling them both up. Bringing them together. Thank you for giving me part of your soul, Derek. Thank you for loving me that much."

"It was just formality, girl. You already had my soul. My heart, and everything else worth having."

She swallowed, seeing the truth of it in his face, and stretched up to briefly press her mouth to his.

"Same goes, cowboy. Now and always."

Raina stepped out onto the porch. The air was thick, heavy, waiting. Moving to the railing, she looked up at the sky. Heat lightning flashed, followed by the distant rumble of thunder.

She placed her bare feet precisely on the steps, interpreting messages through the wood element. Not clear enough. When she reached the stone walkway, she moved onto the grass alongside it. Instantly, a shiver went up into her soul. Way more heat. Electrical. Something was coming.

"Whaaatsuuup?"

At the man's deep voice, she flicked a glance up toward Cathair. The raven was perched on the top edge of the porch swing, his weight settled low, so with the flex of his claws and the help of the rising wind, it maintained a steady, short rocking rhythm.

"Not sure yet. Be still for now."

Normally, an order like that would have been met with an impudent composition of the most obnoxious sounds in his repertoire. Discordant screeches, hoarse coughing sounds, and a peppering of vulgar words strung together in a creative way. But, sensing what she was sensing, her familiar stayed silent, his head cocked.

She focused on the forest that covered most of the acreage of her property. The winding drive to the house was about a mile long, all of it through that thick wood and marsh. Ancient oaks draped with Spanish moss lined the drive. She always imagined them as gray-bearded, gnarled wizards, the great ancients of times past. When she sat on the porch in the early hours before dawn, sipping her wine, she tried to imagine faces shifting in the bark. Of course her familiarity with the normal flow of energy through the old trees was one of the reasons she sensed something amiss now.

The other was she was a witch, just given to knowing these things.

The winding drive appeared to be moving. Sharpening her gaze, she saw it was snakes, coming out of the foliage and marsh. About a dozen of them, copperheads, black snakes, a rattler. They moved toward the opposite side and, a blink later, two alligators followed. Seeing the occasional reptile-pedestrian crossing wasn't unusual. Those coming up the driveway to indulge in the dark delights her house had to offer occasionally had to slow their vehicles until the animals passed. But seeing a full dozen of them crossing, and in the company of alligators, was not the norm. And whatever she sensed coming was not headed in her direction for the pleasures the house had to offer—they were coming for the sanctuary it provided.

She started to walk down the lawn, passing the center drive fountain, a sculpture of a naked man and woman embracing in erotic bliss beneath the glittering fall of the water. As she moved away from the porch, Cathair took flight. In the corner of her vision, she saw him pass across the yellow crescent moon; then he did a loop and came to a landing on her shoulder. She braced herself for his four-pound weight out of habit, and he folded his wings with a minimal mussing of her hair, underscoring the seriousness of the situation.

"Be ready to move," she said, low. "I need to have room to act, and I wouldn't want to ruffle your feathers."

In response, he hunkered down like a soldier settling into a foxhole. It also gave him the right position to launch himself for a fast evacuation if needed. She was tempted to smile at him, but then her empathic senses were hit full blast.

Panic, desperation. Air . . . He was gasping for air as he ran through the swamp . . . on the southwest side of her property. Trying to escape. She extended her senses, pushing past him. He wasn't her main concern. What was following him was the true threat. She didn't identify it right away, but she caught a magical whiff of something strong, deadly . . . male. Something that had every intention of catching up to the fugitive and using lethal means to get what he wanted from him.

Might be good to get a head start on this one. She shrugged her shoulders, cracked her neck. Let her hair down, so it blew down her back in the rising wind and against Cathair. He rasped his irritation in his harsh cadence. "Well, you chose the perch," she said mildly. Closing her eyes, she reached down further in the earth, drew more energy from it. Then she pulled from the light of the moon, the wind scudding the clouds across the sky, and the water of the fountain behind her, such that she heard the water ripple as if hands had swept across it, a momentary interruption of its flow. Her palms heated and energy tingled through her nerve endings, all along her spine.

Automatically, she double-checked the wards on the house, sent them some reinforcement. Inside, those she protected stirred, starting to feel the danger. She sent her succubi and incubi a compulsion to stay where they were. It was Sunday night, the only day of the week they slept at night. She made them do that, because they were better, less frenetic when they observed the Biblical day of rest, literally. The

Bible was a pretty good practical handbook, all said and done. Sunday was a sacred day for a lot of reasons. That would help her now, since those inside would only be in the way. Her demon kin might be lethal, but they were less than useless in a fight.

That blast of emotions, of physical fear, was getting stronger, as if she'd been standing in an ocean tide and it had risen, up to her waist instead of just her ankles now. The fugitive was running, scrambling, fighting to get to her with every ounce of self-preservation he had. He was so petrified, his testicles were shrunk up into his body. He knew if what was behind him caught up, death would be the least of his worries.

Unfortunately, as he was drawing closer, what pursued him was closing the gap, now coming into clearer focus inside her radar. Moving calm, steady, cold.

Oh, shit. A Dark Guardian.

That was bad news indeed. Her lips drawing back in a snarl, she dropped to a squat, putting her hands on the earth to give her full contact.

She loved her Sundays, the quiet of them, the very few roles she had to play. She'd anticipated having a nice night with her latest *Vogue* magazine and a carafe of hot tea, sitting on the rooftop porch, listening to her music and feeding Cathair bits of biscotti. Maybe watch a DVD later. She'd only seen *Titanic* about four hundred times.

Now, a damn Dark Guardian was coming straight to her doorstep. Leonardo and Kate's beautiful scene at the prow of a doomed ship would have to wait.

That just pissed her off.

She sifted the power she'd drawn into the blend she needed, then spun it up fast and sharp, like revving the engine of a street racer right before the light change. It was obviously going to be a shitty night, and she might as well come out fighting.

The fugitive was one of her brethren. An incubus. The

Guardian wasn't going to get him, even if she had to use her dead body to stop him.

There. The frightened male broke out of the forest, racing toward her. He was swift, as their kind could be, flashing over the ground so fast, morphing between corporeal and mist so quickly the human eye wouldn't detect the movement of his legs, but she already knew he wasn't going to make it.

"Duck," she shouted, raising her hands. "*Do it, now!*"

Fortunately, he wasn't too panicked to listen. He dropped instantly. Her volley shot straight over his head like a lightning blast. Twenty yards behind him, just inside the forest line, that power hit a force field. She had braced herself, but it still felt like she'd slammed both her hands against a brick wall, shock and pain reverberating up through every joint and bone from fingertips to collarbone. Cathair let out a shriek and took off.

She watched the backwash of her power spread out, glittering briefly along the full scope of the Guardian's protective shield, about fifty feet wide and that high. Holy Goddess. Never mind. She might not have hurt him, but she'd slowed him down. And her clever incubus hadn't needed further instruction. Almost as soon as she'd loosed her power, he'd been moving across the ground toward her like a veteran Marine, his pelvis glued to the earth and his strong arms and legs pumping like a crab's.

The whites of his eyes were prominent as a cue ball, lips drawn back in a rictus of fear, his body soaked in sweat.

She shot another volley over his head, buying him more time, but this time the Guardian answered. The incubus cringed to a halt as red flame arced through the sky and speared the ground at her feet, sending out a billow of searing heat. Seeing it coming, she'd slammed down a protection on herself and the incubus, and only that kept her from being flung back up on the porch. Even then, it rocketed through her legs and made her sway, but she held fast.

"Get over here," she snarled at the incubus as she doused it. He lifted his head from beneath his hands, shot forward in that same low-level crawl. They could move swiftly on all fours when needed. Especially when highly motivated.

"Damn it." Some of the flame had managed to squeeze through a crack in the protection and the fluttering hem of her dress had caught fire. She doused it, scowling at the scorched edge. She'd have to shorten the dress, and she liked that hem, nearly two hundred inches around, so it flowed just right when she moved. Asshole Guardian.

The incubus staggered over her renewed protection zone and collapsed behind her. He was wheezing like a hunting dog who'd gotten too carried away with a scent and over-taxed his lungs. Or gotten lost from his clod-headed owner and nearly starved in the swamp. She'd nursed a few of those stressed beasts when they'd stumbled into her driveway. Found them nice homes and didn't lose a bit of sleep over the whereabouts of the owner. There was plenty of need and reason to kill in the world if you had the itch for blood and the balls to do it. Blasphemy to be doing it for sport.

Keeping the canine theme in mind, she glanced at the incubus. "Stay," she ordered. "I can't protect you if you move away from me. Nod if you understand."

She asked for the confirmation, because his almond-shaped eyes were half-wild. He wasn't one of the more civilized and tame succubi or incubi, like those who lived in her establishment. Nor even one of those who'd learned to live unnoticed on the fringes of society. Though he had the shape of a man, the glow in his eyes and the sexual energy power signature coming off him said he'd always lived outside human society. It meant he was a scavenger, an opportunistic feeder who'd never known or learned better. She was all too familiar with the story. What hunted him probably held the usual philosophy toward incubi and succubi. Hunt them down, exterminate them. Better off dead.

The old, bitter rage turned over inside her, but she pushed

it back. She'd need her wits about her, because it was about to become that kind of fight. The Guardian had only fired the one volley, and that told her he'd been checking to see if she'd turn tail and scamper back into the house. Yeah, that'd be a cold day in Hell.

She waited, because she certainly wasn't going to him. Small fires scattered across the lawn, the result of their fall-out, were starting to ebb, though she concentrated some small bursts of magic in those areas to finish the job. If he'd damaged her landscaping, particularly the clematis vine on the nearby trellises, she was going to have his ass for dinner.

No sign of him yet. Maybe he'd call it off at this point and head to a Starbucks for an overpriced coffee, chalking it up to a bad business. Sure. And she'd get that *Vogue* magazine fantasy tonight as well.

The incubus stirred behind her, started to speak. "No," she ordered. "Be quiet until Mommy and Daddy finish argu-ing over who gets custody of you."

Her dry humor went right over his pretty head. Definitely a scrounger. She had pity for him, though this was going to get complicated, because a scrounger could be vicious and savage. But she'd take the straightforward challenge of that over the subtle quagmire of cultured and deadly, any day. And that was coming toward her now.

As he emerged, she caught a glimpse of his wings, which she admitted was kind of a thrill. Not many got a chance to see their wings. For one thing, much of their wetwork was done in the dead of night, and the wings were black. Not glossy black like Cathair's, but the deep ash of cemetery statuary at midnight on a moonless night, where the shad-ows seemed to collect in the hollows, offering a mere glimpse of the eerie silhouette.

The wings also only came out on special occasions, like during a pursuit where the Guardian had to exert himself a bit to stay in the race. That meant the incubus cowering behind her had some game. Didn't mean he was clever, of course. Crossing a Dark Guardian, incurring his wrath, was a low check on the IQ scale.

The wings began to dematerialize as the Guardian strode toward her. She noted the texture looked more like a bat than a bird. Sinister-looking. In fact, the ragged edges made her think of the black sails on a pirate ship, loaded with cold-eyed criminals armed with wicked cutlasses and daggers to slit their victim's throats.

When the wings tucked in and vanished, she found herself looking at something altogether different. She told herself she wasn't impressed. She was the madame of a bordello, after all. As a businesswoman, she knew a man's appearance gave away clues to his bankroll, whereas his outer beauty had little to do with whatever lay inside his soul. Most of her clients thought they checked their souls at her threshold, so the latter concerned her far less than the former.

His clothes were custom-tailored. Black slacks, white shirt, black suit coat. What every discerning, fashion-conscious man wore to a hard chase through a Southern swamp, of course. Not a speck of mud or a drop of sweat on him. Not even a spiderweb caught in his beautiful dark hair, which was cut short but had that artful array of strands across a broad forehead, teasing a woman's fingers to touch it.

As he shifted in and out of the moonlight, his dark brown eyes became black, then brown again. His cruel face was precisely chiseled, as beautiful as Creation could make it, because things that were cruel were always beautiful. That was the way it worked; otherwise the being couldn't get close enough to *be* cruel.

He could break anything he wanted, destroy anything he desired. And destruction was not new to him. Actually, it was no more than breathing. She knew it, because she knew him, indirectly. By reputation versus face-to-face meeting.

Mikhael, Dark Guardian of the Underworld, and recently the hugely inadvisable hook-up of her good friend Ruby. Fortunately, Ruby was keeping better company these days, with the wizard Derek Stormwind, the polar white to this guy's dark. She wouldn't be admitting that first part, though, because there was no sense in letting Derek know she liked him. Even if she had gone to their wedding and stood as Ruby's maid of honor. For one thing it would be distasteful and intolerable to have to deal with a reciprocation of affection from Derek.

A Dark Guardian was essentially a cop, just like Derek, and Raina had never had a good relationship with authority. Neither Heaven nor the Underworld particularly favored her decision to open a bordello with creatures known to suck life out of mortals through sexual touch. Hers didn't do that, thanks to her special abilities, but it didn't mean anyone approved. If she ever relaxed her enchantments and her incubi and succubi unleashed the deadly side of their nature, Derek would be the first on her doorstep to take her down. It was his job, nothing personal. She understood it, the way he understood she had to dislike him on principle.

She didn't really give a rat's ass what any of them thought, but she had learned to straddle the fine line between snubbing and being discreet enough about her disdain to be left alone. Unfortunately, standing between a Dark Guardian and his prey was not the way to fit into that latter category.

Ruby had said Mikhael was . . . distracting, in that way the bad boy always was. Actually she'd said, *"He's the bad boy of all bad boys. Rhett Butler lumped in with Sawyer from* Lost, *Alex from* Grey's Anatomy, *Mickey Rourke from* 9½ Weeks *and Nicolas Cage from* Valley Girl"—the best part of that eighties movie, they both agreed. *"Oh, and Antonio Banderas doing the tango in* Take the Lead."

As she watched him approach, Raina agreed, enough that she wondered if Mikhael also had some incubus blood. The man's body—sinuous muscle, broad shoulders and tapered hips, the way he moved, the intensity of his eyes, flex of his hands—were all designed to make a woman think of sex. At the end of his stroll across her lawn, he might try to dismember the incubus behind her, or do something else equally nefarious to her, yet all she could think about were tangled sheets, his slick muscles under her palms, his body moving upon her.

Maybe it was a Dark Guardian thing, because Ruby had been pretty obsessed with him there for a time.

She wouldn't fall under the same spell as Ruby, though, because sex didn't matter. It could be strong, passionate, overwhelming, what have you, but in the end, it was a moment or two, balanced against the whole-rest-of-your-life kind of shit, the responsibilities she had. So she set it aside and focused on what mattered—whether or not she was going to have to kick his ass.

On her home turf, she was unbeatable. Most of the time.

"Dark Guardian." She nodded coolly. "Fancy seeing you all the way out here, and on a Sunday night, no less. We're closed. If you come back tomorrow night, perhaps we can meet your needs."

Mikhael glanced at the incubus cowering behind her. "He took something of Lucifer's. Lucifer wants it back."

You dumb bastard. Raina glanced down at the creature, who was staring at Mikhael as if he held a death notice in his hand. Except for his drop-dead sex appeal, Mikhael actually did look as emotionally invested as a bored collection agent who regularly delimbed individuals.

"I'm sorry," she said. "We didn't get around to names. You are?"

The incubus shifted his terrified gaze up to her, blinked in surprise, probably at her pleasant tone. "R-Reginald."

"A fake name will do right now." She nodded. Spoke succinctly and slow. "Reginald, this is Mikhael. He is a Dark Guardian. You've taken one of Lucifer's toys. They're very possessive of their toys in the Underworld. If you have his toy, you need to give it back, because it's not nice to take other people's toys. Do you have the toy?"

"N-No, I don't have it."

"I see." She looked up at Mikhael. A ways up. The man

was a little too tall for her taste. "Seems we have a conundrum. He says he doesn't have it, you say he does. He has sanctuary here. Until I can get to the bottom of it, maybe you can just go away. Give me your cell number and I'll text you."

Mikhael pivoted, made a gesture. Just that minuscule movement had the incubus whimpering, quailing into a smaller ball behind her, as if he thought her body could completely hide his. However, Mikhael's focus was on her. His head tilt said he wanted her to step away from the incubus, toward him, for a semiprivate word. There was command in that minute gesture, a command that annoyed her, more for the fact that something in her responded to it than the fact he did it. She stepped forward with an arched brow that told him she recognized the command, was unimpressed by it, but she wasn't scared of stepping closer to him, either.

A curve touched his lips, a hint of an uncanny smile that could simultaneously chill and heat a woman's blood to boiling. Because of her shorter stature, such close proximity required that she tilt her head back to stare into his face, which was an advantage she wouldn't give him. Instead she looked past his shoulder, staring at the woods, waiting for what he had to say. He bent his head, not touching her, but the heat of his breath stirred against her ear.

"I can incinerate him where he lies, witch. I can also do the same to you, your house and everyone in it, before you have the chance to cast your next spell. Is he worth that to you?"

She shifted her gaze up to his, locked. "I didn't run when you threw flame at me. Why would you think a few words would make me bolt? You can huff and puff all you want, big bad wolf. This house isn't blowing down."

"You think I'm bluffing?"

"No, I think you're testing. If you were enough of a soulless monster to do such a thing, you'd have already done it. Regardless, I won't lie down and be your doormat. If you want to slaughter us for your information, you go right ahead."

He tilted his head. His face was so close to hers, it brushed those tempting strands on his forehead against her brow, and his gaze dropped with interested speculation to her mouth. She held her ground, though she felt an odd flutter in her throat, a need to swallow she suppressed.

Something in the dark eyes flickered. "All right, Raina. What would you propose?"

"You know my name." That was unexpected, but then she knew his, didn't she? They probably had the same source of information.

"Dark Guardians know everyone's name."

"How lovely for you. You never have that awkward moment at parties where you can't put a name to a familiar face."

He didn't blink. "I can read your mind. That's how I know your name."

"You're lying." She tossed back her hair, stepped back, a deliberate insertion of space, not a retreat.

He flashed a dangerous smile that wasn't a smile. It was a baring of fangs. "You're calling me a liar?"

"If it rubs your fur the right way, yes. Perhaps even if it rubs it the wrong way. Some cats like that."

He swept his glance over her, a gesture that felt like a full-body stroke of that fur. "I'm afraid I'm here to rub *your* fur the wrong way, because I am taking that thing that's behind you. No matter what."